RENEWING HOPE

Books by Jennyfer Browne

In Your World Series:

Healing Faith
Renewing Hope
Finding Love - coming soon

RENEWING HOPE

JENNYFER BROWNE

Volume two of the In Your World Series

Renewing Hope, Copyright © 2013 by Jennyfer Browne

All rights reserved.

Except as permitted under the U.S. Copyright Act of 1976, no part of this book may be used or reproduced in any form or by any means electronic or mechanical, including photocopying, recording or by any information storage and retrieval systems, without prior written permission of the author except where permitted by law.

The characters and events portrayed in this book are fictitious. Any similarity to real persons, living or dead, is coincidental and not intended by the author.

ISBN 978-0-9894966-3-6

When doubts filled my mind, your comfort gave me renewed hope and cheer.

--Psalm 94:19 (NLT)

1

Home.

Coming back to the Berger's farm felt more like a homecoming than any time I had come home in my English world. The Bergers, quiet Amish who allowed me sanctuary the first day, still welcomed me with open arms, asking only the necessities of information in regard to my forced trip back to California, and then hustled us back into the daily routine that I had yearned for every moment I was away. Fannie and Jonah Berger, parents I had always wanted, understood the necessity of looking after family, and in forgetting the past. They loved, unconditionally. It was their way.

As the sun disappeared that first evening, I had a moment's panic in saying goodnight to Nathan Fisher, the man who had saved me from my past and held my heart. His presence had become a comfort while I struggled to find my way. With a reassuring embrace in the cover of darkness, a light touch of his lips, and a whispered promise to be back in the morning, I slipped back into the routine that I would emulate for the rest of my life.

The Amish way of life held more hope for me than anything in my life before its discovery.

With the Amish, little time was spent reflecting on one's past or failures. Instead, they looked to the future. My future was with Nathan, and I could not wait to begin with my new journey.

I slept fitfully beside my new sisters Emma and Abigail. Emma held me close, as if I might disappear at any moment, while Abigail appeared to have grown in just the week I had been gone, her blonde hair creating a web over her face while she slept. In the dark with them beside me, the peace settled over me that I had only felt while there with the Amish.

Once asleep though, the dreams that carried me through the long night meandered through rustling corn and crashing waves, ending with me at the edge of a wide cliff overlooking the ocean. Behind me, the corn parted and in the distance I could make out a familiar white house. I only had to walk through the corn to get there.

I awoke to the sound of Jonah and Fannie walking past our room, and slipped from the warm bed to dress. I didn't want to return to my dreams.

I wanted to forge ahead and start anew.

Fannie smiled as I entered the kitchen, Jonah looking up from some papers as I slid in beside him at the table.

"You did not sleep well," Fannie stated with a compassionate smile as she laid out mugs of coffee for Jonah and me. I shook my head and looked down at my fingers wrapped around the hot mug.

"Too many dreams," I whispered, and left the rest unsaid.

"I suspect it will take some time to settle back into our routine," Jonah said, glancing at his wife.

"I'd rather jump right in," I replied. "I'm ready now. I've done everything the elders requested of me."

Jonah cleared his throat and looked at me with cautious eyes.

"They will be pleased with the tasks that you have accomplished. I do not necessarily agree with them that you should lose contact with your family. But I am certain that they will see your willingness to step away from that life as a positive step to joining ours. This week's Sermon perhaps, we will meet with Elder Ezekiel. He is fond of you. Perhaps we will be able to move things along, if that is your will," he suggested.

"I want to stay here. I want to learn," I reiterated.

Fannie and Jonah both smiled and looked at one another.

"Then we will try our best to see it so," Fannie replied, hugging me tight.

Jonah smiled over his coffee and looked from me to Fannie, as if trying to determine what to say next. Fannie nodded and patted my hand softly, gaining my attention.

"You have become quite special to Nathan," she started, her eyes crinkling a bit when she noticed my awkward readjustment in my seat.

"We do not wish to ask you about your time with Nathan, daughter. That is between you and Nathan. And God," Jonah added.

I shook my head and tried to will the blush to go away.

"Nathan was very respectful of me on our trip," I said, speaking the truth in a way that kept our time together still ours.

"He is a good boy," Fannie said fondly. "I have no doubt he had the same difficult night you had, being apart after you have been together as much as you were."

I nodded, unsure of where they were going with this discussion.

"We understand there may be feelings between you," Jonah ventured. "But we also have to be careful, because of your situation. There are rules to courtship."

"I understand," I said, not really understanding.

"I will speak with him today. Let him know what our expectations are of him. We would just like to know what your feelings are, before we agree to anything," Jonah replied with a knowing smile toward his wife.

I looked from one to the other.

"I care for Nathan deeply. I don't see my life without him. Is that wrong of me to think this way?" I asked, suddenly worried that maybe Nathan and I had moved too quickly in our relationship.

We had been quick, it was true.

But the feelings were there.

"You have done nothing wrong, Katherine," Fannie replied as she brushed away a stray hair by my temple.

"If you are to make a home here, we just want to make sure of your feelings for Nathan. He is as much our son as you are our daughter. We care for you both," Jonah murmured and sat a little straighter as he watched me react. "It is not our business until you make it so. But we hope to hear from Nathan in regard to his pursuits."

I shifted in my seat again and looked up into Fannie's hopeful eyes.

"I think he intends to speak with Jonah soon," I confided, watching Fannie's eyes tear up.

"And what are your feelings regarding that?" Jonah asked softly, reaching out to hold onto Fannie's hand.

"I've already given him my answer. A few times now," I replied, a soft laugh escaping my throat at the happy memory of him asking me again and again.

"Does that mean you would accept him?" Jonah asked.

"Of course," I said, smiling.

Fannie hugged me to her, laughing softly into my hair.

"I have a feeling we will be busy this fall making arrangements," she sighed and kissed me firmly on the forehead.

"I will expect him to come speak with me then, soon, as you have said. We have other matters to deal with first, namely convincing the Elders," Jonah said, his face not quite reassuring.

"Do you think I have a chance?" I asked, worried. "Or do you think they will deny me?"

Jonah simply smiled and patted my hand.

"Things will fall into place. You came to us for a reason and we see that in the way you make Nathan happy again. And in the way you have found peace here. God would not send you here and provide the healing balm we have seen in the two of you only to take it away. I have faith," he said and stood to pour himself more coffee.

"As do I," Fannie added. "You are both home and we can move onward. This is the beginning of a good day."

I sat in the quiet, thinking on what lay ahead while I waited for Emma to come down to start morning chores. I felt a sense of contentment when she joined me moments later. As we neared the barn though, I felt a sudden burst of trepidation as I remembered the last time I had been there. I could hear the chickens, and the corn rustled slightly in the breeze. I froze in place, my breath coming to me in tearing gasps. My dreams from the night before played in my head, and the sounds around me caused me to tremble.

I wanted to run.

"It is all right, Katherine," Emma whispered beside me.

I looked toward the corn, sure that at any moment I would see Sean step through it in pursuit.

"Katherine?"

I struggled to shake my unease, taking a cautious step toward the barn. I felt Emma's hand in mine, drawing me inside. She lit all the lamps, more than we usually did in order to offer some warmth in the darkness. I kept my back to the wall as we milked in silence, my eyes often returning to the door, fearful of seeing movement there.

But we were left alone, the cows contented with fresh grain and relieved of their milk. As we made our way back with the sun breaking over the horizon, I looked to the hill and saw what I most needed making his way down toward us. I breathed a sigh of relief at the sight of him, back in his Amish clothes, his black hat pushed back slightly on his head as he neared.

"Pleasant morning," he breathed when he joined us on our way inside, his deep green eyes taking me in.

"Yes, it is now," I replied, grinning when I noticed him smirk.

He set his hat on the hook by the door and greeted Mark and Jonah, trying his best to keep from watching me. But my constant glances his way were met with his own, and with it a gentle smile, as if he was as relieved as I was to see one another.

He looked tired as well, and I had to wonder just how much sleep he might have gotten alone in his house.

Did he have bad dreams like me?

"You look tired, Nathan," Jonah was saying. "A few days of travel on the road seem to have worn the two of you out."

I smiled behind my hand when I noticed Nathan's fresh-shaved cheeks brighten a bit, but he recovered quickly.

"It was an adventure. I saw more than I would have seen here," he said and smiled back at me when he noticed my blush.

"And still you returned. It must not have been that exciting," Hannah quipped, catching our looks.

"It was more than I could have imagined," Nathan replied, and then his smile softened. "But this is where we belong."

Fannie helped me finish cooking, and brought them to the table, all smiles as she listened to our conversation. Once we were all settled around the table, Jonah spoke morning prayers and we discussed the plans for the day.

Just like any other day.

It was a comfort to have the consistency of the Bergers to help ease us back into our daily lives. I listened quietly as Mark and Jonah discussed the day's chores, while Nathan asked about how things had been while he was away. Every now and then I would feel his leg brush against mine, and I would smile behind my fork at the simple feeling of him beside me.

We were back to discreet touches, and I knew that would be a challenge for us now. But it didn't diminish the warm feeling it sent through me every time he made contact. If anything, his brief brushings were magnified now. It made me wish the day had finished so that we could sit on the swing again and feel that closeness once more.

Before breakfast was finished, Jonah drew his attention back to me.

"Katherine, I must ask about your vehicle. You know that you will not be able to keep it," he said, his gaze thoughtful.

"I know. I was hoping to sell it. I don't know how much it's worth, but it should bring in enough that it could maybe help out here. And I was thinking maybe I could give something to the community too, maybe the school?" I asked.

Jonah nodded and looked at Mark for guidance.

"You have English friends that might help? Someone who might get an honest price?" he asked.

Mark grinned and looked over at me.

"You do not need to worry about that, Katherine. We will get a good price for your car. I have a good friend in town that can help," he beamed.

Jonah clapped his hand on Mark's shoulder and stood.

"Excellent! Let us get our day started then. I would like to be finished with our tasks by midday so that I can go check on the Jorgen twins born night before last," he announced.

Nathan stood and touched Jonah on the arm, stalling him.

"May I speak with you a moment alone, Jonah. It is important," he said and glanced back at me.

"Of course. Walk with me to the barn. You can help me prepare the horses," he said with a wink toward his beaming wife before he left out the back door.

Nathan glanced back once more at me before turning to follow Jonah outside.

Hannah leaned in close to me, smirking.

"Must have been a very fulfilling trip, yes?"

"Hannah!" Fannie exclaimed, but she couldn't hide her grin when she turned back toward the sink to attend to the dirty dishes.

"I only say what we are all thinking," Hannah grumbled.

"It is none of our business what happened on the trip. Nathan deserved his Rumspringa. So did Katherine. It sounds like it was worth it," Mark teased, winking at me.

"That is the kind of Rumspringa I would have wanted. What did you show Nathan of your world?" Emma asked, grinning when I shook my head and turned to help Fannie with the dishes.

"Four days travel. And overnight together. That must have been revealing," Hannah quipped.

"Hannah, I am sure Nathan was respectful," Fannie argued, looking at me with inquisitive eyes, making my face turn scarlet. How had I forgotten how much my new family seemed to know of my secrets?

    Mark kissed his wife and followed Nathan and Jonah outside a few minutes later, walking at an exaggerated pace to give Nathan his chance to speak with Jonah alone. I tried to keep my mind occupied with clearing the table, but Hannah and Emma wouldn't let me have any kind of peace.

    "You will need to learn how to make your own dress," Hannah was saying.

    "We can make ours together!" Emma exclaimed.

    "Of course we will have to space the celebrations out some. Or maybe on the same day would be easier," Hannah mused.

    "Nathan hasn't even asked Jonah yet," I whispered, laughing at how this was becoming a little too much at the moment. We had only just returned and my sisters were suddenly planning things.

    "That is what he is doing now, Katherine. Do not try to deny it," Hannah admonished.

    "Do you think Father will announce it right away? Or will he torture us and make us wait?" Abigail squeaked, all smiles and dancing around the table.

    "Did you know, Mother?"

    "How nervous do you think Nathan is right now?"

    "I think he has been waiting to ask this for some time."

    "Did he ask you on your trip? I wish I was there to see! I am sure he was tongue-tied!"

    "Do you think the Elders will baptize you soon, then?"

    "We will need to go buy more fabric for dresses."

    "Mama, I want a new dress, too!"

    "Do you think the Bishop would allow a double wedding?"

    "Would you stay here that night or go to Nathan's, I wonder?"

    "That is not fair! I think they should stay here, just out of respect for us! We did not get the chance to have a wedding night alone!"

"But if you get married on the same day, that means two wedding couples in the same house."

"Where will I sleep? I wish I had a beau!"

I blinked and tried to follow along with them, hoping Fannie would put a stop to their banter.

But she joined in, albeit under the guise of the mother planning the celebration. It was too much when coming from each and every one of my new family.

"We will need to plan the feast. Perhaps we can do this before the first frost and we can have it all outside with the Jensen's tent. That would be lovely!"

"And the guests. This will be quite the news for the community! Three Bergers married in a few months' time!"

We finally got back to work, setting the idea of weddings aside for the moment while chores needed to be completed. Later that morning, I volunteered to bring the men drinks, wanting an excuse to see Nathan while he worked. I found them behind the house, overturning the earth where the small garden had grown and was now being prepared for winter crops. Nathan slowed the horses as soon as he saw me, his face pink from the morning's labor and the sunlight. Jonah and Mark stepped up and thanked me for their drinks before walking a short distance to give Nathan a chance to have a moment alone.

I looked around at the work they had accomplished, wondering about Nathan's garden. Surely it was dry from being untended the last week or so. My thoughts drifted to what we might plant and I hid my smile at my sudden plans for the two of us. Already, I felt so at ease with making plans for our future together.

Nathan's hand brushed my cheek, my eyes coming to find his. He winked and handed me his cup, his smile never fading as he set back to work with the horses. His conversation must have gone well.

He was smiling and working with so much determination beside Jonah.

And Jonah was eyeing us with the doting eyes of a father.

Midday meal was quiet. My sisters watched Jonah in the hope

that an announcement would be made. Abigail would then turn and scowl at Nathan, perhaps thinking he would announce the result of his conversation. But he remained silent while he grinned around his sandwich and brushed his leg more often against mine. Even I couldn't keep from smiling from all the giddy energy he seemed to have.

The rest of the afternoon passed, in much the same way it always did. Routines changed little. Chores were completed, the supper prepared, and mending finished, I was able to sit outside in the shade of the porch on my favorite swing, waiting for Nathan to return from his chores. The eager anticipation of seeing him crest the hill didn't go unnoticed by my sisters, who laughed and discreetly departed inside when he appeared. Abigail made kissing noises before Emma dragged her upstairs.

I held my breath until he slowly climbed the porch steps, his hat in his hands as he sat down beside me, a small distance between us that felt like a mile. I handed him his glass of iced tea and we sat there in the quiet for a short time, enjoying the afternoon breeze.

His soft snort of laughter drew my gaze to eye him with curiosity.

He glanced down at the separation between us and rolled his eyes. Sliding my hand down to the swing, I let out a relieved breath when I felt his hand brush over mine in a feathery caress before taking it in his own and relaxing beside me.

"This will be difficult," he murmured quietly, taking a long drink of his tea.

"Probably," I said and chuckled when he squeezed my hand.

"We could take a walk," he suggested, his eyes a little dark.

I glanced out to the yard, eyeing the barn and the corn as it waved and rustled in the breeze. Immediately, my good mood faltered from the shiver of fear I had felt earlier when I had neared the barn. The thought of going anywhere near the area where Sean had attacked me still made me fearful. Even with Nathan beside me, the corn's vicious rustling made me hesitate.

"Supper will be ready soon," I said, deflecting the need to explain my fear.

He squeezed my hand with gentle pressure and offered an understanding smile.

"You are probably right," he whispered. "We should behave. We have the Bishop to impress."

I let him think those reasons were why I hesitated. They were valid points. We had rules to follow and I was trying to prove myself. It was for the better. We sat in the swing for a long time and enjoyed the simple touch of our hands. His exaggerated sigh when we had to go inside mirrored the same regret I had when we had to let go of each other.

I missed Nathan's touch. With the fear of the barn now preventing our private strolls, I missed his closeness even more. Nathan didn't question why I didn't want to walk with him, but I could see the want in his eyes every time he suggested it. I continued to let him believe that we needed to behave and left it at that.

His leaving at night left me feeling more vulnerable, like his presence protected me from the fear and danger of my past. The nightmares continued, with the cornfields separating us at every turn. Try as I might, I couldn't navigate through the strangling stalks as they blocked out the light. I reached out for Nathan. My hands slid through open air, finding nothing to grab. Many nights my terror juggled between Sean with his forceful grip, and the dark glare of the Bishop, putting up his hand to bar me from reaching the end of the corn.

This would be much more difficult than I imagined.

2

It was nearly a week before Nathan finally convinced me to walk with him in the waning afternoon. I had run out of excuses to avoid the side of the barn that had once offered us a pleasured moment of privacy. Stepping off the porch with him I held myself stiffly as we walked toward the shade of the barn, my eyes watching the dead stalks for any movement other than the fluttering afternoon breeze.

It was when I jumped at Nathan's hand on mine that he frowned and stopped just out of sight of the house.

"What is wrong?" he asked, concern etching his features. "You look fearful."

I swallowed and glanced past his shoulder to the mocking wave of corn. He glanced behind him, still confused.

"That's where he took me," I whispered. "I haven't been able to get that out of my head. I have nightmares."

Nathan's eyes widened and he pulled me toward the house again with care.

"I did not know it frightened you," he said and continued to hold my hand with a protective grip, even in view of the house. As if daring propriety further, he leaned in and kissed me on my temple.

"I will fix this," he said and sat me back on the swing, his arm wrapped around me.

Although it should have been avoided for propriety's sake, I took comfort in his embrace. It pushed away the tension and for the rest of the night, I felt as safe as I should have when I was with him. I made a promise to myself when I went to bed that night to stand up to my fear so that Nathan wouldn't have to worry about me.

I was surprised the next morning when I stepped outside with Emma to milk the cows and discovered Nathan already in the field closest to the barn, his horses rigged up to one of Jonah's larger machines, and already the first row of corn by the barn had been cleared from the earth. Behind him in the large wagon stood a man I recognized and was surprised to see working amongst the Amish.

Benjamin Yoder. I remembered him from the Gathering, seemingly months ago. Benjamin was the old friend of Nathan's who had helped find me.

The Bishop's son.

He was still dressed in English clothes, his dark hair grown out since the last time I had seen him and a wavy mess from the work. It was obvious he knew how to work the machinery. I wasn't quite sure why he was here, but as Nathan looked up and spoke to him, I could tell the two had somehow resolved their differences. They smiled and called out to one another, working well as a team to complete the task at hand. Both were already soaked in sweat and Nathan's concentration was such that he didn't even notice Emma and me standing to watch him.

I jumped when I heard Jonah beside me.

"I woke up to find them hitching up the horses," he said and looked toward the machine as it drew near. "Nathan is a good man to you."

I nodded and felt my eyes burning as I stood there.

Nathan was clearing the field because it frightened me.

I swallowed and waved to him as he passed, my heart full when his smile broke out over his flushed face. Benjamin turned to see us, and I caught a tremulous smile from him before he returned to his task of spreading out the stalks in the wagon. Jonah hurried us into the barn for our chores and by the time we had returned to the house, I found Nathan cleaned up and sitting at the table with Jonah. Benjamin was nowhere to be seen, and I had to wonder why he hadn't come in to eat after helping.

I slid in next to Nathan, feeling his rough hand take mine in my lap as Jonah recited prayers. While everyone seemed occupied with passing the biscuits and eggs, I leaned toward Nathan and whispered my thanks.

"I promised to see you safe. I will always see to that," he murmured and that sweet smile graced his face before he straightened up when Jonah spoke.

"It is a shame that Benjamin could not join us," he said, looking up from his coffee.

Nathan cleared his throat and nodded.

"He did not wish to put us in ill favor," he mumbled, wiping the top of his biscuit at some of the yolk leaking onto his plate.

"He knows that he is always welcome," Fannie replied, her heavy sigh loud in the quiet room. "Please remind him of that when you next see him. It would help him to see we have not given up hope on him."

"He is of his own mind," Nathan said in a hushed voice, wistful and melancholy. "But I will remind him. Thank you for your invitation, Fannie."

"I miss him reading to us," Abigail said, and even her exuberant voice seemed somber.

Benjamin Yoder had made an impression on many it seemed.

When I asked Nathan about it later that night, he nodded and looked off toward the newly turned earth by the barn.

"Benjamin was well respected growing up. It is not easy to be the son of the Bishop, particularly the youngest son. But Benjamin was charismatic and many loved him," he said and frowned, looking down at his hand in mine.

"And then he lost his way," I prompted. "Was he shunned?"

Nathan shook his head.

"The Bishop wanted to shun him. I remember that clearly. It was a month or so before you arrived," he said and let out a long breath. "Benjamin's mother pleaded with the Bishop not to shun her son. She was so ill with grief at Benjamin's leaving that I believe the Bishop did not do so only out of fear of losing his wife as well."

"The Bishop's wife is ill?" I asked, thinking of how combative the Bishop always seemed.

Perhaps that was his issue. He had to be upset at losing his son and possibly his wife.

"She has been for some time, but with Benjamin leaving, she grew worse. There is much responsibility in being a Bishop's wife, and she has all but become a recluse," he said while his frown deepened.

He was quiet for a while and I didn't push.

The Yoders were a confusing lot.

"I should have helped him."

I looked up to see Nathan's eyes closed tight, his head bowed.

"You weren't in a place to help him, I think. Not then," I whispered and squeezed his hand to soothe him.

"I could have brought him back," he continued. "That night he took me to my first Gathering, I should have insisted he come home. But that night, so much happened."

"It's not too late, right?" I asked.

Nathan shrugged and squeezed my hand again.

"I am not sure of his desire to come home."

"He wouldn't have come to help you this morning if he didn't," I reasoned.

"Perhaps. He has come to visit me every night since we have returned," he murmured.

"Really?" I asked, surprised he was just telling me this now. He seemed to understand and offered a sheepish smile.

"He does not wish to ruin your chance of joining," he explained. "Today he helped because I asked."

"Perhaps there is hope for him, then," I said and squeezed his hand in mine. "Some people just need a reason to come back."

A small smile crept onto Nathan's face and he leaned in close, daring propriety with a tender kiss to my temple.

"There is always hope."

We were quiet the rest of the evening, and I smiled when I watched him walk over the hill, hoping his friend would be there waiting for him.

I lay in bed long after Emma and Abigail fell asleep, thinking about Nathan's friend.

The Bishop's son.

Was he looking for a way back?

Would that change things for us?

Would that help in the healing that seemed necessary in this small community?

I had to hope so.

The next morning, Jonah reminded me of my own hurdles when he brought up my intention to join the Amish.

"With Sermon coming tomorrow, and with your expectations to join our Way, I think I should go speak with old Ezekiel after we finish this near field. With Ezekiel on our side, we can get the baptismal classes started soon. It is late in the season to begin them," he said and tried to hide his smile with a bite of his biscuit.

"You think Ezekiel will agree that Kate will be able to join?" Nathan asked, hopeful.

"I think old Ezekiel will be open to the idea. He more than anyone has the ability to bend the Bishop's ear," Jonah replied and left it at that.

The food lay untouched on my plate, my nerves tightly wound so that my stomach churned and clenched. While I understood what I would have to accomplish, I also knew that the Bishop would need to be convinced. With Jonah's promise to speak with the Elder I had met at Hannah's wedding, the possibility of an Amish life for me was suddenly more of a reality than a dream.

The remainder of the morning was spent helping Fannie with clearing cabinets indoors. It was a welcome distraction and a relief to stay out of the sun that offered perhaps our last day of summer. Soon, it would be fall, and judging by my sisters' grins, I was not the only one with ideas of what the fall would bring. With fall came plans for winter. With the winter came the hope of being Nathan's wife and a life of peace.

Lunch was a hurried affair as Jonah announced he was off to speak with Ezekiel.

He looked my way and nodded.

"I think we will have good news when I return," he assured us and squeezed his wife's hand as he left.

Fannie turned to us then and nodded.

"Well, with the garden cleared and the laundry done here, it seems we should look to taking care of some things that have fallen to the wayside. Katherine, you may go with Nathan if you like, and help see to his garden. I do not think it has been watered in several days, and we need to harvest what we can for preserving. I am sure he needs help with the stalls as well since he was here so early," she said and I gaped at her at the idea that she was letting me go over to Nathan's house, without a chaperone.

She smirked and gathered up the dishes beside her.

"I will send Emma shortly, as soon as we have finished cleaning here," she added.

Nathan stood and held the door for me as we departed, his gait a little faster than I had ever seen as we made our way up the hill. I had trouble keeping up with his long strides and was breathless by the time we crested the hill. He glanced back to the Berger house once before reaching for my hand and breaking out into a slow run, my surprised laughter echoing off the barn as we neared it.

Slowing as we approached the barn, he wrapped his arm around me to pull me close. Stepping inside, it was much cooler, and smelled of horses and clean hay as we walked deeper toward the stalls. He chuckled as he guided me toward an empty stall, his hands sliding up to cup my heated cheeks.

"The benefit to not sleeping at night?" he murmured against my temple. "I was up well before dawn to finish my chores."

His lips found mine, devouring mine as we moved further into the stall.

"I have missed you against me, so much," he groaned and pulled me down into the fresh hay.

"Me too," I sighed and felt his lips glide along my jaw while his body adjusted beside me, his hand sliding along my hip.

His mouth searched me out, his nose nuzzling into my hair before he let out a slow breath and kissed the thrumming heartbeat in my throat. He looked down at me with heavy eyes, his mouth open as he struggled to breathe in his excitement.

His hands moved along my body, fingertips gliding up my ribs until they reached my breasts, ghosting over them with exaggerated care. I moaned and arched my back, desperate for his warmth to envelope me.

"I missed feeling you against me," I murmured.

I felt him shift, his leg moving in between mine, my skirt and apron hindering him as he tried to move closer. He looked down at my clothes and chuckled low.

"I miss your English clothes," he joked and let one hand slip down past my thigh to grasp at the skirt, raising it up to my knee. Feeling his fingertips brush the bare skin of my thigh, I moaned and drew my leg up around his, tugging him closer to me. His lips found mine again, and explored me with more urgency.

"Not enough time," he moaned into my mouth, his fingers gripping my thigh to hold me closer.

I knocked his hat off reaching for his hair, his soft laughter echoing in the stall.

Rolling him to his back, I straddled him as he continued to kiss me along my neckline, his hands searching for the hooks that kept my dress closed. He unhooked two, snaking his hand under the fabric to search out my bare skin beneath. His hot fingertips made my eyelids flutter while they traveled and brushed the swell of my breasts, a pleasured hum escaping my throat at his feather light touch.

I felt Nathan's arm wrap around me and pull me back into the hay, his body pressed to mine with more determination as his mouth tasted my skin, a pleasured moan coming out of his mouth when his middle ground along the right spot against me. His hand slid down toward my knee, guiding it up with a gentle nudge to spread out as far as the skirt would allow.

His body pressing closer to mine.

And then we heard a noise somewhere outside the stall.

Followed by a man's voice I didn't recognize.

"Hello?"

Nathan pulled away in a flash at the sound of the man's voice somewhere in the barn, near the far entrance. I scrambled to cover myself as he pulled my skirt down and straightened himself hurriedly. We were both flushed and breathing heavily, something that would be noticed by whomever was calling.

"Nathan? Are you in there?" the man called again.

He looked down at me, asking silently if I was all right, watching as I smoothed my mussed hair. I nodded and watched as he rose, stepping out of the stall quickly to head off the unknown person before he discovered us. I heard the strain in his voice as he spoke.

"Benjamin, pleasant day. You startled me," Nathan was saying as he moved away.

Benjamin Yoder was here? Again? Why did he have to choose this particular time to come around?

"I am sorry," I heard Benjamin say. "Did you forget I said I would come by this morning? Did I interrupt you in your tasks?"

I heard Nathan cough and the sound of the barn door creaking as it opened.

"Just clearing stalls," Nathan replied, farther away.

"I can help."

"No. Just about finished. How about a drink inside? I am rather thirsty," Nathan continued.

"You do look flushed. You should not over exert yourself. I

would have helped."

I didn't hear Nathan's answer, as they continued out of the barn. I let out a frustrated breath and brushed myself off, sure that I had hay stuck in my hair. I waited a few minutes to let my skin cool, and then headed toward the garden, just in time to see Emma coming down the hill. She drew near, her smile widening as she caught sight of me.

"The garden is looking better," she said in a casual voice, although the smirk on her face gave her away.

I tried to smile as I grabbed the water pail, intent on watering the garden at the very least. She followed along behind me, smiling as she watched me. I had the water gushing out of the pump before she leaned in and plucked a few stray strands of hay from under my cover. The smirk and devious glimmer in Emma's eye told me I would never hear the end of this.

"Spent some time in the barn taking care of the stalls?" she asked coyly.

"Yes," I replied and dragged the water pail away, feeling her fingers in my hair once more.

"You should really put a blanket down next time," she giggled, jumping away from me before I could splash her with water.

She giggled again and I couldn't help but laugh.

I would rather be caught by Emma than by Jonah.

On my third trip to the water pump, I noticed Nathan was sitting on the porch with Benjamin, watching us. While waiting for the pail to fill, I chanced a glance at Nathan's old friend while they talked. Benjamin had not changed: thin and in faded English clothes, his hair shorter than Nathan's, but still a wild mess as it splayed out over his ears and forehead. His countenance was different from the two times I had seen him before. He smiled a little easier as he spoke, and glanced back toward Emma and me time and again with a thoughtful look on his face while he listened to Nathan's replies.

I looked up toward the porch as I laughed with Emma, who was still finding hay, and noticed Benjamin's bashful smile as he realized he had been caught watching us. He turned away from us and toward Nathan, who was watching me with contented eyes. Benjamin said something, making Nathan blush before tugging at his hair and laughing, keeping his eyes on me as I picked up the bucket and turned back to the garden. When we finally reached the porch, the two of them were deep in conversation, Nathan staring at me as I approached. Benjamin turned and smiled, taking off his ball cap and nodding to me.

"Pleasant day, Katherine. Emma."

I nodded and smiled.

"It's good to see you again, Benjamin," I said in greeting.

Benjamin cleared his throat and shook his head.

"It is good to see you well, and back with Nathan," he said and smirked when Nathan shifted in his seat. "I am glad you are safe amongst family once more."

I busied myself with looking down at my hands, muddy from the garden.

"He and I have you to thank. By helping Nathan, he was able to find me. We are most grateful," I said and looked up to find Benjamin looking down at his own hands, wringing his old ball cap.

"It was the least I could do. I am sorry for your hurt."

"That's in the past. We have forgiven and moved on." I smiled when he glanced up at me again, his eyes full of curiosity.

"Benjamin took care of things while we were away," Nathan added and squeezed his friend's shoulder in silent thanks. "He has been coming to check on me since we arrived home, to help keep things from falling behind more than they have."

"Thank you for your kindness, Benjamin. I wondered how the garden seemed less dire than I feared," I quipped, noticing Benjamin's embarrassment at Nathan's praise.

"Well, I wanted to come help Nathan with his chores, but he seems to have them in hand. He made quick work of the stalls, I see," he chuckled, his eyes cutting back at me, full of mischief.

Emma took that moment to chime in.

"Yes, well Nathan was always rather good about getting his work done early so he could enjoy the benefits," she quipped with a laugh, Benjamin joining in.

"I should get going," Benjamin said after he settled down and made to stand.

"I'm sure Nathan would love the company while we head back to prepare supper," I suggested, seeing Nathan's hopeful eyes regard his friend.

Benjamin gripped his hat a little harder, offering a pained smile.

"Probably not the best thing right now," he murmured.

"Fannie and Jonah have asked to invite you to supper when we saw you next," I continued, glancing at Nathan. "Surely you wouldn't deny Fannie a night of filling your belly."

"I really shouldn't," Benjamin said. "If the Bishop learned…"

"It is our way of thanking you for helping us. And for helping to clear the field. Please say you will," I said, earning a resigned sigh and then a brief nod.

"Thank you. A good supper would be nice," he said and avoided my eyes, his mood suddenly very melancholy.

"We will see you soon then, Benjamin," I said, feeling a little guilty for strong-arming him to come to supper.

"We should head back and help Fannie with supper," Emma suggested and turned to go.

"I will be along for supper shortly. I have some things to talk with Benjamin about," Nathan replied quietly.

"All right," I said and waved as Emma pulled me toward the hill.

Halfway up the hill I slowed and looked over at Emma, who was strangely quiet.

"Do you think he will come to supper?" I asked.

She shrugged.

"I hope so. He is worried about being seen," she explained. "I am sure he does not want to tarnish your chances to join us by spending time with you or Nathan."

She let out a long breath.

"It is sad, really," Emma continued. "Nathan and Benjamin were the best of friends. You saw how much happier Nathan was with his friend there. A man needs his brothers, and Benjamin was like a brother to Nathan, as Nathan was to Benjamin. Benjamin's mother misses him. His sister misses him. It is not the same without him among us."

"Maybe Benjamin is seeing that," I suggested, remembering the wistful look Benjamin had that one night as he watched his friend leave the Gathering. It couldn't be coincidence that he was coming around more often.

"Maybe," Emma murmured and remained quiet the rest of the walk toward the house.

Somehow I knew her simple answer wasn't quite that simple.

3

Emma and I chatted about vegetables and winter canning as we walked into the Berger kitchen to help with supper.

"Beans and peas work well for the winter. But you learn to work with what you have. We always have too many canned tomatoes by late winter," Emma replied, sticking her tongue out as if in disgust.

"I could make some tomato sauces with them," I suggested and rinsed my hands.

Fannie walked in just as we were drying off and looked at us, surprised.

"You are back early," she said, a little nervous.

"The garden didn't have anything to take, but it's watered," I replied and eyed her with curiosity. "Benjamin Yoder is joining us for supper."

She paused in the doorway and glanced back down the hallway before motioning to the bucket of beans waiting next to the table.

"Will you cut up these beans so we can cook them for tonight?" she asked.

We nodded and set to work cutting, Emma glancing at her mother as she left to go toward the front of the house, glasses of tea in her hand.

"Mother is acting strangely," she whispered. "She would normally be happy to hear that a stray was coming to dinner."

"A stray?"

Emma popped the beans in half and raised her eyebrow at me.

"You of all people should understand that we offer our home to anyone who needs a place. Benjamin is just as lost as you were that first day. Yet, she did not even seem to hear your words."

I frowned and glanced down the hall.

"Maybe she's just nervous for Jonah to come back with news," I suggested.

I knew I was nervous for that.

What would Ezekiel say about my return?

Would Jonah say something about Nathan wanting to marry me?

I made myself busy in Fannie's absence, checking on the roast chicken and potatoes she had in the oven while Emma prepared the beans. It looked as if the chicken was just about finished. I checked on the other things she had laid out: fresh rolls she had baked earlier in the morning, and the tea that sat on the counter, freshly brewed from the sun.

Everything had its place and time for preparation, so that when the men returned all would be ready. I marveled at how Fannie knew just how to make everything work out with such ease. I smiled at the thought of a much younger Fannie, just starting her home with Jonah.

Learning what his favorite things were.

I wondered what they were like back then.

Were they anything like Nathan and me, happy just to be with one another, and sad when we were apart?

They still seemed so much in love.

Maybe they were a rarity even in the Amish community?

I doubted the Bishop was as affectionate to his wife if he could turn his son away so easily. I wondered what Benjamin's mother thought of her lost son.

I pulled my thoughts from the Yoders when I heard Fannie call for me from the front of the house. I wiped my hands on my apron and smiled at Emma as I walked out of the kitchen. Fannie was not in the front room, but voices on the porch drew me out the door, seeing Fannie there with Jonah.

As well as Elder Ezekiel.

I paused in the doorway, taking in Fannie's nervous glance before finding the courage to step forward.

"Elder Ezekiel," I said in my best voice. "Pleasant day."

He turned and smiled at me from the chair he sat in. He motioned me toward him, his eyes squinting in the afternoon sun.

"Katherine. It is good to see you again. Jonah has told me you are back from speaking with your father," he said, his voice crackling with age.

I swallowed and glanced at Jonah, whose face remained neutral as I nodded, only hesitating for a moment.

"Yes, sir. I have spoken with him," I replied, unsure if perhaps Jonah had left out the circumstances of how I had returned to California.

"Come, sit with me for a while. Fannie and Jonah have invited me to supper and I would like to learn more of your trip," he said and patted the chair beside him.

I wiped my suddenly sweaty hands on my apron and sat beside him, my back straight.

He glanced at Jonah and Fannie and waved his hand, effectively dismissing them.

"Let me speak with Katherine for a moment alone. We will be fine," he said.

I watched as Jonah and Fannie disappeared into the house, one last worried look from Fannie as the screen door closed behind her. Ezekiel's weathered hand on mine brought my eyes back to his. His smile eased the tension.

"Do not fret, my daughter. I wanted to speak with you alone, without the pressure of your adopted parents to interfere," he said and sat back with a groan.

"Can I get you something? More tea?" I asked, thinking of any way to flee what was sure to be a life-altering interrogation.

He let out a crackled laugh, his eyes closing for a moment before their blue depths captured mine once more.

"I am fine. These old bones do not sit as easily these days. But we are not here to discuss my years, we are here to discuss you," he replied.

I nodded and held his steady gaze, trying to slow my breathing so that I appeared calm.

"Can you tell me about your abduction?" he asked, his voice soft and gentle.

I felt my breath catch and I blinked at him for a moment, unsure what to say.

Had Jonah told him everything?

Would my abduction prove to the Elders that I was a bad influence?

"I understand it was frightening, daughter. To be taken from a safe haven, especially after we promised you sanctuary," he said and I could see the sadness in his eyes.

I looked down at my hands in my lap.

"I was afraid I would never be able to come back," I whispered.

"How did he know you were here?" he asked. "We gave strict instructions to keep your location secret."

I kept my head down and my voice quiet.

"He learned about me from an English. And one of the girls in this community."

"Which girl? And which English?"

His voice had hardened and when I looked up into his eyes, I saw the determination in his eyes.

"Is it right to give her up? I find myself questioning myself every time someone else is at stake," I said, unsure if telling on Joanna was right or not.

I was second-guessing every move I made as if each one would be judged poorly.

His hand touched mine and again, his eyes were gentle.

"Your heart is in the right place, girl. You show much more compassion for her than she has done for you. God will decide her fate. We will decide if she should be given the opportunity to repent, as she should, or be turned away. She put you at risk. That is not the Amish way," he replied.

I nodded and let out a long breath, detailing what I had learned from Sean about how he had gotten his information. About how Jeff had taken an interest in me when we had seen him at the party. About how Joanna had challenged me from the first time I had met her, at the Frolic. He nodded and pursed his lips, patting me once before pulling his hand away.

"I had my suspicions of Joanna. It is no surprise she has left her home," he said and sat back in his chair, thoughtful.

"What do you mean?" I asked.

"She left shortly after you were taken. No one has seen her since. And the English boy has not been to work in the mill as well."

I felt my breathing pick up, felt the tremble in my hands as I clutched at them. He noticed and placed his hands over my own to calm them.

"Do not be afraid, Katherine. Jonah and I have spoken already of this. And the English law is looking for them. We are keeping a watchful eye as well. They will not be able to come here without being announced," he assured me.

But I knew that if Sean could find me, so could Jeff.

And Jeff's history told me he would hardly be afraid of a bunch of Amish men with pitchforks. Jeff knew they would not raise their hands to him. Regardless of Mark's anger, Jeff knew the Amish were more like sheep.

"Jeff is dangerous, Elder Ezekiel. He has hurt more than just me. He has no regard for the Amish ways," I said, panicking.

Ezekiel tilted his head to the side and his thick eyebrows knit together with concern.

"How has he hurt others?" he asked.

"It is not my story to tell, Elder Ezekiel. But he's not one to be easily turned away. He's a danger to the community," I said and felt my heart fall.

They would dismiss me from their community, but not because of Sean. It would be from the fear of bringing Jeff here.

"Please don't send me away because of this," I whispered, feeling the tears threatening to fall.

"Why would we do that, Katherine? You are not to blame for another's actions," he chided.

I looked up and took comfort in his doting face.

"You aren't afraid I'll keep bringing danger here?" I asked, scared to hear the answer.

"You have brought much joy in the short time you have been here. Fannie tells me that you work hard and find joy in your daily tasks. That is difficult to find in even the Amish-born youth these days," he confessed, and winked at me.

He put his hat on his lap and tapped the brim of it with his fingers as he continued.

"Jonah tells me that you dealt with your abduction with as much grace as one could, and that your conversation with your father is done. The English boy who took you is in custody and will not be seen or heard from again. And you maintained your Amish beliefs while there," he said.

I blushed and looked down at my hands.

"As much as I could, yes," I whispered.

"And Nathan? He was a gentleman and respected you?" he asked.

"Nathan is the most respectful and kind person I have ever met," I murmured, feeling my ears burning for my feelings for him.

"Nathan has been quite troubled, since his family left him,"

Ezekiel sighed. "It is good to see him smile and find his faith once more. You have been his guiding angel."

"I don't know about guiding angel," I replied, looking down at my hands in my lap.

"I see more of God's light in you than I have seen in all my days. It is my belief that you were meant to find that light, and offer it to those who need it," he said and leaned in, his voice a little rough with emotion.

"You are truly Ruth, come to remind us of our faith and love in God."

"Thank you, Elder Ezekiel," I murmured, humbled by his praise.

He patted me on my knee and clapped his hands together, forcing my eyes up in surprise.

"Now, tell me, Katherine. How have your studies of the Way progressed?"

I straightened up and smiled.

"I read from the Book every night. I have learned a lot from the Bergers," I said.

He nodded and scratched at his beard thoughtfully.

"I must ask you seriously, then. Are you set on making our way of life your own? To give up on the English diversions and embrace the plain life?"

I laid my hand over his, looking into his eyes with all the determination and hope I could muster.

"More than anything," I said. "This is my place. This is where I belong."

"You will need to prepare for the baptism into our way," he said and seemed to pause, deep in thought.

I waited until he spoke again.

"I will speak with the Bishop and instruct him to begin classes with you. It is customary that you take those classes on Sermon days, which as you know, are every other Sunday. But that will put us into the deep winter for baptism. Perhaps he will allow for more frequent classes, perhaps every Sunday," he considered.

RENEWING HOPE

I somehow doubted that.

"How many classes are there to prepare?" I asked.

"There are nine classes. All meant to prepare you in understanding the Ordnung and the Way. After you have completed the classes you may then make the choice to live among us. If we see then what I already see in you, then you shall be one of us by vote of the community. And then, if you wish, you may marry a good Amish man," he said, and I couldn't help notice his eyes crinkle slightly at the mention of marriage.

For a group of people that insisted courtship be secret, it seemed everyone knew Nathan and I had feelings for one another.

It was a little maddening.

"Well. While we wait for supper, and for Nathan to arrive, will you read me some of your favorite passages from the Book?" he asked.

I let out a soft breath, feeling much more at ease than when I first sat down, and slipped Nathan's mother's Bible from my pocket. I paused over it for a moment, touching the weathered cover in deep appreciation. I thought about how I could have lost it so easily when Sean had taken me.

How I had laid it in the window that morning after reading, not wanting to get it dirty when we went to the garden. Had I taken the Book with me, it would have been lost in the corn, or worse, discarded with my clothes when Sean had stripped me of my Amish garments.

Emma had returned it to me my first morning back, and I had never been so relieved.

This Book was precious to me.

It was perhaps the most treasured gift I had ever received.

It was a token of Nathan's heart.

I opened it up, to one of my favorite places, and read to Ezekiel, his eyes closing as I read, a contented smile on his face as he listened. I read to him about Jesus and the Pharisees — about the beggar woman who washed the feet of Jesus when his host would not. She was a sinner and less fortunate than the host and Jesus himself, and yet Jesus forgave her of her sins for her selfless giving. This particular passage always seemed to uplift me.

"Why did you choose that verse, Katherine?" Ezekiel asked, his bright eyes on me.

I smiled and closed my Book, laying it gently in my lap.

"We are all the same in God's eyes. No one is above the other. Therefore we should treat one another with respect and kindness, so that we may receive it in return. That is the meaning of this passage to me. And I try to live by it everyday," I replied simply.

Ezekiel took my hand in his and squeezed it, his skeletal fingers looking small over mine.

"You are a generous and kind girl, Katherine. God's light shines bright in you," he said softly.

He let out a contented sigh then and gestured to the door.

"Will you help an old man inside? Fannie must surely be ready for us," he said, licking his dry lips.

I helped him up, letting him take my arm as we made our way into the house. As I stepped in, all work stopped as the women inside watched me help Ezekiel into a chair. I purposefully sat him next to me, closest to Jonah. He winked at me once he was settled and looked over at Jonah who was coming in from outside, Nathan and Benjamin behind him.

"Ah! I see God has truly brightened this house with His love! Here now! Let me see Benjamin Yoder, we have missed you!" Ezekiel cried out, waving his bony hand toward Benjamin, who stood with terror-filled eyes just outside the door.

He lingered in the doorway, Nathan and Jonah to either side of him while he wrung the ball cap in his hands, eyes darting between the Elder and outside, which offered him his escape.

"Elder Ezekiel," he whispered, unable to form any other response.

"Come boy, come sit with me and stay a while. Fannie has made this bountiful feast. Surely there is room for one more," he said and looked to Fannie for confirmation.

"Benjamin is always welcome in our home. He is like our son," she replied primly.

Benjamin looked from Ezekiel to Fannie, glancing at me briefly before taking a measured step inside. I saw Jonah's gentle smile, and felt a surge of pride toward Nathan when he placed his hand on Benjamin's back, welcoming him in.

I turned to help Fannie with the meal, smiling when she looked my way, as if to silently ask if my conversation had gone well. I nodded and leaned into her arm as it wrapped around me for an instant before we resumed preparations. This family had so much love to offer, and now with Ezekiel offering to help see me enter the community, I felt more at ease than I had the night before.

Nathan and Mark helped Jonah find the inserts to the table, expanding it for the gathered company. Hannah set the table as the men sat and talked quietly.

Benjamin sat with a stiff back directly across from Ezekiel, but the Elder's eyes were kind as he spoke with Benjamin. Nathan caught my glance once or twice, trying to be discreet at watching me work, but the few times our eyes met, it was difficult to not smile.

When it came time to sit down to eat, Ezekiel and Jonah were smiling and enjoying the company of the extended family. I took my seat between Ezekiel and Nathan, seeing Benjamin's wistful countenance when I glanced over at him. I had a feeling he was remembering the love that this group of people shared. No matter what happened during the course of the day, supper was a time to come together with those you loved.

I wondered how long it had been since Benjamin last felt that.

Jonah spoke the mealtime prayer, Ezekiel reaching over to grasp my hand as the prayer was said. When I lifted my eyes, he was smiling.

"Jonah," he said as the food was passed around. "You are truly blessed with your family and friends. You make an old man feel at home with the love that shines here."

"You are always welcome, Ezekiel," Jonah replied.

We ate and talked as the evening progressed, and all too soon I was helping to clear the dishes. I felt a hand on my shoulder, and glancing up saw Ezekiel's blue eyes shining down at me. I turned to give him my full attention.

"I will speak with Bishop Yoder. Tomorrow you will begin your lessons. I expect you to show everyone your kindness, as you continue to show me. They will see that you are made for this life. You are made to make those who care for you happy," he said, nodding to Nathan, who stood off by the door, hat in hand.

"Thank you, Elder Ezekiel. I won't let you down," I murmured and smiled when his eyes crinkled.

"I look forward to seeing good things from you, child. Thank you for keeping me company today," he replied and turned to wave at Nathan and Benjamin.

"It is good to see both of you in better spirits. Benjamin, do not remain long in the English world. Your mother misses you. Nathan, dear son. Come, keep me and Jonah company while he delivers me home," he announced and tugged on Nathan as he made his way down the hall.

Nathan shot a worried glance over his shoulder at me before he disappeared. I stood there for a few minutes, lost in my thoughts. It wasn't until I heard Fannie say my name that I shook myself from thoughts of gardens and uncovering furniture to take in her words.

"Let us sit in the front room for a bit. Benjamin? Will you sit with us until the men return?"

I followed Fannie's smile to where Benjamin stood leaning against the door, looking out at the cleared field. He nodded absently and followed us to the front room, where Fannie lit the lanterns to cast a soft glow around the room. I sat quietly in a chair near the window, pulling out the Bible to read. Benjamin sat across from me, watching as Emma and Hannah mended a few of their dresses and Fannie set to knitting something that looked like a cap. Mark was keeping busy behind a newspaper, but I could see he was smiling and making faces at Hannah, who pretended to ignore him.

I noticed that Benjamin sat there awkwardly, not having any real reason to be there. He glanced at the door every few moments, I was sure inwardly praying that Nathan would reappear to take him away from the room he was now in. The conversation with Emma about him earlier and the way Ezekiel seemed to treat him kindly had me baffled. It seemed many around us wanted Benjamin to return, but he still held his own reservations.

Benjamin was also familiar with my old world, and how hard it was to transition from the English to the Amish. Perhaps we had met with a purpose, to help one another figure things out. If anyone understood my struggles, it was Benjamin. And maybe I could help him as well with his return.

"Benjamin?" I asked, startling him when he heard his name in the quiet.

I could feel everyone's eyes on me as I looked up from my Bible to look intently at the Bishop's son.

"Yes, Katherine?" he asked, his voice a little rough from being quiet for so long.

"I have a question about something I am reading," I said, feigning innocence.

He turned to me, his English clothes belying the timidity of his face as he looked at me.

"What do you have a question about?" he murmured, scooting his chair a little closer.

I set my Bible down, knowing I had to be careful with Benjamin and the subject I wished to address. I leaned in and tried to keep my voice down in the quiet room.

"The prodigal son."

He pursed his lips and sat a little straighter, distancing himself from me a little.

"It is not something I can describe clearly," he muttered, his defensive walls going up.

The room was silent, and I knew I was leaping when I should be tiptoeing. But I liked Benjamin. He deserved a second chance. He just needed a bridge to get back.

"I don't understand how a son could think his own blood would think him so lowly, when God says that forgiveness and love are the keys to salvation," I replied, trying to seem vague.

He shifted in his seat, no ball cap to grab at as he sat there.

"Sometimes the sins are more than the blood can bear."

I shook my head at his explanation.

"Blood is blood. But love and forgiveness wipe away what may have been," I stated, looking into his conflicted eyes. "If I am reading this right, forgiveness is necessary in order to know His love. The prodigal son wanted only to have some place in his former world. Any place so that he could return; it didn't matter if it was only as a servant, and not as the loved son. But there is more, regardless of what he expected. His family saw that and offered him more. They offered him their love. Because we can forgive and embrace those we love, for all their faults. The prodigal son returns to love because we know that there is more. We can look beyond the past."

He looked at me for a long while, his face unreadable. I sat there and waited in the tense silence; wanting him to see that he had the chance to return to this life if he chose, regardless of his father's obstinate behavior toward him.

"Sometimes, life does not reflect what we have read," he whispered and looked away.

"That's a matter of choice," I replied and he looked at me askance.

"Sometimes, Benjamin," I continued, "I think we must ask for forgiveness by offering what we can to those that must forgive us. They will or they won't. But we won't know unless we try, right?"

He nodded and looked out the window behind me, deep in thought. When he finally turned back to me, his eyes conveyed all the sadness and regret I knew he felt from having turned from his life here.

"It is difficult, Katherine. To ask for forgiveness when you have strayed so far and are turned away," he whispered.

I leaned in and touched his arm, feeling him tense at my touch. I didn't care that touching a man and speaking my mind was not the Amish way. I needed to get through to Benjamin. He needed to know he deserved a chance.

"You won't know unless you ask. Courage is an admirable trait," I replied softly.

He stood and stared down at me as if to argue, before turning to Fannie.

"I should go. I need to be at the mill early. Will you let Nathan know I will be here Monday if he needs help?" he asked, keeping his eyes away from me.

Fannie nodded and smiled at him as he prepared to leave.

"Please, Benjamin. We would be happy to have you for supper tomorrow, if you like," she said.

He nodded and grabbed his ball cap that had fallen on the floor while talking. He glanced back at me, his eyes contemplative as he fiddled with putting the cap over his unruly hair. He made his way to the doorway, turning to look my way.

"The Bishop will want to test you, Katherine. You need to be true to yourself. You must prove to him that you see the goodness of this life, as you do. I have faith that you will shine," he said and then turned and disappeared down the hall.

I let out a breath and smiled to myself, hoping that maybe he had seen that we saw him as a good man. Regardless of what the Bishop thought of him, everything I knew of Benjamin was good.

We waited until Fannie began to yawn, deciding to retire so that we could be alert for the next morning. Hannah and Mark stood together and said their goodnights, walking upstairs quietly. I stretched and was tucking my Book into my pocket when I heard the door open in the back and straightened, my senses suddenly more alert.

Fannie shook her head and said her goodnights as well, followed by Emma who merely smiled and gestured to the kitchen. I stepped into the kitchen just as Jonah was hanging up his hat. When he heard me, he turned and gestured to the door leading to the porch.

"Nathan is waiting outside to say goodnight. But it must be quick, for you have an early day tomorrow. Ezekiel will honor his statement in starting you with your lessons," he said quietly.

"Ezekiel approves?" I asked, smiling.

Jonah came to me and put his hands on my shoulders, his eyes bright.

"Ezekiel approves. Whatever you said to him, he dotes on you like a granddaughter," he replied.

I blushed and shook my head, embarrassed.

"I only spoke the truth."

"That is all that is needed."

Jonah stepped away and turned down the lamp by the door.

"Just a few minutes with Nathan, my daughter. You have a busy day on the morrow."

I waited until Jonah disappeared up the stairs before opening the door to find Nathan waiting, his face full of joy. He took my hands and drew me out onto the dark porch. I sighed when his arms wrapped around me, drawing me close.

"Did your trip go okay with Ezekiel?" I asked, watching his lips as they drew closer.

He smiled down at me and shook his head.

"I do not know what you do, but you seem to beguile those around you," he whispered.

"What do you mean?" I asked, leaning into him a little more.

His lips were so close.

"I think you will have no issue with Ezekiel. He wanted to make sure I was respectful of you," he murmured, his lips brushing mine, taking his time to explore my bottom lip with a swipe of his tongue.

"So what are you doing now, then?" I asked, teasing him by pressing my body closer.

He chuckled and his hand moved to hold my head in place as he drew his lips along my jaw.

"I needed to be sure to give you a proper goodnight," he whispered and moved back to my mouth, offering me a slow, deep kiss that lasted much longer than Jonah's idea of a moment alone. When he pulled away, we were both dazed.

"I will come and take you to Sermon in the morning, Kate," he sighed, his eyes still shut.

"You can do that?" I asked, fuzzy headed.

"Yes. I am courting you now. As allowed by your father and Elder Ezekiel," he replied, grinning as his eyes opened up, playful.

He leaned in and kissed me once more before whispering his goodnights. I watched him as he turned into the darkness. The sadness I felt every night at his leaving still lingered, but he walked with more purpose as he disappeared over his hill. We were making steps toward our future together. And Ezekiel approved of me. I couldn't help but smile at that. I only needed to win over the community and complete my lessons. So far, it seemed that I had won over some. Ezekiel and the Bergers were a start.

I turned off the kitchen lantern and tiptoed my way up to my bedroom. I tried to be quiet as I stripped out of my dress in the dark. Emma shifted in the darkness, the pale light moonlight catching in her eyes as she regarded me.

"He loves you," she whispered as I slipped into bed beside her.

"I thought Hannah said you couldn't hear anything from the porch," I hissed, a little embarrassed.

"I did not need to hear the words," she whispered. "His eyes throughout dinner spoke for him."

I felt her hand grip mine, and her smile glowed in the darkness. I hugged her fiercely, her soft laugh a confirmation that she knew how I felt. Tomorrow would be Sermon day.

My first day of Baptism classes.

I knew it would be a big day.

It was a long time before I could even think to close my eyes.

4

Breakfast couldn't come fast enough.

I felt overly sensitized for the day, preparing for the Sermon and for my first lesson with the Bishop. To say that I was nervous for the interaction was an understatement. Between the troubling dreams I seemed to have inherited from leaving my old world, to the stress of being judged by the one member of the community who didn't want me there, I had slept little and woke up early once more, joining Fannie and Jonah before the rest of the family.

I felt like I was invading on their private time. But their open arms and welcoming smiles belied any disappointment they might have of being interrupted. I worked with Fannie to prepare the breakfast, waiting for Emma and Abigail to come down so that we could begin our morning chores.

Routine.

It was so easy to find peace in it.

Milking the cows, filling their stalls with hay, gathering eggs for the morning meal.

Seeing Nathan coming down the hill to intercept us.

Feeling the calm with him nearby as we ate. I wondered how it would feel with him apart from me at the Sermon.

Nathan watched me throughout breakfast, the food on my plate never disappearing, only moving from side to side. It was quiet at the table this morning, as if everyone knew I was getting ready to stand up to my biggest obstacle. I forced a few bites down my throat, knowing the Bergers would worry if they knew how nervous I really was.

Fannie saw it all, though, and excused me from cleaning up in order to accompany Nathan to the Bishop's home, where the Sermon would be held. I took a deep breath when I felt Nathan's hand wrap around mine as we stepped out onto the porch. He guided us out into the morning sun, the walk up the hill quiet as we both lingered in our own thoughts.

"You did not eat much," he finally said as we neared the barn.

I shook my head and tried to offer him a reassuring smile, but he was as perceptive as Fannie.

"You are nervous. I can understand. But there will be others there. It will not just be you and the Bishop," he explained and let me go so that he could pull an open buggy out enough to get his horse harnessed into. I studied it for a moment, having never seen it before. He turned and watched me as I touched the seats.

"It is sometimes called a courting buggy. Young men are given these in order to openly court a girl. Without the walls, it will be obvious of my intentions," he said, grinning.

I blushed and looked up at him through my eyelashes.

"So everyone will know you are courting me, then?" I asked.

His smile widened and his ears pinked up as he looked away bashfully.

"I think many already assume, Kate. I think this will just confirm their belief in it," he teased.

I looked away, suddenly nervous for what that meant. I was already under scrutiny for simply existing in their community.

"Kate, it is all right. People will see how beautiful you are," he whispered close to me.

I turned and felt his fingertips graze across my jaw before his lips came down to brush across mine. His energy passed through me, settling some of the nerves I had. He always seemed to make me feel better. His lips brushed alongside my ear, his voice soft.

"I know you will do well today. I have no fear," he murmured and pulled away with some effort to go and get his horse.

I watched as he stepped inside the stall, speaking low to the big black horse, Magnus. I took a tentative step back when he came out with the horse, its massive size making me feel tiny in comparison. My head barely met its shoulder. The horse stamped with impatience as Nathan strapped him in, the horse's dark eyes watching me as he stood there.

The dark horse was a bit intimidating.

I had never been around horses much before coming to West Grove.

They were big animals. Much bigger than the cows in Jonah's barn.

"Ready to go?" Nathan said as he stepped around the horse.

I nodded and took his hand as I climbed into the seat of the open buggy. It felt a little unsafe, wide open with no sides to hold us in, but with Nathan next to me I remained quiet about my nerves and held onto the side of the seat discreetly. He smiled as if he knew I was nervous and urged his horse forward, a quick flick of the reins and a sound from his mouth that sounded almost guttural.

The buggy jostled along, lightweight enough to bump along every little hole. But Nathan kept us to the side of the road, steering clear of some of the larger potholes. He sat beside me, hands on the reins, smiling into the morning sun, eyeing me time and again as I took in the landscape. That sense of peace relaxed me, knowing that when we were together, Nathan always seemed to be content. I looked at the day then not as a challenge, but as the next step in our lives. I had classes to go to, to learn this new way of life.

My peace didn't last long.

I felt my nerves spike at the sight of the house ahead, buggies situated along the road. I had no idea the Yoder's house was so close to the Berger's. It had felt like mere minutes that we had ridden. Nathan pulled his buggy up close near the shade, helping me out of the seat with his hands securely wrapped around my waist. As soon as I touched the ground, he released me, let out a disappointed sigh as he looked down at me.

"We may be courting, but I miss not being able to touch you," he whispered.

I fought my smile and stepped away, knowing that we needed to keep a respectable distance. He walked beside me as we neared the house, more buggies arriving as we slowly mounted the steps. Nathan paused at the top, his fingers touching my arm to halt me. He licked his lips, his brow furrowed as he pulled his thoughts together.

"I will not be able to sit with you. But when you are in your class, remember that I will be there with you, regardless of the space between us," he said.

I looked at him, confused.

"I thought you had taken these classes," I replied, stunned.

He shook his head and looked down at the ground.

"I would have started them this spring. I chose not to," he replied.

I understood. He had turned away from a lot after his family had died.

"That makes me feel better, knowing you are doing this too," I whispered and fought again to hide my smile.

"I do hope Elder Ezekiel spoke with the Bishop about allowing us to take the classes privately. I do not think I like the idea of waiting so long," he said with a sigh.

I couldn't help but chuckle.

"Well, I have a feeling we will need to learn that patience is a virtue," I mused.

He pretended to scowl at me and shook his head.

"You learn much from the Book," he replied and opened the door for me to enter.

I didn't have time to respond. As we stepped into the front room of the Bishop's house, I heard my name and turned to see a young woman rushing toward me. Her face was brilliant as she looked at the both of us, nearly bouncing before me as she took my hand.

"Katherine! I am so happy to see you! I am Naomi, Bishop Yoder's youngest daughter. Elder Ezekiel was here this morning, and told us the great news that you will be preparing for baptism! I am as well!" she exclaimed and nodded to Nathan as he disappeared down the hallway, leaving me with the Bishop's young and exuberant daughter.

"Come! I want to get a good seat!" she exclaimed and pulled me down the hall.

I glanced back to Nathan, but saw he was already in conversation with one of the deacons.

Naomi pulled me along into the kitchen, where the hustle and bustle seemed rather frenzied. I saw Sarah Jensen there again, the woman who always seemed to be at every function and handled herself in the kitchen well every time. She offered me a fierce hug and loud welcome before returning to her tasks, too busy to make small talk. A number of women I had met at the Frolic looked up from their duties and smiled my way as we passed. I felt much more welcome in the Bishop's house than I had expected to.

We navigated to the back of the house, away from the busy kitchen. Naomi reminded me of her brother, Benjamin, with her dark hair and eyes. But her energy rivaled Abigail after too much pie. She was perhaps Emma's age, a few years younger than me. And she was chatting away beside me.

"I had heard you had gone, but now you are back and I am so happy to hear you are staying and taking the classes. I heard Old Ez asking to hurry the classes. Have you and Nathan made plans to marry then?" she asked as we walked through the crowded house.

I shook my head, feeling uncomfortable talking about our plans to marry.

Naomi merely shrugged and held my arm a little tighter.

"Well, I am sure we will hear about it soon enough. I am excited for you! And to think that Papa thought I should marry Nathan!" she said and laughed at my shocked face. "You have no idea how relieved I am that you came along! He is nice, but Nathan Fisher is not for me!"

I stumbled along behind her as we neared the end of the long hallway and nearly ran into the youngest Yoder when she turned quickly to face me.

"My mother was excited to hear that my brother was at the Berger's last night," she whispered and slowed by a closed door, looking at me intently.

"He was. He looked after the Fisher farm while Nathan was away," I explained, cautious not to give away anything Benjamin may not want to reveal.

Her eyes closed and she let out a slow breath, possibly the first one she had taken since I had met her.

"Then maybe he will come back," she murmured and opened her eyes once more, wiping away a tear. "He looked well?"

"Yes, healthy and earnest in helping his friend," I replied and squeezed her hand.

She nodded and motioned toward the door.

"My mother wanted to meet you, but she was not feeling well enough today to come down. I may have told her about you a bit," she said and blushed when she predicted what I was thinking. "Women talk. You have been a topic since you first arrived. Papa has his own thoughts, but keeps them to himself, mostly."

I swallowed at that.

So it was public knowledge that the Bishop despised me. That wouldn't help me in winning over the community to allowing me to remain, I was sure. But then, Naomi and others had welcomed me with open arms. It was confusing.

Naomi and I stepped into a small room, a couple of benches laid out on either side of a chair set at the front of the room. Nathan and another young man sat at one bench, two girls at the one opposite. Naomi directed me toward the bench with the girls and sat down next to me. As soon as we had settled, I heard the door close off the voices of the congregation that had started singing. Glancing back, I watched as the Bishop strode forward and sat in the chair before us, his lips set in a thin line as he regarded me. His dark gaze lingered on mine for just an instant, a brief quiver to his lips as if he thought to smirk. And then he straightened his back and looked away from me purposefully, and spoke.

"Gottes Liebe umgibt uns. Wir leben um ihm zu dienen, so wie es uns die Bibel lehrt…"

I sat rigid on the bench and forced my face to remain neutral. To steady my breathing as I listened to the Bishop speak.

In their language.

I understood that brief smirk he had given me now.

He had agreed to teach me, but by his rules. I didn't dare look at Nathan. If I did I was sure to see his worry. Or his anger that I wouldn't understand the Bishop.

Really, I didn't.

I heard maybe half of the words, understood even fewer.

God's Love. Serve him. Live simple. Refuse the outside world. God in our heart.

But so much of it I couldn't translate. I could understand some of the context, but hearing it was harder than reading it. Some of it sounded like English, only muddled with the guttural prose of their language. Both Emma and Nathan had assured me that I wouldn't need to learn their language to be allowed to join the Amish. But they also didn't know that I knew a little of what he said. I seemed to remember something about the Amish speaking Pennsylvania Dutch.

Was that why I was having such a hard time? It sounded something like German but not quite. He was doing this on purpose. He was trying to make me fail. I listened as well as I might, paying attention like I did in my physics class, trying to piece together words to gather context so that maybe, I could prove that I belonged.

Always proving.

Always striving.

And at that moment, feeling so inadequate.

I felt the inner turmoil bubbling to the surface, my breath struggling to tear out of itself, when the Bishop turned to me, smiling.

A smug look that said he thought he had me at last.

Challenging me.

He directed the next question to me, still in his language.

I held my breath, working the words in my head to translate as well as I could.

What reason to live simple, and reject modern life?

That was what I could gather, and he expected me to come up with an answer. I was never good at answering a teacher's question. I always felt put on the spot; and speaking another language, to one who knew it so well. It was so much more than replying, *"the ball was round or the bier garden was close by"*. I swallowed and opened my mouth, knowing I had been silent too long. He was turning from me as if he knew I did not understand. That snide look, the one that no teacher or man of God should have on his face, made something in me snap.

The shy girl disappeared, and from my open mouth I spoke.

I said the words as best I could manage, praying that they were correct in context and form. All in German, and hoped it translated well.

We reject the outside world because of our desire to be close to God. God is here, not there in that world.

I never let my eyes leave him as I spoke, even when my voice trembled and I stumbled once or twice on the way my tongue needed to move. I watched as his eyes widened, his own mouth opening in surprise, then it clamped shut and he turned an accusing eye toward Nathan.

As if Nathan could teach me their language in a month.

I chanced a glance at Nathan, and saw his astonished face before a smile crept in. It was all short-lived though. As if my revealing that I could speak German was a deal breaker, the Bishop stood abruptly and stalked toward the door.

"Lesson is over," he rasped. "We will continue on the next Sermon."

He left, leaving the door open for us to join the congregation that was singing once more. Naomi stood beside me, her face a mixture of confusion and resentment.

"I cannot understand why he did that," she muttered. "And to instruct this class in the Old Word. He rarely does that. It is a good thing you know a little something of our language, Katherine."

My response was a curt nod, afraid that if I spoke, I would break down. I had only made matters worse by speaking at all. The Bishop was more enraged than ever, more than likely assuming I made him out to look the fool. Nathan stepped near me, as if to question me over what had happened, when Naomi pulled me away to the door.

"Come, we should sit for the remainder of the Sermon or he will be upset with us," she said hurriedly and pulled me out the door before Nathan could open his mouth.

I glanced back long enough to see the worry in his face. He knew I was upset, but this was not the place to bring up my fears. This was not the place for me to question him about whether this would work.

5

The Sermon seemed to last forever. Even though we had missed the first hour while in our class, it seemed the Bishop wanted this Sermon to go on forever. He alternated between English and their words, directing Nathan and the man I had seen with him earlier to sing more songs than I remembered.

Naomi had pulled us into a seat in the back, near the open door. I was glad for that, as it allowed for a breeze into the hot room, and a chance to hide from the group as my mind wandered while the Bishop spoke. I tried to ignore Nathan's constant glances our way, afraid I would only upset him further if he saw my own fear.

I found myself looking outside more times than not.

At the landscape that just this morning had been so welcoming, and now I felt something akin to panic rising up inside of me. What would I do if the Bishop refused to let me into the community? Would Ezekiel stand up for me like he suggested? How would I get through eighteen weeks of the Bishop's steely glares and obvious plots to turn me away?

Why would I let him?

I alternated between wanting to fight him at every step, to then cowering and wanting to run away again. I didn't really want to run. Given everything, I wanted to stay. Even if it meant learning so much more than they had shown me. I looked out at the drying fields outside and spotted movement near the house. I watched as the corn rippled, my heart stopping at the thought that Sean had somehow returned and found me.

But then the stalks parted and I saw another man, his eyes drawn to mine instantly.

Benjamin.

He stood at the fringe of the field far way enough to go unnoticed by many. He was dressed in Amish clothes, his straw hat low over his head, as if to hide whom he was. He stood there, unmoving, never letting his eyes pull away from mine. I could tell he was contemplating coming closer. I could see it in his eyes and how he chewed his lip with his teeth.

Another hymn was being sung, the closing hymn of the Sermon. It was then that he let his eyes close, tipping his head up toward the sky. The music seemed to wash over him, his hands, tight and clenched earlier, hung loosely at his sides. He opened up his eyes when we finished singing, and I could tell he was looking up at the upper floor, perhaps toward his mother's room. A look of sadness flitted across his face, one hand rising in a tentative gesture as if to wave to someone. He looked back at me and shook his head slowly, as if to answer my unspoken plea for him to join us.

Then he was gone, drifting back into the field.

I turned back to the room, feeling so confused about the Yoders. Benjamin wanted to come home. Mrs. Yoder wanted him home, but some wedge between himself and the Bishop had forced him stay away. This rift made their entire family sad and broken. Something was wrong with the Bishop, if he could do this to his own family. It was no longer just about me anymore. I had a feeling he was angry about a great many things, and he believed I was a good punching bag for it.

People were standing and starting to find places outside to

congregate while they waited for lunch, many of the women going off toward the kitchen to help out. I walked with Naomi, Emma joining us when we reached the kitchen, and set about grabbing food to take outside.

"How was the class, Katherine?" Emma was asking.

"Fine," I grated and avoided her perceptive stare by heading out behind Naomi to the food table.

The Bishop had more help than ever, so it didn't take long to have food out and ready for people. Our tasks completed, I could only put together a plate and go in search of Nathan and the Bergers. I didn't have to look hard. Nathan was by my side in an instant, taking my plate gently from my hands and motioning toward Emma and John under a shaded tree.

"You are tense," he whispered as we walked.

I kept my face passive as we passed several older men, all watching Nathan as he walked close to me. But I remained quiet.

"I did not know you spoke our words," he continued as we drew close to Emma and John.

I looked up at him then, fighting back any emotion that would alarm him.

"I don't," I forced out and sat down beside Emma, who was watching our interchange. Nathan frowned and sat down alongside me, handing me my plate of food.

"You spoke in class, Kate. It was not perfect, but you understood what he said. I am sure you surprised him," he said, a slight smile on his face.

"Yes, I probably did. Which is just one more reason for him to be angry with me," I replied and poked at my food.

"What happened in class?" Emma asked, interrupting.

"The Bishop held the class in our language," Nathan explained. Emma's eyes grew wide.

"He did not! That is too much! What did you say to him, Katherine? Did you argue with him?" she asked, suddenly nervous.

I shook my head.

"She spoke. In our words," Nathan revealed.

Emma looked from me to Nathan in astonishment.

"Have you been teaching her?" she asked.

He shook his head and they both looked at me again.

"You know how to speak our language?" she asked, smiling.

"No. I took two years of German in high school. I know about enough to say my name and ask where the bathroom is," I muttered and stabbed at one of the meatballs on my plate.

"She knows more than that," Nathan said, grinning.

I looked up at them, frustrated.

"No, I really don't, Nathan," I retorted, my voice clipped. "I only understood about a third of what he said, and to be able to answer a question was nearly impossible. He knew it would be too much. Do you all speak it more than you have when I am around? I just felt like he was proving to me that I don't belong because I will never learn everything."

John leaned in and put a calming hand on my own, looking at me with reassurance.

"Katherine, some of us speak it in our homes, but it is not who we are. We are whom you see, every day. Bishop Yoder had no right to do this. We speak both languages, and not knowing is no measure to keep you from learning our way," he said, his kind eyes offering some comfort.

I nodded and rubbed at my eyes, trying to keep from crying. I didn't want to show them how much this bothered me.

"I'm sorry. I didn't mean to sound ungrateful. I'm just worried he'll do anything to keep me out," I said.

"Something should be said regarding this," Emma declared and rose from her place.

I looked at her with wide eyes.

"No! You can't do that! Please, he hates me enough!" I pleaded.

Emma looked down at me with determination.

"I will not chastise him, Katherine," she started and then looked over her shoulder. "But I think you should speak with

Elder Ezekiel. Perhaps he will say something."

I looked past her to see Elder Ezekiel sitting with the Bishop and the other Elder, Eli.

"I can't."

"No, not in the way you think, Kate," Nathan said and stood as well, a devious smile on his face.

He held out his hand and helped me up, looking toward the Elders, deep in thought before he nodded and steered me toward them.

"We will simply go over and speak with them, tell the Bishop we are happy to be in the class preparing for our life. And then you should thank him for his diligence in showing you properly. Leave the rest to me," he said and continued walking to where the Elders sat.

Ezekiel saw me first, smiling and waving us over. My throat was dry. I had no idea how this would go. I somehow knew the Bishop would make some excuse against me.

"Katherine! Welcome!" Ezekiel exclaimed and took my hand when I was close enough.

"Pleasant day, Elder Ezekiel. How are you today?" I said, trying to stall.

His smile widened and his grip tightened in mine.

"I am well, better having heard you started your classes today. How did you enjoy them?" he asked, glancing briefly at the Bishop.

I offered him my best smile.

"I learned much today. I am so appreciative for the Bishop's dedication to make sure I learn in the truest form," I said and felt Nathan step a little closer to me.

"It was certainly enlightening. I was surprised when you held the class in our language; we do it so infrequently now. And I had no idea Kate spoke German so well. How did you know, Bishop Yoder?" Nathan asked.

There was a tense silence, the Bishop looking at me with a mixture of irritation and fear, while the Elders looked at the Bishop in shock.

"Samuel?" Ezekiel asked, his voice low and guarded.

I felt myself tensing at the frustration I saw in the Elders. Why couldn't this be simple? Why was it a fight? Particularly with the Bishop?

"Katherine," Elder Eli said, interrupting the silence. "Please, if you and Nathan would excuse us. We have matters to discuss."

Nathan and I nodded, my heart hammering as Nathan pulled me away, his hand brushing my shoulder as he walked me toward the house.

"It will be all right, Kate. Come, I will take you home," he whispered, steering me further away from the Elders.

"He's going to be so upset," I murmured, trembling at the thoughts of the Bishop's retaliation.

"Yes, he will. But it is time for him to see he is the only one opposed to you being here. It is time others see that he has strayed," he replied.

We made our way back to the people sitting, finding Fannie and Jonah at a table with Hannah and Mark. Jonah stood and came to us quickly.

"Emma told us what happened in your class. I will speak to the Elders, Katherine. This is not to be permitted," he said, his voice stern.

I shook my head and felt myself shrink inward.

"I don't want this to get out of hand, Jonah. Please, I just want to do what I need to. If I need to learn German, then I will. Why should I get special treatment?" I asked.

"You do not get special treatment, Katherine. We speak English in our home because we choose to. We will teach you our language in time, but it is not a necessity if you are to live among us. There are those here that do not speak it. We are a young order. Some of us have not lived in the Old Ways. He was out of line," Jonah said.

"What do you think the Elders will say about this?" Nathan asked.

"We will see. I know that Ezekiel is disappointed in Samuel's actions towards Katherine before today. I do not see this new trouble being well received," Jonah replied.

I looked over toward the Elders, seeing that the Bishop had left, leaving only Ezekiel and Eli there. I had to wonder then if they had sent him to go find me. I didn't want another confrontation with the Bishop today. I just wanted to go home.

"Jonah, may I have permission to take Kate home? We could wait with you if you prefer," Nathan asked, sensing my tension.

Jonah looked between the two of us and nodded.

"We will be along shortly. Perhaps, Katherine, you can pull the last of the melons from the garden to eat tonight?" he asked.

I nodded and felt Nathan's hand on my back, pulling me toward the buggies.

Situated back in his open seat, we were off, the trip taking hardly any time at all before we were back at Nathan's house. I waited as he slipped the harness off of his horse, guiding him into the nearby paddock to graze. The more I watched him work, the more I wondered what I would do when I became his wife. He had said he needed help.

Would that include more than what Fannie did, since she had daughters to help out?

How would life be with Nathan when it was just the two of us?

What would he expect of me? Would it be more than I could handle?

"You are deep in thought."

I looked up to see Nathan standing before me. His fingers traced along my jaw delicately before slipping back into his pockets, his look tentative. I shrugged and looked around him, at the farm that was struggling.

"It's just, with the Bishop showing me how little I really know of your world, I am wondering what it will be like, truly," I explained.

He took my hand and led me back toward the hill, his pace slow to allow us time to talk.

"What do you wonder will be different?" he asked.

I looked up at him and gestured toward his house.

"You need help here, Nathan. I don't know anything about farms or gardens. Don't you want someone who knows those things? Someone who won't slow you down?"

He frowned and shook his head.

"I want you. The rest will come with time and learning, just like how you are learning our Way. You will learn," he replied, looking out at his fields, now a mixture of drying stalks and freshly turned earth.

"What if I'm not any good?" I asked.

He smiled and laughed.

"I think you are very good, Kate," he teased.

I frowned at his sudden bravado. His laughter guttered out when he noticed I was not laughing.

"You are nervous that you will not do well as my wife?" he asked, stopping half way up the hill to turn toward me.

I blushed at his words. I had a feeling we would be fine as husband and wife. It was the daily routine that I worried over.

Planting, farming, mucking out the stalls.

He cleared his throat and threaded his fingers through mine, his grasp almost desperate.

"I must confess I am fearful that I will not make a good enough husband for you," he whispered.

I looked up at him in surprise.

"I don't think that."

He looked back at his house; his eyes had turned melancholy, a reminder of how he had been when I first met him.

"Look at it, Kate," he murmured. "My father would have sown all the fields, and I barely made one field prosper this year. I do not have food stores made for winter; I do not know how I will feed my horses, much less myself. I cannot take care of myself, let alone a wife. It will be difficult. How will I take care of you?"

I touched his face, drawing it a little closer to mine. I leaned up and placed my lips over his to offer him some of the comfort he always shared with me when I doubted. He let out a soft sigh and leaned into the kiss, but I pulled away, pressing my palm onto his cheek so he was looking toward his house once more.

"Do you know what I see?" I asked near his ear.

He shook his head.

"I see a home that needs two people to make it thrive. I see your hard work in those fields. And I see a home that is beginning to shine again. Maybe what I am most afraid of is that I don't know what you expect from me. I want to learn, but I need to know what to do in order to be a part of it. I see a beginning for both of us," I whispered and held him a little closer.

"You will not turn away?" he asked, looking down at me. "If it becomes too difficult?"

I shook my head and smiled.

"Teach me and we'll do it together," I replied and laughed when he grinned down at me.

He leaned in and sought my lips and capturing them in earnest, letting out a low moan when he finally pulled away.

"We should hurry back. Jonah will not be long behind us," he murmured.

I nodded and we made our way back to the Berger house, the sun casting long shadows across the grass as we crossed the yard toward the garden. We picked three of the ripest cantaloupes and retreated into the kitchen, enjoying the coolness of the house after the day in the sun. Nathan hung back while I washed up and prepared the melon, smiling his way every now and then as he sat and watched me.

I cut the melon into small pieces, tossing them into a bowl as I worked. I tried one or two pieces, realizing I was hungry. I hadn't eaten much during the day, but as we stood there in the quiet, my calm allowed my body to feel hungry once more. I glanced back at Nathan again as I popped another bite into my mouth, pausing when I noticed him staring.

The heat of his look made the air in the room seem much colder as my skin heated. How could someone as innocent as Nathan offer such a lusty stare? And why couldn't we get more than a few minutes alone?

I was spoiled from my time with him outside the confines of the Amish.

As if to prove the point, we heard the buggy pull up, carrying the Bergers.

Nathan let out a slow breath and scrubbed at his jaw before standing to walk outside, distancing himself from temptation. I let out my own sigh and returned to finishing up with the melons as Fannie came in.

We fixed something light for supper, the heat of the day making everyone quiet and thoughtful. When the meal was done, we finished cleaning and I settled onto the swing with Nathan, Emma and John relaxing as they found a place in the fading light away from us. We sat there and read quietly, Nathan pulling me close as he read near my ear, lulling me as I closed my eyes. I had not slept well since returning; my dreams clouded and often included corn and running.

My mind wandered, and this time the Bishop stood before me with the Bible in his hand. He looked up from the Book, glaring at me before slamming it closed. I jolted awake and upright from Nathan's arm.

"Sorry, I didn't mean to fall asleep on you," I whispered and rubbed my face, trying to get my bearings again.

"Was it a bad dream?" he asked.

"I'll be fine," I assured and moved to get up. His hand on my wrist made me pause.

"You do not need to be afraid anymore. I will be here for you through everything," he said.

I nodded and squeezed his hand.

"Together, right?" I asked, referring to the conversation before.

He grinned and stood.

"Always. No matter how long it takes," he said and stretched. He was beginning to lean in to offer me a kiss when we heard voices inside. He pulled away with a jerk, just in time.

We watched in surprise as the Bishop came through the back door, Jonah and Fannie on his heels as they followed him. Jonah's eyes darted over us as if to be sure we weren't doing anything the Bishop would find inappropriate.

"It is late Samuel. This can wait until tomorrow," Jonah said.

The Bishop looked back at Jonah and shook his head.

"I must say what I came to say tonight," he demanded and turned to me. "Katherine, I will speak with you in private," he said.

I blinked at him, all fatigue gone as I recalled my dream and wondered if he was here to tell me I must leave.

"She does not need to be alone while you speak with her," Jonah started but the Bishop waved him off.

"What I have to say to Katherine is for her alone. And God."

Nathan stepped a little closer to me, his hand moving to encircle my shoulder. The Bishop watched as Nathan wrapped a protective arm around me.

"Please," the Bishop requested, his voice much softer.

I looked up at Jonah, who hesitated before nodding and holding the door open for Nathan.

"We will give you a few minutes alone. Nathan, come inside and have some tea with us," Jonah requested and waited for Nathan to move. He seemed reluctant; his eyes remained on the Bishop before he looked down at me and smiled.

"I will be just inside," he whispered and let me go with some reluctance.

I waited until they were safely inside before I directed my gaze back at the Bishop. I couldn't read his face. It was a cross between agitation and pain. And maybe even resignation. He gestured to the swing and followed me to it, sitting after I had sat. He kept his distance and pulled off his hat, looking off into the evening.

When he spoke, his voice was rough.

Surly, almost.

"I must ask your forgiveness for my actions today."

I blinked at his words and after a shocked moment, I nodded.

"You have it. I understand why you did it," I murmured.

He paused, as if he had expected me to balk at his apology. The old me would have, but the new me had learned that it was necessary to forgive in order to move on.

"You are not upset with my reason?" he asked finally, keeping his eyes on the field.

"I can't understand why you treat me badly when I have done nothing to earn your scorn. You don't know me to judge me," I confessed.

He was quiet once more for a long time. I waited for him to continue.

"You seem to have won over everyone around you."

I straightened and held my head a little higher.

"I haven't won anyone over. I am just trying to make a life here, Bishop Yoder," I replied.

"Are you? I think you are here to steal young Fisher from us," he stated, refusing to look my way.

His tone was starting to make me angry. I took a breath, struggling to remain calm.

"I am here to find peace and a life I can understand. Nathan is part of that, yes. But it is with Nathan and this lifestyle I wish to make a life," I started, but he put up his hand to stop me.

"And your trust in God? You come from a world that is Godless. How can I trust that you are not here to hide, and have not found God?" he asked.

"I may be new to this community, Bishop Yoder, but the outside world has God as well. If you are asking if I have found Him while I have been here, the answer is yes. I may see it a little differently than you, but I have seen it here," I replied.

"To live with us is to live with God," he preached.

I pursed my lips and eyed him carefully, not sure if I should say what I felt. But he continued to judge me. Without knowing me.

"To live with God is to follow His words. Words like love and forgiveness and acceptance," I argued. "To know God is to open your heart and your home to others, to help those less fortunate, to offer friendship and peace to a stranger. To forgive those who have wronged you, to know that God will send justice, not man. God rewards those who follow His path."

My heart was beating fast while I waited for his response. So much of what Nathan spoke of at night were these things exactly. And these things I had witnessed every day. But the Bishop had shown me none of that. He was further from what he preached than I was.

"You speak well, but do you mean what you say?" he whispered.

"I have always been honest and true. That has never changed. Not all English are bad, Bishop Yoder. I wish you would see that. Whatever your bias, it's not fair to judge me based on that," I whispered and stood.

He sat there looking out at the field while I stood, waiting for him to speak. When he did, it was barely a whisper.

"Your world sucks the innocence from ours. I have not seen any good come of your world."

"That's like the outside world saying that the Amish are all backwoods ignorant occultists," I replied, watching his face contort in anger at my words.

"It's not what I think," I added. "But you see the prejudice? It's not fair to lump me into that world when I so desperately want out of that."

"You are too worldly for this life. You will tire of it here. And you will drag Nathan with you out into that evil. Just as I have lost my son, we will lose Nathan," he hissed.

"Whatever happened between you and Benjamin is your own issue. It's not about the English world. And Nathan is old enough to do what he likes. I won't tire of this life. You don't know what my life was like before. What I know is that this is what I choose. Even with you making it difficult at every turn. You will not dissuade me, Bishop Yoder. I will do my best to make you believe that I am worthy," I said and started to leave.

His next words made me stop.

"I do not approve of you, Katherine Hill, because you are a woman with strong opinions. Your world has made you willful."

I turned and shook my head at him.

"If anything, Bishop Yoder, that world has made me more determined to seek out what will make me happy. It made me run, and I found this place. It made me see where I needed to go. There is nothing I want in that world. Not when I can find peace and happiness here," I replied and stepped inside.

I heard him following after me, and saw the looks of surprise on the Bergers' faces as I stepped in. I put myself at a safe distance from him, close to Nathan as the Bishop lingered in the doorway. He looked at each of us, holding his hat tight in his hand.

"I was told to meet with both of you weekly, so that we may complete your baptism classes before first frost. I will do so, but it is under duress," he said, refusing to look at me.

"Samuel, you know this is right," Fannie said as she stood beside Jonah.

He shook his head and turned to leave.

"It is not for me to decide when the community has spoken. Therefore I will abide by their wishes," he said and paused in the doorway, looking back at us.

"I will expect you at my home this Tuesday evening. We will meet for an hour, and then discuss a time to meet from there. It is inconvenient, but it must be done," he said and made to leave.

"Thank you, Bishop Yoder. We will try not to burden you," Nathan said.

The Bishop glanced over his shoulder, eyeing Nathan hard.

"We will see. But you must remember your responsibilities, Nathan. Your baptism brings with it many responsibilities," he said and disappeared into the night.

I looked up at Nathan, whose eyes were now downturned and thoughtful.

"What did he mean, Nathan?" I asked, my voice sounding fragile in the silent room.

He tilted his head up, his eyes unreadable as he stroked my chin lightly. His smile seemed a little sad, but his eyes had turned soft as he gazed down at me and sighed.

"It means," he murmured, "that you may soon be a Bishop's wife."

6

"What? What does that mean?"

I knew my voice sounded a little too high-pitched and shocked. I had been having a hard enough time figuring out how to make tomatoes grow, so the idea of becoming some pillar to the community was way out of my league.

Nathan guided me toward the table, sitting down beside me as Fannie and Jonah looked on.

"Every man baptized into the community is eligible to become the next Bishop," he explained, watching me with trepidation as I tried to close my mouth and swallow.

My throat was terribly dry.

Couldn't we have just one day without something new coming up?

"It was always imagined that Benjamin or Nathan would make fine Bishops," Fannie explained.

"In truth, the Bishop had hoped to get Nathan baptized soon, as he has wanted to retire from the position since his wife grew ill," Jonah added.

"She would not be so ill had he not sent her son away," Fannie grated. The heat in her voice surprised me. She had never seemed angry before.

"Calm, Fannie. It is not our business," Jonah chided.

"Wait," I interjected and raised my hands to halt their conversation. "I'm still stuck on the Bishop thing. We can come back to Benjamin in a bit."

I turned in my seat and looked at Nathan, who was rubbing at the clean tabletop distractedly.

"The Bishop wanted you to be his next in line?" I asked.

He shrugged and nodded.

"It is not for him to decide, but that was his hope, yes."

"If it's not for him to decide then he can't threaten you with the plan of becoming Bishop," I said.

Jonah leaned in and took my hand.

"It is for God to decide, but the community can vote on who is to be chosen. You can be sure Nathan's name would be amongst the chosen," he said, confusing me further.

"Every year," Fannie continued. "We meet in Council to decide on our laws and ways. This is a means of renewal for us. And at that time, if a new Bishop is to be chosen, the community puts in names of those deemed worthy of the leadership role of Bishop."

"Those men who are baptized and voted in are taken with the Elders to choose from several Bibles. In one, a slip of paper is hidden, that signifies the chooser as the new Bishop. In this way, although we may have chosen whom to nominate, God ultimately decides who is to be our new Bishop," Jonah explained.

I thought about it for several moments, trying to work my mind around their voting policies. Even if Nathan were to choose the Way and become a baptized member, it was not a guarantee that he would be Bishop. Or that he would be chosen once married to me.

"It seems far-fetched that the community would vote in a man with a wife who had once been English," I argued.

"Perhaps we do not see you as English at all, Katherine, but always meant for the Amish life," Jonah mused and made to stand. "True, it is not common, but if the voice of God is in the pairing, who is to argue it? And there are some who would see that as a blessing for Bishop."

"This is all speculative and will only cause more worry. It is not in our hands to decide," Fannie said and stood up with her husband.

Nathan nodded and stood, holding onto my hand as he did. I stood with him and walked to the doorway, wanting to say goodnight. He turned back to Jonah, pausing in putting on his hat.

"May I speak with Kate for a moment? I will be quick," he asked.

Jonah nodded and let us leave, Nathan pulling me toward the barn on his way to his hill. We saw Emma wish John a good night and slip into the house, careful to give us a wide berth as Nathan led us to the barn. Once on the far side of it, he turned and looked down at me, eyes intense.

"Does this news trouble you?" he asked.

I could hear the fear in his voice, the uncertainty.

"You don't want to be the Bishop," I reasoned, understanding his fear when he shook his head.

"It was always Benjamin. He was always deemed more appropriate for the position. At least prior to his falling out with his father. With him gone, there are very few the community would consider. Many would have chosen Benjamin," he said, holding me a little closer.

"Is that why he's afraid to return?" I asked, thinking about the looks he gave when mentioning his return.

"It is more than that. He let his father down by staying amongst the English. The Bishop feels he failed his son, and that is difficult to admit. And even now, many still wish the Bishop's son would return. But when we are baptized, it will be assumed that I should be voted in," he explained.

"And the Bishop may try to do that before we are married?" I asked, thinking about a new way to try and scare me off.

"I would not doubt it. I do not see us married before the next Council. Baptized, perhaps, but a wedding would need to happen immediately," he said, glancing off toward the house.

I turned in time to see Jonah's silhouette in the doorway.

"I should get back," I said softly.

"Wait," he said and took me by the shoulders, gripping me with care. "I do not wish to put us in a bad position, Kate. I should have discussed this with you before asking you to be my wife. I should not have withheld this possibility from you. That was unfair."

I smiled and leaned up to kiss him. It was short, much shorter than both of us wanted.

"I will still be your wife," I whispered. "Being a Bishop's wife doesn't scare me."

He smiled and deepened the kiss, pressing into me a little harder.

"You truly are stronger than many see. You are my rock. I hope I can be that for you as well," he murmured, his mouth covering mine a little more earnestly.

"I need to get back," I mumbled against his lips, sighing when they traveled to my ear, his breath hot there.

"I will not be able to sleep without thinking of you next to me," he said and pressed his lips just under my ear.

I grinned and tightened my grip around his shoulders, holding him closer.

"Well, at least he agreed to offer classes sooner. That means a quicker wedding," I said, tipping my head back to wink up at him.

He pulled away and laughed.

"That will be a benefit," he sighed and then sobered up quickly. "I will manage this. It is perhaps a sign that I will find a way to make it through the winter, Kate."

I pulled his hand, drawing him back toward the house.

"There is still my car to sell. And I have a little money left from Dad. Not much, but if the car sells well, we'll have something. And I can make anything out of just about nothing.

You'd be surprised what I can do with noodles and an imagination," I said with a smile.

He stopped at the base of the steps and held my hand for a moment longer.

"We will see what is provided for us. Perhaps tomorrow you can help me to clear part of the garden and we can plant something to grow before the frost?" he asked.

I glanced up at the shadow of Jonah in the window and nodded.

"I'll see if they'll let me," I replied and kissed him one last time before he drew away.

"I will see you in the morning then, Kate. Pleasant dreams," he said and walked backwards until I closed the door. His profile was still visible through the window as he turned and walked slowly up the hill and disappeared.

Heading to the kitchen, I found Fannie and Jonah sitting at the table, looking my way.

"You must think this unjust," Jonah said softly.

I frowned and tilted my head to the side, silently asking what he meant.

"He means how we choose our Bishop," Fannie clarified.

I sat once more at the table with them.

"What if it's not something that is in his heart?" I asked quietly.

"Every man must have God in his heart. Every man knows that he may be chosen, and must accept it if it falls on him. The responsibility will be immense, on both of you. But it will be Nathan's duty if chosen. Every man understands and agrees to it upon his baptism," Jonah explained.

"The community wanted Benjamin Yoder," I stated, trying to work through my thoughts.

"Yes, that is true."

"What if he rejoined the community? Would he then be in line to become Bishop?" I asked, looking up into Jonah's compassionate eyes.

He glanced at Fannie, a look of uncertainty crossing his face.

"He would need to convince the Bishop that he was worthy of his baptism. He has not accepted our path yet," he said, ducking the issue.

"But if he did convince Bishop Yoder, before the Council convened. He could be chosen and not Nathan?"

Fannie patted my hand and tried to smile.

"You seem to like Benjamin, we all do. But his history with his father is what makes him hesitate about returning," she said.

"What did he do to make the Bishop turn him away? Nathan told me that he's not been shunned," I said, their smiles widening at my observation.

"That is Benjamin's story. But I will say he fears more than he should. It is true; the community has not shunned him, as much as the Bishop may have wanted to. His wife convinced him otherwise. And for that there is hope. It is time for him to come home and face his demons here," Jonah said and stood up.

"So how do we convince him to come back?" I asked, wanting to figure this out.

Fannie smiled and pulled me in with her arm.

"What makes you think we are not already succeeding in that? He came to supper this evening, when before he would not. Is that not a success?" she asked, grinning.

"Enough talk now. It is late," Jonah said, putting an end to the conversation. "Tomorrow will be a busy day."

I nodded and hugged them goodnight, my mind overwhelmed by what had happened during the day. I struggled to find a solution for everything. It appeared the simple life wasn't really all that simple. I barely slept; the early morning came too quickly to offer much rest.

Nathan was quiet throughout breakfast, answering only a few questions from Jonah, most of them with nods or a shake of the head. He looked tired, as if he had not slept well either. I was silent beside him, finishing my breakfast in preparation for a busy day. I was sure that there was much to do not only at the Bergers' house, but at the Fisher home as well, and I wanted to dive in and assist in any way I could. I stood and cleaned up, rushing through the washing so that I could convince Fannie that I should go to Nathan's.

It was wash day after all.

"Yes, Katherine," Fannie said, exasperated. "You can go, but I will be by to help as soon as I have Emma started with the wash."

I said my goodbyes and grabbed the basket we had made for a meal later, following Nathan out into the early morning sunlight. We kept that respectable distance we had cultivated while in public. But even with a foot between us, I could feel him beside me. When we were out of earshot, Nathan spoke.

"The morning sun plays in your hair nicely. Like spun gold," he offered.

I smiled and glanced his way. I could tell he was watching me, although his head remained forward.

"That is the first thing you have said all morning to me," I replied, smiling.

He frowned and shook his head.

"I apologize for that. My mind has been many places this morning," he said.

"Don't apologize. I understand," I soothed, reaching for his hand as we crested the hill. "It's nice to hear a compliment as the first thing."

His lips curved into a timid smile and he tilted his head my way, green eyes swallowing me up.

"I wrote you something last night. But I dare not show it to anyone."

"Why would you tell me that and then not want to share it?" I asked, laughing.

His ears reddened and his smile grew wicked.

"I will share it with you on our wedding night," he replied and squeezed my hand a little tighter.

We walked to the house, so that I could put away the food. Nathan watched me from the doorway, taking in every movement as I set things in their proper place. When I turned around to face him, he was looking down at his feet.

"What's wrong?" I asked.

His head shot up and he looked surprised, like I had caught him somehow.

"I am trying to make things work in my head and I cannot seem to make it all coalesce," he admitted.

"Are we talking about what happened last night?"

He nodded and looked down.

"I should not have told you I did not want to be Bishop. I sound ungrateful and selfish, but it is my duty if Benjamin does not return in time and I am voted on. And now I must think how to convince him sooner than I expected," he said, his voice troubled.

I moved to him, wrapping my arms around his waist. His arms engulfed me, and we stood there for a moment enjoying the comfort of each other.

"I have been thinking about Benjamin and how to get him back. I didn't sleep much last night," I said.

"I did not sleep either, thinking about the same thing. We are selfish, you realize?" he whispered.

I looked up into his guilty demeanor and shook my head.

"No, we are being practical, and sensible. Benjamin needs to come home. Not just for us, but for him as well. And the community. He was at the Bishop's yesterday, did you see him?" I asked.

He shook his head.

"He was back in his Amish clothes, and he stood just at the edge of the field, listening. He wants to come home, Nathan. But whatever happened is making him doubt himself. I have no idea if he wants to be Bishop, but at the very least he needs to come back where he can thrive," I reasoned.

"I offered him a place in my home, Kate. He has not taken me up on the offer," Nathan murmured into my ear.

"Well, perhaps we need to make him a place here, already

made up for him, so he feels comfortable about it. Maybe he feels he would be putting you out? Which I can't understand since you have this big house," I said, stopping myself before I commented on how it was just Nathan living in the big house.

"We should set up one of the rooms for him," he suggested, and I could hear the pain in his voice.

"I think it would be good, for both of you," I said and leaned up to kiss him across his pursed lips, hoping to comfort him.

"Will you help me? I cannot do it alone," he said.

I slowly drew away and took his hand, guiding him through the house, ignoring the cloth-covered furniture for the time being and heading up the stairs. I didn't know whose bedrooms had been whose. I took one glance at Nathan's tidy room and moved to the next closed door, looking up to him askance.

He shook his head.

"That was Rachel's."

Holding his hand a little more firmly, we went to the next door.

He shook his head again and swallowed hard.

"Mary and Ruth's," he croaked.

The next door, at the end of the hall had him shaking. I pulled him back down the hall to the door across from his. He let out a long sigh and looked at the door as if remembering the memories the room held for him. I figured, based on deduction, that this must have been his brothers' room. He had told me that David, his oldest brother, had died the year his youngest brother, Jason, had been born.

"This room has seen changes, right? Maybe this room is the right one," I offered.

I felt him shudder beside me and he let out a long breath.

"I know things will need to change. It is just difficult to give them up," he whispered.

"Then let's give Benjamin the chance to change things. To give you that step into a new life," I suggested.

Nodding, Nathan took a halting step at the door, his breath

RENEWING HOPE

becoming more irregular as he drew closer. His free hand lingered on the doorknob, contemplating. I watched as he closed his eyes and turned the knob, the door opening with a slight squeak. He kept his eyes closed as the door opened, revealing his youngest brother's room, as it was the day he had died.

Sunlight poured into the room, swirls of dust floating in the air from the movement made by the door. Inside was a room similar to Nathan's. The room was simply furnished with a twin-sized bed, a small chest of drawers, and a writing desk that looked to still have papers strewn across it. The bed had been made, tidy and quilt-covered, just like Nathan's. But unlike Nathan's room, this room had bits and pieces of the occupant's life around it. Tucked in the corner lay a pile of books, a small wooden horse, and on the wall, hand-drawn pictures of farm life. I recognized the big black horse immediately. But there were also drawings of the fields, the hill I had grown to adore, and white puffy clouds over fields of green.

Jason had been an artist of sorts. His drawings, for a small child, were quite good, and my heart hurt looking at the shrine that had been left of him. His last thoughts, his last boyish dreams were littered throughout the room. I looked back at Nathan, who stood frozen, his eyes clenching shut.

"I cannot go in," he whimpered, shaking his head. "I am sorry. But I cannot."

I squeezed his hand in reassurance before letting it go, turning to the room with the solemn sense of duty. I stepped in, feeling the warmth of the sun hit me as I entered. The air was a little stale from having been shut for so long. I moved silently to the window and eased it open, feeling the morning breeze wash over me. Glancing back to Nathan, I found him watching me with pained eyes, arms folded around himself.

I turned back to the task at hand; already the tears blurred my vision while I worked to strip the bed. I could feel Nathan's eyes on me as moved around the room. I took my time, taking care his brother's things while I packed them away, to make room for the future. I wiped my tears away before I turned toward Nathan. I didn't want him to see how much this affected me, too. I wanted him to know I could do this for him. I needed to be the strong one this time.

I worked in silence, pulling down the pictures with care and laying them on the desk next to the unfinished pictures there. Moving to the wardrobe, I found a box of other pictures, older ones that Mrs. Fisher must have been keeping. I placed everything into the box and looked back at Nathan.

"We should find a special place for this. Someplace that won't ruin the pictures," I suggested, my voice rough from holding back the tears.

He swallowed and took a tentative step into the bedroom, stopping half a step in. He extended his hands, silently requesting the box from me. I closed the distance and handed it to him with care, his eyes downturned as he fingered the box in his hands. He then turned and walked out without a word; I watched him as he entered his own room and closed the door.

I let him have some time to himself while I worked to clean the room, able to do it a little faster without him watching. It was still difficult to do, fighting back tears every time I found something that would have been the little boy's. Jacks under the bed, the baseball bat leaning against the desk. I wiped down the dust, opened the window further as the sun heated the room, and gathered up the discarded linens. I left the door open, a symbol that we were moving on.

When I dropped off the linens at the back door, I prepared some tea to set out in the sunlight on the porch and quietly made my way back upstairs. Nathan's door was still closed. I tapped on the door, calling out his name. When he didn't answer, I cracked the door open, seeing him on the bed, fast asleep.

I swallowed hard and watched him for a moment, curled up around the box, his eyebrows drawn tight as he slumbered. He looked like he was a little boy who had cried himself to sleep. I knew he was tired, and that this had been a dramatic event for him, so I let him sleep. I tiptoed into his room to grab the clothes I could find that needed washing, glancing back at him one more time before easing the door closed and making my way downstairs. I searched out the washing machine.

It looked as if the Fishers didn't have one of those nice machines that the Bergers had. I let out a soft breath and set some water to boil on the stove while I traveled back and forth to fill the old fashioned washtub I had found on the back porch. The sun peeked in between the clouds while I worked, my mind drifting as I thought about how sad Nathan had been.

I knew now more than anything that we needed to get Benjamin back. Benjamin was his friend, and he might help bring Nathan out of his mourning for his family. It seemed we all needed one another for some sort of healing. Perhaps it was meant to be.

I wrung out the clothes one by one, humming to myself while I worked, relaxing in the quiet. About half way through the washing, I saw Fannie at the top of the hill and waved. I couldn't tell her expression as she looked down, she was too far away. She waved in reply and turned back around toward her house. I snorted at her checking in and pulled the wet clothes to the clothesline.

Nathan didn't have many clothes this time, so I made quick work of his personals before jumping into the sheets I had pulled off the bed. The quilt was harder to manage, but I wanted it clean for Benjamin when we convinced him to stay.

I knew we would.

I had it firmly set that we would.

The laundry done, I decided to look around to see what else I could do outside before it got too hot. Nathan had still not emerged, and I didn't want to wake him if this nap would ease his worries. I watered the garden, pulling some meager tomatoes and a half basket of beans from the vines. His squash was late but starting to blossom, and it looked like he had planted carrots that were starting to show. I smiled at the idea that perhaps all was not lost in his garden.

Too soon, I was feeling idle once more. Alone with no one to guide me, I supposed it was the best chance for me to learn about the Fisher farm and its goings-on. How much did Fannie do that I had no idea about, and what would I do with just Nathan here? Surely I could help with some of the usual chores. Maybe not get on a plow and dig some trenches, but I could be of help somehow.

It was late morning by now and I could hear the soft nickering of the horses in the barn as I neared it, in search of my next task. I tensed at the noise, unsure of the animals inside. The horses were much bigger than me, and I had no idea how to handle them, really. I walked back to the garden, to the apple tree there and plucked a few good-sized apples from it. I had remembered feeding the horses at a petting zoo when I was little.

They had been little horses, not nearly as big as these. I had been five then as well.

I was older and surer of myself now.

As I stepped into the barn, the big black poked his massive head from his stall and shook his mane fancifully at me as I neared. I hoped that was his way of saying hello and not a warning for me to back off. I whispered to him, his eyes regarding me with a depth I found intimidating for an animal.

Magnus was very aware of the world around him.

I stroked his muzzle with a tentative hand, his lips chewing on my fingers for a second before he nickered and nodded his head, as if telling me to stop teasing him. I chuckled and pulled out one apple, laying it in my open hand for him to take. He took it eagerly and munched on it as I stroked along his neck, looking into his stall to see if it needed cleaning. I had no idea what I was looking for really.

How dirty was dirty to a horse? My personal judgment was it needed to be cleaned, but hadn't Nathan just cleaned it a few days ago? Was this something he did daily?

I offered Magnus another apple and patted him on the neck before moving to the other horses, the tan pair that Nathan used for the bigger wagons. They greeted me much as Magnus had; enjoying the apples I gave them eagerly. I noticed they had nothing but hay in their stalls, and their water was low. Feeling more relaxed with the smaller horses; I opened one stall and spoke in a soft voice with the mare, coaxing her out easily with my hand on her halter.

Maybe she was guiding me out. She seemed to know where to go as we walked toward the other open door leading to the enclosed pasture I had seen them in a few times on my visits. She lingered near the barn, looking back at me as I stepped back in, coaxing her mate out, again with ease. Once together, they ventured off toward the waiting grass, grazing on it as if perhaps this was their only meal available to them.

I thought again to what Nathan had said about not being able to feed his horses, let alone himself. Looking around, I couldn't find anything other than hay and more hay. What else did horses eat? Oats, right?

"What does he feed you, Magnus?" I asked as I returned to his stall, his dark eyes following me as I approached.

He nickered again and pawed at the ground. He made me nervous, towering there even in the stall. I had to wonder if he would get angry if I left him in the barn while the other two grazed. Do horses have feelings like that? I was thinking too hard on the idea of equine psychology.

I let out a huff and stood a little straighter to Magnus, knowing that animals could feel when we were afraid. I didn't want a one-ton animal knowing I was afraid of him. I pulled out another apple and gave him a gentle pat.

"You're going to be a good boy, right?" I asked, my voice calm and sure.

He took the apple from my hand and merely looked at me while he chewed.

I opened the stall door and rested my hand on his halter, guiding him out. I had to almost tip toe to even touch his halter when he started to walk. He paused just outside of his stall and shook his mane again, before turning in the opposite direction of the pasture, toward the other door.

Was there any chance I would have to stop him?

I panicked for a brief moment that he might bolt and run away. Nathan would be angry that I had let his horses loose. I'd ruin it all with a lost horse. But just as we neared the door, Magnus stopped and nodded his head, letting out a loud rumbling sort of sound. I eyed him warily, standing beside a large steel basin. He nodded again and dipped his head down into it, then back up when he saw it was empty. Another nicker and this time he caught me by surprise when he lowered his head and nudged me.

Nudged was a nice word for batted me with his head hard enough to make me stumble, but not so hard to knock me over. He wanted my attention.

"So where are the oats then, you big beast? Show me if you want to get fed, otherwise it's nice tasty Iowa grass for your big butt," I replied.

He nickered again, and I could almost swear it was a great rumbling horselaugh. He nudged me again, pushing me toward a pile of canvas bags opposite the basin. When I found them, I opened them up to find the oats.

"See? I knew you were good for more than pulling a plow," I joked, dragging the bag along the ground toward the basin. He followed, his head dipped close to the opening. He nudged me a little harder as I struggled to get the sack over the edge to pour out the oats.

"Watch it, buddy. Or I'll stick you back in your stall," I grunted and heaved the bag into the large tub.

I poured some out, not knowing how much he could eat. I was probably underfeeding him, but Nathan could always show me later. I dragged the bag back to where I found it and patted the giant beast until he had had his fill; eating everything I had given him. As if to thank me, he left me a pile to clean up as he sauntered away toward the pasture.

I scowled at him as he headed out to graze, separate from the others. He watched me for a moment as I closed the gate, and then steadfastly ignored me to feast on the grass. I sighed in relief and settled into trying to figure out how to clean the stalls. There was a wheelbarrow there, and a pitchfork and shovel laying in it. I grabbed the wheelbarrow, heading to Magnus' stall first, somehow knowing he was the king of the barn, and would need to be satisfied.

Only a couple attempts at the pitchfork and I knew I was in for a challenge.

Hay was a lot harder to catch with a pitchfork than I had thought. And it was heavy when you had a good bit on it. Add to that what the horse left behind and I was sweating by the time I had the wheelbarrow half full. I was trying to think where the wheelbarrow full of Magnus' muck went when I heard my name being called.

Stepping out to the door, I called back to Nathan, who was on the porch looking around. He looked a little frazzled, his hair messed up and gleaming like golden threads in the midday sun. He saw me and pulled his hat on, walking quickly over to me.

"You let me sleep. Why did you do that? There is so much to be done," he rushed out, the panic clear in his voice.

"You needed it, Nathan. I'm sorry," I said, feeling guilty for letting him sleep. He looked down at me, as if to say something, and then stopped, a perplexed look crossing his face.

"What have you been doing?" he asked, and brushed off some of the stall dust from my shoulder.

I thumbed back toward the stalls.

"Mucking out stalls, Nathan Fisher. What did you think I was doing?" I asked, fighting a grin.

He craned his neck to look around me, to inside the barn.

"You are?" he started and then followed me as I turned to return to my job.

He surveyed my poor attempt at clearing Magnus' stall, at the wheelbarrow that thankfully had more hay and refuse in it than the floor around it, and then back at me. I shrugged.

"I'm terrible, I know. But it's my first time. I'll get better," I said looking away, embarrassed now that I had even attempted this.

I wasn't prepared for his hands reaching out for me. He startled me, making me jump as he pushed me up against the stall wall and kissed me hard. His lips attacked me with such enthusiasm; I was left breathless and gasping for air when he pulled away.

"How am I supposed to be gentlemanly when you do such incredible things like this, making me want you so badly," he groaned and hugged me to him. I felt his heavy breaths, through his chest and across my ear as he let his emotions go. I hugged him to me in return, keeping quiet as he battled his feelings. I whispered softly in his ear, to offer him love and comfort. When he finally pulled away, he was smiling again. He looked around the stall, chuckling and pulled me around so we could survey my work.

"It is not bad, Kate for your first try. I do not know how you handled Magnus. He is particular about who handles him," he said, eyeing me in curiosity.

I waved him off and pretended I had it under control.

"That silly horse? Putty in my hands," I scoffed.

"Really?" he asked, unconvinced. "I think you bribed him, perhaps."

I shook my head and laughed.

"How do you bribe a horse? He was even helpful and showed me where the oats were," I continued and picked up the shovel to continue my work. Nathan gently took it from my hands and smiled as he swapped the shovel for a pitchfork leaned against the outer stall.

"I will have to show you the daily business out here, I suppose. Feeding and care, and maybe I can convince Jonah to allow me to have a cow back," he said and illustrated how to properly muck out the stall.

I stood there and watched him for a moment, trying hard to listen to him as he detailed the daily morning duties, but it was difficult when his back turned and stretched and his arms flexed as he tossed manure into the wheelbarrow.

Horses fed and watered.

Stretch, push, flex and flick.

Hay bale moved from somewhere and something or other.

Stretch, muscle ripple along the forearm. Lift and toss.

Clean the stalls, something about every other day...

Scrape, bend and watch the suspenders tighten as he leaned, pulling the waistline of his trousers up, accentuating his backside against the tight fabric.

"Kate?"

I jerked my eyes up and could feel the heat on my face. It

didn't matter how close we were. I was still caught ogling.

"Do I need to show you again?" he asked, his voice deep and his playful grin telling me he knew exactly what I had been doing.

"Um," I said, trying to rein in my feelings of just wanting to explore the hay with him again.

He stepped closer to me, the heat radiating off of him as he leaned in. His lips brushed across mine, feather light. I let out a sigh and leaned in, wanting more. But he pulled away and licked at his lips.

"I do not want to be found out again in the barn, not without a blanket," he mused and kissed me quickly before stepping back to return to scraping the last of the stall, the smile remaining on his lips.

"I will show you where we put the used straw. I use it for compost," he said, back in teaching mode.

I nodded and walked with him as he pushed the wheelbarrow through the back door and to an area that was obviously used for disposing of the horse waste. A pile of hay, slowly decomposing, sat there a good distance from the barn. He dumped the wheelbarrow and mixed it a little with the other hay already there, blending it in.

We returned to the barn and I worked in the mare's stall while Nathan worked in her partner's. I cried out when he threw a clump of hay at me, contemplating throwing a good dry piece of horse manure. In no time we had the stalls cleared out.

I had even tried my hand at pushing the wheelbarrow.

Some things I just wasn't good at. Nathan caught it before it toppled over and laughed. I'd be sure and strong enough, one day. We ate our lunch out on the porch, catching sight of Fannie once more on the hill, offering a wave and then disappearing once more. Nathan looked out after her in amusement.

"She must trust us, if she is only now coming to check on us," he commented as he chewed on his sandwich.

"She did the same thing while you were sleeping. While I was at the wash," I replied.

He nodded and was silent for a while, eating his sandwich in quiet contemplation.

"I am sorry I left you to do all the chores," he said finally.

"You didn't leave them to me, Nathan. I wanted to do them. I need to learn," I replied.

He sighed and looked down at his hands.

"It was just more to deal with than I thought. Seeing Jason's room again," he murmured.

"I know," I whispered and touched his hand, clasping it in mine.

"I know I need to let it go and move on. It is just difficult to do so," he explained, refusing to look up.

I touched his chin, drawing his eyes up to mine.

"How about this, Nathan? We will open one room once a week," I suggested. "It is not about letting go, it is about allowing it to emerge into something else."

He sighed and thought about it for a second.

"One room every week?" he asked. I nodded.

He looked at the house, as if seeing it in a new way.

"That sounds like a good idea," he murmured and leaned in to kiss me.

"We'll deal with it together, okay?" I offered. "And we'll convince Benjamin to come back. Things will be better, you'll see."

He pulled me close and rocked us gently in the swing, letting the early afternoon breeze cool us as we relaxed before returning to our daily chores. It was a nice bit of quiet for just the two of us.

Nathan showed me the seed stores they owned, his mother having collected many good seeds for her garden, many of which we would hopefully be planting in the spring. We picked out some beet seeds, finding a space in the garden to start them with the hope that they would grow in time before the first frost.

Everything seemed to be determined by the first frost.

Nathan left me so that he could check on his crops in the fields, young growing pumpkins and winter squash. I watched him now and again as I sat up to stretch from digging and filling holes.

He walked with care through the field, squatting every once and a while to touch at the plants growing there. He seemed at peace there amongst the dirt and the green.

This was his life.

I continued on with the planting, watering as I went, relieved at the cloud cover as it started to shade the sun from my neck. For September, it was hot. September back home had been rainy and cold. But that was most of the time. These clouds were darker than I had seen though upon coming here, and as I stood to stretch, I felt the first fat water drops as they hit my face.

I wiped at my hands and rushed to the clothesline, grabbing at the clothes in haste and tossing them into the basket unfolded. The storm seemed to rush in, the darkness a little unnerving as I grabbed the last of the sheets and hauled the basket into my arms to rush inside. As I stepped onto the porch I saw Nathan in the pasture, herding the horses back into the barn. I dropped the basket and ran out to help him just as the heavens opened up and the thunder boomed overhead.

He had Magnus beside him as he guided him in, the horse stamping angrily as they stepped into the barn. The other two horses came trotting after. I helped to get them back into the stalls, offering them more oats in one of their basins. As soon as they were settled, Nathan shut the stalls and wiped his face, the rainwater dripping from him.

"Ready to make a run for the house?" he asked as we both looked outside at the sheets of water falling.

My answer was drowned out by the loud crack of thunder, but his hand grabbing at mine propelled me into motion. We dashed across the yard, mud and water kicking up as we ran. Jumping up onto the porch, we stood under the overhang, watching as the rain continued to come down in sheets. Nathan helped me with the basket of clothes and set it down on the kitchen table when another rumble of thunder sounded through the house.

"The window upstairs!" I cried out, realizing I had forgotten it was open to air out the room.

I rushed up stairs, shutting the window quickly before any

more water seeped in.

Looking around, I shook my head at the mess. The water was not as bad as the mud I had tracked up the stairs with my soiled shoes. I took them off with a rough tug and was about to look for something to wipe it up with when I saw Nathan in the doorway, holding a towel.

"I'm sorry. I didn't mean to track mud into the house," I said, getting on my hands and knees to wipe up the mess.

"It is all right, Kate. That is why we have wood floors. They are easier to clean. Come. I will finish that. You should dry yourself," he said and took a measured step inside the room.

He looked around the space, clearly uncomfortable, before taking another step in and squatting before me. His hand reached out slowly, taking the towel in my hands.

"Go and get dry. You will catch cold," he whispered, and the look in his eyes made me realize he was concerned about me. Of course he was thinking about his family and their sickness.

I could see it in his eyes.

I nodded and stepped out, grabbing my soiled shoes and finding the clothesbasket back in the kitchen. I searched through it and found a towel to dry off with, taking off my cover and letting my hair down to dry it. I heard Nathan come down the stairs and as I turned I blinked at him, bare-chested and walking toward me.

"You need to dry off, Kate. You are soaked," he said, taking the towel from my hands and wiping down my arms and neck.

I stood there dumbly.

I was wet, not particularly cold in the moment while he touched me. He seemed to realize the effect he had on me and paused, looking at the towel in his hands. His eyes drifted up the length of me, my breath coming faster as I watched his eyes darken under his wet hair that had fallen down onto his forehead.

"Your dress is soaked through," he said, his voice husky.

"I'm just wet. I can just take the dress off and let it dry," I replied, trying to ease his concern.

"You do not have a change of clothes here," he said, his eyes widening some.

"You've seen me in less than my shift Nathan," I replied and started undoing the hooks. His hand stopped me.

"I don't have the strength today to keep my distance, Kate," he whispered. "I have been struggling all day to behave."

"Oh," I said, not realizing he had been in such dire straits with me. I knew it had been an emotional day, but I didn't know I had been part of the cause.

"I'll wrap up in the quilt, okay?" I said, starting to feel the chill as the cold settled in.

He nodded and pulled the quilt out of the basket holding it up for me as I undid the hooks on my dress. His eyes never left me though. I paused and smirked at him.

"Nathan, if you are struggling, then why are you staring at me while I strip?" I teased.

He blushed and closed his eyes, cracking one open before I swatted at him. He bit at his lip and closed his eyes again, letting me pull off my dress so that I stood in only my shift. It was damp as well, but I didn't want to suggest taking that off too. I reached for the quilt and wrapped it around me, covering me better than any toga at a frat party would.

Nathan opened his eyes again and smiled.

"Much better," he said and grabbed a dry shirt to put on. I watched in dismay as he dressed, rather liking him standing there half naked before me.

It seemed both of us had issues with behaving.

We stood there in the darkening kitchen while we waited for the rain to let up. As the minutes passed, the storm seemed to worsen, the sound of pelting raindrops slapping loudly against the porch roof. Looking out, we noticed the hail. I wondered idly if this was God's way of warning me to be good when Nathan took my hand and pulled me close, the two of us standing in the doorway as we watched the yard in the back of the house turn a muddy grey. Perhaps God was giving us a little time alone in a place that wouldn't normally allow it.

I liked that idea better.

Nathan held me a little closer, dipping his head down to kiss the top of my head before looking out again at the storm. His fingertips drifted across the bare skin of my shoulder, making the skin prickle there.

"Are you cold?" he asked, tracing the skin and watching it pebble under his touch.

I shook my head and glanced up at him, his eyes dark once more.

"Why are you shivering then?" he asked.

I let out a slow breath and turned away from the torrent outside.

"You know why," I breathed and leaned into him, enjoying his warmth.

"Jonah and Fannie will worry over you. They may come, even in this rain," he said, his hand slipping down and around the back of my shoulder, stroking.

"So stop touching me then, if you're afraid," I whispered and stood on tiptoes to kiss him.

He groaned and wrapped his arms around me, pulling me back into the kitchen, the storm and everyone in the world falling away. I felt one arm wrap around me high, the other low, and I had just enough time to brace for it before he picked me up and carried me up the stairs. I cried out in surprise when he tossed me on his small bed, following after.

His mouth covered mine with an urgency he rarely allowed, his hands twining into my hair while mine traveled down the length of his back. He groaned and pressed me into the small bed, partially covering me with his hard body while we explored one another in the darkening room. Lightning flashed outside, thunder rolled, and the rain kept hammering down, as if this was the first day of forty of the great flood.

He broke away from our kiss with a panting groan, and let his eyes wander to where the quilt had fallen loose, exposing my dampened shift underneath. Looking down I could see the shift was almost see-through. He slid his long body beside me so that his head rested against my breast. He wrapped his arm around my waist and pressed himself to me, letting out a contented breath.

"Perhaps we can just stay like this for a time? As much as I want to finish what we started the other day, I think I like just laying here like this with you," he murmured, his breath hot against my skin.

I let one hand play in his hair while the other stroked his arm around my waist. As much as I wanted to go further, it was nice knowing that Nathan could enjoy simply being together. Not needing to do anything more than lay in one another's company, even if our bodies asked for it.

Temptation could be kept at bay.

We lay like that until the rain slowed, the thunder growing more distant, the two of us quiet in our thoughts. Occasionally Nathan would squeeze me a little closer, or speak softly about something he wanted to show me in the spring. Or about what he wanted to plant in the next year. Or I would mention something about what I wanted to grow in the garden.

It was a quiet bit of time where we could share our hopes for the future.

Our future.

"Kate?"

I hummed in response, feeling at peace with his heat against me. I felt him lift up and opened my eyes to see him looking down at me in the waning light.

"If I do become the Bishop, you will be all right with that path? Truly?" he asked, his voice rough from having rested for so long.

"If you are to become Bishop, I will support you as I should. But I worry that it's not something you want," I replied.

He looked at the window and chewed on his lips, deep in thought.

"It is my duty if Benjamin does not return in time. Our classes will be over by November. It will not be easy to get him back that soon I think," he said.

I sat up and touched his cheek, bringing his worried gaze back to me.

"We'll try, Nathan. It's all we can do. But Benjamin needs to want to come home and face his future, too. It's ultimately up to him," I said and moved to get up.

"He feels guilty for many things. I am not sure how to help him with those."

I folded up the quilt as I thought about it.

"I think he needs to see how much he is needed here. To know that he has a purpose. Maybe he hasn't felt that in a while," I suggested, and smiled when Nathan leaned in and kissed me.

"I think if we must go the route of the Bishop, you will make a very good Bishop's wife. You have such well spoken thoughts," he chuckled and kissed me again.

"We need to get going, Nathan," I sighed as his lips trailed to my neck.

One last kiss at the base of my neck and he pulled away, smiling.

"A good Bishop's wife that knows when to do right," he sighed.

I changed in a rush, grabbing the vegetables I had gathered that day and walked hand in hand with Nathan back to the Berger's house. Supper passed with some talk about why Benjamin did not join us, but Nathan and I both understood. It would take time. And we would be there to help him.

I settled into bed next to Emma that night, who hugged me and watched me as I thought about it all.

"Are you worried about Nathan?" she asked.

I shook my head slowly.

"Not so much. More about Benjamin, actually," I replied. "He wants to come home, Emma. He has a purpose here and I'm worried he didn't show up tonight because yesterday spooked him." I said, explaining about how I saw him in the field during Sermon.

She nodded and thought about it.

"We are going into town tomorrow to drop off some of the corn cakes we made today and to go shopping. Perhaps we will see him in town, and invite him again," she suggested.

"Maybe. I just want to see him happy again. He was happy at Nathan's. So was Nathan," I replied.

"They were best friends, like us. They need each other," she said. "Promise me you will still be my friend when I go off and make a home with John."

Her words caught me off guard, and I felt an instinct to hug her.

"Of course. I will always be your best friend, Emma. And your sister," I whispered into her hair.

"Good," she sighed and settled into bed, her smile mischievous. "Now I assume since you did not come home with hay in your hair, you did not spend any time in the barn?"

Her eyes were sparkling in the lantern light.

"Actually, Emma, I spent a while in the barn," I quipped, stifling my laughter when her eyes widened. "Mucking out stalls, Emma. I cleaned stalls today."

She giggled and rolled over to turn down the lantern.

As we sat in the dark, waiting for our eyes to adjust, I heard her chuckle.

"Do I want to know what you did while you waited out the storm?"

"Nope. Goodnight, Emma."

She giggled again and I felt her hand squeeze mine once before letting go.

"Goodnight, sister."

I sat in the dark and for the first time in many days, I felt like perhaps we were heading in the right direction.

7

"Katherine."

I cracked my eyes open, squinting at the glare of the lantern near me. Blinking, I could see Emma and Fannie, Emma rubbing her eyes as well. Fannie was fully dressed, but it felt early yet.

"What's going on?" I mumbled, the sleep lingering in my brain.

"Jonah and I must go and help with the delivery of the Lapp baby. I am leaving it up to you girls to take care of the chores and take the food to Eli to sell. Mark and Hannah will be here in the morning," she whispered.

"Of course, Mother," Emma said, her voice a little more awake than my own.

"We will be home as soon as we can," she whispered and closed the door, our room plunging back into darkness.

I groaned and tried to roll over. Every muscle in my body hurt. The work I had done at Nathan's was showing up in all the aches and pains of my body. Somehow I knew this day was going to be long when we woke up earlier than usual, having double the chores than we were used to.

Abigail volunteered to get the eggs; I was not going anywhere near there in the dark. I had a hard enough time being in the barn by myself while I milked the cows. We were ahead of time, so I missed seeing Nathan coming down his hill. He arrived just as I pulled biscuits out of the oven. The sausage and eggs were done, and as he put his hat up, he looked around, confused.

"Evie Lapp is having her baby," Abigail explained and Nathan nodded, his brow puckering slightly.

"I suppose I will be taking the corn to market alone then, unless I can convince Mark to come with me," he said as he took a cup of coffee from me.

"Mark is going with us to town," Hannah said as she entered.

Mark strolled in behind her, inhaling the air as he did.

"You can go without me. I can go to the mill with Nathan after we offload the corn," he said and snuck a piece of sausage off the plate as Emma laid it on the table.

"But you also have to help Katherine with her car. You said the man wanted to make a deal," she argued and smacked his hand when he reached for another sausage.

"I can go and ask John," Nathan replied. "I am not sure I like the idea of the girls going to town by themselves."

Hannah pursed her lips at Nathan and shook her head.

"We are not three, Nathan. We can take care of ourselves," she said, her tone cutting.

"I love being the wanted man in the crowd!" Mark joked, patting Hannah's hand until she leaned back and glowered across the table at Nathan.

We ate and spoke about the course of the day, Nathan wanting to be sure I was back in time for our baptism class later in the afternoon.

"We have to drop off the food at the general store. I know Fannie wanted to pick up some more flour and basic items at the market. And then there is Katherine's car," Hannah was saying.

I was a little sad about seeing the car go. But if it fetched a good price, it meant that Nathan could relax a little about the winter. I was clearing away the last of the dishes when I felt Nathan's hand on my shoulder. I looked up into smiling eyes.

"How are you this morning?" he whispered.

I returned the smile and busied myself with the dishes while I spoke. It was nice having him this close. We both knew Emma and Hannah would understand. And luckily Abigail was distracted with pretending to arm wrestle Mark.

"I'm a little sore from the stalls," I admitted but laughed and shook my head. "I have to start working out or something."

He let out a soft chuckle and let his fingers slip up onto my neck, their warmth feeling nice on my sore neck.

"I imagine you will be sore for a few days. I am grateful for your help, though. I could not stop thinking about yesterday, all night," he breathed near my ear.

"Enough flirting, Nathan!" Hannah admonished. "You will see one another plenty soon. We must get ready or we will not be home in time for your class."

Nathan straightened and let his hand slip from me. But as soon as Hannah had turned, he leaned in and chanced a swift kiss on the cheek, grinning.

"Be careful. I will be thinking of you today," he murmured and took a step back before Hannah intervened once more.

He and Mark disappeared out the back door while we packed up the treats Fannie hoped to sell at the general store. There were several pies she and Emma had made the day before, as well as her prized corncakes. It took us several trips to the buggy to pack them all in, with crates crammed between us and under our feet for the journey.

I sat in the back with Emma and Abigail, while Mark and Hannah sat in the front. I took a brief look back toward the hill, my smile playing on my lips until Emma spoke up, laughing.

"You two are inseparable now. I cannot imagine what it will be like once you are married," she said.

I pretended to scowl at her and turned back around to watch as the road took us to town. I was eager to get there. I was determined to see Benjamin today to be sure he returned to the

Berger's for dinner, and hopefully to stay with Nathan. Emma and Hannah chatted about Emma's upcoming wedding. They still had not planned a date, waiting for when they were baptized. Emma had revealed that John would be going to the Bishop to ask for the two of them to be baptized within the month, so that the wedding could take place in November.

"That does not leave you much time, Emma," Hannah was saying. "And you need to work on your dress. Both of you do. Then there are the invitations to family and friends, coming out and planning the feast. It is more work than you realize."

"I know that, Hannah. I was planning on starting my dress this week, now that most of the crops are done. Besides the canning, we have more time for that," Emma said and smiled over at me.

"Katherine will need help. She has never sewn a dress before. Or did your mother show you?" she asked.

I frowned and looked out at the fields, many clear or in the process of being cleared.

I hadn't thought about my mom much since arriving here.

"My mom didn't show me much of anything before she died," I murmured and continued to look out the window. I felt Abigail lean in and take my hand, her bright blue eyes taking me in with more wisdom than any ten year old I had ever known.

"We will show you. That is what sisters do."

I wrapped my arm around her and held her close, happy to have the support of my new sisters. It made me think wistfully of Stacie, and I had to wonder where she was and what she was doing. It would be sad to not have her here when my own wedding happened.

I missed her with a sudden, sharp pang of loss.

Perhaps Nathan had been earnest in his words to her that she could remain a part of my life. I needed to write to her and tell her the news, knowing she would worry about me.

It's what family did.

The buggy pulled up to a car yard, tearing me away from my idle thoughts. Old cars littered the property near a large garage, many beyond their years and looking more like junk for parts than serviceable vehicles. Inside the covered work area was my car, sitting there as Mark and I passed it on our way to the office. Seeing it there, knowing I would never drive again, was a dose of reality to what my life would be life before long.

A life with no technology, no cars. Simple things. No luxuries.

"Are you all right, Katherine?" Mark asked as we stepped into the small office.

I forced a smile and nodded.

I wasn't going to dwell on things I was leaving behind.

I was looking ahead to what there was to build here.

"Mark!"

I looked up to see an older man, greasy and weathered from working on cars, stepping in from a door behind the counter in the office.

Mark leaned over the counter and shook the man's hand. The man glanced at me for a moment before turning his attention to Mark as he spoke.

"I hear you have an interest in the car we had brought in," Mark said with an easy going smile.

The older man nodded, his face becoming that of the businessman as it grew serious. He wiped some of the grease off his hands with the work towel while he discussed my car.

"It needs a lot of work. Not a bad body but under the hood, it will need a lot of tender loving care to bring the best price," he was saying, his voice sounding a little wearied, like my car was too much work for him to fix up.

I bristled at his words.

If there was one redeeming quality about Sean, it was that he knew cars. And he took care of mine like it was his child. He had even haggled a price for it when I bought it. He had inspected it thoroughly and berated me when I didn't change the oil or rotate the tires per his orders. It wasn't the newest and greatest, but it was in far better condition than this man was letting on.

Mark was listening to him, his reaction contemplative as the man ticked off the problems.

"The engine will need a rebuild. The tires are worn. Cracked radiator. New brakes, and I would think probably work on the struts..."

I shook my head and put my hand up.

The man stopped talking at my reaction, his eyes trained hard on me when I opened up my mouth.

"The engine was still under warranty. The tires do need to be replaced, I agree. But the radiator is most definitely not cracked and the brakes have less than five thousand miles on them. It is in much better shape than you are telling us," I said firmly and watched his eyes slowly widen.

He stood there in silence for an instant before looking over at Mark, poking his thumb in my direction.

"Is this your wife?" he asked, and I could hear the bite to his words.

Mark cleared his throat and shook his head.

"She's my sister-in-law and the owner of the car," he mumbled and glanced at me as if embarrassed for my speaking up.

Had I done something wrong?

The man was trying to short us. And I wasn't having it. Not when this sale might get us through the winter. The man looked me over once more, obviously confused as to why an Amish woman would own a car. But I tilted my head up in defiance and stood my ground.

"The car is worth Blue Book, which last I checked was over twelve thousand. It's been taken care of and all the receipts are in order for repairs. I won't take less than," I started but was cut off by Mark, who put his hand on mine that gripped the edge of the counter.

"We're asking seventy-five hundred. That would give you a tidy profit with a fast turn around," he interjected.

I clenched my mouth closed and let him haggle.

It was obvious I was only there to sign over the papers to it. And truth be known, Mark had asked for more than I was going to. I didn't want to ruin this deal by putting my foot in it.

The man thought for a moment and then finally nodded, shaking Mark's hand.

"Let me go get the paperwork together and I'll cut you a check. I can't let this one go," he mumbled and disappeared through his door, leaving me alone with Mark.

"Did I say something wrong?" I asked in a forced whisper, looking up into Mark's tense jaw.

He scratched at the vinyl cover on the counter, avoiding my eyes.

"You just have to learn how to speak like an Amish woman in public, Katherine," he explained, and blushed before looking up at me. "Do not misunderstand me. I think you are very brave and strong for what you are doing. But you are very vocal. People are not used to that. At least not here."

I frowned and looked away from him, feeling myself withdraw as the mechanic returned with paperwork for me to sign. He spoke with Mark while I signed several papers, glancing at me several times until I slipped the title of the car out of my bag. Looking at it for a moment, and at my father's signature there beside mine, I let out a soft breath.

"You cannot take it with you," Mark said, jarring me out of my brief memories of the first day I had seen my car. I had spent all of high school working to pay for it. And now it was going to something worthwhile.

"No, I can't," I whispered and handed the mechanic the car's title.

"Whom should I make the check out to?" the mechanic asked, leaned over his checkbook.

My instinct was to tell him my name; it was my car. But Mark's words played in my mind. I was too strong, too brazen for an Amish woman. More and more I was seeing this man's world I was entering into and that scared me.

But Nathan didn't treat me like that. We were partners.

"Make it out to Nathan Fisher, please," I replied.

I had faith.

My check tucked safely into my bag, we were on our way into

town, my thoughts mulling over that interaction with Mark. It was difficult for me to understand why he thought I was so forward, when looking at Hannah and how she spoke around him. She was very vocal about her feelings, except when she was around others outside of the family. I remembered her at Sermon. She was quiet and helpful. She never once scoffed or spoke out that I had seen.

I had so much to learn.

Mark pulled up before the general store, where my journey had all started for me seemingly so long ago.

"I will walk to the mill and see if they have the order ready," Mark said as we climbed out of the buggy. Hannah nodded and offered him a demure smile.

We were just starting to pull our boxes out when I heard someone behind us.

"Well look at this. The Berger girls."

I turned around sharply when I heard Hannah gasp, dropping her box to spill across her shoes and the pavement. On instinct, I stepped in front of Hannah as she shuddered and withdrew further up against the buggy.

Standing there, grinning like the cat that had the mice cornered, was Jeff.

"What do you want?" I hissed, staring him down.

His grin widened and he looked down at the mess at our feet, licking his lips hungrily.

"Dear Hannah. You dropped your pies. I always liked your pie. Your cherry was especially nice," he purred and I felt Hannah shudder against my back, her hands fisting into the fabric of my dress.

"You're not wanted here, Jeff," I grated and stood a little taller in front of Hannah. Emma and Abigail stood beside me, helping me to block her from view.

He chuckled and wiped his mouth with one finger, eyeing me in an amused air.

"Oh? But I haven't tried a taste of yours yet, Kate. I bet you have the most flavorful cherry pie," he said and took a step toward me, his eyes roaming over me.

I didn't waver. I held my ground.

It didn't matter what Mark said about a docile woman.

He wasn't here.

I was.

"Come on now, Kate," Jeff cooed. "You picked Fisher over my buddy, Sean? I thought Sean had convinced you?"

Just mentioning Sean had my insides turning. I would never be free of him.

"He's in jail where he belongs. And aren't you wanted for questioning?" I seethed, trying hard to keep from trembling as he slid a little bit closer.

He opened his mouth to speak, when another voice interrupted.

"Leave them alone, Jeff."

His eyes narrowed as he turned to see Benjamin striding toward us. I let out a relieved breath when he drew close enough to stand between Jeff and the four of us. Jeff stared at him hard, shaking his head.

"Is this where you've been? Are you seriously considering that backward life, instead of here?" Jeff asked, incredulous.

"Perhaps. It's none of your business, just like these girls. Leave them alone," Benjamin said, his voice strong and sure.

Jeff took one slow step back, eyeing me from around Benjamin's stony frame and winked.

"I'll see you around, Kate," he said and then turned and walked away, as if on an afternoon stroll.

I felt Hannah's breath on my neck, her hand clenching mine hard when we were alone again. Benjamin's eyes followed Jeff until he had turned the corner.

"Thank you," Hannah whispered from behind me.

"Let me help you clean this up," Benjamin offered when Jeff was gone. "You should get your sister inside and calmed down before her husband returns."

Emma and Abigail grabbed Hannah around the waist and pulled her inside the general store, leaving me alone with

Benjamin.

"Thank you, Benjamin," I said and squatted down with him to scoop up the remains of the pies back into the collapsed box.

"He just got back in town today. I saw Joanna in the diner, and then I saw you here with him. I am sorry he accosted you," he murmured, frowning at the mess between us.

"He wouldn't do anything out here in public. Just rattled us, is all," I rebuffed, although my hammering heart said differently. Jeff was a bully just like Sean, and therefore drew the same fears out of me.

Benjamin shook his head and looked off toward the general store.

"You should attend to your sister. The Bishop is watching from the window. He will see your actions as improper," he whispered and pulled the box toward him.

I grimaced and started to glance up but Benjamin stopped me.

"We are not used to such forwardness. Do not openly defy my father. It will not end well," he said and stood. I stood with him.

"Will you come to supper at the Berger's tonight? Nathan was sad to not see you last night," I whispered, watching as he looked down and grimaced.

"I do not wish to intrude," he started.

"You are always welcome. Nathan needs a friend, Benjamin. This is going to be a rough time for him," I replied. His head shot up, concern on his face.

"What do you mean?"

"We started opening rooms yesterday, Benjamin. He still misses his family terribly."

"I understand."

I saw the pain etched in his troubled eyes. He also knew what it was like to lose things.

"He's alone in that house, Benjamin. It isn't helping him to move forward and he is struggling. But he was smiling and happy when you were there the other night. He needs his friend back," I continued.

He pursed his lips and I thought maybe I had gone too far.

"Perhaps I should not put that burden on you," I whispered and turned to leave.

"Katherine," he said, calling after me. I turned to see him nodding as if to drum up the courage. "I will be there tonight."

I smiled and stepped into the general store, pretending not to see the Bishop watching me as I made my way back into the bathroom where my sisters were. By the time I got there, she had stopped crying, but her eyes were swollen and her cheeks still flushed.

"I cannot let Mark see me like this," she was saying, running cold water over her face.

"You stay in here and get settled. Abigail and I will bring in the baked goods," I volunteered and stepped back out when she and Emma nodded.

We made quick work of the boxes, bringing them in one by one. The Bishop seemed to have disappeared while I was in the bathroom, and for that I was grateful. I didn't want to have yet another altercation. My mind was buzzing over having confronted Jeff and for arguing over my car.

So many things.

And the day was hardly over. It was just noon and I still had the baptism class to endure through late in the afternoon.

Hannah and Emma came out just as we were finishing; Hannah's eyes still a little red but much more calmed down. Hannah touched my arm, as if in silent thanks, a tremulous smile on her face. I knew she still must have fears about Jeff. I had to wonder how long my past life would haunt me.

Would I continue to bring trouble or would I bend to the ways I must learn?

The happiness I had found was worth the sacrifices I would make; Nathan treated me well and for that I would do what I needed to.

If I had to be the quiet wife, then I would.

I'd make whatever changes I needed to.

We arrived back at the house in the late afternoon, Jonah and Fannie still not home from where they had gone. Hannah had suggested we buy something in town for supper, which was a brilliant plan with so little time to make anything, and with Nathan and me leaving for our class so soon.

He arrived just as we did, his buggy stopping beside ours in the yard. He smiled and helped us pull everything out, his eyes watching me with concern as I grabbed the flour and grain we had purchased. I winced at the soreness of my muscles, thanking him when he offered to take the heavy grain bag from me.

I said my goodbyes to Hannah and Emma, Mark busy with unhitching his horse. Nathan helped me into his buggy and we were off to the next stressful part of my day, the Bishop's class. I wondered if he would mention the altercation with Jeff. I wondered if he would make an example of my willfulness.

"You are very quiet," Nathan said after a moment. "Are you all right?"

I nodded and frowned.

I didn't want Nathan to be upset over Jeff, but I didn't want him to hear about it from the Bishop, either.

"Jeff was in town today," I said quietly.

"What happened?" he asked, alarmed.

I shook my head and tried to smile.

"He didn't get to say much. Hannah was upset. But Benjamin stepped in and made him walk away," I replied.

Nathan slowed down and stared at me, the worry clear in his knotted brow.

"Did he threaten you? He didn't touch you, did he?"

I shook my head.

"No, he just wanted to scare us. Benjamin was there at the right time," I said and touched Nathan's hand to console him.

He sped his horse once more, his eyes straying from the road back to mine.

"So you spoke with Benjamin then?"

"He'll be at dinner tonight," I said trying to change the subject from Jeff.

Nathan remained quiet for the rest of the ride, thoughtful as he looked straight ahead. When we reached the Bishop's house he unhitched his horse and tied him off near the pasture. When he turned to me, his smile was sad.

"I should have gone with you today."

"You can't be with me every moment, Nathan," I replied and frowned again over how he had worried about us going on our own.

"But I can keep you safe."

"I am safe here, Nathan. You do keep me safe," I murmured and tried to smile as we walked toward the house.

I started up the steps to the door, Nathan behind me. We stepped onto the porch just as the door opened and Naomi smiled, motioning us inside.

"We can start early! Father is letting Bishop Zachariah Ropp from Friendship speak with us for a bit while he deals with business. Come!" she said and took my hand to guide me into the room we had been in for the last baptism class.

Only instead of benches, a table was set up for us to sit at, and a young man, whom I assumed was the Bishop from Friendship, was standing and smiling as we came in.

"Welcome! Please come and join me! Katherine, Nathan, it is so pleasant to meet you," he said with open arms and sat us down, Naomi sitting beside me while Nathan sat across from us with the new Bishop.

"Are you helping Bishop Yoder with the classes?" Nathan asked, curious.

I was curious, too.

Was this the Bishop's way of avoiding us?

The young Bishop's smile grew a little as he cast a quick glance toward Naomi and cleared his throat. It was obvious by looking at how Naomi blushed and beamed at the young Bishop that some feelings existed between the two of them.

"I was here today for personal reasons, and am happy to help

Bishop Yoder. But I think he intends on resuming on Sundays. I may help if he asks again. If it speeds up the process," he said and I couldn't help noticing his brief glance again toward Naomi.

It seemed we were not the only ones hoping for a wedding before the frost.

I sat and listened quietly as Zachariah discussed the rules of the Ordnung, driving home some of what I internally struggled with. An Amish family was made up of the husband and the wife, and children.

The wife was there to be the overseer of the house, to assure it was well kept and in good running order for her husband. A wife was there to serve her husband. A wife followed her husband's decisions without complaint. The husband was head of the household. His word was law. The husband was there to provide for his family. Children were a blessing from God. A large family was a good Amish family.

Time and again, Nathan would glance my way. I could see his eyes in my periphery. But I didn't dare look at him. The Bishop's might make Naomi swoon as she sat there and smiled, but I felt nothing of the sort. I had to wonder if perhaps the Bishop and the others had been right.

I was outspoken, when an Amish wife should be quiet and obliging.

I was stubborn, where an Amish woman would be gracious.

Perhaps I wasn't made for this life.

When the lesson was over, I offered my thanks to the young Bishop just as Naomi did and walked out in a rush, following Naomi onto the porch to wait for Nathan while he spoke to the young Bishop for a few moments. When we were out of earshot from the men, she let out a long exasperated breath and looked over at me shaking her head.

"There are many things I agree with about our way, but I plan on being my husband's partner, not his slave," she muttered.

"But the Ordnung says," I whispered, my words trailing off at her eye roll.

"God made man and woman to serve together side by side. Not one over the other. This is a man's way of holding something over us," she said and pulled me down off the porch so they could not hear us.

"Do not fret, Katherine. Nathan understands this. He does not see you beneath him," she said and patted me on the shoulder while I frowned at her contradiction to what we had learned and how she had reacted in the room.

How was I supposed to know which rules really applied and which ones could be bent? And why would they have such rules if people didn't believe in them? Why weren't they written down somewhere? Things would be easier if they had been written down.

"That is so they can change them to suit the community's needs," she explained when I asked.

"Well that's confusing," I huffed and wrapped my arms around myself, feeling more lost than ever now.

"Naomi! Come inside before your father returns for his supper!"

Naomi rushed inside at the young Bishop's call, past Nathan as he stepped outside with Zachariah. The young Bishop watched as she passed, saying something low to Nathan, who smiled timidly and glanced my way. He shook hands with the young Bishop and placed his hat back on his head as he walked toward me, his smile faltering as we walked in silence to the buggy. He hitched Magnus to the buggy in a rush and let me get up into the seat before he followed.

"You are worried," he said as we started off.

I let out a breath and shrugged.

"I'm confused, I guess," I murmured and glanced at him.

His brow creased and he slowed the horse to a walk so that he could look at me more carefully.

"Is it regarding what we discussed tonight?" he asked, worrying his lip.

I nodded, hesitant to reveal my fears.

"Some. But things that happened today, too," I said and tried to make my words less worrisome for him.

"Nathan?" I started. "Am I too outspoken?"

He seemed taken aback at my question.

"How do you mean?"

I sighed in frustration and told him what happened at the garage, and then what happened at the store with Jeff and Benjamin. He stopped the buggy on the side of the road and turned to me.

"Kate, you are everything I want in a wife and a partner. I understand Mark's point, even Benjamin's. A traditional Amish woman is quiet in her tasks while in public. But if you were quiet and reserved like the other girls here, we would not be where we are today. Your courage brought us together when I had none. Your bravery and outspoken ways kept you alive when I could not get to you. And I would not wish you to be any other way," he said, his voice strong as he spoke.

"But that's not..." I started but he shook his head and interrupted me.

"Kate, you will be my partner in life. We stand beside one another, not above or below. God made Eve from Adam's rib, because he wanted Eve to be Adam's equal. Not above or below. Had he wanted Eve to be Adam's servant, he would have made her with the bone of his foot. The Amish way is to love and respect one another. Not to serve. The only one we serve is God. Do you not see that with Jonah and Fannie?" he asked, his voice softening at the mention of his aunt and uncle.

I nodded, feeling my throat tighten in his proclamation.

"It's just been a difficult day. I keep feeling like I'm messing up," I whispered.

He took my hand and brought it to his lips.

"You have not done anything wrong. I want all of you, Kate, just as you are. Do not be upset over what you have heard tonight. Zachariah Ropp was brought up much as our Bishop was. And if I am destined for the role of Bishop, do you not think we will have some sway to change that?" he asked, raising his eyebrows in challenge.

He leaned in and offered me a brush of his lips on mine, his sincere eyes allowing me to relax some.

"I would not have you any other way, Kate," he whispered.

I nodded and smiled, watching him as he flicked the reins, putting us back on the road to home. I thought about what he had said. He wanted me as I was, regardless of what the Ordnung said. He wanted me as his partner, and for that he put my mind at ease. He was right. Jonah and Fannie lived as they wished, and they were well thought of in the community.

I just needed to learn to temper myself around others.

We arrived at Nathan's house just as the sun was setting. Nathan showed me how to unhitch Magnus from the buggy and grinned when he watched me guide the horse back to his stall. Again, it was really more a matter of the horse simply knowing where to go as I walked beside him. But he nickered softly when I closed his stall, his head poking out to nudge me before I could step away.

"He is taken with you," Nathan chuckled and pulled me into his arms.

"He's not so tough," I joked, feeling the horse snort behind me.

Nathan pulled me from the barn and we walked at a slow pace back toward the Berger's.

Before we made it to the top of the hill, Nathan pulled me to a stop and kissed me, soft at first. The kiss deepened for only a moment before he hummed and drew away, a playful smile playing on his lips as he pulled something out of his pocket. I looked down at the cloth-wrapped package in his hand, confused.

"What is that for?" I asked, looking back up at his mirthful face.

"I cannot wait until after supper to give you this. I have been wanting to give it to you all day, to make your day special," he murmured and placed the package in my hand.

I could tell it was a book of some sort, judging by the weight of it.

"But what's it for?" I said, smiling at his mysterious air.

"Do you not give your love a keepsake on their birthday in the English world?" he asked.

I looked at him, thinking hard about what day it was. Was it my birthday? I couldn't remember the date. How did he know?

"It's my birthday?" I asked in a small voice.

He nodded and brushed his lips to my forehead.

"You did not know it was today?"

I shook my head and looked down at the present in my hands, feeling the tears in my eyes. I felt his thumbs wipe away the tears, his hand tipping my head up so he could gaze down at me.

"Why are you crying?" he asked.

"I'm not used to someone remembering," I whispered and touched the present again.

His brow puckered and he pulled me close.

"Well, then this will be the first of many with me. I will celebrate your birthday, with happiness in my heart that you are here with me," he said and kissed me again sweetly.

"Will you open it?" he whispered against my lips.

I chuckled and pulled away, looking up at his excited eyes when I pulled the fabric wrapping back to reveal a small, leather bound book. Opening it up, I gasped when I read what was inside the first page.

To my Kate.
To my Beloved.
Forever.
Your Nathan.

I turned the page and smiled when I read the poem there.

The first poem he had ever written me, the one I had found on his desk that first day at his house.

"It's your poetry," I said, looking up at him with all the love I felt in my heart.

"It is a little something of me for you to carry with you always," he whispered.

"I love it. It's perfect," I said and reached up to kiss him once more.

He held me to him as the sun dipped past the horizon.

When we finally made our way toward the house, it was nearly dark. Walking in to the kitchen, my day only seemed to get better when we found Benjamin there with Emma, Abigail, Hannah and Mark. Nathan clasped his hand tightly, happy to see his friend with us once more.

With supper served, we sat and ate, enjoying one another's company. Benjamin seemed more at ease as he sat and laughed with Nathan, the two of them lighter in their moods than we had seen them since I had been with the Bergers. My sisters asked about my studies while we cleaned up, the men relaxing outside on the porch while we worked inside.

Mark came inside, drawing Hannah upstairs with his arm around her as if to protect her. She still seemed reserved from her day, and it seemed Mark either knew or sensed it. I was hoping he would put her at ease once they were upstairs and alone to talk about it. More than anything, Hannah needed to feel safe again, and only Mark could do that for her.

Emma winked and disappeared with Abigail upstairs when it was time to retire for the night, leaving me in the kitchen alone with Benjamin and Nathan speaking in hushed voices just outside on the porch. I couldn't catch all of what they said, but I watched as Benjamin leaned in, embracing his friend. Pulling away, he clapped Nathan on the back and turned to leave. Halfway down the steps, he turned back, nodding toward the door.

"I will see you soon. Thank Katherine for asking me to come," he said and turned to leave.

He waved as he left, calling after Nathan as he disappeared into the dark.

When Nathan came back inside, he was smiling.

"What was that about?" I asked, curious about their conversation.

Nathan pulled me into a warm embrace, his head dipping into my hair as he sighed and nodded.

"He is bringing his car around to the house. He will stay with me," he whispered.

I hugged Nathan back, feeling his relief at having his friend back.

"I have something for you before you leave," I whispered and pulled away to grab my bag and dug out the check for the car.

He eyed it for a moment, wide eyed.

"This is from your car?" he breathed.

I nodded.

"If we can, I'd like some of it to go back to the community. But we should have the money for the winter," I explained.

His smile broadened and he held me close. His lips were soft as they pressed against my own. His hands spread out across my back, hugging me close against him as his mouth explored mine. He took a deep breath and shook his head, looking down at me.

"You amaze me every day. We will do well this winter. Thank you, Kate. Do not worry. We will be fine because we will do it together," he whispered and tucked the check into his pocket, shock still on his face.

We heard the door to the front of the house open, pulling us apart on instinct.

Fannie looked in on us and smiled, her face tired. She nodded once and disappeared upstairs, Jonah following after he offered us a cursory nod. It was later than I had realized. Nathan took my hand and walked back out to the porch, pulling me into another warm embrace.

"I need to leave, to settle Benjamin in. I am sorry I cannot stay longer. It is late, but I would have liked to thank you fully for all your love and support," he said, drawing away to look down at me.

"It's okay. Make him comfortable, and tomorrow bring him to breakfast. We'll have time together soon," I replied and kissed him before he pulled away.

"Happy birthday, Kate. And do not worry over what happened today. You are what I want, nothing else. Tomorrow will be a new day," he said and kissed me once more before stepping away.

I watched as he walked away, back up his hill and to his house. But for once I smiled as I watched him go. Because I knew, tonight he would not be alone.

"I am glad Benjamin is staying with Nathan," Emma whispered when I closed the bedroom door.

We settled into bed, and I kept the lantern by my side, so that I could read from the journal Nathan had given me. I read until I started to yawn, learning more of how much Nathan cared about me. I extinguished the lantern and closed my eyes, smiling into the dark at the thought that he had given me the best present ever.

He had given me his heart and his life.

8

I looked up at the sky again and wondered how the storm clouds could roll in so fast. Another afternoon with the rain threatening, and I hurried inside with my basket of vegetables before I got wet again. Hearing the distant thunder, I wondered if maybe I should head off to the Berger's. But that would leave Nathan alone. And I liked the idea of remaining with him in the rain again.

Last time had been wonderful.

That had been a week ago, and we had been occupied with so many other things that alone time had become scant. Now that Benjamin was living with Nathan we only had our evenings together, and those were becoming more of a threesome of reading and lectures on the Ordnung than pleasant walks around the barn.

Not that I was complaining about Benjamin.

He was opening up and beginning to feel comfortable again. I could sacrifice alone time with Nathan if it meant bringing Benjamin back where he belonged. But I could tell in Nathan's eyes, he missed our stolen moments.

Another rumble of thunder, this one closer, and I knew it would be only moments before the rain started. Outside, the air seemed to be electrified, and there was a golden hue to everything as the grey of the clouds covered the sun. Benjamin was at the mill late today, leaving Nathan and me alone for most of the afternoon, but we had not seen much of one another.

He was behind on repairs to the barn, and I had been clearing away old growth in the garden and mulching some of the new plants in preparation for the cooler nights. But with the threat of rain, perhaps we could find a moment or two alone.

I smiled and busied myself in the kitchen to finish my duties there.

I washed off the strawberries I had found bursting to life under some of the old bean vines, and grabbed the thermos of tea that Nathan had forgotten in the kitchen before going out to the barn to fix the siding. One last thought occurred to me on my way out; I grabbed the old blanket I had found in the closet upstairs and headed outside.

Outfitted for a mini picnic, I grinned and hurried toward the barn, just as the rain started to fall. I found Nathan near the back of the building, pulling out rusty nails from some old planks of wood he had stacked beside him. A gaping hole in the side of the barn was letting in a cool breeze from the thunderstorm that was rolling in.

He looked up from his task to smile and raised an eyebrow at the items in my hand before returning to the board. He pulled out the last of the nails and tossed the plank onto the stack of finished boards. He was dirty from the work of the day, his shirt damp around the neck from the hot humid air. He had rolled up his sleeves so that his arms were bare and glistening with sweat. He licked his lips and took a step toward me, wiping his forehead with the handkerchief from his back pocket.

"Please tell me you have a cold beverage in your arms. I forgot your drink after lunch," he said, grinning when I produced the thermos.

He thanked me and took a long drink, some of the tea

dribbling out the side of his mouth and down his neck.

Sweaty, dirty Nathan Fisher was quite a sight to behold.

Add to that the rivulet of liquid running down into his shirt, and it was all I could do to swallow down my want and try to think of November. We had six more weeks of baptism classes and then the rush of the baptism itself before the wedding.

It was still so far way!

"What are you thinking?" Nathan whispered, standing a little closer to me.

"November," I whispered and felt my face turning hot.

"The winter vegetables should be ready by then, yes?" he said innocently, then his eyes widened and he let out a low chuckle and took another drink to cover his flushed face.

I loved his simple innocence so much.

I wondered if he would remain that way even after we were married. Not really the innocent part, obviously. But the simple, tender ways he spoke that were honest and genuine.

I hoped so.

He cleared his throat once more and handed me the thermos, eyeing the strawberries in the basket I carried.

"Do you want some?" I asked.

He looked down at his hands and wiped them down his chest, only managing to smear the dirt on himself a little more. I plucked one of the bigger berries out of the basket and held it up for him to bite. He looked from me to the fruit, his mouth hesitant for a moment before he leaned in slightly to take a bite. Juice dribbled down his chin as he bit down, forcing him to pull away to wipe his chin with his bicep.

He was a mess.

He was beautiful and smiling down at me.

Leaning in once more, this time past the berry in my hand, he hummed deep in his throat and kissed me at a leisured pace, keeping his body distanced from my own. I edged closer, wanting to feel him, dirt and sweat be damned. He drew away at my movement, licking his lips as he took a tentative step back.

"I am dirty, Kate. I need to wash up before I touch you," he murmured.

"I don't care about that, Nathan," I whispered, his groan rumbling through him as he looked down at me.

"I still have work to finish," he sighed when I stepped in and traced my finger along one of his suspenders.

"Okay," I pouted and took a step back, watching as he stood there, one hand lingering on my arm.

"Do you want to help? Perhaps we can make quick work of it," he suggested, glancing back at the boards.

"What can I do?" I asked, suddenly excited to help with anything.

He took my hand and drew me toward the workbench. I eyed the hammer with suspicion when he handed it to me. He laughed and took it back to demonstrate.

"It is not too difficult. Let me show you. Then you can remove the nails and I will replace the boards over there," he said.

I watched as he showed me how to pry the nails out of the boards.

"Why did you take the planks off just to put them back on again?" I asked, somehow managing to curl the nail in the fork of the hammer.

It was more difficult than he let on.

"These are not the originals," he explained as he looked on in amusement. "These are reclaimed from another barn. My boards had termites. I still have many to replace. You could put a hammer through much of that wall there without much effort."

He gestured to the wall he was working on. It seemed sturdy to me, but I was sure he knew best. He chuckled at my slow progress and kissed my cheek before picking up a few of the finished boards and another hammer. I watched as he ducked out of a small door near the back of his workshop area and watched his shadow as it made its way to the gaping hole in the wall.

He pulled some long nails from the apron at his waist, placing them into his mouth with care while he lined up the first board. It was raining now and his cream shirt grew damp as he worked. The sound of the hammer striking the nail into the wood resonated in the barn, much like the thunder as it rumbled overhead. Nathan glanced up at the sky, grabbing another board and hammering with more determination.

I could tell he was trying to work fast to beat the oncoming storm. I was sure having a hammer in his hands in the middle of a thunderstorm was not the best idea. As soon as the pile of wood ran low, I picked up what I could and handed it to him through the hole. His grin was awkward around the nails as he took the boards from my hands. In no time, only a small strip remained open, too small for anyone to slip through.

He ducked back into the room, flinging the hammer and apron onto the table as he moved with purpose toward me. He grabbed me up into his wet arms, hands slipping up to my neck as his lips descended to capture mine.

"Where are those strawberries?" he whispered against my lips, drawing me deeper into the barn.

I mumbled something and let my hand wave in the general direction of where I thought I had laid the basket down. I felt the wall against my back, Nathan's damp body close to mine while his lips moved along my jaw, nipping and sucking a trail to my earlobe.

"Grab the blanket and berries. You see this ladder?" he whispered, gesturing to the ladder I just then noticed was beside us. I nodded and he grinned.

"It is much less visible up there and more comfortable than perhaps the stalls. I will be up in a moment," he said and kissed me quickly before pulling away to disappear down back toward the stalls.

I grabbed the blanket and threw it over my shoulder, gripping the basket in one hand while trying to grip the wooden rungs of the ladder that led up to a loft. Trying to climb in a long skirt, with only one hand, was harder than it seemed. I felt hands beneath me, and looking down I found Nathan close behind me again. He had taken off his shirt, the undershirt slightly damp but clean. And it looked like he had rinsed off. He took the basket from my hand, allowing me to climb a little easier.

I managed to get to the loft and climbed up onto the hay-covered floor, pulled the blanket from my shoulder and opened it up, the size of it more than enough for Nathan and me to relax upon. I had just laid it out when I felt his arms wrap around me, pulling me down into the soft makeshift bed. He laid the berries down by my head and leaned in close, allowing his nose to skim across my jaw.

"It will rain for some time yet," he whispered near my ear.

I sighed and let him slip his hands along my ribs, his eyes merry as my hands drifted across his chest. My fingers slipped up along his suspenders, pulling them off his shoulders easily. He moaned against my neck and gripped me a little harder around the waist, tugging me to him.

"I love the feel of you against me, Kate," he sighed and rolled us over, his hand slipping down to work my skirt up until it was bunched up along my thigh. We lay like that, kissing and exploring with our hands until Nathan's breath became a little heavier, his mouth a little needier. After a moment his hand gripped my hip and pressed his body tight to mine.

"Kate," he whimpered and closed his eyes to the feel of us so close to one another.

His mouth open, breathing in long tortured breaths, he moved against me. His fingers slid up my back until they twined into the hair at the base of my neck.

"You have no idea what you do to me, Kate," he murmured against my temple.

"I think I have some idea," I said, smiling while I took in the flush along his chest and throat.

"It is so much more than that," he replied. "Although that is always amazing."

His smile was bright as he looked up at me, letting his fingers trace along my collarbone and the neckline of my dress.

"I cannot wait for you to be my wife, Kate. So much, I want to feel you against me every night, and wake up to you every morning," he whispered and pulled me in for another kiss that left me breathless.

The sound of the thunder continued to echo around us while

the air was laden with the fresh scent of rain. Nathan's soft whispered words were only interrupted when he would snatch a strawberry and feed it to me before popping another into his mouth with a joyous laugh that sounded throughout the loft.

That sound was the best part of the rainy afternoon in the loft with Nathan. I would never get enough of Nathan Fisher.

November needed to come.

Soon.

~~~~~

I rubbed at my eyes in the dim light. Looking down at the fabric, I sighed and set it aside, knowing I wasn't going to accomplish much more on the dress tonight. My mind wasn't on seams and hems and gathering of fabric.

It was on Nathan.

He had missed supper so that he could help Benjamin. Fannie and I both had been disappointed that they had not come. But with the continued rain and the need to move Benjamin's belongings out of his rented room, there was little to be done for it. I sat on the bench seat by the window, looking out as the occasional lightning flash lit up his hill and I wondered what they were doing.

It had been two weeks since Benjamin agreed to stay with Nathan. It had taken him almost that long to finally switch back into his Amish clothes for good. With each night spent at supper with the Bergers, we saw a little more of Benjamin open up to our way of life.

Nathan smiled more, Benjamin helped more, and everything seemed to be going well.

On nights like this, when the rain forced us to retreat into the house instead of on our walks, Benjamin sat with us and reviewed what we were learning in our classes. Alone, my mind drifted to other things.

Like the soft words Nathan would murmur against my ear whenever we were alone. Or his voice when he recited some of his poems from my journal. I pulled out my journal and smiled at the page I turned to. Every word from Nathan's mind was something to savor.

Simple joy
In seeing your smile
Delighted breath
In catching your scent on the breeze.
Contented sigh
Having you in my arms.
Mirthful
That I have you.
My Angel.
My Kate.

I smiled and turned the page, my eyes tearing up at the desperation of the next passage.

Lost.
My heart.
My soul.
Gone.
Everything I have.
I will risk.
To find you.
My heart.
My soul.
My everything.
My Kate.

The magnitude of his affection was limitless. How had he been able to write while I was away? I didn't know, but I cherished every word. It solidified his dedication to me. How did I show him my dedication?

I smiled and thought on every time he smiled and laughed now, having changed so much since my arrival. Even through the worst of our time together, he had been able to commit to us. And I had been able to make him smile again and again.

Perhaps I did show him how much I cared.

In everything I did, I proved my love for him. As we continued to progress through time slowly, I dug into my studies, wanting so much to see him smile every day. It didn't always mean I understood my lessons. Sometimes, the Amish ways baffled me just as much as they reassured me. There was many a night that I sat with Nathan and Benjamin and tried to be patient while they explained things to me.

"It is something of a quiet understanding, Katherine," Benjamin said, offering a consoling smile my frowning face.

"It's just," I said, sighing in exasperation at the latest baptism class. "If you are supposed to practice what the Bishop and the Elders say is the law, but the Bible says something else, isn't that going against God?"

Nathan and Benjamin both sat, silent, and thought hard on my question.

Our class that evening had been about following the Ordnung and the Elder's orders. But some of what they discussed tonight went against what I thought the Bible stated. It was confusing when they told us one thing but the Book said another. And I wasn't about to vocally question the Bishop, although I could tell as he watched me every class, he expected me to say something.

To be willful.

But I had been the exact opposite. I had been quiet and reserved, modest even, at least when we were in public. But the double standards of their teachings, and seeing it in how the Bishop acted, was frustrating. He didn't practice what he preached at all.

"It is complicated, Kate," Nathan started, looking at Benjamin for help.

I sighed and knew I wouldn't get much out of them for this section of the classes.

Just nod and agree, Kate. You'll figure it out.

So I did. I nodded and smiled as if I understood their complicated ways. After all, did I understand or accept everything I had been taught in my old life? There were some battles you just did not fight.

Nathan offered a timid smile and leaned back in his chair to stretch. We had been discussing everything we had learned for some time now. Benjamin watched me while I cleared away the glasses and came back to sit, pulling out my Bible. We were quiet for a time, Nathan and Benjamin both watching me. When I couldn't take the scrutiny any longer, I lifted my eyes from the Ephesians passage to regard Nathan expectantly. He chuckled and tugged on his ear.

"It is always interesting to watch you read," he whispered.

"Why?" I asked, suddenly self-conscious that perhaps I mouthed the words while I read.

It was difficult to understand some of the passages without rereading many times.

"You seem very determined to understand what it is you read," Benjamin replied, grinning.

I blushed and looked back down at the book in my hands.

"I'm a little behind. You've had years to learn, I have weeks. You guys know it better than I do," I whispered.

"I think you know more than you realize," Benjamin replied and glanced over at Nathan, a silent conversation between the two of them.

"How do you mean?" I asked, curious.

It was Benjamin's turn to blush.

"I just mean that you have a pure spirit. It seems to come naturally to you. You seem to see the Spirit in much of what you do. More so than I do," he murmured.

"I don't think that's true," I said, touching his hand as it sat on the table.

He shrugged, suddenly shy.

"No, really, Benjamin," I continued. "You see how it applies to the community. I see absolutes, and you see the grey of it. You explain it much better than I could. You've experienced so much, and know how to apply it to live the way one should. I am still causing people to question my being here."

I frowned at the last.

The Bishop in particular continued to have his doubts.

"I think the opinion of you is far higher than you figure," Benjamin said. "You have better standing than I do at the moment in this community."

"I doubt that, Benjamin. You are missed," I whispered and patted him on the hand again, smiling.

He let out a soft breath and eyed me for a moment, like a scared animal afraid that I might swat at him. I had to wonder again just how bad his fight with his father had been. His mother wanted him home. His sister missed him. Surely the rest of the community missed their future Bishop as well.

"I may be missed but that does not change that I am outcast," he said after a moment in silence.

Nathan pursed his lips and stared at his friend.

"You were never shunned, Benjamin," he said and shook his head to silence Benjamin's argument to the contrary. "Your father sees you as outcast, but you are not truly shunned, otherwise you would not be sitting here with us."

I looked from one to the other, trying to gauge the conversation. It wasn't until Nathan slapped his friend on the back that I relaxed.

"I will never understand shunning," I muttered and looked back into my book.

"It is not an easy thing to understand," Nathan started and looked to Benjamin to pick up the conversation.

"We shun to keep the community free of the blight that the English world would force upon us by disobeying the rules of our Ordnung," Benjamin said, an air to his voice not unlike his father's.

I wondered how many times he had heard it recited to him.

"What happened to forgiving of transgressions?" I countered.

"Sometimes it is done, when the offender has properly repented," Benjamin replied and looked away from my searching eyes.

"That doesn't seem so hard," I challenged.

"It is harder than many understand," Benjamin countered, brows furrowed.

Nathan cleared his throat and nodded toward the door, signaling it was time to go.

I watched as they walked up the hill together, heads pulled low and jackets tight as the rain fell. They disappeared and I closed the door, deep in thought.

I didn't understand shunning, really. Both Benjamin and Nathan tried to explain it to me, but the idea of it baffled me when looking at the context of Amish life. Everything I had learned and read about my new life seemed to contradict the idea of Shunning.

The Amish life was about forgiveness.

Loving one's family.

Never being proud.

So why did Bishop Yoder remain so stubborn about his son? Why had he not forgiven Benjamin of his transgressions while living in the English world, and accept his son's desire to come home, to the Amish life?

Both had too much pride to admit their own faults, and both held onto the belief that their reasoning was right. The Bishop refused to accept that his son was a good and honest man, made for this life, but had simply strayed. Benjamin wanted to come home, but refused to believe that what he had done should matter. And if I had learned anything in my baptismal classes, it was that really, what he had done did not matter in retrospect. He had yet to be baptized and accept the Way. In true Amish faith, he would be washed of those past sins upon his baptism.

If only the Bishop could forgive.

We had a few weeks of baptism classes left and the Bishop continued to eye me with contempt. Benjamin still avoided integrating back into the community. He would close himself off at the mention of the coming baptism Sermon for Emma and John.

This week I had told him his mother was more distant than usual. I thought perhaps she was ill. Naomi wouldn't say anything, and I couldn't ask the Bishop. Word from the women in the kitchen for Sermon was that she was worse than ever.

Benjamin wouldn't talk about it and I didn't push. I understood his fears. He was afraid of being cast out, by more than simply his father. I understood that feeling because I saw the eyes of the community on me wherever I went, whether it was with Nathan in his courting buggy, or with the Bergers at the weddings that had begun with the start of autumn. People watched me and spoke in hushed tones after I had passed. I don't think many knew I understood some of their language, for they spoke to one another in Pennsylvania Dutch.

Things I heard from some made my spirits fall. I tried to keep my disappointment from Nathan, but he always saw through me. Or maybe he heard those same words following after me.

English infiltrator.

A danger to the Way.

Temptress.

People like Sarah Jensen and Naomi Yoder were a comfort to my self-confidence and I was welcomed again and again at gatherings, but just one disparaging whisper clouded my determination, regardless of Nathan's assurances. Time was running out.

If we were baptized before the yearly Council met, then things would change even more.

The Bishop would vote in Nathan to ultimately replace him. Perhaps he saw it as a way to keep me from marrying Nathan. He knew I would be looked down upon, and that the stress could be too much. The community might not allow me to even be baptized, even after all the work I had done to learn. They might try and coerce Nathan to not marry me. It seemed as though all the forces were set against us.

I shook my head with a resolute determination. We would see ourselves through this winter, together. I would show the doubters that I cared about this community as much as they did.

9

With the fall came more baking and a push to sell our goods to the markets before winter fell on us, limiting our means of making money while the snow and cold kept us close to home. I had learned of the Amish market in Friendship, a monthly market that Fannie prepared for eagerly by baking and cooking for long hours. Hannah had made a name for herself with her quilts, enough to develop a nice little business to help support Mark and herself.

Fannie thought it would be good for me to help this time since my pies had begun to have quite the reputation amongst our own community. What better way to prove oneself than through one's baking?

So for the last few days, we had baked nonstop.

"Katherine, can you pull down the bag of sugar in the pantry? We have run out in here," Fannie called from the kitchen.

I set the box of cornstarch down and looked for the sugar. Finally looking at the upper shelves, I saw the bag of sugar and reached to get it. It was just out of my fingers reach. On tippy toes

I could just grab the edge of the bag with two fingers. I strained a little higher, dancing on my toes when the bag slipped some in my fingers.

I settled down and was just about to reach again when a hard thud hit me on the head, and then the fine shower of tiny granules fell over me like an avalanche. I let out a screech and waved at the pouring mass, trying to reach up to stop it. I felt someone behind me, felt the waterfall of sugar cease, and struggled to wipe my eyes when I heard a soft chuckling near me.

"Katherine, I think perhaps we should restrict you to the lower shelves."

I sputtered, my mouth tasting overly sweet before I could speak.

"I'm sorry, Fannie! It just slipped!" I moaned, still wiping the sugar from my face.

"It is all right, Katherine," Fannie replied, taking me gently between the shoulders.

"You should go outside and try to dust yourself off. I will clean up in here."

"I'm sorry," I murmured, embarrassed and upset with myself for wasting so much sugar.

"Go on, daughter," she chuckled, and pushed me out the door.

I groaned and stepped out into the yard, brushing off the sugar that had collected on my dress, grumbling when I realized the thin sheen of sweat from baking had made the skin on my arms and neck only collect the sugar in thick clumps. I was finding sugar in my pockets when I heard a loud nicker behind me. Turning, I almost bumped into Nathan.

And Magnus.

"What is wrong, Kate?" Nathan asked, looking over me curiously.

"I was clumsy this morning," I muttered, and continued to dust myself off.

He laughed and put his hands up when I glared at him.

"Jonah needs me on the roof. Would you take Magnus to the

paddock? Mark said he would be by sometime before midday meal to borrow him for the delivery of our hay today," he said and leaned in to peck me on the cheek. He pulled away grinning.

"What?" I groused.

"You taste sweet," he whispered and kissed me again, this time on the neck.

"I dumped sugar all over myself."

He hummed and let me take Magnus' rope lead from his hand.

"And I thought you could not get any sweeter," he replied with a grin as he stepped away.

I smiled at his playful words.

Only Nathan could make my embarrassing moment better.

I patted Magnus on the side of the neck, and started to lead him over to the paddock, feeling his breath blow past me as he walked close behind me. I startled when I felt warm soft lips nuzzle at the sticky skin of my neck. I squirmed away, swatting at my wet neck and glared up at the big animal's dark eye.

"Hey now, just because Nathan does it, doesn't mean you can, too," I said, to which he made a noise like a snort.

I huffed and tugged him a little harder, opening up the gate and letting him follow close behind me. Once inside, I reached up to unclip his lead from his halter. I stood there for a second as the big black looked down, one great eye watching me. I rolled my eyes and dipped my hand into my sugar-clogged apron pocket, opening my palm to his muzzle.

His soft lips greedily moved across my open hand, blowing half the white goodness from my hand before he looked up and stamped his hoof.

"Nathan is going to kill me for spoiling you, you know that right?" I asked him, as if he'd understand.

I dug out the rest of the sugar and held it out to him, stroking along his neck and speaking softly to him as he ate up the sweet treat from my hand.

"Don't expect this in the winter, big boy," I said. "It's slim rations this winter. Besides, you're getting kind of fat."

He snorted again, looking up and shaking his mane as if to argue with me. I laughed and gave him a good pat on the shoulder.

"Go on, go flirt with Patience before she starts to think you don't like her," I said and made the clicking noise Nathan always did when he had unhitched his horses from their harnesses, signaling them to go.

Magnus let out a low guttural noise and threw his head back, far above me, nodding it before turning and bolting away, tail high and head proud as he pranced along the fence line and back again. He slowed a little just as he came close and then turned and pranced away again. I shook my head at his playful attitude and closed the gate behind me, wondering if perhaps horses suffered from sugar rushes.

Magnus was certainly enjoying himself as he pranced and waved his head about.

Close to the house, I heard laughter above me. Looking up I saw Nathan and Jonah sitting on the roof of the front part of the house, watching me as I approached. Nathan pointed his hammer toward the direction of the paddock and shook his head.

"He is spoiled with you. You have turned my proud stallion into a prancing pony!" he admonished, fighting hard to hide his smile.

"I don't know what you're talking about. Your horse was always like that," I replied before glancing back at Magnus, who was now trotting around Patience before settling in beside her to graze on the mound of hay laid out for them. I grinned and shrugged when I heard Jonah and Nathan chuckling above me.

At least Magnus didn't hate me.

I finished dusting off in front of the porch and went back in to help Fannie with boxing up the pies and cakes we had made for the market. We had the buggy hitched and the food loaded before Jonah and Nathan were done repairing the roof, so Fannie settled into the seat and let me slide in beside her. Waving the men goodbye, we set out for the market.

"So is this an Amish-only market?" I asked as we rode.

"Mostly it is made up of several communities surrounding

ours. The English farmers come as well. But aside from the general store, it is a good place to sell our goods, and a fine place to stock up on some of our pantry goods," she said, turning onto a side road I had never been on.

We chatted as we rode, Fannie offering me ideas for what to buy at the market to help build up Nathan's kitchen. I knew there was next to nothing there, and had made a list of things to buy for him when we arrived. I was excited to make the first purchases for the house, but was a little apprehensive about making sure I did it right.

And of course, I could still end up being denied amongst the Amish, even though we had almost completed the baptism classes. I still had to prove myself worthy to the rest of the community. I didn't think I could do that simply with pie at a market.

I let out a steadying breath when we pulled up to a large open warehouse, buggies and trucks lined up along the side of the market. We unloaded our food quickly, the booth set up for our community close by. Sarah Jensen and an elderly woman supervised the booth, their smiles widening when they saw the number of pies we had brought.

"I have heard of your pies, young Katherine," the old woman said, squinting to investigate one of my apple pies. When she looked up again, I noticed one of her eyes was blind, clouded with age and cataracts.

"Ethel, she puts my pies to shame," Fannie replied, holding me close.

The old woman laid the pie back down on the table and patted me lightly on the arm.

"Well, that should make the young Fisher boy happy. Fatten him up. He is far too thin," she said, nodding seriously.

"I will do my best," I murmured, smiling at the idea that perhaps I could make him happy with more than simply my pies. And even more so, that Ethel already approved of me to do so.

Perhaps pie was the way to the Amish heart.

"Bishop Yoder, pleasant day."

I froze with a pie in my hand at the name on Ethel's lips.

Turning, I found the Bishop standing in front of the booth, eyeing the baked goods and jams. When he looked up to find me standing there with pie in my hands his friendly face faltered and a slight sneer appeared. It only lasted an instant before the man standing beside him spoke. I hadn't even noticed the young Bishop, Zachariah Ropp, standing there.

"It is good to see you again, Katherine Hill," he said with a courteous nod of his head. "I have heard many say your baked goods would make a fine addition to this market."

The Bishop's eyes narrowed at the young man's compliment.

"I am happy to offer whatever I may, Bishop Ropp," I replied, my voice soft.

Fannie came up beside me and transferred the pie in my hands to the table.

"She is blessed in her baking," she replied simply.

"You have taught her much then," Bishop Yoder stated, never taking his judging eye from mine.

"No, she was blessed before she arrived with us, Bishop Yoder," Fannie replied. "I dare say she outshines my own skills."

"Really?" Bishop Ropp asked, his eyebrows rising slightly. "Naomi Yoder has said that no one can cook like you. Your cakes and dishes are always the first to go at your Sermons, I hear."

Fannie wrapped her arm around my waist and smiled.

"Not any longer, I think," she said. "I do believe Katherine's pies disappeared while the main dishes were still hot on last Sermon."

"You will make an Amish man very happy one day," Bishop Ropp said before jerking his head toward his elder Bishop, who made a strangled noise in his throat.

Clearly Bishop Yoder didn't think so.

"An Amish wife must know more than how to fill her husband's belly," he muttered and nodded his goodbye before stalking off toward the horse auction.

Bishop Ropp looked after him for a moment before offering his clipped farewell and following after. Ethel patted my hand and gestured toward the retreating Bishops.

"Do not worry over Bishop Yoder. He has just forgotten what a meal made with love tastes like."

"I do not think Nathan Fisher starves so," one of the other women teased.

"Leave her be, Mary," Sarah said, winking at me as my blush deepened.

"Shall we shop?" Fannie interrupted, pulling me toward the main floor.

I waved my goodbyes and Fannie walked me around the warehouse floor, my embarrassment subsiding as we walked amongst other Amish that smiled and nodded along our way. She pointed at booths that we would come back to, and booths to avoid for their steep prices. By the time we had returned to our own booth, we were laden with supplies and had several young boys assisting us to our buggy.

I was rather happy with myself, my interaction with the Bishop forgotten. I had managed to get quite a lot with only about half the money Nathan had given me that morning. We still had a trip into town on our way back, during which I hoped to get a few other things. But our money seemed to be stretching better than I had hoped. Fannie seemed to be pleased with my success as well. Our buggy was crammed full of goods that would last us for quite some time into the winter.

Our pies had sold quickly, earning us a bit of money Fannie said would help with making clothing purchases for the cold weather ahead.

"Nathan will need more thermal underwear, as will you," she said as we climbed out of our buggy once again. We were in front of the feed store, Jonah and Nathan wanting us to place their order for animal feed.

"How cold does it get in the winter?" I asked, dreading her answer.

"There will be days it will be difficult to even step out to the barn, but chores must still be done," she replied and opened the door for me into the front office of the feed store.

I knew it would be rough. The only saving grace to that would be staying warm with Nathan throughout the winter. That thought made me smile. We ordered what we had been asked to order, my eyes widening a little at the prices of feed for the horses and cows. I wondered how many meals I could make with just milk and eggs, as that would be what we would have on hand and could afford little else if we expected to keep the horses and cows fed.

"It is not so dire, Katherine," Fannie assured me as we walked back out. "I have many canned goods in the cellar I intend to offer you so that you may have something there."

We walked to the general store down the street, Fannie wanting to check with the shop owner about future cake orders when a flash of orange caught my eye. I turned a little too slowly, but swore I had seen a woman with red hair duck into the alley next to the diner. A cold chill ran up my spine at the memory of that alley and the time Nathan had come to my rescue.

But more than that, I felt the prickling of fear at having possibly seen Joanna.

Was she spying?

Or was she simply in town? She had not yet returned to her parents' house, as far as I knew, and with the appearance of Jeff earlier in the month, I had my suspicions.

"Are you ready, Katherine?" Fannie asked, coming out of the store. "We need to still empty our goods when we return home."

I nodded and was quiet as we made our way home. Dozens of thoughts ran through my head, all dark and fearful, as I pictured Jeff's predatory smile, Joanna's narrowed eyes, and Sean's rough way. Every time I thought of Jeff or Joanna, I thought of Sean.

Why hadn't I heard anything?

Would they mail me a notice of his conviction?

He had to be here in Iowa by now, awaiting trial or in prison already.

I had been thinking about him a lot lately, perhaps because I knew at some point, there would be a question of whether I had forgiven him. The idea of doing so made my stomach turn. So perhaps that is why my stomach lurched when I saw the police car in the driveway of the Berger's farm as we rolled in. And when I saw the sheriff listening to Jonah and Nathan, I knew something was up.

This was not a simple call.

I could see it in Nathan's panicked eyes when they met mine.

Something had happened.

Nathan's fingertips hovered around my elbow and he directed me to the swing, where the sheriff detailed the news he had to share. My head swam as I sat there, Nathan's arm preventing me from falling. It was hard to breathe, difficult to concentrate on what the sheriff was saying. When he told me Sean had escaped, I nearly collapsed there in front of them. If not for Nathan's strong arms holding me, I would have crumpled.

I hadn't really heard how he had escaped.

Something about feigning sickness.

Something about a switch at the hospital.

Things you only hear about in movies, never in real life. But somehow he had slipped away and now they had Sean's friend Brendan in custody instead of Sean. Brendan had been there the night I had run. Brendan and Sam had held me down. Brendan had pulled at my clothes while Sean had hit me.

"Miss Hill, you need not worry," the sheriff was saying. "The Arcata Police Department has had sightings of him in their jurisdiction. He would be an idiot to come back here, with federal marshals looking for him."

"You are sure he is not in the state?" Nathan asked beside me.

"As much as we can gather. He was seen near Arcata last week with a group of his friends who appear to be helping him hide, like they did before he was arrested."

"Kate, breathe."

I looked up at Nathan, the worry in his eyes making me feel more lost as I tried to pull myself together.

"Miss Hill, he won't come back here. He has only made his case here worse. I wouldn't be surprised if he makes his way to Mexico," the sheriff said, trying to comfort me.

"You don't know Sean," I mumbled and closed my eyes.

"If you like, we can have an officer camp out here for a few days. Will that make you feel safer?" he offered.

Would I feel safer if an Outsider watched as we tried to go about our peaceful way?

Would this drive the wedge further between the community and me?

"What of his friends here?" Jonah asked, concern lacing his usually kind features. "Have you investigated them?"

"They claim to know nothing. They deny having helped him in the first place."

"Is there any threat to Katherine?" Jonah pressed.

"I don't think there is. He is gone. The Feds seem pretty sure of that."

"Kate?"

I opened my eyes and turned to see Nathan and Jonah watching me, the worry clear in their eyes.

"I don't know what to think," I whispered sighing in defeat.

Sean would never be out of my life it seemed.

Nathan tucked a stray hair behind my ear and turned to the sheriff.

"We appreciate your coming out to let us know. But if he is gone as you say, I think having an officer watch us will only make Kate more nervous," he said and held me a little closer.

"We will keep our daughter safe," Jonah added.

The sheriff straightened and put his hat back on his head.

"I understand. If you need anything, you know I am always happy to come out," he said and moved to leave.

Jonah and Nathan thanked him, while I nodded and stepped inside to give myself some distance from what I had just heard.

Sean was loose.

I would never be free of him.

Regardless of what the sheriff said.

I would always be looking over my shoulder.

I heard Nathan behind me before I felt his hands slip around and hold me in the dark hall.

"It will be all right, Kate," he whispered. "I will not let him hurt you again."

"After next Sunday, Nathan, you won't," I replied into his shoulder.

After we were baptized, Nathan would have no recourse to defend us. We didn't raise our hand to fight, even in self-defense.

"He will not come back. If he is hiding in California, he will not dare come back."

I nodded and pulled away as the door opened and Jonah came through, patting me on the shoulder.

"You will be safe here, Katherine. God will look after you," he said and disappeared into the kitchen.

"He is right," Nathan whispered. "God would not see you hurt."

I let it go with a nod, not wanting to argue with Nathan. Maybe this week or this month, we would be safe. But what about in six months, or a year? Even as Nathan assured me time and again that night, I just couldn't believe that we would never see Sean again.

Sean wouldn't give up that easily.

He would come back.

10

Nightmares of the corn had no time in my mind when I was too exhausted to dream.

As the fall crops and preparations for winter kept us busy, my studies and struggles at learning the Amish life forced thoughts of Sean into the back of my head. We had so much to do; it was difficult for me to think much on anything except my studies and my daily tasks. With Emma's and John's baptisms to prepare for in the coming day, all our energy and thoughts were for our sister, and the celebration to come. I was hopeful that everything I had learned would earn me a bit of the same nervous energy I saw in Emma all week leading up to her baptism.

Soon, Nathan and I would hopefully be committing to this life. Emma was alive with excitement beside me as we finished up on our dresses for the weddings. It had taken me a month and it was almost finished. Hannah helped when she could, but she and Mark were staying at the Bowman farm now, settling in as the elder Bowman began construction on an addition to the house there.

It was Mark and Hannah's addition.

Several men had come together to pour the foundation for the multi-room addition to the farmhouse there and then laid out the skeleton framework for the two-story house. We had organized the feeding and care of the men, so that by the end of the two-day build, the beginnings of their house had been completed. Needless to say, Hannah was busy in preparation for her new home, while we prepared for the next step in our journey.

I sighed in relief when I finished the last hook and eye on my dress, watching Emma as she bent over to finish her own.

A knock at the door brought our heads up. It was well past supper; Nathan and Benjamin were talking in the kitchen while we worked in the front room. Jonah and Fannie were away helping with another birth, leaving us alone. I stood and walked with Abigail as she made her way to the door. Another knock, this one more pronounced, had Nathan and Benjamin coming down the hall. When we opened the door, we took a tentative step back, surprised to see Naomi Yoder there, tear-streaked and breathing heavily. She grabbed at us, her eyes wide.

"I must speak with Elder Jonah! My mother!" she croaked and nearly collapsed into my arms.

I felt Benjamin behind me in an instant, his hands reaching out for his sister, gathering her in his arms as she cried out and clutched at him.

"Benjamin! You have to come! Mother is very sick! We need a doctor!" she wailed.

"Mother and Father are at the Snyder's for their baby," Emma said, looking at me in a panic.

"What is wrong with Mother?" Benjamin asked, his eyes burning with a need for information.

Naomi shook her head and cried a little harder.

"She started throwing up day before yesterday. She has had a fever that will not break. She has become weaker than I have ever seen her!"

I glanced at Nathan; he had that pained look on his face he wore whenever he thought of his own family. This was just another reminder for him. It didn't help that we had opened the last room yesterday, his parents'. I leaned down and touched

Naomi on the arm to get her attention.

"Come on, we'll take you home. Nathan will go let Jonah know. You need to be with your mother," I said firmly, pulling brother and sister up from the floor where they had collapsed.

Benjamin looked at me in fear.

"I will go with Nathan, to get Jonah," he stammered.

Nathan's hand on his shoulder, pushing him gently into the wall, made him pause. I could see the pained determination in Nathan's eyes. The death of his mother was still heavy on his mind.

"You will go see your mother," Nathan said, his voice low and dangerous. "You will not delay this any longer. You may not get the chance again."

"He will be there," Benjamin breathed.

"You will be there for her. Nothing else matters."

I held my breath at the interchange; Nathan's demanding nature was surprising. But the intense fear in Benjamin's face was even more so. He stared wide-eyed at Nathan, his mouth moving but no noise coming out.

"You will go," Nathan affirmed. "Go with Kate and Naomi. I will bring help."

Benjamin looked my way while I held his sister in my arms. I nodded in encouragement, and watched as his resolve set. The fear slid away at the sight of his sister, limp and crying in my arms. His family was in need. His mother needed him. He swallowed and nodded, taking deep breaths as if to prepare himself to dive into deep water.

Perhaps he was.

Nathan snuck in a kiss to my cheek and rushed out through the back door while Emma, Abigail and I helped Naomi into the Bishop's buggy. Benjamin followed with sluggish feet, his face ashen as he slid into the seat and grabbed the reins. A hard swallow and quick flick of the wrist to the reins and we were off into the darkness toward the Bishop's house. The full moon lit our way, the air eerily quiet and still making the sound of the buggy seem loud and jarring as we rode the short distance.

I watched Benjamin as we rode, his lip tucked in his mouth, his eyes too large. Fate had forced his hand and perhaps this was what was needed to drive him back home. I had no idea if he was ready; I could only hope that he was.

As soon as we pulled into the yard, the Bishop came out of the house and moved toward us swiftly, only to pull himself up short when he saw Benjamin helping Naomi out of the buggy.

"What?" he said haltingly. He glanced at me, then at Naomi, narrowing his eyes.

"Why is he here?"

"He wants to see Mother. He needs to see her," Naomi stammered, and clung to her brother a little more closely.

"What makes you think you are welcome?" the Bishop spluttered.

"It is time I saw Mother. She is in need," Benjamin said in a soft voice and walked past his father, never looking him in the eye.

He watched in shock as Benjamin half carried his sister into the house, Emma and Abigail not far behind them. He whirled around to face me while I unbuckled his horse from the buggy.

"What do you think you are doing? Bringing him here! This is your doing, I know it!" he hissed.

"She is sick. He wants to see her, in case," I started, only to have the Bishop silence me.

"She will not die! I sent the girl to fetch Jonah and she brings back Outsiders!" he yelled and raised his arms into the air.

The horse startled, pulling me hard until I had it calmed down. As soon as I had a firm hand on it, I turned to the Bishop, propriety and the quiet Amish female image I had tried to cultivate for over two months dashed by his anger.

"Jonah was not at home. Nathan is running now to get him. Benjamin is your son, not an Outsider. He deserves to see his mother!"

"You do not understand. You do not know this boy like I know him," he sneered and stepped forward, as if his height would intimidate me.

But I was the willful one, and so many years of accepting the berating of Sean and my father, and now the Bishop, made something in me snap.

"You are right. You know him better than I do. He is your flesh and blood and yet you discard him like a piece of ruined meat. You make him out to be a lost cause, Bishop Yoder, but I have seen his kindness. I have seen his charity. Do you not preach to us that family is the basis of our Way? Is it not in the Book that if one does not provide for his relatives, he has denied the faith and is worse than an unbeliever?" I asked, my hand tightening on the horse's bridle when the Bishop stepped closer again.

"How dare you throw my teachings back at me, English!" he seethed. "How dare you say I have no faith? I was born into this life. I accepted it with open arms. I did not spurn it so that I could sow my oats to an English whore that defiled that most precious thing as life by getting rid of it! I did not fill my soul with the Devil's drink and turn from His word. I remained faithful! I did not defile Him by cursing His name and turning from God and from my duty! You do not understand because you are an Outsider! You will always be an Outsider!"

He was towering over me, his breath hot in my face as he yelled. There was so much anger and hatred in this man.

And so much hurt.

I could see it in his eyes, beneath the ire. He was battling his demons and they were winning. He stared down at me with fire in his eyes, and inside of me I felt a sudden surge of pity for this man. He didn't live by his teachings. Everything he had lectured me on came back in a rush. Weeks of the Amish Way opened up my thoughts and it all became crystal clear to me, the meaning of this life.

"Our Way is love and forgiveness, Bishop Yoder. We are sinners by nature. But we are forgiven by God and by those who love us. Family is our life. Without it, how can we hope to flourish? I see that in the struggle that Nathan faces every day working his farm on his own. It is impossible without family. Naomi will be getting married soon, Bishop Yoder. And if you turn from your son, you will be alone. There is nothing more tragic than to turn from your family. I know. I have said goodbye to my blood by choice, because I choose this life."

Benjamin did not get that choice. He had been cast out, by his own flesh and blood.

"Where in the Bible does it say this is right? When your son needs so much of your love and guidance on the path of righteousness, you turn from him, you who are his spiritual advisor and his father. You refused him when he needed you most, when he needed a guide from the darkness of Rumspringa you toss your youth into. You cast him out for struggling and making his mistakes. Where is that in our Way?" I asked and took a step toward the Bishop, his former stance now less forbidding as he stepped back from my advance.

"When he wants to return, and when he wants to make amends, when he desperately wishes to return to that love and guidance, you shun him?" I asked, taking another step. "When he needs a father most, he is left alone and discarded? How can you be a man of God and shun your own son, who has suffered so much and only wants to return to the love of his family and his faith?"

I was whispering by the time I finished, my throat tightening at the sheer horror that was this man. I never broke eye contact with him as he stood over me while his horse nickered and pawed at the ground nervously. The Bishop raised his hand to point at me in accusation, the horse and I both flinching from the sudden movement.

He narrowed his eyes and leaned in, his breath washing over my already-heated face.

"You do not know what you speak of. You will never understand the true meaning of the Amish Way, the simple way that God intends. You are as tainted as he is, with your English ways. You do not exemplify the Way. You will always be an Outsider, and looked down on as such. With your violence and your sin and your outspoken ways. You will never be of the Amish Way, no matter how many you charm and manipulate," he grated.

I took a step back, pulling the horse to the side to walk around the Bishop. I paused a few steps away and turned back, my energy to stand and fight gone with his biting words.

"I may always be viewed as an Outsider, and I may never be

able to live amongst you for that reason. But Benjamin has struggled to find his way home, on his own. That shows how honorable and true his desire to live as an Amish man is. He has been tested, maybe by God Himself. I may not have been born into your Way, Bishop Yoder, but Benjamin was. He belongs here, and only hopes for your forgiveness," I said quietly and walked away, leaving the Bishop gaping by his abandoned buggy in the moonlight.

I settled the Bishop's horse into a stall, unsure if it was the right one or not. It didn't matter. The horse was happy to be in a stall with oats and water. I made my way back toward the house, unsure whether or not to enter, so I remained outside in the cool night, sitting on the steps leading up to the house, deep in thought.

The Bishop had made it clear that I would always be an Outsider. There was no winning him over. I felt my determination crack from his scathing words. There would be no baptism for me if he had to choose. I would not be able to marry Nathan, and I would be forced to leave, I was sure. Would Nathan walk away from this life, like he had said on our trip back, or would he choose the Amish Way over me?

I couldn't think ill of him if he chose his faith over me.

This was his life, and while I wanted to be with him more than anything, I wouldn't force him to choose.

I thought of leaving this all behind and I felt my breath catch. I would be lost without this life.

I fought back my tears; it would just hinder me further to have the Bishop discover he had cracked my resolve.

It was a long while before I heard the sound of hooves on the gravel in the dark. I made out the silhouette of a buggy, hoping it was Nathan with Jonah. My hopes were dashed when I saw the dapple-grey horse pulling in close. A man jumped out of the buggy, walking around to help someone out of the other side.

Gleaming white beard and stooped-over figure — I recognized Elder Ezekiel immediately. I stood awkwardly, my legs numb from sitting for too long. Ezekiel took the man's hand and walked at a crawling pace toward me, smiling when he was close enough to see me.

"Katherine. What a surprise to see you here, of all places. Has the Bishop cast you out of his house?" he asked, a bit of biting humor in the timbre of his voice.

I blinked back tears at his words, unsure how to respond.

Ezekiel frowned at my startled expression and gently took my arm, leaning in as I helped him up the stairs.

"I am sorry, girl. I did not mean to make light of a troublesome worry you undoubtedly face. Let us go in and see how the Bishop's wife is," he whispered and patted my arm as he hung on it a little heavier. I had a feeling the Bishop would have another opinion of me entering his house.

As we entered the bedroom, the Bishop turned his head from me. He stood off in the corner, his eyes trained hard on Benjamin as he sat beside his mother, who cried softly and clung to his hand as he whispered to her. Naomi sat on the other side, her head on the side of the bed, her hand in her mother's hair as she stroked it lightly to calm her mother. Emma busied herself with applying cool compresses against Mrs. Yoder's forehead.

I found a chair for Ezekiel to sit in and took in the scene around me until I felt restless from the tension in the room. Ezekiel noticed my nerves, bending me toward him to whisper, asking for a cup of tea. Given an occupation, I disappeared into the Yoder kitchen and made myself useful. It was going to be a long night, and still Jonah and Nathan had not arrived.

I set the water boiling for tea. I cleaned the dishes that appeared to be left from a hasty supper. I kept myself busy, cleaning and supplying drinks as needed. And when I had nothing else to do, I set about making breakfast. Emma came down regularly to retrieve more cold water, whispering to me how she thought things were progressing. But aside from the Yoders standing vigil, no other efforts were made to heal the family's issues. No one spoke, unless Mrs. Yoder requested it.

I was leaning against the counter, nearly asleep while standing when I heard the front door open. I straightened up in time to see Jonah make his way up to the bedrooms. I saw Nathan in the doorway, tired and disheveled, taking in the scene of me alone in the kitchen.

"Emma told me her fever broke an hour or two ago. She's sleeping last I checked," I whispered.

"And Benjamin?" he asked, concerned.

"Sitting beside his mother."

He nodded and stepped into the kitchen quietly.

"The baby was finally born a few hours ago. Fannie is staying with the mother until daybreak. I am not sure Jonah has slept in two days," he said and sat at the table, groaning as he rubbed at his neck.

"It will be a long day," I replied and poured him a cup of coffee. He took it gratefully and watched while I worked, pulling out biscuits and the breakfast casserole Fannie had shown me.

"Have you not slept?" he asked.

I offered him a tense smile and shook my head.

"I don't think I could sleep even if I tried. Too much going on," I replied and wiped my hands.

Nathan opened his mouth to speak, closing it when he heard footsteps coming down the stairs. Naomi came in through the doorway, going straight to Nathan to hug him tight.

"Thank you, Nathan. Jonah says she should be fine now that the fever has broken. Thank you for finding Jonah. And for my brother," she whispered.

Nathan hugged her back awkwardly before pulling away at the sound of more footsteps. Jonah and the Bishop entered next, Jonah speaking in a hushed tone as they sat at the table. One look at Jonah told me that he needed some coffee. I poured cups for the men, setting them down on the table before returning to get cream and sugar. Emma came down next and helped Naomi and me to prepare dishes for everyone. The Bishop watched us as we brought the plates over, looking down finally at his plate as his daughter placed it before him.

"Thank you, Naomi," he murmured and never looked up toward me when I laid out the remaining plates.

"Is Elder Ezekiel still here?" I asked.

"Upstairs in one of the bedrooms," Naomi replied.

"And Benjamin?" Nathan asked, earning a scowl from the Bishop.

"He is sitting beside Mother," Naomi replied, glancing sideways at her father.

I sat beside Emma, quiet as the Bishop recited mealtime prayers. When he was done, Jonah glanced from him to me, taking in the tension in the air. He cleared his throat and looked my way, smiling.

"Thank you, Katherine, for making this bountiful breakfast. You are so much like Fannie," he said, offering me a sympathetic smile.

I nodded and pulled my eyes back down to my plate, not wanting to say anything in the moment. I had made my opinions clear the night before. I knew the Bishop would sooner die than compliment me after what I had said to him. We ate in silence, the light of the lantern falling away to darkness around us in the early predawn. With breakfast completed, we cleaned up while the men spoke about the Sermon for the coming day and the baptism.

"I will be along shortly. I want to make sure my wife is comfortable. Naomi will stay with her during the Sermon," the Bishop announced.

"We should go to prepare for our guests. We are behind on our daily chores," Jonah said and nodded toward me when I turned from the dishes.

The Bishop looked toward Emma and allowed a terse smile.

"Emma, thank you for your assistance last night. My wife is better for your hands. And Nathan, for bringing Jonah when you did," he said, never looking my way.

Nathan regarded me for a long moment, perhaps hoping the Bishop would open up. I remained quiet by the sink.

I knew better.

The awkward silence was interrupted by footsteps and voices coming down the stairs. We turned to see Ezekiel and Benjamin as they entered, the old man leaning into the other as he spoke.

"I think your arrival was a Godsend, boy," Ezekiel was saying and then turned to smile as he took in the room. "Are we late for breaking fast? I could smell it, but these legs do not work as well as they used to."

Naomi and I busied ourselves with making plates for the two new arrivals.

Ezekiel had pulled Benjamin down to sit beside him at the table, gripping his arm with amazing strength for an old man. When I set the plates before them, Ezekiel smiled and thanked me quietly. Looking over at Benjamin, he patted his arm and motioned to the food.

"Will you say morning prayers, boy?"

Benjamin swallowed hard and glanced at his father from across the table, murmuring the words softly beside the old man. When he was done, Ezekiel nodded and dug into his breakfast, speaking to the Bishop as he ate.

"It is good to see your son with us once more, Samuel. He has given us renewed hope in family and love. Your wife was the happiest I have seen her in a very long time," he said, looking down at his meal while he spoke.

The Bishop looked at his son, his eyes unreadable.

Blank even.

"She was happy last night," he finally conceded, frowning and drinking the last of his coffee to cover his frustration.

"The prodigal son returns," Ezekiel said and looked up at the Bishop with an intensity that I could feel from across the room.

The Bishop sat a little straighter but said nothing.

Ezekiel nodded as if the Bishop had answered him and turned back to his meal.

"Benjamin," he said after a moment. "I speak for the Elders when I say we are grateful for you showing the courage to return. We hope that you will stay and formally accept our Way, as God intended. The community will be here for you should you choose it. And if God so chooses, a path to lead."

Benjamin flushed and looked up at Nathan.

"I do not mean Nathan, Benjamin. God has other plans for him," Ezekiel continued and put his fork down, the intensity in his eyes never wavering.

"It is time to come home and take your place, son. The community needs this," the old man said, his voice soft and crackling, but the meaning clear.

"It is time for this poison that eats at the two of you to be expelled, and for you both to take God's purpose to heart. It is time for this family to be healed and for you to become the man God intends."

The image of Benjamin as he sat there while Ezekiel told him he had to come back played in my head again and again while I hastily completed my morning chores before the Sermon. We left before the heated argument that must have followed. Nathan took my shoulder while Jonah made our farewells. Benjamin looked after us with the countenance of a young man going off to fight an unwinnable battle.

His eyes beseeched us.

Or cursed us.

I wasn't sure which.

But if he didn't run now, after Ezekiel's words, I would be amazed and relieved.

Nathan was quiet on the ride back; Jonah only spoke for a moment before he too fell silent. Emma held a sleeping Abigail in her arms, but had glanced at me with those perceptive eyes of hers.

Could she sense the guilt I suddenly felt for pushing Benjamin to go see his mother?

Now he was being told that he had to return. Could he still refuse?

If he refused, did that mean he would no longer be permitted in the community?

I shook my head and concentrated on the milking of our impatient cows. They sensed my frustration, or perhaps they were upset we were late in milking. I wasn't paying attention. I was worrying over the idea of Nathan losing his friend. I was worried once again about Nathan becoming Bishop. I was worried I would be denied, based on all the words thrown around the night before.

Did Ezekiel tell Benjamin he had to come back for Nathan's sake? Because no one would allow their future Bishop to marry an Outsider?

My head hurt from all the questions and lack of sleep.

I couldn't think, couldn't concentrate. I sat beside one cow long after she had been milked and struggled to understand why I was sitting there. My mind had shut down.

My body wasn't much better.

Carrying two large pails of milk, I tripped and spilled most of one over into the grass. I watched it disappear into the soil, struggling not to cry at the loss. We'd be short milk now for all the food we needed to make. How would I possibly be able to juggle milking and gardens and stitching and being the Bishop's wife?

Fannie gave me a tired knowing smile when I walked in. Either she had seen me trip or she just knew. But she remained quiet and focused instead on kneading the bread for supper after the Sermon. We worked in silence, filling and emptying the oven until just before services. When the other wives showed up to help out, Fannie sent me upstairs to change.

After a quick sponge bath and change into clean clothes I stepped out into the hallway just as Emma emerged from Hannah's old room. She pulled me close and hugged me, her breath labored.

"It's okay, Emma," I soothed, feeling her pull away at my words.

She touched my cheek and smiled.

"I am not worried about today, Katherine. I am sad for this morning. He does not see you," she said.

I frowned, confused. She let out an exasperated breath and rolled her eyes.

"I mean the Bishop," she explained and my frown deepened. I hadn't thought much on him ignoring me this morning. Only his accusations and what they meant for my future.

"That doesn't matter, Emma," I said shaking my head and forcing a smile. "Today is your day. Yours and John's."

We hugged again and walked downstairs together, Emma

growing more nervous as people began to arrive. Emma took my hand and sat me down by the aisle, so that when called, she could make an easy exit. I looked around for Nathan, finding him with John as they stood near the door adjoining the other room.

Ezekiel was led in and seated a few rows in front of us. He smiled and nodded in our direction before leaning over his Bible, pushing his glasses up to his forehead to read. The room filled quickly, and at the Bishop's entrance, people found their seats and quieted down.

I watched the Bishop as we sang the opening hymns for baptism. His face was unreadable once more, which was disconcerting coming from him. It was easy to interpret his outward contempt for me, but today he was a mask of neutrality. I had to wonder if that was due solely to the conversation we had left that morning.

Had Ezekiel convinced Benjamin his place was here?

The Bishop walked out with Emma and John, her hand tightening on mine for a brief second before she slipped out. As we settled, I looked around for Benjamin, hoping he would be here. I couldn't find him, which made my heart sink at the idea that he was running away once more.

Nathan stood tall and sure as he started the next song. His face was solemn and focused as he led the congregation. I wondered if he felt the same as me. In a couple of weeks, we would be doing this also if everything went well. To that end, he would accept a duty he neither wanted nor could afford to take should he be chosen.

With his Outsider bride to cause extra stress.

The song ended and we sang another, his eyes catching mine briefly during the verse. I thought I saw a ghost of a smile before he looked away to concentrate on the singing. I was sure he was trying to provide me with strength. He knew me so well, I was sure he knew I was battling my fears as I sat at the end of the bench, alone in a room full of people.

The congregation finished the song just as the Bishop re-entered. I slid to the side as Emma returned, her hand gripping mine tighter than ever, her smile near bursting. I knew that those who were to be baptized met one last time with the Bishop, to offer those joining one last chance to step away. Judging from Emma's death grip and nervous excitement that coursed through her body, I was sure she had all but shouted her agreement to this way of life. I glanced at John, and caught him looking our way, a smile on his face that seemed to light up his side of the room.

I felt a calm wash over me at their enthusiasm. As the Bishop spoke the introductory words to the baptismal Sermon, I thought on how this would change everything for the person making the leap.

No going back.

No retreating.

No breaking the rules.

That person was casting off any thoughts of a different life and choosing this one.

An Amish life.

There was no way to separate from it except to be excommunicated once one was baptized into the Amish way. By taking the vow to live the Amish life, Nathan and I would agree to live by their rules, and to support one another and our way of life. I could feel the build up of excitement coursing through me just as Emma must.

This was the moment she had waited for.

The Bishop paused in his Sermon, as if to gather his thoughts. Taking a deep breath, he looked straight ahead, his voice detached as he spoke.

"Today we see members of our youth take the final step, by accepting in their hearts and in their souls the Way. With each new member, our community grows stronger. With each baptism, a duty fulfilled. Today's baptism is no different. For we bring into our community the means to continue on, to strengthen and to remain true to the Way. As God demands."

He paused and took another breath, this time more resigned as he opened up his arms, eyes closed.

"Today we shall celebrate the baptism of three of our youth, who shall now come forward and present themselves to their community and to God."

I blinked and turned to Emma, whose grip had tightened until it was almost painful at the Bishop's words. She held her smile for a moment before pulling it into that quiet mask that was expected and stood to move forward. John was standing and moving to the front of the room where the deacons were preparing the pails of water.

But I was lost in the Bishop's words.

He had said *three*.

I turned when I heard soft murmurings behind me.

And there, walking down the narrow aisle, was Benjamin.

I held my breath as he walked toward the front, his head held high and his back straight. As he neared, his gaze flickered over to Nathan, and I watched as his eyes turned from something of solemn duty to determination. Glancing down at me, he offered me a soft smile before passing to kneel beside John. He bent his head in preparation for what would change his life forever.

And possibly the community as well.

Benjamin had come home.

11

I watched Benjamin walk out of the house, surrounded by men and women I didn't know, but who looked ecstatic to see him back. Only a few people looked alarmed by the Bishop's son returning, and interestingly enough, those were the same individuals who spoke ill of me when they thought they were being discreet. I felt Emma beside me, her hand coming up to grab at mine, her smile brilliant as she pulled me outside. We were barely off the porch when she leaned in and let her words flow.

"I could not tell you, Katherine! But oh, how I wanted to! When we walked back to make our pledge, he was there! His father was so brusque with him, but he stood tall and determined as he spoke his pledge, and I am just so happy for him, Katherine!" she exclaimed and continued to pull us out toward the sunlit benches.

I followed along in a daze, my body tired and my mind whirling too quickly for me to think on one thing for any amount of time. Benjamin was back, there were celebrations to be had for the baptisms this day, and what that meant for my own future with Nathan. Emma sat me down on one of the shadier benches and moved to step away.

"Where are you going?" I asked, confused. She smiled and leaned in to hug me.

"You worked hard last night. Relax for a moment. I will bring us plates," she replied and bounded off toward the group of women laying out food for midday meal.

I sighed and let my eyes close, feeling the sun peek through the leaves and cast shadows across my eyelids as I sat there. There was a sense of peace that lay over the land. A warm gentle breeze blew to amplify the smell of food and crisp dry grass. The sound of children running around and playing filled my ears, along with the conversations filtering around.

Sometimes I wished I didn't know German.

My head dipped down and I hid my frown, my eyes concentrating on the explorer ant that was moving in a zigzag across the table. I wanted to concentrate on anything other than the conversation closest to me that seemed to continue on in blistering fashion. I could feel my face heat up, and my heart hammering.

I was tired.

My nerves were worn raw from my dealings with the Bishop.

But the words I heard near me made me feel frustrated and question the meaning of "love thy neighbor".

He should never have been allowed back.

I am sure she had something to do with bringing him home.

She sits there as if to be waited on.

Not a good match for young Fisher.

She is charming our good men, drawing them away.

His farm will falter.

I stood abruptly, causing their voices to silence and their eyes to look over at me. I threw on a false smile, and like the quiet Amish woman I wasn't, spoke out.

"Es tut mir leid. Bitte entschuldigen Sie mich," I said, offering my apologies and excusing myself while their eyes widened. I was pretty sure I had said it all right.

I turned from their reddening faces and sought out Emma before she made my plate. I wasn't hungry anymore. I expected animosity to joining the community; I even expected a direct lashing out when it was my turn to be baptized. But seeing and hearing it be directed to one of their own irritated me.

Benjamin deserved better.

Sarah Jensen caught sight of me as I trudged closer, her eyes narrowing as I drew close.

"What is it, Katherine? You appear aggravated. Be at peace today," she said and wrapped her arm around me. I blew out a long breath and tried to smile.

I was sure it looked like a grimace; she held me a little more firmly and pulled me with her toward the kitchen.

"Today is a monumental day, Katherine. We have seen a miracle today. From what I hear from Ezekiel, you and Nathan will be next. We are truly blessed," she said, smiling.

"If the Elders allow me," I murmured, feeling the fatigue and my worries begin to overwhelm me.

She stopped and looked down at me, her eyes full of concern.

"Why would they not?" she asked. "You have put forth more effort in learning our Way than many of our own children. You are a light that has awoken many, Katherine. I have no doubts in your acceptance."

I nodded and looked down at my feet, afraid to believe her. She had always been civil, since the moment I had met her. She was kind like the Bergers. But the words from the others, time and again, left me doubting.

"I know there are some who may be upset if I marry Nathan," I whispered and glanced back toward the group I had overheard. Sarah looked where my eyes had traveled and she let out something like a snort.

"Oh my, Katherine, do not worry over the Schrocks," she replied and leaned in to whisper. "They have no right to question you. They come from Ohio, from an Old Order community that I believe shunned them. We took them in with open arms. It is our way, and they should have no reason to act as they do. They were new to us not so long ago."

I glanced back once more, frowning.

"Why would they think less of Benjamin, then? I understand why they are upset about me," I started but Sarah shook her head, huffing hard.

"They see our present Bishop as a man to bring back some of the old ways they agreed with. Do not worry, Katherine. Having Benjamin home is a Godsend. And perhaps things will change for the better soon," she muttered and directed me inside toward the kitchen.

I found Emma there, as well as Fannie, who looked about as tired as I did. Fannie nodded to Sarah, who left us alone with a nod and an encouraging pat on my shoulder. I met Fannie at the counter and felt her warm arms wrap around the two of us. She hummed quietly in our ears while she held us.

"I am so happy for my daughters," she said and pulled away, placing her palms on our cheeks.

I looked at her, abashed.

"I didn't do anything," I murmured.

Emma grunted and shook her head at me.

"That is not true, Katherine. Not only did you take up duties to care for the Yoders this morning, but you finally told the Bishop what he needed to hear!" she said, nodding firmly.

I glanced from her to Fannie, nervous now that they knew of the tongue-lashing I had given to the Bishop.

"I know it was wrong to say those things, but he just made me so mad," I stammered.

Fannie hugged me tighter and let out a soft laugh.

"Katherine, from what Emma tells me, you said what many have wished to say. You are unconventional, but we love you for that bit of new courage you give us," she replied.

"You should have seen Benjamin's face while we listened," Emma chuckled.

My eyes widened.

"He heard it too?" I squeaked.

She nodded.

"I think you might have given him the courage to do what he did today, regardless of what Elder Ezekiel may have said. I think Benjamin knew he needed to come back," she explained.

I wasn't sure how to feel about that. Was he feeling guilty? Did he go through with it for himself, or because he felt Nathan would suffer? Or that I would suffer?

"Katherine, do not worry," Emma said. "Come, let us get some food and relax for a little while. This is a celebration, not an inquisition."

I nodded and made up a plate, relaxing some when we finally sat down across from Nathan, Benjamin and John.

"Where did you run off to?" Nathan asked, a little concerned. "You seemed frustrated when you stood up and walked away."

I waved my hand around dismissively.

"I couldn't sit there alone," I replied, not wanting to bring up what I had heard in front of Benjamin.

Even still, Benjamin was looking toward the Schrocks with a knowing eye. He glanced back at me and then concentrated on his meal. Nathan pursed his lips, seeming to understand that there was more to the story, but left it alone while we ate. I somehow knew we would discuss it later.

As a distraction, I turned to Emma and John.

"So now that you are officially committed to the Way, how long do we have until the wedding?" I asked, and laughed as Emma blushed.

John was unfazed by the question. He simply pulled the chicken apart in his hands slowly and offered me a lazy grin.

"I do not think we wish to wait until you and Nathan are ready. It will be late winter by then," he said, his smile growing. "So we plan to announce it today to those we intend to invite."

Nathan's eyebrows raised in surprise.

"You mean to be wed in a few weeks?" he asked, looking from John's smug grin to Emma's beet red face.

They both nodded.

"That is the plan," John replied and rubbed at Emma's hand

to calm her. She seemed to relax in an instant and her blush diminished. It was amazing how in tune they both were with each other.

Nathan cleared his throat and glanced at me.

"I do not believe it will be winter when we speak our vows," he said, his lips quivering.

It was my turn to blush and feel Nathan's soothing touch on my hand.

"Yes, well. You still must have the Bishop ask for Katherine's permission, Nathan," John replied, his smile sobering quickly.

Nathan pulled my hand into his and held his head higher.

"I have hope and faith," he replied, confirming for me that somehow, things would work out.

Even if the Bishop fought us tooth and nail.

Nathan's faith in us made me believe.

It carried me through the rest of the afternoon.

I watched as people eventually dispersed, shaking hands with John and nodding politely to Emma as they left later that afternoon. The formal announcement had been made about their impending wedding, with many congratulations and well wishes. It was nice to see so much affection toward the two of them. A few asked Nathan about his plans to take a bride, their playful banter in German causing him to blush and glance my way with a timid smile, as if asking me if it was all right to announce our own plans.

He refrained, which I was glad for, and the older women teased him about needing a good woman around his house before they glanced at me thoughtfully and went on their way. I simply smiled and remained quiet, trying to emulate the Amish Way.

Nathan excused himself at some point to offer his help in packing the wagon that carried the Sermon benches, and so I sat on our swing, the chores complete and the sun dipping toward the hill. I was exhausted from avoiding the Bishop's intense scrutiny most of the day and shattered from trying to ignore the looks and whispers of everyone else. My nerves were raw, and I tried desperately to hide it so as not to worry Nathan or the Bergers. The day had been maybe the hardest since coming into my new world, and that was saying something after learning how to muck out stalls and wash clothes by hand.

I just wanted to crawl upstairs and sleep, and hope that the following day showed me more grace and acceptance. My eyes had closed at some point, but I heard the tentative footsteps near me. I opened my eyes, expecting Nathan. I was surprised to see Benjamin there, looking down at his hat in his hand. I slid over and patted the swing, offering him a seat. He looked as tired as I felt.

He shook his head and moved to lean on the porch railing across from me. I watched him as he picked at a worn spot on his straw hat, his eyes remaining there as if only the mark on the brim existed in his world. I remained quiet, unsure in my present state that I wouldn't say something awkward or inappropriate. He cleared his throat and glanced up only as far as my own feet.

"I wanted to thank you, Katherine."

I shifted in my seat and shook my head.

"I don't know what for. I haven't done anything," I murmured, forcing his eyes to find mine.

"I have everything to thank you for. I would not be here, if it were not for you."

I made to argue but he put his hand up, silencing me.

"I only hope I will be half of what you expect of me," he said and barked out a harsh laugh.

"I don't expect anything that you are not already, Benjamin," I murmured.

"You see more than anyone I know, Katherine. You seem to know how to inspire," he continued. "You have no fear, you leap into the lion's den, and still you continue on. I have witnessed you stand up to the man who terrifies me, and still you smile and persevere. You stand up for things that should be natural for me to do. But I could not. I walked from my mother's bedside this morning with the idea that I had to do something, after last night and your words. I have run for long enough. You did that for me, Katherine. You made me see God again."

I looked down from him, embarrassed and uncomfortable.

He was putting too much credence into my being.

The same being who was seconds from crying and wanting to run away as well.

"You did that yourself, Benjamin," I murmured. "You just needed to see that people do care about you being here and being well."

"But you made me see that. Your desire for this life makes you unafraid of the wrongs you have been dealt," he said and when I looked up at him, I noticed his pursed lips as he looked off toward his father. He let out a long sigh and turned back to me, his eyes somber.

He tilted his head to the side and regarded me thoughtfully for a long moment.

"You shoulder too much of a burden that is not yours, Katherine," he whispered. "And for that I am sorry. For much of it is my fault."

"It's not your fault," I started.

"Yes it is. My father has never appreciated the wonder of the English world. His father refused him his Rumspringa. My father works in the modern world with his furniture store, but he is not a man of that world. I think he simply refuses to acknowledge it on principle now, because his own father shunned it. My desire to remain in that world meant I could have what he was refused. He did not appreciate that. His children should never have better than he did," he explained ruefully.

"I'm not sure if it was better, Benjamin. But a parent should want the best for his child," I replied.

He shrugged and picked at his hat again.

"I was angry at him for denying me. For insisting I give up the things I had discovered in that world. Better things. I found a girl I thought I loved. Whom I thought loved me," he whispered and kept his head down. He swallowed and cleared his throat. "My father could not fathom me loving anyone outside our Order. He could not see past his own experience."

"That's his fault, not yours," I argued.

He laughed and nodded.

"But I did not help to temper his view of English women. I know he harbors ill feelings for you because of me. I am sorry for that," he murmured.

I stood and took a step toward him. I couldn't handle much more deep conversation today.

"I irritate him for many reasons, Benjamin. Please don't feel responsible for how this community feels toward me," I said, trying to brush off the emotions I felt at having to continue to prove myself, probably for years to come.

He looked up at me, his eyes dark and deep and full of regret.

"You have proven to him that someone can stand up to his hurtful words. It should have been me last night standing up to him. But I was afraid and you were braver than I. I fear I will fail in my faith. I do not know if God still wants me," he said in a low voice.

"I don't think you would have stepped forward today if that was true, Benjamin. You knew it was where you needed to be, even if Elder Ezekiel gave you the nudge you needed. Sometimes we need a push to get us going in the right direction," I explained and allowed him a tender smile when he chuckled.

"Elder Ezekiel is quite persuasive. You do not say no to him," he said, nodding gravely.

"No, you do not. He sees your purpose clearly, I think," I replied.

He sighed and continued to nod, like the movement would help him admit it to himself.

"It will be determined when Council meets," he said.

I remained quiet so that he could continue with what I knew was coming.

"Elder Ezekiel and Jonah have already said they would vote me in for next Bishop."

"Are you afraid you will be chosen?" I asked in a whisper.

He let out a soft laugh and shrugged.

"My father never wanted the position. He was chosen late, when our old Bishop died. He was a successful businessman, and the role of Bishop is consuming. He never fully embraced it. But I have always enjoyed my time doing God's work. In truth it was something I hoped for before my Rumspringa. But I am my father's son. I live with the notion that I will be scrutinized always for my father's failures."

He straightened up looking at me directly, as if in solemn declaration.

"But if chosen, I will strive to live right and do well by you, because you have shown me there are things worth defending that are honest and true. You are worth defending, Katherine, because already you are Amish in God's eyes. Nathan was right. You are an angel from Heaven to enlighten us all. You will make a good partner for my best friend, and will provide the light he needs, just as he does for you," he said.

I swallowed and took a deep breath, his words resonating profoundly after such a long and troubling day.

"Thank you, Benjamin," I whispered and smiled in appreciation. It was nice to hear from someone other than family and Nathan.

Benjamin nodded and looked back at his father once more.

"I must give hope and kindness to my flock if I am to make a good Bishop, now, am I not?" he asked and smiled.

"I think you are a natural, Benjamin Yoder," I breathed, proud of my friend.

He let out a nervous chuckle and took a deep breath.

"Perhaps. We shall see. But your bravery gives me the strength and courage to succeed and I thank you for that," he said and was quiet for a moment, pulling his thoughts together as he fidgeted with his hat once more.

I watched, as Benjamin seemed to transform before my eyes from the scared lost boy to a man of faith.

"I am renewed by your hope and faith in our Way, Katherine Hill. And it is time you see that you are made for this life," he said, his eyes focusing on me intently. "Do not try to live in the expectation of others. To thine own self be true."

I laughed and shook my head.

"That's Shakespeare, not the Bible," I teased.

His smile warmed and he nodded.

"One thing my father did not learn was that there are other wise prophets in the world from whom we may glean advice," he explained and then looked at me seriously.

"Shakespeare was a wise man. The words provide a truth we should all follow. Follow what is in your heart, because that is where you reside closest to God's way."

"Shakespeare was a wise man indeed, then," I replied.

"And so you shall see your new Bishop bring in fresh thought to this congregation if I am chosen," he said. "Because you and I have seen the evil in the world. We understand what beauty there is here," he replied, a little wistful.

I touched his hand lightly, not wanting to overstep any rules.

"You will be a better Bishop because of that, Benjamin. I am sure of that," I said smiling.

"You will see, Katherine," he murmured. "Things will be right once more. I promise you peace and kindness."

I knew in my heart as I looked at Benjamin that God would choose correctly. He had been a lost sheep. He had endured the trials of fire, and now, standing before me, he was a better man for it. Afraid to fail, worried he would falter. Educated in the ways of loss and suffering.

That made him more a man of God than his father was. He strived to live better, more honestly and more faithfully. What made me most proud was that Ezekiel and those who mattered had seen it, too.

Things would be better.

Our world would be better.

12

Days moved on, with the fall deepening with each sunrise. Each new day greeted me with the familiar forms of Nathan and Benjamin walking down the hill in the predawn. The autumn, with its chilly winds and resting soil, brought with it new beginnings when the rest of the world settled in to rest. With each step toward winter, a new joy could be found.

Today, that joy would be Emma's wedding day. .

"We could have waited a few weeks, Katherine. Then you and I would both be wed on the same day. It would have been something special for us," Emma said in the early dawn.

I yawned and shook my head to try to wake up. It was difficult this morning; Emma had tossed and turned all night.

"This is *your* day, Emma," I explained for the tenth time. "We have time."

The truth was, the days were coming faster and faster. Perhaps with the sun going down a little earlier and with less time to spend with Nathan, I simply felt that it was going faster.

Sooner than I could imagine, Nathan and I would have our

last baptism class, and the Council would meet to discuss not just changes in the Ordnung, but whether I would be allowed to join the community. And maybe even the choosing of a new Bishop. Just a couple of weeks now and everything could change.

For better or worse.

I sat on the bed, Emma in front of me as I brushed her hair and pinned it up to look fuller than it was. It had grown out well, but was still short compared to other girls our age. It seemed like just a few weeks had passed since I had run away, only to discover my true home in this world. I smiled and pinned Emma's hair deftly, having learned so much in the few months I had lived with the Bergers.

How had I lived before this?

In fear, and in denial.

My smile faltered as I thought back on my life before that fateful buggy ride. Sean had always smothered me and made me feel insignificant. My dad had never supported me.

Escaping that life was the greatest achievement of my life so far.

So far.

I had my entire life ahead of me now.

I would forget about Sean Miller.

Forget about my old life.

I would conquer my nightmares of being trapped in the corn, always running from Sean.

He was my past.

My past could not hurt me anymore.

I hoped.

"What are you thinking about?"

My smile picked up and I resumed pinning Emma's hair, having not realized I had stopped.

"I was thinking about how beautiful you are going to look standing there beside John when you are presented to us today. And how I can't wait for that day myself," I whispered and leaned in to offer her a little hug.

She turned and grinned at me, her eyes filling up with tears.

"I am only sorry I will not be able to be here with you tonight!" she said and I laughed hard.

"I think you'll be happy where you are sleeping tonight, Emma," I retorted, watching her face brighten.

"It will be strange to be there instead of here," she murmured, suddenly a little forlorn.

I leaned around to see her face fully.

"John is excited to take you into his home, and his father seems excited to welcome you. We'll be fine," I replied, and hugged her again.

"I can milk the cows and get the eggs!" Abigail stated, acting much more mature than I had ever seen her.

"And the washing and the cooking, *and* the mending?" Emma teased.

"Mother will still cook. And I am still a better seamstress than Katherine," Abigail argued.

I nodded and laughed.

Perhaps Abigail would do well without all of us.

"I am sure we'll manage, Emma. Who knows, maybe Fannie and Jonah will discover what they have missed all those years with a full house," I replied and giggled with them when we both thought about Fannie and Jonah being romantic again.

Not that they didn't now.

One hears a lot of things when one can't sleep.

But somehow I wasn't disgusted by the idea of my adoptive parents being intimate; it just made the idea of growing older with Nathan more alluring. The Amish seemed very amorous with their spouses. At least Fannie and Jonah were, and I somehow knew that Nathan fashioned himself after the likes of Jonah.

I couldn't wait for that with Nathan. If I would be allowed, that is.

I sighed and pulled away from Emma, smiling at how much her hair had grown in the last few months to afford her a simple bun under her cover.

"You are beautiful," I whispered. "John won't know what hit him."

Today was going to be a magical day.

I stayed with Emma until it was time to let her and John speak their vows privately with the Bishop, anxiously waiting with Abigail and Naomi Yoder on a bench as Zachariah Ropp led the congregation in song. Nathan sat with Mark near the front of the room, glancing back toward me once in a while to sneak a smile before turning back to listen to the young Bishop's words.

It seemed like an hour before Bishop Yoder returned, Fannie and Jonah slipping onto their benches quietly. I could tell Fannie had been crying and I felt a moment's contentment when she leaned in and squeezed my hand. We all turned in our seats to see the newly married couple when the Bishop announced them. Emma held John's hand like it would disappear if she let go, and John grinned from ear to ear, nodding in acknowledgement of the quiet blessings offered them as they entered.

The Bishop presented them to the room, and a final song of marriage and duty to one's community echoed throughout the room. It didn't escape my attention that we sung about how many children would be a blessing. I hid my smile when I noticed Nathan glancing my way with his pink tipped ears. It was the Bishop's pursed lips as he eyed me that made Nathan turn his head away, his face matching his ears.

Bishop Yoder glanced my way, a smug look on his face as he walked past.

"He is trying to intimidate us," Nathan whispered near me as we claimed our plates for the meal.

"It's working," I whispered back.

"Only if you let it."

I forced a smile on my face and tried to put Nathan at ease, but I knew what the Bishop had said to me. There was no way he would ever allow me to join. It would take an overwhelming vote of the community to allow me to commit to this life.

"His opinion of you will not sway everyone," Nathan said as we sat at the table with the Bergers.

"There are many who would see you a happily married Amish

woman," Fannie added. "Everyone who has met you has seen your kind heart."

"Do not fret, Katherine," Jonah said. "When we meet at Council, it will all be decided. You will see."

Jonah's words didn't ease me. Especially when he didn't explain himself.

It wasn't until I was alone with Nathan late that afternoon that I expressed my concerns openly.

"What happens if they deny me?" I whispered into his chest as he held me.

"It will not happen," he maintained.

I looked up into his eyes and saw the determination there.

"They will think that all I bring here is violence every time something from my old life comes back," I whispered. "They have to be upset that Sean is loose."

"Jonah and Ezekiel will speak for you, do not worry," he soothed. "We have one last class and then it is a matter of choosing."

He offered me a chaste kiss, groaning when he moved to step away.

"Only a few more weeks and then it will be our turn to marry," he murmured and deepened the kiss. "I cannot wait for that day."

"Me too," I murmured and put aside thoughts of being denied.

He pulled me along, away from the house and toward his hill.

"Where are we going?" I asked.

"There is a little place across from my home that I wanted to show you. It is not far. And we have a little while before the sun dips too low," he explained and pulled me a little closer when the house fell away behind his hill.

We walked in silence, the air full of the smell of late autumn, with its dried plants and crispness of the waning afternoon. I wrapped my shawl a little tighter to keep out the cold breeze.

"Are you cold?" he asked.

"A little. I get cold easily," I replied, wondering how I would stay warm in such a cold place during the winter.

"Nathan, how do you keep the house warm all winter?" I asked, hoping for central heat but knowing that probably didn't exist.

"We have a furnace, and the fireplace in the front room. We close the registers in the rooms we do not use, but it does get a little chilly, especially at night," he explained and then chuckled.

"What?" I asked, smiling at his continued good mood.

He laughed a little louder and tugged on my hand, pulling me closer still.

"It will mean we will have to remain very close to one another at night," he said, grinning down at me.

"I think I'll like winters here," I replied happily.

We came upon an old gazebo, long abandoned along with the land that grew wild around it. Nathan helped me up the steps and brushed off the long bench that looked to have withstood the neglect. Sitting, I was able to look around and take in the vines that grew up around the sides of the gazebo.

It looked like something out of a romance novel. Perhaps a gothic romance novel with the tattered beams and floorboards, but the air seemed to have a special energy as we sat there. It was private and closed in and quiet, surrounded by a thick bramble of bushes, still dense even without the leaves.

"Do you like it?" he whispered and leaned in to let his lips brush against my temple.

"It's lovely. I didn't even know it was here," I breathed, closing my eyes for a moment to imagine the bushes full of flowers and the warm breeze in summer.

"It is overlooked and private," he murmured, letting his hand slide up my arm until it cupped my cheek, drawing me to his lips.

He let his lips move against mine with such ease; it was as if he had always known how to kiss me, that there had never been reservations. Every kiss reaffirmed that we were made for one another. I felt his hands move along my back, drawing me closer as his kiss deepened. Having him pressed against me was the most amazing feeling ever, warm and safe. He sighed and broke off the kiss, burying his head into my shoulder as he held me tight. My fingers found their way to the nape of his neck, playing with his hair there. Nathan groaned and nuzzled a little deeper into my neck, the heat of his breath causing me to shiver.

"I cannot bear to let you go just yet," he whispered. "I continue to count down the days until you will be mine wholly."

If I hadn't been worked up already by his kiss, his words would certainly do me in.

"A touch to last forever, a smile to get me through the day," I whispered.

He pulled away to grin at me, his eyes sparkling as he took me in.

"You are quoting me now?" he asked, amused.

"It's my favorite so far. I read it every night," I murmured, his poem forever etched in my mind from the number of times it calmed me from missing him at night.

He kissed me gently on the forehead, his lips brushing along my skin as he whispered.

"I must refrain
I must do well by you
I must be the man you need
But I wish so much more.
I will keep you in my thoughts
I will not act on impulse
I will treat you as you deserve
But I wish so much more.
So I will remember those brief moments
And let them carry me through.
Because you give so much
I wish to give you so much more.
A touch to last forever
A smile to get me through the day
A kiss to seal my fate with you.
My heart beats for you.
My Kate."

His lips had trailed down my cheek, his final words against my lips before he captured them once more, a little more insistent than before. I was at his mercy; his words from his mouth had rendered me breathless and I melted in his arms.

For someone who had never pursued girls, he was amazing at wooing a woman. His body and his mouth expressed to me just how much I mattered as we sat in the gazebo, kissing and whispering to one another until the sun began to set, signaling it was time to re-emerge from our hideaway.

With his hand in mine, we walked back to the Berger's farm, just in time to see Emma and John off. Emma ran toward me when she noticed us walk up, her eyes full of happy tears.

"I am going to miss you," she whimpered into my ear, holding me tight.

"I won't be far away, Emma," I chuckled and hugged her back.

She pulled away from me and looked up into my eyes, her own serious for a moment.

"Whom will I tell my private thoughts to in the middle of the night?" she whispered.

I chuckled and shook my head.

"I think that job belongs to John now," I replied, watching out the corner of my eye as John's smiled widened at our interchange.

"Whom will you talk to about Nathan?" she asked, a hint of a smile on her face at my blush.

John cleared his throat and stepped close, wrapping his arm around his new wife.

"I think she will be fine in that regard. Soon she will not have to whisper about him, but to him," he replied, winking at Nathan who stood just behind me.

"Well, that is still a few weeks hence. We will manage," Jonah chimed in, causing me to blush at his knowing smile.

I was beginning to think Jonah had a mischievous side to him.

Emma hugged us once more before climbing up into John's

buggy. Her trunk of clothes was settled on the back of the open buggy, a clear reminder that tonight would be a new beginning for them both, and I would have the bed to myself. It was a weird feeling. I had grown used to Emma sleeping in the bed with me for almost two months. Abigail squirmed in her sleep, so I hoped she stayed in her own bed.

And hopefully in less than a month, I would share Nathan's bed.

It got cold at night alone.

I said goodnight to Nathan and watched him walk up the hill alone, Benjamin having left earlier in the evening. He glanced back once and waved, his smile visible in the waning light. And then he disappeared behind his hill, leaving me alone on the porch to look out over the darkening fields. It was a moonless night, and the cold was quick to bite through my clothes as I stood there, arms wrapped around myself as if to capture some of Nathan's warmth from earlier.

The cold air won out, sending me inside to help finish the dishes with Fannie. She yawned and rolled her neck a few times before she finally let out a long sigh and patted me on the shoulder.

"It has been a long day. We can finish the rest in the morning. Come, my daughters, let us get some rest. Tomorrow will be a new day," she murmured and turned from the sink.

I put the rest of my dishes into the water to soak and followed her upstairs, Jonah following along behind us. When I reached my bedroom, I turned to Fannie and hugged her, feeling her arms hold onto me a little tighter.

"Thank you for allowing me into your home. And for allowing me to see what true Amish kindness is. I love you," I whispered, those words not so awkward and unfamiliar when spoken to Fannie.

"I love you too, Katherine," she murmured and held on to me for a moment longer.

When she pulled away her eyes were wet and her nose a little red.

"I am happy that you found your way, but will be so sad

when you leave us, even if it is only over the hill," she said, and wiped at her eyes discreetly.

"I'll always be here for whatever you need, Fannie. Even milking the cows at predawn," I replied, and laughed when she did.

"Let us hope Nathan takes his cows home when he takes you. I do not want to have to milk a dozen cows on my own!" she retorted.

She hugged me once more and let me go, letting me slip into my room that I now only shared with little Abigail, who was already asleep in her own bed. I slipped out of my dress and hung it up on the hooks by the door, and laid my cover down on the bare dresser. Gone were Emma's few trinkets, her brush and her pins.

She had started her own life just as Hannah had started hers. And soon, it would be the same for me. The bed was cold without Emma beside me. And no matter how I tried, I couldn't venture over onto her side. In the darkness, I heard Abigail move, my bed jostling slightly as she slipped under the covers with me. I smiled into the dark when she scooted up against me, her warmth more than welcome.

I drifted off to sleep, images of another bedroom in my mind.

One that would soon belong to Nathan and me.

I hoped.

13

"Marriage is the sacred union between a God-loving Amish man and his obedient and Amish wife."

Bishop Yoder had chosen the subject of marriage as our final baptism class.

With a smug look on his face as he regarded me the entire time.

Most of what he had to say Bishop Ropp had covered weeks ago, in the same authoritative manner that made my spine straighten and my mouth remain shut.

Obey.

Serve.

Provide.

Being a wife of an Amish man in Bishop Yoder's terms sounded more like swearing in as a law enforcement official.

He never mentioned love, or partnership, or even the fact that the word union in its truest form meant to make as one.

One spirit.

One mind.

One body.

One heart.

Never that.

"A good Amish woman will bear many children for her husband so that the community can thrive and grow with a pure Amish spirit. Her husband will provide for his large family with humility and perseverance. Never will he stray from his duty to exemplify the true Amish spirit, and honor God's will."

I sat quietly and listened.

I didn't pay attention to Naomi while she squirmed in her chair beside me, nor at Nathan's red ears when the mention of many children entered the lecture time and again.

"An Amish woman will sacrifice much for her husband. She will keep a tidy home. She will discipline her many children as God sees fit. She will do as her husband commands."

I remained still in my seat, my mouth shut.

I didn't offer examples from the Book about how a wife would be the husband's rock. How the husband would honor his wife as he would be so honored.

That the husband would please his wife, as she would do for him.

I knew in my heart how Nathan felt.

Marriage was not a step into servitude.

It was a partnership.

There would be love.

There would be honor between us both.

"Katherine Hill," the Bishop said, drawing my eyes up. "Are you prepared to live as God intends? To serve your husband as he so wishes? To provide him with the means to provide and serve God and his community?"

All the loaded unstated requirements were not lost on me.

"I am prepared and willing to do as my husband wishes, and as the community requires," I replied, tempering my voice to be the soft and timid woman that the Bishop assumed I wasn't.

He pursed his lips at me and continued his interrogation.

"You would supply him with many children, without the benefit of your English medicine to mask the pain God has prescribed?"

"I would provide as He wills," I replied. "With humility and honor."

One last look and then he was interrogating his daughter.

Similar questions, but less severe.

Nathan chanced a glance my way and a hint of a smile creeped across his lips.

In his eyes, I had successfully answered the Bishop's questions.

In mine, I simply saw another round of ways to accuse me.

"Should you choose the Way, your life must follow with the laws or the Ordnung," the Bishop continued. "You will live an honest and humble Amish life. You will not allow the blight of the English life into your home. You will live by God's law and you will honor the Amish life."

He glanced at me once more and that smug smile returned.

"Should you choose and we accept."

I held his gaze, my face passive while he scrutinized me.

A long moment passed, a silent face-off between the two of us, until a noise from the kitchen drew the Bishop's attention.

A woman's laughter.

Somewhere deep in the Bishop's eyes, a warming flickered at the sound, until his face blanketed once more into that cold mask of disapproval when we heard Benjamin's voice alongside the laughter. I assumed it was the Bishop's wife, and that Benjamin had come to visit.

Clearing his throat, the Bishop stood, looking at each of us with a measured look.

"To be Amish is to follow His word and live humbly. This is how we live. You have the option to turn from our ways, but only now. Once you have chosen the path, you are Amish for life.

There is no going back to the world of sin," he stated, his lips turning up slightly in a sneer at the last.

"This concludes our baptismal classes. Should you choose to follow the path, your baptism will occur at the next Sermon," he said and stared at me, eyes narrowing. "After the Council meets."

With that he turned and left the room, the laughter faltering when we heard him enter the kitchen. A few garbled words were spoken and soon we heard the door close to outside, the house falling silent. Naomi rose and quietly excused herself, following after her father and leaving me in the room alone with Nathan. I was preparing to stand when we heard footsteps in the hall and turned to find a frustrated Benjamin in the doorway.

"Class is over then?" he said, his brow tightly knit.

"Yes, he just finished," Nathan replied and stood, taking my hand to help me up.

"Congratulations," Benjamin said and offered a small smile toward me.

Based on his somber expression, I had a feeling I knew the interchange he and the Bishop must have had. I knew it would be a long road to walk for both himself and his father before forgiveness was had. For a moment, my own worry about joining had nothing on Benjamin's trial.

As we made our way out, the Bishop's wife intercepted us.

"Please, stay for supper," she asked, her eyes hopeful.

Benjamin swallowed and glanced toward the barn where his father was emerging.

"I am not sure that would be wise, Mother," he started, only to have her wave her hand dismissing his excuse.

"Nonsense," she rebuffed. "It is not only you whom I wish to spend time with. As Bishop's wife, I would like to spend time with Katherine Hill."

My eyes widened at her comment and I hesitated in following her before she took my hand and led me back inside. Glancing back at Nathan and Benjamin, I could see their shock as well. Mrs. Yoder simply continued talking as if we had agreed to stay.

I supposed I couldn't deny the Bishop's wife when my place

in the Amish community depended on it. I followed her into the kitchen, Naomi grinning when she noticed me in the room.

"I knew Mother could convince you to stay!" she exclaimed. "Come help me with the vegetables while the men talk outside!"

I turned to notice that Nathan and Benjamin had not followed us in. Looking around, it was just Mrs. Yoder, Naomi, and myself. Nervous, I prepared for a new interrogation of sorts. I laid on a smile and rinsed my hands in the sink, turning to busy myself with a task. Mrs. Yoder moved to the oven and pulled out a roast, chatting as she did so.

It was good to see her up and around, when only a few weeks prior she had been on her deathbed.

"Naomi tells me that the classes went well. She is eager to announce her betrothal to Bishop Ropp," Mrs. Yoder chirped from the table.

I turned to Naomi in surprise and noticed her blush.

"I didn't know," I said and returned her embarrassed smile. "Congratulations."

Naomi shrugged.

"We are to be married a few weeks after my baptism."

I nodded and hoped that the conversation would switch to mundane things such as baking or mending, but of course this was the only chance the Bishop's wife might have to question me.

"And you, Katherine Hill," she said. "Have you met a good Amish man yet?"

I stammered and struggled to say something, unsure if I should incriminate Nathan so soon.

"Mother," Naomi whined. "Everyone knows that Nathan Fisher has her heart and she his."

Her mother's eyes widened and she looked away suddenly, chuckling to herself.

I glanced at Naomi but she just shrugged again.

"I just thought," the Bishop's wife began and then shook her head. "Between my husband's disdain for you and the way you have helped Benjamin, I thought perhaps my son had taken an interest."

I openly gaped at the Bishop's wife for a moment before I could come to my senses.

"Benjamin is a friend," I said, my words a little stuttered.

She waved her hand at me and nodded.

"Probably for the best," she said and offered me a sympathetic smile. "Your past would not have garnered fair judgment from my husband should you wish to wed my son."

I stood there frozen at her words.

My affection toward Nathan had done nothing to help my cause, either.

She seemed to sense my concern and came over to me, placing one frail hand on my shoulder.

"Sit with us for supper," she said. "My husband will see your heart and will bless you. You will see."

I swallowed and simply nodded.

Perhaps this was the last test for members wishing to join the Amish — supper with the Bishop's family to dissect the candidates one last time. So as the men entered the kitchen, with Nathan and Benjamin nervous under the Bishop's critical eye, I tried my best to show everyone all that I had learned and lived by.

I was quiet.

I prepared a plate for the Bishop before anyone else.

I kept my gaze solidly on my water glass unless spoken to.

I spoke softly.

I didn't dare look up at Nathan although I could feel his eyes on me.

I could feel every eye on me.

"What do you plan for the spring, Nathan?" I heard the Bishop ask halfway through the meal.

"I hope to increase my crops for the spring," he said, his voice timid. "Perhaps wheat this year, or soy."

"How do you plan to do more when it is only you?" he asked.

Nathan cleared his throat and I could hear his fork slide on his plate.

"I have hope that I will not be alone come spring."

The room was quiet for a moment, the only sound that of chewing and forks along dishes.

"My son has his job at the mill. I do not see him offering much aid come spring."

"No sir, I do not intend to rely on Benjamin to help in my tasks," Nathan replied and cleared his throat again. "I hope to have my wife to help."

Another awkward silence.

"And if you do not marry?" the Bishop asked. "You have hardly any stores for winter now. Jonah has taken your livestock to help you, but even he cannot support you."

"I intend to marry, Bishop Yoder."

I made the mistake of chancing a glance around the table, my eyes going wide at the scene.

Nathan stared intently at the Bishop who waged his own war glaring at me, while Benjamin looked to his mother for help. Naomi was the only smart one in the group, keeping her eyes on her peas as she pushed them around on her plate. Finally the Bishop's wife let out a noise and placed a hand on her husbands arm, pulling his searing gaze from me.

"It is time for Nathan Fisher to marry. That house has seen its mourning. It is time to fill it with children once more," she said and smiled my way. "Katherine Hill may have a past we do not know, but she has brought our son home and his friend back from a darkness that would have swallowed him. I look forward to spending time in the sewing circle with her."

The Bishop turned his gaze slowly back toward me, his look an unreadable mask once more as he spoke.

"We shall see."

I supposed that was better than outright denying me in front of his wife, but as we walked home that evening in the cool air, I couldn't quite share in Nathan's good mood. Benjamin sensed my reserve and placed a light hand on my shoulder as we walked, offering me his sympathetic smile. He knew his father, and what his words meant more than anyone.

A silent conversation passed between us, and I gained some solace in my friendship with Benjamin Yoder.

Once cast out.

Now Amish.

A good man returned to where he belonged.

He understood the path ahead of me.

And his path gave me renewed hope.

"You will see, Kate," Nathan was saying as we took the steps up to the Berger house. "The council will decide next week in your favor. The Bishop's wife likes you, and that means much."

I simply nodded and smiled, inwardly wondering if I would have to always do that.

Nod and smile. Hold my tongue.

"Kate."

I looked up to see Nathan's deep gaze on me, a tender smile on his face. Benjamin slipped inside quietly while we stood on the porch, Nathan tipping my chin up so he could see me better.

"It will be all right," he whispered. Leaning in he brushed his lips across mine, sighing when I his warmth enveloped me in an embrace. When he finally pulled away, his eyes were closed and he was grinning.

"Just think, in a week, we will be baptized and then I will marry you," he said and opened his eyes, full of joy. "And then I will never have to walk away from you at night again."

I hugged him fiercely, hoping that he was right.

Watching him leave every night was always the worst part of my day.

"I should go."

I was reluctant to pull away from him, only doing so when Benjamin came outside again. He winked as he passed and waited just out of earshot, allowing Nathan to say his goodnight. One quick kiss and another reassurance, and Nathan joined him, waving to me before they made their way toward the hill, once again leaving me to stand alone as they disappeared into the night.

I stood there with my thoughts, the day's events flashing through my mind in the cool night.

Nathan had hope.

Even when the Bishop threatened, he still held hope that I would soon be his wife.

If not, where would I go?

Since my escape that night, my life had taken a very different turn. While I couldn't think of anywhere else I would rather be than amongst the Amish here in Iowa, I had to worry what would happen should I be denied. I had my sister, but that life in the city didn't appeal to me as it once had a long time ago.

I felt safe here, Sean a fading memory.

As if to mock me, I heard the rustling of the chickens, a few angry squawks, and then silence. A shiver ran through me that wasn't from the cold, thinking about the last time I heard the chickens upset. How long would it be until I forgot Sean, truly?

I looked out into the night, an unsettled feeling of being watched working through me. The moon was hidden behind dark clouds, and the landscape looked barren in the dim light. Nothing moved and the chill crept in, forcing me to retreat inside, into the comfort of the warm home the Bergers had offered me.

In one week, I would learn my fate, and hopefully, put my past to rest and look forward to the future.

14

Every day that drew closer to Sermon and the Council Meeting that would determine my fate, the more on edge I became. Every night I said good night to Nathan, I feared the next day would bring me closer to having to say goodbye forever. Regardless of the daily chores, and my visits with Nathan, I spent my nights thinking about the future. Most nights I slept restlessly and awoke from varying nightmares. Not even Nathan's soft words at night could temper my fears. Every night closer to Sermon, the dreams grew more frantic.

I awoke with a start, the nightmare still playing in my mind. Sean, reaching for me. Nathan bloodied on the ground at my feet. Sean's big hands grabbing, hurting me. A sheen of sweat chilled me as I tugged at my covers that had twisted around my legs while I had struggled to get away. I rubbed at my eyes, glancing at the window at the approaching dawn. An orange glow was already ghosting over the hill.

How had I slept so long?

I struggled out of bed, knowing I would be behind on my chores. I was running late enough to be asleep until sunrise. We rarely slept through dawn. It meant Nathan was already up and probably here already, which meant I missed the image of him as he walked from his home.

I stopped short of grabbing my dress at that thought.

The east was opposite of Nathan's hill, his face always lit by the sun ahead of him, not behind.

I rushed to the window, thinking my eyes were playing tricks with me in the dark.

The sun didn't rise over his hill; it set over his hill. But an orange glow flickered dimly over the rise, setting the hairs on the back of my neck on end. I knew that eerie glow from my last year in California when we had suffered from the brushfires from the drought inland.

"Fire."

My whisper jogged my frozen body into action, my feet propelling me out of my room in a flash, dress and shoes forgotten as I flew to Fannie's and Jonah's room, knocking on the door frantically.

There was no time to waste.

"Jonah! Please! Wake up! Fire! There's a fire!" I cried out.

Their door flew open, Jonah in nothing but his underpants, eyes alert.

"What is this, Katherine?" he asked his voice rough from sleep.

"There's a fire over Nathan's hill! I can see it from my window. We have to hurry!" I cried and tugged him to my room, so that he could see. His eyes widened when he saw the glow, knowing what I did.

"You are right," he breathed and bolted for his room.

"What is wrong?" Abigail murmured, waking from the noise.

I couldn't waste a second to explain. The glow was getting brighter. And I could hear a bell ringing.

"The bell is being sounded," I heard Fannie say from the room as I dashed down the stairs and through the door, barefoot and in only my shift as I bolted for the hill.

"Nathan," I panted as I dashed across the yard.

"Katherine! Wait!"

I couldn't wait, though. I ran at full speed, the worn ground cold and prickly under my bare feet. I crested the hill and gasped at what I saw.

The barn.

The front of it going up in flames. The two Haflingers were running in the field, their silhouettes dancing in the orange glow of the barn. I barreled down the hill, screaming Nathan's name in the hope that he was on the far side of the barn. I noticed movement by the house and heard the distinctive ringing of a bell, loud and cutting in the night, even over the cracking whoosh of the fire that leapt at the sides of the barn.

"Nathan!" I cried, rushing toward the water pump where I saw shadows. I stopped in a panic when I saw the Bishop and Naomi filling buckets.

"Where is Nathan?" I cried. "Where is Benjamin?"

"I heard shouting in the barn," Naomi whimpered and pulled the bucket out of the basin.

"In the barn?" I breathed and turned to look.

The front part of the barn was ablaze, the doors wide open. But the back looked to still be untouched. I sprinted to the back of the building, hearing the Bishop shout out after me. I reached the other sliding door by the paddock and struggled to open it, but it wouldn't budge.

"Nathan!"

"Kate!"

My heart clenched when I heard my name coming from inside, near the front of the barn.

"Nathan!" I screamed and ran to the other door, a single door on the side.

I reached for the handle, finding it chained shut.

"Kate! Get away!"

"Nathan! Where are you?" I cried and made my way around to the front of the barn, standing as close as I dared before the flames. I could just make out two people moving around inside.

Oh God, no!

"Katherine! Go and help Naomi with the water!" Bishop Yoder yelled beside me, flinging the water toward the doorway in an attempt to clear a path.

"They're in there, Bishop Yoder!" I cried, his arm pulling me back to the pump.

"I know, girl. Now help with the water or we cannot give them a clear path!" he hissed and shoved the empty bucket in my hand as he took the full one in Naomi's grip.

"Katherine!" I heard behind me, seeing Jonah and Fannie running toward us.

Behind them I could see more movement. People were coming to help. Women with their hair roughly tied back, men in pants and undershirts, hastily put on. The community was rushing to help.

"Katherine!" Fannie cried and threw a quilt over my body as Jonah grabbed my full bucket.

"Fill the buckets!" he yelled as more men began to form a fire brigade line with their buckets.

"They're in there!" I cried to Fannie, struggling to break free to the front of the line.

"Who?" she said, her worry apparent.

"Nathan and Benjamin!" I shouted over the noise as more men came to help, shouting orders.

"We will get them out, now help fill the buckets as they come," she said and reached for the buckets as they piled up.

I felt helpless as the men sloshed water on the ever-growing fire. I watched as Bishop Yoder disappeared around the side of the barn, coming back in a rush to shout over the noise.

"They are barred shut! Every door! Hurry! We must get them out!"

"Nathan," I breathed.

Something was terribly wrong. Sean's name played in my mind in an instant.

My nightmares had turned to reality.

Somehow, he was here, and he had done this. Who else would see to barring the doors to the barn and doing harm to the one man I loved?

I turned and tore the quilt off of me, dunking it deep into the basin.

"Katherine, what are you doing?" Naomi cried out, but I didn't answer as I snatched the quilt and threw it around me, the weight of its wetness nothing to me. I felt it soak through my shift, glad for the bracing cold to knuckle down my nerve. I grabbed the full bucket in her hands and ran hard toward the opening of the barn.

"Katherine!"

"Wait! Stop her!"

I dodged past the man in the front, my bare feet sliding in the mud as I neared the doors. I wrapped myself up tight with my soaked quilt, covering everything that I could. The flames licked at the sides of the barn, and inside that I could see, but the floor was concrete and clear as I held my breath and leapt through the flames, my bucket of water streaming out before me.

It was insane, what I did.

But I knew that this was entirely my fault.

I couldn't let Nathan burn to death at the hands of Sean.

"Katherine!"

I felt the scorching heat as it burned my eyes, closing them on instinct as I tumbled to the floor several feet in, knocking the wind out of me. I struggled to get up, my eyes tearing up from the smoke and the heat. In the noise I could hear the terrified shrieks of a horse, and then a voice.

"Kate! No!"

I turned toward the voice, trying to see Nathan through the thick smoke.

"Nathan," I choked out when my lungs filled with smoky air.

I scrambled toward the voice, on hands and knees to stay low under the smoke.

"Just grab her, man, and let's get out of here!"

I startled at the second voice, just as a rough hand grabbed me and hauled me up off the floor. I was turned and shoved hard against the stalls. The tears cleared enough to see black eyes staring down at me.

"I told you, Kate, you are mine. Nothing is going to keep you from me," Sean growled as he held me hard against the door.

"Sean," I sputtered, fighting to break free. "Let me go!"

"Kate!"

I turned at Nathan's strangled cry, to find him tied up against a beam further into the barn, in his workshop. He struggled in his bonds, his eyes wild as he watched me. He had blood on his face and down his undershirt. Beside him on the floor lay Benjamin, unmoving and bleeding from the head. Standing above Benjamin was Jeff.

"Grab her and let's go, people are showing up," Jeff called, wiping his hands of the blood on them.

I turned back to Sean, whose eyes had never left me.

"Please, Sean, let them go," I begged.

"This ends here, Kate," he seethed, and pushed me harder into the stall. I felt it jolt forward against my back, an angry whinny at my ear.

Magnus was still in here.

"Sean, let them go and I'll go with you," I wheezed, choking and coughing on the thickening smoke.

"No, you'll run again. Just like you do every time. This ends here. He dies and you go with me willingly," he yelled and fisted my shift to drag me off the stall door.

I grasped onto what I could, the bars of the stall holding me where I stood.

"Kate! Please, just go!" Nathan cried out, struggling again to break free.

"Please, let them go!" I cried out, and reached around to grasp the door with both hands.

Turned around, I could see Magnus' wide eyes as he pushed

and tossed his head back and forth in anger, nostrils flaring. He rammed the door again, almost forcing me to lose my grip.

"Just leave her and let's go! This place is going up fast!" Jeff hollered, and slipped into the darkness near the back of the barn.

"Come on, Kate!" Sean screamed, and reached around to pry my hands loose.

"No!"

I kicked at him, his curses muffled against my hair as he tugged at me. Magnus struck at the door again, jarring one of my hands loose. I grabbed at the lock, hoping to slip it loose and set Magnus free. I felt Sean's hand wrap around my hair, forcing my head back just as my fingertips wrapped around the lock.

Another angry whinny and Magnus reared at the stall door, throwing it wide open and catapulting me away from it with Sean tangled with me. I broke from his grasp and tumbled away, hearing him yell after me. I turned to ward off his attack when a large, black mass blocked my view of him.

An angry rearing black horse and the sound of bone crushing filled my senses, followed by the bloodcurdling scream harmonized with an equine cry.

"Kate!"

I sat frozen, fallen on my side, watching in horrific disbelief as hooves and hands tangled. As the smoke swirled around the big black horse.

"Kate!"

I screamed and fought back my nausea as Magnus reared again, striking a killing blow. I scrambled back, not sure if Magnus would, in his fear, trample me as well. He huffed hard and turned toward me, head down as he whinnied and nudged at me almost tenderly. My terrified cry choked in my throat when I felt him nudge me with more urgency, pushing me toward the back to where Nathan was tied up.

"Kate, please, get yourself out of here!" Nathan cried, straining in his bonds when I fell at his feet.

"I have to get you out," I said, struggling to untie him. He had deep cuts along his wrists, and his lip was bleeding from being hit at some point.

"There is no time," he hissed, looking at me hard. "Go. Jeff left by the back door there."

He motioned with his head at the door behind him. I darted for it, praying it was still unchained. Throwing my weight against it, it wouldn't budge. I tried again, feeling it give only a little before it slipped back into place.

Jeff had locked it from the outside.

"It's locked!" I cried out.

"The wall, Kate!" Nathan choked out, coughing in the smoke as it engulfed us. "The wall I repaired! There are many boards still weak! Grab the ax!"

I coughed and looked around in the haze, fumbling in desperation to find the ax.

"I can't find it! Nathan!" I wailed, searching as my eyes watering from the smoke making it hard to see.

"Please, get out of here, Kate!"

My hands found a handle and pulling it off the wall revealed an ax. I turned to find Magnus pawing at the floor beside me. His head batted against me and he let out an angry whinny, trying to edge me toward the locked door.

"The wall!" I cried out, rushing for the gap in the wall that Nathan had left unfinished. The hole was too small of anyone to get through.

I swung and felt the jarring force of the steel hit the wood, making my teeth chatter in my mouth.

"Further to your right!" Nathan cried out, coughing uncontrollably through his words.

"Nathan!"

I looked behind me and saw him sagging in his restraints. I wheeled around and swung again, to the right. The ax cut through the rotted wood enough that I stumbled when the blade went through. I tugged it free and swung again, making a hole. Again I swung, and again, the hole growing wider. I could hear voices outside.

"Nathan! Just hang on! I'll get you out!" I yelled as I swung, until Magnus' flank shoved me aside and he reared at the wall.

Magnus' bloody hooves came down on the wall, sending splinters of rotted wood flying. He shrieked and hit it again, the hole big enough for me to get Nathan through. I rushed back to him, his breath ragged as he coughed and sagged against his restraints. I felt around on his workbench behind him, finding a blade amongst the old nails and planks.

Voices called for us at the hole, mingled with Magnus' screams and the cracking of the wood and roar of the fire surrounding us. All I could think about was getting Nathan and Benjamin out of harm's way. Flames had engulfed the hayloft above us; I could feel hot ashes burning at my skin as flaming straw landed on me. Nathan's bonds were taut as he bowed forward, unable to hold himself up any longer. When they broke free, he tumbled to the ground, coughing and wheezing.

"We have to get out of here!" I yelled over the noise.

Any second the hayloft would collapse and topple down onto us.

I pulled at both Nathan and Benjamin, my bare feet slipping in the dust and straw. They were too heavy for me. Nathan struggled to crawl beside me, trying hard to move while he coughed. Magnus gave one more burst of his hooves, opening the hole enough that he barreled through, crying out and disappearing into the night. I dragged Nathan to the gaping hole, just as hands grabbed at me.

I turned and could make out Bishop Yoder and another man reaching for us. I shoved Nathan at them, working myself free of the Bishop's grasp.

"Katherine! The barn is coming down! You must come!" he yelled.

I pushed Nathan through, and tumbled back in to the barn.

"Benjamin!" I cried out. "He is here! I need to get him!"

"Katherine! It is too late!"

I turned back into the flames, the heat unbearable as I fell over Benjamin, unconscious on the floor. I shook him, trying to jog him conscious, but he was out cold. Grabbing at his arms I tried to drag him toward the wall, his weight too heavy for me to do much good. I heaved away from him again, moving him perhaps a foot.

The fire had taken over the worktable near us, the heat of it forcing my eyes closed.

I wouldn't be able to stay much longer.

"Please, please help me," I whispered, praying to be heard.

I pulled again, letting out a strangled cry that burned my throat when I inhaled.

I was going to die in here.

I pulled again, gaining another few inches. The sound of the fire drowned out the yelling, and the smoke obscured the hole in the wall as I struggled with Benjamin's limp body, hoping I was going in the right direction.

"Please. Help me," I croaked, yanking with all my weight to get Benjamin to move.

I felt hands behind me, an arm reaching around me to grasp at Benjamin. Turning my head, I could make out the Bishop beside me in the smoke. He had the weight to help tug Benjamin toward the hole, one hand on me to drag me as well. When we reached the hole, hands reached for us, hauling me out into the night, followed by the Yoders. I coughed and wiped at my eyes, the smoke and debris blinding me.

I shivered and gave into the hands as they carried us further from the fire, my strength evaporated as soon as the cold air seeped into my heated skin. I couldn't stop coughing long enough to call out to Nathan. The hands carrying me seemed to know where to take me, though.

"Kate!"

I turned to the hoarse voice, finding a shadowy figure seated in the grass away from the house and the blazing barn. I worked my way free of whoever was carrying me and rushed to Nathan, his body collapsing when I fell into him. His arms wrapped around me, uncaring how it might appear amongst the people around us.

"Nathan," I wheezed, refusing to let him go.

"I am all right, Kate," he groaned, his hand moving over my arms and back to survey my injuries. "Why did you go back in? You could have died!"

"Benjamin," I croaked.

"Is he?" he stammered, pulling away to look around. He let out a strangled whimper when he looked behind me.

I turned to see Bishop Yoder and Jonah lay Benjamin down with care beside us. We let out a sigh of relief when we saw he was still breathing. Women rushed around us with purpose, bringing water and blankets while the men wet down the house and trees beside the house. The barn was a lost cause. Where they had pulled us out was well under fire now, the last quarter of the barn catching as I watched. I saw headlights coming down the driveway, wondering how the fire department had been called.

As they drew close, rushing out to haul hoses that hooked up to their tank truck, their purpose now was clear. Save the house. The water shot out of the hoses immediately, helping the Amish men considerably.

A blanket was wrapped around me, and I opened it up to wrap Nathan with it as we listened to Jonah giving orders to those around us.

"I need more water, and we need my bag from the house. Go!" Jonah called, the voice of authority.

"Is he okay?" I whispered, my voice raspy from the smoke. I coughed hard from breathing and took a drink of water, wincing at the burn as I swallowed and coughed. The water tasted like smoke.

"I believe he has a concussion. It appears nothing is broken," Jonah replied, going over Benjamin's head and body one more time before taking the water a young girl brought. We watched Jonah while he worked, having never had the chance to really see him at his job as a healer.

I held Nathan close to me and felt the tears slide down my face as the Fisher barn flared for a moment before it toppled in on itself. The brightness of the fire hurt my sensitive eyes, but the destruction of it was difficult to turn from.

And with its fiery destruction, so was the end of my past- a grisly funeral pyre for Sean Miller.

Another minute in there and we would have perished as well.

Jonah turned to us, checking us over quickly. He pursed his lips when he noticed my bare feet, and the burn marks that had worked their way through my bone-dry shift.

"You burned your feet, Katherine. We will need to clean and wrap them," he said, looking up at me with pained eyes.

"I'll be fine. Is Nathan okay?"

He looked Nathan over, rinsing off his wrist wounds, and nodding.

"You will be tender, Nathan, but I believe you are well. You are both in shock. We will need to get you inside where it is warm. I will put some ointment on your wounds to ease the pain," Jonah replied and stood to wait for his bag. He stepped back over to Benjamin, checking his breathing and leaving us alone in our thoughts for a few moments.

"I couldn't stop it."

Nathan's soft whisper pulled my eyes down to his bowed head.

"It's all right, Nathan," I soothed, brushing away the damp tendrils that lay haphazardly across his sooty forehead. He shook his head and closed his eyes.

"I should have known. It came so fast. So fast," he murmured.

"I know. It's okay. It wasn't your fault, Nathan," I whispered, wrapping my arms around him when he started to shake.

"I should have been able to do more. And you are hurt," he groaned and shut his eyes again.

I held him closer to me, my mouth against his ear.

"Listen to me right now, Nathan Fisher. I am all right. You are here in my arms and we are together. We will be fine. We are alive," I whispered, feeling his body slowly relax against me.

"I'm so tired," he mumbled.

"A lot happened, Nathan. Just relax," I whispered, cradling him in my arms.

"I am sorry, Kate. My father's barn. What will we do now?" he asked, his voice a little garbled.

"Shhh. We're safe. Barns can be rebuilt," I murmured and held him a little closer.

He shifted against me, his hand slipping out of mine.

He mumbled something else, but it was lost against my shoulder, his head growing heavy on me. I brushed the hair from his forehead again, looking into the darkness beyond. I swallowed down the pain I felt and took in the damage around us, letting out a long breath. Clean up would be exhausting, and we wouldn't know just how bad it was until daylight. I closed my eyes to it all and hugged him a little tighter.

Somehow, tomorrow, I would need to assure him that we would be fine.

Regardless of what we found at daybreak.

We'd be all right.

Sean was out of my life forever now.

I opened my eyes at the sound of someone approaching. Bishop Yoder knelt down and pulled a bucket close to us, wringing out a rag in his hands. He glanced up at me and then off to his son, who was being carried to the house by four men.

"You saved his life, when your Nathan was safe," he said, his tone measured.

I swallowed and held Nathan a little closer to me.

"I couldn't let Benjamin die."

He dipped the cloth back in the water, pausing to wring it out again. His brow was furrowed, as if troubled by his thoughts.

"You would risk your life, when your love was safe from harm? For my son?" he asked, looking up at me with large dark eyes.

There was so much pain in his eyes.

Conflict. Turmoil.

And anger?

"He is family, Bishop Yoder," I answered softly.

"Benjamin is family to you," he stated, not asking.

I nodded.

"He is like a brother to Nathan. And he has been kind to me. He *is* family," I replied.

He was quiet for a long moment, wringing the cloth in his hands once more.

"Your feet need to be cleaned," he whispered, looking up again, askance. "May I?"

I blinked and nodded, hesitantly, caught off guard by his soft voice.

He bent over and pulled back the blanket, exposing my feet. In the dark they looked dirtied from the mud. I was afraid what they would look like when I saw them in the light. They didn't hurt yet. I had no idea how badly I had burned them. The water was cold when it touched my skin, causing me to shiver. He looked up, feeling me shudder.

"It's okay. Just cold," I mumbled, uncomfortable sitting there in the dark with the man who had caused me so much turmoil.

He worked slowly, rinsing and wiping away the dirt with great care. My eyes never left his face, concentrating on his task with solemn duty. He finished one foot, gently laying it down and covering it before moving to the other. He spoke as he worked on the second foot.

"It was considered a great honor to wash the feet of esteemed people. Jesus wiped away the sins of a beggar woman who anointed his feet with her tears," he said, never looking up.

I knew the story. I had recited it to Ezekiel, citing my place in the world.

But I had been the one unworthy, wishing to be accepted.

This wasn't how Bishop Yoder saw it.

"I am not esteemed, Bishop Yoder," I murmured.

"You are more esteemed than I," he whispered. "You would sacrifice yourself for another. You see what is right while I have been blinded by my prejudice. I am but a beggar wiping the dirt from one who has the power to forgive me of my most abominable sins."

He rinsed out the dirtied cloth and let out a soft breath when he resumed his task.

"Did you know that we wash the feet of our fellowship every year? To ask forgiveness of any sin we may have done?" he asked.

I shook my head when he glanced up for my answer.

"Well, it should have been covered in your baptismal classes. I suppose we missed some things, given your circumstances," he said quietly.

He wrung out the cloth and placed it on my foot, looking up at me, the anger gone.

"I can only pray for God to forgive me, as I hope you will do one day. I have acted out of fear and pride. I doubted you. It is clear to me tonight that you are what Nathan believes you to be. I beg your forgiveness, child, so that I might find a path back as you have done for my son," he said, his voice rough with emotion.

He looked away when he saw my uncomfortable frown, wringing out the cloth one last time before standing with the bucket. I cleared my throat and tried to speak what was on my mind, but my head hurt from the smoke and the adrenaline.

"Perhaps you and I both have forgiveness in our hearts tonight? You saved your son tonight, which shows me that you do care for him. That you and he can make amends. Family is important, and Benjamin needs his family. Whatever pain made you lash out at me, I hope it has passed," I whispered.

He nodded and his voice was softer when he spoke again.

"You are more than I thought you to be, and for that I am sorry to have judged you," he said.

"I forgive you, Bishop Yoder."

He let out a long breath and glanced back at me, the raging emotions diminished in his glassy eyes. He watched me for a long moment before nodding toward the house.

"We should get you inside. Nathan needs his rest, as do you. You have a choice to make before the Baptism," he said, and waved over a few men.

I couldn't open up my mouth for the surprise of his words. Before I could take a breath and clear my throat to thank the

Bishop, he was walking away to follow after his son. My heart was much lighter, despite the pain of the last hour or so. The Bishop's words, instead of instilling fear of rejection, offered me the hope that Nathan had held onto for so long.

Now it was simply a matter of recuperating enough to make it to Sermon.

I nudged Nathan gently, rousing him from his sleep. The men helped us up; once standing I could feel the tenderness on the soles of my feet. I limped toward the house, hearing the firemen discussing the clean up.

"You're sure no one was left in there?" one was asking Jonah.

I slowed and turned to them.

"There was one person in there," I said, feeling Fannie slip beside me, holding me up.

"One more?" Jonah asked, his eyes wide.

I nodded, looking off at the smoldering pile before us.

"He was already dead," I replied evenly, my mind numbing the reality of the memory. "Trampled."

"Trampled?" the fireman asked.

I watched Jonah's face as I explained what happened. It was important that they knew. We needed to move on.

Sean was gone.

Jeff had escaped.

But we were alive.

"I'll let the sheriff know about this Jeff Biggins. We'll have to send word to him about the body as well," the fireman replied and walked away to his crew.

I nodded and slumped into Fannie's shoulder, exhausted suddenly.

"Come, Katherine," Fannie whispered, pulling me toward the house. "You need to rest."

"I want to make sure Nathan is all right," I said as we made our way up the stairs.

She nodded and pulled a chair close to Nathan's bed,

remaining with me while Jonah saw to Nathan's cuts and my burns. Nathan fell asleep almost immediately, his hand in mine while I watched him in his small bed.

"I will see to Benjamin. You need your sleep, Katherine," Jonah said.

"In a bit."

They left me there, understanding my need to simply sit beside Nathan in the quiet. Outside I could still hear the firemen as they threw water on the barn, and downstairs I could hear women in the kitchen. I could only assume they were trying to figure out a meal as the morning drew close.

I dozed for a time in the chair, but at first light, I slipped from Nathan's room and made my way back downstairs, a blanket wrapped around me to ward off the cold. My feet were sore but I ignored the pain as I made my way out into the early morning, over the scorched grass until I stood near the ruined barn, a few tendrils of smoke still filtering up from the depths of blackened wood. The horizon looked strange without the barn there; I could see into the field that had been trampled and flooded in the night. I turned my attention to the charred structure once more, my thoughts on only one thing.

Sean lay there somewhere, deep in the debris. Hugging myself from the chill, I let out a long breath, feeling a sense of finality in his passing now that the daylight could confirm the events of the night. My past had taken care of itself, in the most horrible of ways.

"Goodbye, Sean," I whispered in the breeze and clutched at the blanket a little more tightly.

I stood there for some time, watching as men in uniform sifted through the rubble, putting small items into bags and sending it off to a police van nearby. A familiar nicker behind me drew my attention from the devastation, and up into wide black eyes. Magnus limped toward me, his head low. He was caked in ash and dirt, the dried blood around his hooves almost disappearing in his black coat.

"Come, Magnus," I whispered and held my hand out to him.

He stepped up to me, his head nuzzled into my stomach as I

stroked his neck carefully. Along his neck and shoulders, fresh cuts from forcing himself through the wall had barely scabbed over in the dirt and grime.

"You have earned yourself all the oats I can sneak you, sweet boy," I whispered and stroked him a little harder, my tears falling over his forelock as he nickered against me.

Jonah stepped out onto the porch, watching me as I held the big black horse against me. He wandered over when I waved him to me. Jonah was silent as he looked over the horse's wounds, specifically the blood along his hooves.

"He will be all right. We will need to clean his wounds. But he is a sturdy horse. Maybe a few scars, but he will be back to work in no time," Jonah replied.

"He saved us last night," I murmured, stroking the horse's cheek slowly.

"He is fiercely devoted to you and to Nathan. I am always amazed at the defensive nature of our beasts," he replied, eyeing me thoughtfully.

"You think he trampled Sean for a reason?" I asked, the idea a little frightening.

"I think your ties to Nathan are more understood by this beast than by many. Magnus would not let anything happen to you."

I nodded and held my hero a little closer.

He would most certainly be getting more oats from here on out.

15

The day was a rush of activity, men from the community coming to help clear away the wreckage of the barn, while the women brought food and helped with clearing away the dirt and ash that had filtered into the house. I barely made it to midday before Fannie and Mrs. Yoder were ushering me up to the bedrooms to get some rest. It didn't even register in my head that they had put me in Nathan's parents' room.

So much had happened; my mind had processed very little. Nathan had slept most of the day. Every time I had checked on him, he had been fast asleep. All I wanted was to see him awake so I could be sure he was all right. Fatigue finally won out. It was no surprise that my dreams were murky and tense while I slept. It was dark when I awoke with a start, Nathan's name on my lips.

"I am here."

I turned to his voice beside me, his body leaning from his chair to brush his fingertips over my arm. He smiled and stood, leaning over to kiss me softly against my forehead.

"You should try and sleep, but I know Fannie wishes to

return home," he whispered.

I groaned and managed to sit at the edge of the bed, still groggy when I felt Nathan slipping my shoes on loosely. My energy was difficult to dredge up. The bed had been much too comfortable.

"Do your feet hurt?" he asked, looking up.

I shook my head and tried to stand. They were only a little tender when I first stepped on them.

"How are you feeling?" I asked, touching the angry cut on his bottom lip. He shrugged and tried not to smile too wide, lest the cut open up once more.

"I'm sorry about the barn," I murmured, sitting back on the bed heavily.

Nathan sat beside me, one arm wrapping around my waist to comfort me.

"Why would you apologize for that? It was not your fault," he said.

"Sean is my fault, though. You would still have a barn if you hadn't pursued me," I replied, looking down at my hands.

"Well, that is over now. We need never think about him again," he said, his voice rough. "I am just thankful that I did not lose you last night. A barn can be remade. You cannot."

His words rang of the familiarity of what I had said to him to calm him that night. I smiled at the thought of how we tried to console one another. I was quiet for a moment while he held me, contemplating the angry series of lines and bruises on his wrists.

"I didn't ask you how it all happened," I whispered. He sighed and held me tighter.

"We heard the horses carrying on. When we stepped into the barn, Benjamin was struck with a shovel. I had time to dodge, but only a second. I was struck hard, lost my balance, and then they tackled me," he explained.

He let out a grunt and shook his head.

"There are some days I wish I was from your world, Kate," he whispered.

"What do you mean?"

He looked down at me and I could see the dangerous glimmer in his eye.

"When he grabbed you, all I wanted to do was kill him," he breathed.

I looked down and shook my head.

"You wouldn't have been able to live with yourself," I murmured.

"It was too smoky to see how he fell. One minute, you were being grabbed, the next I heard Magnus and then his screams," Nathan said and paused. "Magnus killed him, didn't he?"

I nodded. I had no idea how Nathan would treat Magnus after knowing that.

"I will need to see to buying his favorite treats for the winter," he whispered.

"Well, I plan on spoiling him. He'll be a fat horse come spring," I replied, feeling Nathan hold me tighter.

"I love you," he breathed, kissing the top of my head before slowly drawing away. "I would have died had something happened to you."

"Me too," I whispered and pressed my lips to his, mindful of his damaged lip.

"The past is in the past," he murmured and sighed. "Let us get you home so that we may begin the future, tomorrow."

He helped me off the bed, walking beside me with care as we made our way downstairs where Fannie waited.

"I will see you tomorrow. It is a big day for us," he said as we neared the door.

"I am looking forward to it. I can't wait," I replied, earning a curious grin across his face.

"You are not worried?" he asked.

Thinking on the Bishop's words, I shook my head.

"Then you need to sleep well tonight. Everything changes tomorrow."

We said our goodnights, and for the first time since I had come to this world, I walked away from him, Nathan watching after me as I left him for the night. I glanced back to find him watching us as we crested the hill, and I took in the landscape.

It looked different with no barn.

But that could be replaced.

Nathan's smile could not.

I silently offered my thanks as I lost sight of him, glad that he was still there to bring me joy. I wasn't sure how I would able to sleep that night, but I did. I had a dreamless night and for the first time in a long time, I felt at ease.

My nerves picked up some when Nathan and I walked to the Yoder house the next morning, waiting outside while members of the community passed us on the way in for the Council meeting. I watched as several men took turns leaning in to speak with Nathan as they passed, his demeanor reserved and often almost hesitant as they spoke. He nodded and shook hands several times, the men continuing in for a place to sit.

It was strange to wait outside with those who had not yet made the choice to join the Amish yet, mostly children much younger than us, with a few men and young women scattered around the buggies, bundled in coats to keep warm.

"Are you cold?"

I looked over to where Nathan leaned against the porch column, smiling in the morning light.

"Not really, just nervous," I said and wrapped my shawl around me a little more securely.

"This meeting should not take long," he said and glanced back at the front door leading into the Yoder home. "Changes to the Ordnung are rare. I think they have little to decide upon."

I let out a breath and looked out at the fields, long cleared and dry in anticipation of the coming winter.

"Just our future, Nathan," I reminded him, winking.

Before the night of the fire, I would have been more panicked. But the Bishop's words had given me hope that he would be on our side. After all we had been through, the idea of leaving it all behind was an impossibility for me. If denied, I would simply wait and show them all that I was indeed made for this life.

"I cannot see them denying you, Kate," he said and moved closer to me, wrapping his arm around me to offer some warmth in the cool morning air. "You have proven yourself to all."

I smiled and let out another long breath, my nerves still working their way into my stomach. As the minutes turned into an hour, and then longer while we waited, my nerves continued to grow. Nathan and I took a short walk to help to distract us, but every time we looked back, the doors remained shut to those not baptized.

It was close to midday when the doors finally opened and a deacon called for us to come inside. Nathan took my hand for a brief moment before walking with me up the steps, trailing behind the other youth. With a quick smile he left me at a bench near the front, making his way to sit beside John and Mark. Alone on the bench, I felt as if my judgment was at hand.

I was taken by surprise when I felt a light hand on my shoulder. Looking up I recognized the woman standing beside me from previous gatherings, but had never formally met her. She smiled down at me, the wrinkles around her eyes accentuated as she regarded me. Behind her, several other women stood, many I had never met.

"I am Marta Jensen, Sarah's sister," the one closest said. "I want to welcome you. Please forgive me for having not spoken with you before. Thank you for your courage."

I wasn't quite sure how to respond. I was a little dumbstruck. Having been in the community for over three months, I felt even more exposed in the moment. I understood their reservations, but I couldn't understand why she was thanking me.

"Thank you," I replied quietly, knowing I probably looked uncomfortable.

"We would like to bring some things you might need to the Fisher farm before the frost. Would that be all right?" she asked.

I blinked and nodded my head, still confused by the surrounding women as well as their words.

"We thank you," I said, my nerves growing when I heard a

murmuring behind me from the women.

"We will see you then, Katherine. Let us say the day after the wedding," Marta said, patting me on the shoulder with a wink.

Sarah's sister continued to smile and step to the side, where another woman stepped forward, touching me softly and speaking her name, only to step aside as the next woman stepped forward. Some offered a welcome, some offered thanks. I grew more nervous with each woman's greeting.

As they left to find seats, whispering and nodding to one another, I chanced a glance toward Nathan, who was smiling over at me. I looked at him askance, only to be interrupted when Emma and Hannah sat beside me. I felt their arms wrap around me, my discomfort wiped clean in my sisters' embrace.

"We are so sorry we did not speak with you last night," Emma said against me. "Mother said you were in need of rest after everything."

"You look much better this morning. Are you ready for today?" Hannah asked, effectively steering the conversation away from the pain of the last few days.

"I was," I mumbled and glanced back at the women sitting behind us. "Why are they thanking me?"

Emma squeezed my hand and leaned in to whisper into my ear.

"They are grateful for your courage the night before last," she whispered. "If you had not done what you did, we would be in mourning instead of celebrating."

I shook my head and frowned. What I had done last night had been selfish and idiotic. I had gone in to get to Nathan and Benjamin because I would have died myself if they had perished because of me.

"Don't they understand why the barn caught fire?" I whispered.

It was Hannah's turn to lean in.

"They know everything. It was not your fault, Katherine. They know and understand that you are truly one of us," she replied.

I looked between the two and their shining smiles told me everything.

"They have agreed to allow you, Katherine," Emma said and leaned in to hug me tight. I looked past her to see Nathan grinning, shaking hands with Benjamin. I watched as Benjamin turned around, catching my eyes and nodding in silent conversation.

"There is something else, Katherine," Hannah said, interrupting my thoughts.

I swallowed and pulled away from Emma's embrace to hear the news Hannah had.

"The Council ran long for a reason," she started and glanced back to Benjamin, who was making his way forward to his father, the Bishop, who stood at the front of the room. Hannah leaned in and whispered in my ear.

"The community is thankful to you because today you gave us the opportunity to welcome the new Bishop to this Sermon."

My eyes widened and I watched as the two Yoders bent their heads together to converse before turning together to quiet the congregation. Benjamin glanced over at me once more, and I saw the determination in his stance. He nodded to me, as if to remind me of his promise that day he had been baptized. The congregation quieted down, many smiling at the sight of father and son standing at the front of the room. The elder Bishop Yoder cleared his throat looked around the room, his voice clear and sure.

"As many of you know, I have asked to step down as Bishop, as I believe my need at home has made me forget what is important to this community. Love, and faith — something I had lost along the way until recently," he announced, looking my way in silent acknowledgement.

"The Council has met and agreed," he continued. "And four men were nominated this morning; voted in by their peers, and God has chosen. It is with a humble heart that I can present to you the new Bishop, my son. With this most special Sermon today, which shall strengthen our flock with the addition of its new members, I think it fitting that this be his first of many

Sermons for those of us in West Grove. We are truly blessed today."

With an agreeable murmuring of the crowd, the elder Yoder stood beside his son, holding the Bible for Benjamin so that the younger man could begin the Sermon. Benjamin glanced over at me for a brief moment and smiled, letting his eyes close as he spoke, his voice soft, but clear in the quiet room.

"Today is a special day, in that we welcome two young people into the Way," he began. He opened his eyes, looking around the room.

"We have been blessed this year, after such a difficult year past. Many losses, and so much heartache. But today marks a new day for these young people, as well as our ever-growing community. Our strength comes from our love and our faith. From courage and commitment. Today we gain all these things by blessing our friends, Katherine Hill and Nathan Fisher into our community."

I swallowed at his well-spoken words, feeling an overwhelming sense of duty and acceptance wash over me as Benjamin motioned for us to follow him out of the room to recite our pledges. I walked in front of Nathan, keeping my head lowered so I could not see the eyes on me as I passed. We walked into the room we had taken our baptism classes in, Mrs. Yoder welcoming us with a broad smile on her face.

I stopped when Benjamin turned around, taking my hand and Nathan's in his own. He looked from me to Nathan, his voice soft in the room while the congregation sang in the other room. I could feel his nerves coursing through him as his hand tightened around mine.

"As a Bishop, I welcome you into our fold, into the heart of God, who loves you as you love Him. As a brother I welcome you as family, to forever have a home, to forever have a shoulder to lean on, for as long as you live in our Way. And as a friend, I welcome you into my life, for only by your love and perseverance was I saved."

I kept my head down, the tears rolling down my cheeks at his kind words. Never before had I heard such acceptance as I had in coming to this place. For everything that had transpired in my life,

I finally felt the love I had hoped for. Benjamin's hand squeezed mine, drawing my eyes up to his. I watched him swallow down his emotion as he addressed me.

"Katherine," he murmured, his voice thick. "You have the chance to step away from our world, with no one to judge you for your choice. Or you may choose to be one with us. As a daughter, as a sister, as a wife and as a friend. In your decision to accept the Amish Way, you choose to live as we do, and will gain from that the love of your family. You will be washed of all sin, and pledge to live an honest and good life in our Way. I ask you now, if you so choose to be one with us, to live in His light, and practice peace as we do. What say you?"

I swallowed, trying to form the words. This moment was what I had struggled to reach since I had arrived. And it was finally here. I felt his hand squeeze mine once more, offering me some courage.

"I choose this, the Amish life," I whispered, hiccupping as the monumental decision of my vow took root in my heart.

Benjamin grinned and turned to Nathan, asking him the same question. Nathan didn't even pause.

"I choose this, the Amish life," he replied, his voice wavering some. I turned to see him emotionally worked up as well.

"Join hands, my brother and sister, and be of the Way," Benjamin said, my hand slipping into Nathan's and gripping it tightly.

Mrs. Yoder stepped close and raised her hands to remove the cover on my head, leaving my head bare. Benjamin cleared his throat and tightened his grip over our hands.

"I will walk in ahead of you, and you will follow," he began, looking at each of us individually. "Come to the front of the room and kneel before me. We will recite our pledges once more for everyone to hear, and I will then baptize you. Once done, you will be whole, and washed of all sin. I am so honored to have you as my first baptism."

One last squeeze of encouragement and he was walking past us, back out into the room. I took a breath and walked out ahead of Nathan, feeling his fingers brush my arm before following behind me. We took our places on the floor before the congregation, Benjamin leading everyone in a song for baptism. We recited our pledges one at a time, and upon saying the words out loud once more for all to hear, I awaited the final step.

I didn't bother to hide the tears, understanding at last how one must feel at this moment. Everything was washed clean; my past to be washed away and forgotten. I had only to look to the future that offered love and peace and family.

I felt the water as it hit the back of my head, a light drip that soaked through my hair just above my bun and trailed to the sides of my head, to be intermingled with the tears that dropped to the floor. They mixed as one, and as I felt a light hand on my shoulder, I raised my eyes to see Benjamin smiling down at us.

"May I present to you our two newest members, Katherine and Nathan!"

The rest of the sermon flew by in a blur, my mind whirling with the ecstatic feeling of being a part of something real and special. Emma and Hannah held my hands, surely keeping me from floating away in my joy. As we settled into a bench for lunch, the immensity of it all finally came to me.

I was no longer an Outsider.

I was no longer English.

I was Katherine Berger.

And I had chosen the Amish life.

16

Being welcomed into the community after the Sermon was overwhelming. People I had met once or twice in my time came to welcome Nathan and me for much of the afternoon, leaving us both a little hungry as we never seemed to have time to sit and eat before a new person came up to congratulate us. It was nearing the end of the day when Benjamin could break away to sit with us, his grin difficult to erase all afternoon.

"Bishop Yoder," I greeted, laughing when he gave me a strange look.

"I will need to get used to that," he replied, chuckling to himself as he stretched on the bench seat next to us.

"I'm happy for you," I said reaching over to grip his hand. "Thank you for your words today."

"Thank *you*," he replied, emphasizing the word to let me know he meant more than simply choosing this life.

"So what are your plans, now that you are Bishop?" Nathan asked, happy to see his friend so at ease.

Benjamin scratched at his bare chin and looked around at the congregation, seemingly in thought.

"Marry a few, baptize some, and hope that I can bring this community the guidance they need to be successful in the Amish Way," he said, winking at me when he noticed Nathan's bright smile.

Benjamin leaned in, drawing us close.

"So when am I marrying you two so we can see that house fill up?" he whispered, laughing when Nathan cleared his throat, embarrassed.

"Benjamin, I think you need to work on your subtlety," I teased.

He rolled his eyes and looked between the two of us.

"It is my job to get your permission to have Nathan marry you, is it not?" he challenged, amused.

"I am supposed to ask you first before you formally ask her," Nathan chided.

"Fine," Benjamin replied, sitting up to clasp his hands between his knees, waiting on Nathan.

Nathan looked to me, and I to him before he laughed.

"Bishop Yoder," Nathan said, grinning wide, unable to hide his joy. "Will you ask Katherine Berger for her permission to marry me?"

"Maybe you should go away so I can ask her in private," Benjamin suggested with a gleam in his eye, laughing when Nathan huffed and rose from his seat. Under his outer frustration I could see his excitement, though. He winked at me and gestured toward the dessert table.

"I will see if they have any more of your pie while you speak with the Bishop alone," he said and slipped away, a slight bounce to his step.

I turned to Benjamin and pretended to glower at him.

"You already know my answer, Benjamin," I said.

He nodded gravely and put up his hand.

"That's Bishop Yoder to you, Katherine Berger," he said, fighting a smile.

I sighed and rolled my eyes at him, waiting for him to continue.

He cleared his throat dramatically and looked me in the eye and paused, suddenly very serious.

"Katherine Berger, I must ask you a serious question in regards to Nathan Fisher," he started, his lips trembling only slightly.

I pretended to act innocent.

"What of Nathan Fisher?" I asked sweetly.

He glanced over to Nathan, his eyes taking on a distant look for a second before turning back to me, all traces of humor from before gone from his face.

"I am here to ask you if you would consider him as a suitable husband," Benjamin said, his voice low.

"I would," I whispered, feeling the immensity of this conversation in that moment.

Benjamin nodded, patted my hand lightly, and suddenly stood.

"Very good," he said, his grin breaking out across his face. "I shall go ask your father and we can plan to get you two married before the month is out."

Before I could say anything, he was off to clap Nathan across the back as he marched off toward Jonah on the far side of the yard. It wasn't long before the chatter brimmed with the excitement, the word spreading almost instantly. Nathan came back to sit beside me while we watched the news pass from family to family.

If I had learned one thing since coming to live with the Amish, it was that nothing was secret for very long. In less time than it took for us to share a slice of pie, everyone at the Sermon knew.

I was officially betrothed to Nathan Fisher.

~~~~~

I was exhausted when we finally made our way home. It was late, for we spent much of the early evening receiving congratulations from everyone at Sermon for the upcoming wedding. Apparently the wedding of Nathan Fisher and Katherine Berger was an eagerly anticipated event, especially when Benjamin announced that it would be in the coming week.

I was not shocked that Nathan had suggested it.

We were more than ready to move ahead with our lives, together.

With the Bishop's blessing and my adoptive father's permission, we would be married in a matter of days.

As I climbed the stairs to the bedroom, I was confused when Emma and Hannah snuck out of Hannah's room to usher me out of the hallway.

"We are staying the night, Katherine," Emma explained when she closed Hannah's door. "There is much to do in the next couple of days."

"I can't sleep in my own bed?" I teased.

"I do not think Abigail should be involved in some of what we have to say," Hannah said, grinning as she helped me out of my dress. I eyed her warily, afraid of what she might have to say to me that Abigail had no business hearing. I fought my yawns and climbed into bed, Hannah and Emma cuddling with me to get warm. I laughed at the idea that they might sleep there with me.

"Won't your husbands get lonely?" I asked.

Hannah waved off my question while Emma snorted.

"They can live one night without us. Perhaps we might even get a little sleep," Emma said.

"You're not sleeping?" I asked, concerned that maybe Emma was having troubles settling in to her new life.

She laughed again and pushed back some of the hair that had worked loose from my braid.

"It is difficult to sleep when John wishes to remain up with me," she replied.

Hannah snickered.

"Mark gets tired, but he is certainly energetic."

All at once, I knew why we had left Abigail in the other room. This conversation was a little embarrassing, and not something I really wanted to discuss with my sisters, knowing that my private time with Nathan was perhaps more intimate than they realized.

"You will see," Emma chimed in, giggling when she took in my shocked face.

"Yes, I am certain Nathan will be very attentive, if not a little too eager," Hannah said, biting her lip to keep from laughing.

"I don't think I want to talk about this," I mumbled, embarrassed.

"It would not be fair of us as sisters if we did not help you through what will be a stressful evening," Hannah replied, sitting up a little in the bed.

"It is true," Emma said, nodding. "With Nathan's lack of experience, you could be disappointed if you do not take certain precautions."

Precautions?

I was not having a sex talk with my Amish sisters!

"I can figure some of that out," I rebuffed, shifting in my covers to fall asleep.

Hannah shrugged.

"That is fine," she said, sighing dramatically. "It is too bad it will only last a moment, given his nerves."

Emma snorted again and settled in next to me.

"You will be lucky if it is a moment, and that it does not hurt."

I sat up and put my hands out to stop the conversation that had become most decidedly awkward.

"I know what to expect on our wedding night. I think we will be fine," I huffed.

Hannah rolled her eyes and crossed her arms over her chest.

"Well I should hope you know. But he will not and will burst from the nerves when he first sees you," she said.

I looked at her for a moment, shocked by what she was alluding to.

"Although I am sure Nathan will rebound quickly," Emma said, chuckling. "He has always been one to complete a task."

They both burst out laughing.

"Yes, I am sure he will be more diligent! Mark wanted to try for perfection."

I closed my eyes and shook my head, embarrassed.

"Please can we stop talking about this?" I moaned.

"Just think about helping poor Nathan that first time, Katherine," Emma said, hugging me close. "He has no one to tell him and if you want the night to be a good one, he will need to be calm when he takes you to his bed."

"Maybe then he will make it through the night," Hannah added, slipping off the bed with a grin when I moved to slap her.

"Okay, I get it. Calm his nerves! Can we please just go to sleep now?" I pleaded, mortified and desperately wanting to put the conversation behind me.

"Yes, you need your sleep," Emma said, trying to be serious until a giggle escaped her lips. "Because you will not be getting any sleep in a few days!"

She leapt off the bed and followed Hannah out of the room, the two of them laughing down the hall as I slunk down into the covers. I heard them giggling in my old room, enough to have awoken Abigail so that she whined, wanting to know what they were laughing at.

Served them right for embarrassing me.

Let them try to explain it all to Abigail.

I wrapped myself deeper into the covers, thinking over what they had said.

I had faith in Nathan. We had been close enough that we could help one another out that first night. But I wondered if perhaps they were right, that Nathan would be too nervous. He would be so upset if he had trouble on our first night together. I let out my breath and resolved to surprise him then.

I just hoped that I didn't traumatize him. I grinned into the covers as my mind drifted, thinking about being Mrs. Nathan Fisher in a few short days.

My dreams were more vibrant that night, leaving me eager to spend a quiet moment alone with Nathan the next day. But I didn't see him much at all, the two of us so busy making preparations that we hardly had time to even speak to one another. Nathan stayed at his house to clear what remained of the barn, while I helped Fannie clean and make room in the basement for the next day's festivities.

Even when Amish weddings were simple, they were quite a lot to deal with. Emma and Hannah helped with cleaning the basement, a wide-open space often used for social gatherings in inclement weather. Since the weather had grown much colder with the coming winter, Jonah and Fannie both agreed that having the ceremony inside was better.

I had been with them for three months and had no idea the basement had even existed.

"Most of our homes have them, Katherine," Fannie explained as we mopped. "Even the Fisher house. We use it for canning, quilting, and laundry as well when it gets too cold out."

I made a resolution to look around my new home. I had a sneaky suspicion the Fisher clothes washer was somewhere in the basement I had not known existed.

Thoughts of moving in with Nathan flitted through my head all day, especially when I delivered lunch for the men at the Fisher farm. I laid everything out in the kitchen, smiling at the thought that in a day, I would be there instead of at the Berger's. Looking around the kitchen, I knew I would love my new home. Where once there had been ghosts in the shadows, now there were possibilities.

Fannie didn't let me linger long, though.

After lots of cooking, ironing of tablecloths, and double-checking my dress, I was tired from the long day as night crept in. Nathan pulled me out onto the porch before he left, wanting at least a few quiet minutes alone before he retreated to his home. He pulled me to a darker part of the porch, arms wrapping around me to keep me warm in the chill air.

"Are you nervous?" he whispered against my cheek. I closed my eyes and smiled into the roughness of his jaw.

"A little," I whispered, refusing to admit what exactly I was nervous about. The ceremony was not really something I worried over.

This time tomorrow night, however...

"I cannot wait to take you home," he murmured, his face growing hot against me.

He chuckled softly and angled his head to catch the flush on my own cheeks.

"I did not mean it that way at first, but now I do," he said, looking down at me with those playful eyes of his.

I touched his cheek lightly and stretched to kiss him.

"Tomorrow will be a good day," I said and let him kiss me more firmly. My heart sped up with his lips on me, anxious and excited for tomorrow night when his lips would be allowed on me completely.

"I should let you sleep," he whispered. "Pleasant dreams, Kate. Until tomorrow."

He took a step back, so familiar now as he retreated into the dark.

For the last time.

Tomorrow, I would go with him.

I would never have to watch him walk away from me like that again. I smiled into the dark, his body disappearing into the night. I waited for a moment, hoping to perhaps see his silhouette on the hill. When I could not, I let out a breath and turned to go inside. I was rather tired, and I was sure to get more advice from my sisters tonight to make me more nervous. We said our goodnights, Hannah and Mark leaving for home. John and Emma walked upstairs with me. I watched as John slipped into Hannah's old room, leaving me alone with Emma for a moment.

"Any last questions, Katherine?" she asked, grinning.

I shook my head and reached for my door.

"I think I'll figure things out, Emma. You guys kept me up most of last night with too many thoughts," I retorted.

She hugged me tight, and when she eventually let me go, I could see tears in her eyes.

"I am so glad you chose to stay. I told you that you were meant for something. Tomorrow will be a new beginning," she said, smiling brightly.

She hugged me one last time, and then finally let me disappear into my room, joking about my need to sleep. She had no idea how much I wanted to simply collapse and get through the night as fast as possible. Of course my mind would not let me, regardless of how my body wished it.

Thoughts of Nathan and the following day made me restless, nervous and smiling at the idea of finally being with him.

Tomorrow.

17

Tomorrow became today much swifter than I imagined.

It was the day.

What do they say about nervous brides?

Emma had drawn me a bath before dawn, scented in lavender and vanilla. The bath energized my tired body, and Emma's urging to get dressed woke up my drowsy mind. In a matter of a few hours I would be Mrs. Nathan Fisher.

Kate Fisher.

Mrs. Fisher.

Married.

I was getting married.

My stomach wrapped itself in knots.

I didn't eat much, sad that Nathan and Benjamin did not join us. I wanted to see if Nathan was as nervous as I was. Perhaps it was just how things were. Brides were always nervous. I swallowed and breathed the best I could, adjusting my new dress repeatedly. Had I stitched it wrong? Why was I fidgeting so much?

The neckline felt strange. I was sure I had sewn it too tight. And it was hot in the basement as people began to arrive.

There was only one way out.

"Katherine?"

I turned to see Fannie coming down the stairs, a bemused look on her face.

"Come, Katherine," she whispered near my ear and took me by the waist, steering me to the small room near the back that stored all the Berger's quilting and laundry supplies.

I held my chest and sat down hard on a small stool, trying not to hyperventilate.

I couldn't breathe.

"Katherine, you look pale. Poor Nathan looks almost as nervous as you do," she chided, fanning me to give me air.

I looked up at her in surprise.

"He's here? He's nervous?" I asked.

She laughed and kissed my forehead.

"I forget sometimes how nervous I was when I was married. And Jonah. Yes. Nathan is very nervous," she said.

She tucked a hair back around my ear and shook her head at me.

"The two of you are just too much," she admonished. "I will tell you what Jonah is telling him right at this moment, Katherine. Nothing will keep the two of you apart. You are meant to be together."

I let out a shaky breath and nodded.

"Is it wrong that I am relieved he is nervous?" I breathed, feeling my nerves lessen somewhat.

Fannie laughed and shook her head.

"No, it is not. I think he is more nervous about the after than the here and now," she whispered, looking down at me with the mischievous glimmer I had once seen in Jonah's eyes when he had mentioned bringing his mare to Nathan's.

I didn't think I could take hearing the sex talk from Fannie at this moment.

She smiled and shook her head.

"You will love one another no matter what, Katherine. Just remember that young men like Nathan are apt to be nervous and fumbling. He cannot help it."

Nervous and fumbling.

He would not be the only one, regardless of our previous encounters.

"Just be patient and loving," she continued. "And do not be afraid to quell his nerves. He trusts you so much."

There was a knock at the door, drawing me up quickly.

I didn't want to look like I was nervous.

Well, more nervous than usual.

Fannie hugged me, letting me take a quick breath before she opened the door, revealing a smiling Emma.

"Ready?" she asked, her smile widening when she heard me breathe out once more.

"It will be fine, Katherine," Fannie whispered.

I knew it would be.

He was nervous, too.

I took that as a sign that what we felt was normal for couples.

I just hoped I didn't throw up.

As I stepped out of the storage room, I found Nathan sitting near the front, his knee bouncing with pent up excitement while he spoke with John beside him. Emma took my hand and drew me to the free seats across the aisle from Nathan. When I sat down, I glanced his way to see him grinning at me. I offered him a quick smile before hearing Benjamin quieting everyone in the room.

Suddenly things became very serious. I may have stopped breathing when he called my name. And then Nathan's. I had not been expecting him to get right to it. I had figured he would begin with a song or two, maybe a grand speech about love and commitment. Instead he called us up to stand with him. He reached out to take our hands, an affectionate squeeze to offer some ease to our nerves, and then he was speaking, loud and sure.

"A few months ago, a girl, lost, broken, and fearful, took shelter with the Bergers. We know Fannie and Jonah Berger to have such great love in their hearts; they took the girl in as one of their own. She was alone in our simple world. But with a loving heart and an open mind, she embraced our life, and found something worth fighting for, because God works to right the wrongs in our lives. What better way for Him to do this than to unite two lost souls destined to be together?"

I felt Benjamin squeeze my hand again, willing his strength into me as I struggled to breathe.

"Katherine quite literally fell into Nathan Fisher's life. And like a mighty storm, she shook him with her determination to discover what this life had to offer, even when he himself had doubted. Two souls hurting from their own pain and loss, found one another. Just as He intended. Katherine, his Angel, and Nathan, her Healer. Never have I seen His work more than when I look upon these two," Benjamin proclaimed, taking a big breath as he looked from me to Nathan.

"I have been blessed to know Katherine and Nathan. They are my dearest friends. They helped me find my own way back home, and I am so grateful for the love they have not only for one another, but also for those around them. With them, there is no hate. There is no judgment. There is only love and acceptance. They live and love as every man and woman should. Each day I feel inspired to live a little better. To forgive, and to find peace in everything around me. It only seems right that I join them today in marriage."

He smiled and looked around the room, taking in the faces behind us.

"Today I see family and friends, here to witness their union. I cannot express the joy I see in your faces. There is so much love in this room; surely we are truly blessed this day," he said and turned back to us, his gaze falling on me. His voice softened when he spoke.

"Katherine Berger. You have chosen this life. You have committed to the Way, and by that choice, you have offered yourself to live in peace and love. You stand here today, to share in that commitment with the man beside you. What say you? Do you take Nathan Fisher as your husband, to love and support, to guide and to nurture, to listen to and to comfort, for all of your days?"

I swallowed and inhaled, terrified I would somehow mess up those two words.

"I do."

I could feel the smile spreading across my face. Benjamin grinned and squeezed my hand once more before turning to Nathan. I looked over to find Nathan looking down at me, his eyes so full of love I thought I might falter from the intensity of them. I was lost in those eyes, hearing only his affirmation to his pledge, followed by a brilliant smile. I felt the familiar heat of his hand in mine, looking down to see Benjamin had joined our hands before us, his own above and below.

"We have heard their vows confirmed to one another, and as husband and wife they shall go into the world and live as is our Way. Be completely humble and gentle; be patient, bearing with one another in love. There is nothing more precious than their love for one another," he said and paused, squeezing our hands once more before drawing away to lift his arms up to the congregation.

"Let me now present to you Nathan and Katherine Fisher," he said in a loud voice to announce throughout the house.

We turned to our guests, my eyes returning to Nathan's adoring gaze when he pulled me a little closer beside him. I never let go of his hand, no matter how many people came to congratulate us. We smiled and thanked so many people it was all blurred memory. My cheeks hurt from smiling, and my heart swelled with each gentle squeeze of my husband's hand.

My husband.

My Nathan.

Everything may have passed in a blur, but Nathan remained clear and true beside me.

His joyful eyes.

His mirthful laugh.

I vaguely remember smelling food.

I may have eaten.

I don't know.

I only remember my husband and his soft words when he leaned in to whisper into my ear whenever we had a moment alone.

"My wife."

"My husband."

His face would light up and he'd hold my hand a little tighter. I was never letting go of him. So as the afternoon began to wane, and as our guests wished us well as they departed, the feeling of what lay in store for us made my stomach flutter once more. Nathan's fingers flexed and tightened more frequently with each blessing offered, until at last we were standing on the Berger's porch, tearful goodbyes said as we prepared to depart to our home.

Emma and John stepped in first; Emma's hug nearly crushing the breath from me.

"I will miss you, my sister," she whimpered.

"Emma, she will be a short walk away," Hannah snorted before leaning in to hug me tight.

"I love you both," I said, feeling the tears building once more. I had made it nearly all day without crying.

Abigail came rushing up to us, catapulting into our embrace so that we stumbled together, laughing quietly against one another.

"Sisters always," Hannah whispered, the four of us holding onto one another before we drew away.

"All right, let these two get home. I am sure they are exhausted!" Mark exclaimed, his wink obvious as he pulled Hannah apart.

John and Mark chuckled when they noticed both Nathan and I look down bashfully. I didn't want to think that perhaps John and Mark had spoken with Nathan about tonight. Perhaps that was why he was so nervous. Everyone had an idea of how our night was going to end up.

Except, perhaps, for us.

Everyone needed to have faith that whatever happened, it was on our terms. Whether Nathan lasted a moment or all night. Whether it hurt or was magical. We had enough to be nervous about without everyone's suggestions. So I held Nathan's hand a little more firmly, never letting go of it when I hugged Fannie and Jonah and turned to Benjamin, who had a small suitcase in his hands.

Fannie then stepped forward and handed Nathan one very similar.

"Your wife's clothes. You may pick up the rest tomorrow," she said simply.

I looked over at Benjamin as he turned toward the house. Jonah was already waving him in.

"A good night to you, Nathan. Katherine. Do not worry about Benjamin. He will take Hannah's old room," Jonah explained, winking at us.

Nathan's hand squeezed mine almost as hard as I did at the very same moment.

"Let us go before they say anything else that makes us any more uncomfortable," he whispered near my ear.

Fannie remained on the porch to watch us go. It was such a strange feeling to walk into the dark, Nathan at my side.

"Is this what it felt like every night when you left?" I asked as we crested the hill.

"No," he replied. "Because my heart is here by my side this time."

He had no idea just how incredible he was. I pulled him closer, his lips meeting mine for a brief kiss while we walked. I couldn't wait to show him just how much he meant to me. We walked the rest of the way in silence, the sound of my heartbeat thrumming in my ears when we stepped into the dark house. Nathan's hand slipped away for just a moment, the striking of a match lighting him in a dim glow.

Nathan lit the hand lantern by the door, his voice a little shaky when he turned back to me.

"I have not had a chance to fill the other lanterns, and the gas lamps are still shut off from the fire. I have candles upstairs," he said, licking his lips when he glanced up to the second floor.

"All right," I whispered and eased my suitcase from his grasp, taking his free hand in mine and smiling.

"Are you thirsty? Or hungry?" he asked, gesturing toward the kitchen with the lantern. "You did not eat much today."

I shook my head and gripped his hand a little tighter.

"We can go upstairs, Nathan," I said, hearing him let out a long breath, as if trying to draw the courage.

He nodded and together we made our way upstairs, down the hall to his parents' old room. We paused in the doorway, Nathan taking a deep breath before guiding me in. It was another milestone in the reshaping of the Fisher home — saying goodbye to the lingering memory of what this room had been, and welcoming what it would now become. No words were necessary to remind him of the past and the need to let go, his slow tracing thumb along my wrist an unspoken desire to forge ahead into the future.

"It is dark, one moment," he murmured and his hand slipped from mine so that he could light the candles by the bed.

I stood in the middle of the room, my suitcase in my hands while I watched him illuminate the room. The candles offered inviting warmth, and made his hair glow in the darkness. When he turned to me, he gestured toward the bathroom.

"Do you want to change? I brought up fresh water earlier, in case you wanted to wash first. Before," he stammered, letting out a nervous laugh before looking down at his feet.

"All right. Thank you," I replied, trying to diffuse his nervousness. "I'll just be a minute."

He nodded and watched me close the door before I realized too slowly that there was no light in the bathroom. I opened the door quickly, startling him. He already had one side of his suspenders dangling at his side, the other caught up in his fingers.

"Sorry. It's dark in there, too," I said, laughing softly when he fumbled to give me the lantern.

I closed the door once more, well aware that he stood just on the other side of it, waiting for me.

I took a deep breath and jumped into action, pulling the cover off of my head and releasing the pins to let my hair fall over my shoulders. The dress came off next, to be hung on the peg by the door, a daily routine that had become second nature to me. Stripping down to nothing I splashed the cold water over my face and washed in a rush, shivering in the chill air. I freshened up as fast as I could, wanting to be back in the room with Nathan. I rummaged through my small suitcase and found a fresh shift to put on.

I smoothed my hair one last time, taking a steadying breath before opening the door.

I found my husband standing there, dressed in only his underclothes in the middle of the room, watching me as I stepped out. In his hands, his shirt hung limp in his fingertips. I drew close, and pulled the shirt away slowly, watching as Nathan's eyes followed my movements.

His fingertips traced up my arm, the backs of his knuckles dragging over my shoulders before sliding through my hair and drawing me close. Warm lips brushed across my temple, moving down to my cheek, until they found my lips. They barely grazed, his breath spilling out over my mouth as he sought to control his nerves.

When he pulled away, I could see his heart beating hard in his chest.

He was trembling.

I watched as Nathan struggled to pull off his undershirt. So many times before, we had seen one another in less. But tonight was different.

Tonight we would be one.

We were both nervous.

He was breathing heavily, his mouth open slightly as he looked down at me with timid eyes.

"I am a bit nervous," he admitted softly.

I touched his cheek, drawing his eyes to my own.

RENEWING HOPE

"Me too," I whispered and gently guided him to the bed, touching the waistband of his underpants. "Will you let me do this for you?"

He swallowed and jerked his head in a nervous nod.

I held my breath and slowly pushed the material down his thighs, feeling his breath hitch when I bared him. One hand on his chest, I eased him to sit on the edge of the bed. He looked up with dark eyes, licking at his lips as he watched me pull the shift over my head, revealing myself to him fully for the first time.

"You are so beautiful," he groaned, reaching out for me with a trembling hand.

I took his outstretched hand, kissing it gently, and placed his hand on his knee.

"Let me do this for you?" I asked again, kneeling between his legs.

He let out a stuttered breath when he felt me move closer, my hands sliding up his bare thighs. When I reached where I wanted, he let out a long groan and let his eyes roll back into his head.

"I will not last. Oh, Kate," he moaned.

"I know," I whispered and leaned in to him, hoping that this would settle his nerves.

Then we would have the chance to go slow afterward.

One touch of my lips and he jolted, crying out.

I smiled and continued on, purpose driven to please my husband.

Always.

I kissed him again, my hand sliding languidly along the length of him as my mouth carefully took him in, the sharp taste of him hitting my tongue when it glided over him, his low moan spurring me on to try a little harder. Our eyes locked upon one another, the desire clear in his while he watched me pleasure him. He leaned back against one elbow, his hand threading into my hair desperately, and his breath coming faster. He adjusted under me, his hips rising slightly from the bed, a whimpered cry the only warning I had from him.

He shuddered and held my head still, panting my name until

his head lolled back onto the bed and he melted into the blankets. I crawled up alongside him, smiling when he wrapped his arms around me, his body all but jelly as he lay, spent. I could feel his hot breath at the base of my neck. He had not lasted long at all, the tension of the day surely winding him tight. Now he was much more relaxed.

He pulled away some, letting his eyes wander over my body. I lay there in nervous anticipation, his hand tracing along my neck and dipping down to trace a line down and in between my breasts. His fingertips never left my flesh, grazing lightly as they circled around one breast, and then the other. He seemed to be memorizing every single inch of my skin as he touched.

My heart raced at the heated look in his eyes as he watched my body react to his touch. His voice seemed to drip with want.

"You have no idea how much I have wanted to be with you like this," he whispered, his head lowering to lay a tender kiss over my heart.

His breath tickled the swell of my breast, just before hot lips touched the skin, causing it to pebble from his touch. I moved against him, my body tense with excitement from his touch, coupled with the joy of having brought him pleasure before.

Of feeling him lavish my breasts with his fingers and mouth.

The heat of his mouth enveloped one nipple, sending delicious shivers through me, making me cry out. He pulled away, as if to check to be sure he had not hurt me, only to smile and turn to the other nipple. I gasped out his name, grabbing at his hair and writhing underneath him in my desperate need for more.

He continued to tease my breasts, a hand on one while his mouth sucked the other, his tongue moving against me much as I had done to him minutes before.

His teasing mouth was too much. I needed more.

I began to wonder why I had thought I should offer him a quick release, when I became so worked up.

How long would it be before he was ready again?

I needed him.

Needed to feel him there.

"Need," I whimpered, rolling into him slightly to wrap my arms around him, drawing him close.

Feeling him already begin to harden, I moaned and looked down at the beauty of my husband's awakening need.

Tugging on his hip, I urged him to roll over with a groan against me. I could feel his heavy pulse against my thigh. Sliding my hands down his back as he hovered just above me, I watched his eyes trail down until we were both watching him stir and grow. Nathan let out a measured breath, moving slightly so that he lined up close against me. I gasped at the shiver that shot through me. He was barely touching me but already I could feel the heaviness of him as he slid closer, his body almost nudging on its own.

Our bodies knew exactly what they needed; it was just the matter of our minds letting go.

"Kate," he whispered and coaxed my legs to relax, allowing the heat of him to press against me.

I whimpered and flexed my legs around him, trying to draw him closer. But he held himself away enough to drive me crazy with the need for more. My hands traced across his back, feeling every muscle quiver as I worked my way down, until my fingers spread across his buttocks.

Still he remained just far enough away to keep my body strung tight.

Looking up, my eyes widened when I was met with his staring down at me. In them I saw so much need, and hesitation.

"It will be all right," I soothed and stretched to kiss him with a reverence that belied the nervous heartbeats in our chest.

His eyes tightened and he groaned when he felt me move against him, sliding closer and closer. As if testing the water, his fingertips skirted downward across my stomach.

He paused and looked up at me, his lip between his teeth. I reached down and guided his hand, both of us sighing when we felt his fingers slip against me, edging his length against my entrance with care.

"Please," I whispered, stretching my neck to allow my lips to brush across his neck. I felt him swallow and groan quietly, sliding against the slickness of me. He hovered there, pressing against me just enough that I could feel his thunderous pulse vibrate along the sensitive skin there.

Nathan's breath grew more labored at my temple. The tension inside me was becoming too much. I didn't want to push him; I knew he worried.

I knew there would be some discomfort.

But that passed. People had sex all the time and enjoyed it.

For thousands of years couples had survived this first moment.

The pain wouldn't last. I had felt pain. This would be nothing like that. There was such a thing as pleasurable pain.

I knew this would be so.

"Please, I need to feel you," I pleaded and arched into him, his reaction too slow for my movement.

Pressure again and a gasp from both of us as we felt him slide inside just enough to feel everything, a tingling stretch that was not exactly painful, perhaps just a little uncomfortable for only a moment. Burning hot and smooth, he inched slowly forward, the tight, stretching feeling only eclipsed by the quivering ache that blossomed deep inside at feeling him inside of me. I let out a forceful breath and clutched at him, his progression halting.

"Kate?" he croaked, hot breath panting beside my ear. He was tense everywhere I could feel him.

Wound up. Coiled.

Cautious.

"I'm fine," I breathed, scared he would withdraw and I would feel the vast emptiness of where he had joined with me.

Nathan's hand gripped my thigh, holding me to him as he flexed forward until I felt his hip grind into me. Fully and completely, we were one.

"So much, I cannot," he groaned and buried his head deeper into my neck. He held himself deep inside of me, not moving but breathing as if to calm himself.

Every place we touched seemed to thrum from our heartbeats, pulsing in a harmonious rhythm. This was what it felt like to be complete with your lover. To feel that amazing moment when you connected, no space between one's bodies. His lips touched the racing pulse in my neck, his deep groan moving down through his body and into mine. With a tortuously slow movement I felt him pull away, making me whimper when I felt the air cool me along my stomach and breast when his skin separated from mine.

And then he pushed back toward me. My hands felt every tense contraction in his hips, the slight forward rotation accompanied with a tightening of muscles, and then a softness of flesh as he pulled up into my hands.

Slow, measured. Deep. Long.

Tattered breath in, low moan out.

Lips against my neck, capturing moist flesh.

Flex. Tense. Groan.

"Nathan."

My breath came in short bursts, because every time I breathed, I felt him tremble and his chest would connect with mine. The rough hairs of his chest would scrape across my nipples and I would feel that ache inside coil tighter with each breath.

And then he pushed through that tightening and entered me a little harder, a little deeper and paused.

Slow. So unbearably, deliciously slow.

We trembled against one another, quiet except for our labored breaths.

The hand on my hip hugged me tighter to him, and in response I wrapped my legs up and over his waist, opening myself further to him and holding him to me. His responsive flex into me was more persistent, making me gasp. He pulled away to look down at me worriedly.

"Did I hurt you?"

I could only shake my head and urge him on with the gripping of my calves along the small of his back. The resulting thrusts made both of us whimper.

Slow and deep was unbelievable.

But that short firm thrust made my stomach tense and quiver.

"Again," I whispered, my eyes closing when he pushed against me, again with a little more enthusiasm.

"Too good," he groaned and moved again, a little faster.

"More," I moaned and let my fingers dig into his flesh just a little, like spurs to a stallion, willing him to go faster. He obliged, and soon he was moving with more vigor, panting with each thrust.

He rose up onto his elbows, his hands on either side of my shoulders, watching in wonder as he disappeared inside of me. I forced my eyes to remain on his face. On Nathan's dry lips as they pouted while he breathed in heavily. On the quick lick and tug on his bottom lip when he groaned. On his eyes as they traveled up my body and then fixed on my own. His dark eyes traveled to my own mouth, and then he leaned in and kissed me, his movements only slowing long enough to find my lips before breaking off to watch us moving together once more.

He worked up a sweat, the flickering glow of the candles enhancing his rippling muscles, shown in sharp relief as he moved to. I was enraptured by his body — forearms tight, stomach taut, his heaving ribs ridged as he curled and twisted above me.

Watching his intense concentration caused a deep trembling wave inside of me, like a quaking shiver that ran as far as my toes and then up into my scalp. It prickled and drenched every cell in me, like a wash of icy hot liquid running over me, making me shudder and whimper.

His eyes closed for a moment and his body slowed, as if he could feel the reaction his body created in me. And then he moved with more energy, and the quivering inside me grew, radiating from the center out.

Blossoming as I cried out.

A clenching that made him thrust into me harder with a rough series of grunts.

Losing control.

Faster. Whimpering.

Uncoiling.

Teetering.

Crashing.

Shaking.

"Kate," he whimpered, his eyes fluttering closed and his thrusts quickened, shallow and erratic.

My hands grasped at his shoulders, needing him against me, but the shaking made it hard to hold on. He leaned in, arms sliding up around my shoulders to draw me tight against his jolting and heavy frame. I felt his body tense, my name caught in his throat.

Every muscle tightened, as if he was frozen like a statue for a split second.

And then he shook, his voice deep and almost pained as he called out my name, long and loud against my hair. His body grew heavy against me, the delicious weight of him against my hips only serving to keep him deep inside me, even as I felt him relax every muscle. He struggled to hold himself up by his forearms, breathing hard along my neck and down to my shoulder, laying trembling kisses along my hot skin.

When he was finally able to lift his head up, his eyes were half closed as if drunk, and his mouth was turned up in a relieved grin.

I returned the smile and stretched to kiss his dry lips.

"I do not wish to leave this spot," he murmured, angling his hips slightly, and felt him slip from inside me.

I moaned at the loss.

It was a strange feeling — a foreign emptiness when he was not a part of me.

Having him there felt so natural. Now, as we held one another close, spent and quickly cooling in the chilly air, I wanted nothing but to feel him there again.

For all eternity.

He sighed and nuzzled his mouth against my shoulder, holding me tightly against the length of his body. His eyes followed his fingers as they wandered along my body, taking in every inch of my skin.

"Did I hurt you?" he whispered, tracing along my hip and pulling me closer to him.

I looked into his eyes and shook my head.

"No," I replied and let my lips trace over his jaw until they found his lips, his mouth opening up to my searching kiss.

"Did I please you?" he murmured against my lips and nibbled on my bottom lip lazily.

"Oh yes," I breathed, giggling when a bright smile broke out over his face.

I sighed into his mouth while I threaded my fingers into his damp hair at the base of his neck. His lips moved to my ear, delivering slow open-mouthed kisses as he hummed and adjusted me against him, crushing my breasts into his solid chest.

"I love having you against me," he whispered and rolled us over until he was laying partially on me, his eyes closed while his lips trailed down along my collarbone.

My limbs felt weak, but my heart beat a little faster, even as he laid his head gently against my breast and sighed contentedly.

"I am happy to feel you here," he murmured against my breast. The roughness of his stubble felt good against my soft flesh.

"I wrote you another poem for tonight," he murmured, lifting his head just enough so that he could look up with heavy-lidded eyes.

"Are you going to recite it for me?" I asked, grinning.

I was already sated, but his words would be the perfect way to complete our joining.

He sighed and kissed my lips slowly, his tongue entering for a moment before he pulled away.

"My love has lips I shall taste again and again, for her lips taste like heaven."

He dipped down, taking one nipple into his mouth, sucking on it languidly.

"My love has nectar that floats on her skin, for she is an Angel and she tastes divine."

His hand slid across my stomach, fingertips skirting lower until he found me, wet and needy once more.

"My love is always ready for my touch, for her body is made for me as if by His plan."

He pulled me tight against him, his body lining up with mine, truly as if we were made for one another. He let his lips wander, from my ear to my jaw, finally finding my lips to offer me a tender kiss.

"My love will always have me wanting, because she and I are one, together forever and always."

I threaded my hand through his hair, enjoying his low groan vibrate through me.

His fingertips skirted along my side and down my hip absently, finally slowing at my thigh and grazing the inside of it, pressing it slightly to open me to his exploration. The backs of his fingers trailed up the fleshy part of my leg, making me moan at the warming inside me.

My heart had barely slowed from our first foray of making love, and then with his beautiful words I needed him again. My mouth found his, and I kissed him until I felt him melt against me. He sighed and adjusted his head, laying it along my shoulder, his face relaxed in a contented smile.

"If you are not too sore, I would like to feel you again?" he mumbled, clearly sleepy.

I giggled and traced my fingers down his sturdy back, enjoying the extra weight of him when I pressed my palms to his buttocks.

"You have me forever, my husband," I whispered against his temple.

He hummed into my skin and kissed my heart sweetly.

"I just need a moment to rest," he replied, his words already garbled.

I felt around with one foot and slowly worked the blankets up over us to keep warm. Nathan tucked in against me, his warmth lulling me into a relaxed and satisfying sleep.

Or more like a brief nap.

I wasn't complaining.

Waking up in the middle of the night to Nathan's lips while he gently nudged my thigh around his waist would always be welcome. Feeling him move inside me was far more fulfilling than only dreaming of it.

And with the initial fear of not satisfying the other behind us, we both relaxed and enjoyed one another at a more leisurely pace. Soft touches, gentle exploration.

Perhaps we would skip breakfast in the morning.

Slow and attentive Nathan was much more satisfying.

There was nothing like finally being one with Nathan Fisher.

18

The sunlight filtered through the window, catching on the crisp white sheet that covered me at my waist. A glint of gold caught my eyes and I focused on the light shining through Nathan's hair, tousled and tickling against my stomach as he lay curled against me. One arm draped low on my waist, his head heavy on my stomach while he slept.

The rest of him lay tucked in close to me, one leg tangled with my own in the sheet that had worked its way down in the early hours. Or perhaps that was where it had ended up after the last time Nathan had awoken and made love to me.

I smiled into the air at the memory, still a little dreamlike in the middle of the night.

He had been eager to prove his fourth wind sometime before dawn. My body was mildly sore from the events of the night before, but nothing I could say bothered me enough to want to move from my spot.

Nathan's warm naked body on mine was how I always wanted to wake up.

Unfortunately, the Amish had a daily routine.

And as if that wasn't enough, there was never any time for a honeymoon with the Amish.

I was contemplating staying in bed with my husband all day when I heard a noise outside. Horses nickering and men talking, and someone downstairs in the kitchen.

I could even smell bacon.

"Nathan," I hissed, nudging him lightly so as not to panic him.

Even though I was panicked myself.

I was naked, with my husband happily sated on top of me.

This was not how I wanted Fannie to find us.

He hummed and hugged me tighter, his body stirring to life in ways I knew we wouldn't be able to quell, given the activity outside.

"Nathan, wake up," I said a little more insistently. "There's someone cooking downstairs."

"Good," he murmured. "I am famished."

His head jerked up then and he looked around, his face pink where it had been resting on me.

"Someone is downstairs," he said, as if I had not just said it.

I slid out from underneath him and snatched up my shift off the floor, hustling to get some clothes on before someone came up to serve breakfast, or worse, ask us why we were not up to do chores.

"It sounds like the whole community is here," Nathan said, walking to the window and looking out. He chuckled and I watched as he waved before turning back toward me, naked and glowing in the light through the window.

Given any other day, I might enjoy the beauty of him.

But at the moment, there were people to attend to. I peeked out through the window and gasped at the sight below. What looked like a gathering had begun in our yard, men and wagons coming and going with supplies, while women walked in and out from our porch with armfuls of food and clothes.

"We had best get dressed. It looks as if our Bishop has plans for us today," Nathan said, laughing as he found his clothes on the chair and started getting dressed.

I disappeared into the bathroom, splashing water on my face hurriedly before I drew my hair up under my cover, trying to look at least presentable when I greeted everyone. I somehow knew it was clear what we had been up to, based on Nathan's smile and my flushed cheeks as we made our way downstairs. People I had only just come to know greeted us as we passed down our hallway, smiling pleasantly and keeping their opinions quiet as we stepped out onto the porch.

Sarah and Mrs. Yoder took me by the arms, away from Nathan. I glanced back at him to see him smile as he watched me, his eyes bright and filled with so much joy I swore that they shone in the shade of the porch.

"You look very well this morning, Katherine," Sarah was saying, smiling when she noticed my blush deepen.

"The men wanted to come early," Mrs. Yoder scoffed. "Clearly they do not remember their wedding night."

The two women laughed a little loudly and squeezed me when I cleared my throat, trying to come to terms with their frankness.

I was beginning to understand now why it seemed so normal for the wedded couple to remain at the parents' house for several days. I was instantly grateful for having my time alone with Nathan now.

I didn't think I could handle Fannie or Jonah speaking so easily about how fresh and glowing I seemed, or perhaps how joyful Nathan was. There was certainly a bounce in his step and his smile was wider as he made his way toward Benjamin near the barn.

We looked like Mark and Hannah had their first morning!

I chuckled and shook my head, resigned to the fact that everyone knew, because they had been there before. So I held my head a little higher and smiled a little brighter, because in truth I had never felt as good as I did today. And now the community had come to our aid and was showering us with the things we most needed.

How perfect was this group of people?

I was stunned by their charity.

I had expected Sarah and some of the women to come by today with a few canned goods perhaps, maybe a quilt or two. I had not expected over a dozen women with their daughters, and crates upon crates of goods for us.

"This should help with the winter," Sarah was saying as she instructed the stream of women into the house.

"It's too much," I breathed, overwhelmed as the counters began to fill up, the table long covered by so many crates.

Sarah and Mrs. Yoder both scoffed and shook their heads at me.

"It is something we would have done regardless, Katherine. But with your strength and courage, it was important that we show you how grateful we are as well," Mrs. Yoder said, hugging me tight.

I let out a breath and fought to hold back my emotions.

"It was important to outfit Nathan and his new bride," Sarah continued as she pointed some young girls toward the cellar with crates of jarred goods.

She turned to me and looked a little sad.

"When his family died, we tried to offer him this same charity but he pushed us away," she said, and then looked around the room wistfully. "I am so happy to see life here once more."

Her eyes captured mine for a moment, and I suddenly understood just how close so many must have been to the Fishers when they were alive. This community was tightly bound. More than just Nathan had suffered when his family died. I could see from Sarah's welcoming spirit and her unabashed support of both Nathan and myself that she was a close member to the Fisher family. I wrapped my arm around her and held her close for a moment.

"We'll see this house is full of life again, Sarah," I whispered and laughed when I heard her chuckle.

I knew what she thought.

And strangely, the idea of having a house full of children running around didn't sound nearly as terrifying to me as it might have a few months ago. I knew I had family here to help out.

"All right," I said, trying to change the subject. "Let's see about putting some of this away!"

We set to work, filling up the cabinets with jars of vegetables and fruits and canned meats as well as bakery goods. I was shocked at how much there actually was. Sarah told me each of the families of our community had donated a crate of food to us, and I was learning that every family traded with one another when someone would grow one type of food, allowing for quite a varied array of stores for the winter. Our cabinets filled up quickly, and soon we were walking crates down into the basement.

Finally I was able to find the basement and laughed when I saw the nice washer near the back of the large room. I shook my head when Mrs. Yoder looked at me questioningly. They didn't need to know that this was my first time in the basement of my house. When we finally made it up to the kitchen once more, I noticed that the table top, which had been cleared away of all the crates, was now covered with bundles of clothes.

Mrs. Yoder cleared her throat and looked through them with careful attention.

"We know you came with little when you arrived into our lives, Katherine. Some of the women thought you might like some of their dresses and coats for the coming winter. It can get quite cold, and you will not want to depend on only a couple of dresses to get you through," she explained.

I looked at the mounds of clothes there, seeing some that were most definitely not for me.

There were small clothes for children, as well as a few sweaters and pants for Nathan as well.

"There is enough here for an entire family," I whispered, fingering a small boy's shirt.

"Well, we do hope that there will be a need for some of these clothes soon. Sooner than later, I think," Sarah said, chuckling.

I could feel the blush in my cheeks again, and I pretended to scowl at her.

"We'll work on that," I said, making her blush at my words.

That made me feel better.

I could still surprise my neighbors.

I walked with them as they made their way back outside, going to each of the women there to thank them for their generosity. On many occasions, they hugged me and offered me the same congratulations they had just the day before at our wedding, but it felt richer somehow seeing just how much this group cared for their members.

As they started to depart, many waved and wished us well, calling after that they would see us the next day. I turned to Mrs. Yoder to ask what they meant. She pointed toward the bundles of lumber that lay stacked by the concrete slab of our old barn.

"Tomorrow you will experience a barn raising, Katherine," she said and leaned in close. "I would suggest getting an early sleep tonight, for it will be very busy in this house tomorrow, with you organizing all the women in order to feed the men. I hear all the community will be here for it."

I looked at her in shock.

The entire community?

"Like the Wittmer Frolic?" I asked, more than a little overwhelmed.

Sarah and Mrs. Yoder both nodded.

"Do not worry, Katherine," Sarah said soothingly. "We will be here early to help. Fannie is already at home baking for tomorrow."

They said their goodbyes, leaving with the other buggies. I watched them for a moment, still a little dazed by how much had happened in the last few days.

Glancing over at the bundles of lumber again, I saw Nathan and Benjamin bent over the pipes by the house. They straightened when they heard me, Benjamin looking a little bashful while Nathan grinned at me with a mischievous air about him.

I knew they had been talking about me, because Benjamin had trouble looking me in the eye suddenly.

"Are you two gossiping like a couple of teenagers?" I asked, teasing the two of them.

I knew Nathan wouldn't reveal the specifics about our night. I had a feeling perhaps Benjamin and the others thought we would have been more awkward with one another.

They had no idea just how incredible Nathan really was.

My smile broadened at the thought of Nathan, and how he made me feel.

For all his nerves, he had done very well.

"I should go see how Jonah is doing, I told him I would help around the house until you came over," Benjamin said quickly, wiping his hands of the grease from the old pipes they had been working on.

Nathan chuckled and shook his head, amused.

"Thank you for the help with the propane tank. Hot water will be nice to have tonight," he said lightly.

"Yes, it will!" I exclaimed. "I'm dying for a nice hot bath."

Benjamin blushed again and stepped past us, tugging his hat low over his head.

"I am sure," he mumbled and nodded, looking at Nathan briefly before letting out a nervous laugh and wishing us a pleasant day.

I turned to my husband and eyed him suspiciously.

"Do I want to know why he seemed so nervous to get out of our hair?" I asked, hand on hip.

Nathan laughed a little harder and stood up to wrap his arms around me.

"He seemed a little nervous, didn't he?" he asked, grinning.

"You're like a couple of girls after a first date!" I said, smacking him lightly on shoulder.

"I did not tell him a thing!" he said loudly, laughter causing his words to jumble together.

I quieted him down with my lips on his, so happy to hear the joy in his voice.

I didn't care what people thought, really. I was happy to see

Nathan enjoying himself.

Let them think what they would.

We were content.

"Are you done out here?" I whispered.

He hummed into my lips and slowly drew me toward the house.

"I need to relight the water heater and appliances," he murmured, kissing me again at the top of the porch steps.

"We should go over and help Fannie and Jonah some," I said as we stepped inside, never letting him go.

"True," he replied, closing the door behind us and sighing into my hair.

"Apparently, there's a barn raising tomorrow," I said, giggling when he nibbled at my jaw.

"So I have heard," he replied, kissing me until we entered the kitchen, a joyful look on his face when he finally stepped away.

I watched as he lit the stove and started the refrigerator, his eyes taking in all the stores we had accumulated. His smile never faded while he continued with his tasks, heading down into the basement to light the water heater and the furnace. When he came back upstairs, he took my hand as we made our way to the front door.

I knew we had to see Fannie and Jonah today. It wouldn't be fair to leave them with so much to do, even if Benjamin was there to help. It was past midday and surely there was still a lot of baking to be done for the next day. At the door he paused, leaning in to kiss me once more.

"You know that Hannah and Mark will have something to say about us just showing up only now?" he asked, smirking.

"Good," I replied simply and pulled open the door, looking back at him in challenge. His ever-present smile widened and I guided him outside, toward the hill I knew so well.

After climbing the hill so many times alone or unable to show our adoration for one another, it was a new experience now. With Nathan's hand in mine, openly showing the world how we felt for one another, I smiled into the sun and enjoyed this new feeling.

Walking with my husband to my parents' house.

Loving the laughter and the joy on his face as we stepped into the kitchen, all eyes on us.

Of course, Hannah and Mark would say something.

Of course, we would see those knowing looks from Jonah and Fannie.

Even Emma seemed to be bursting with excitement when she saw us walk in hand-in-hand.

But we kept calm regardless. Nathan kissed me lightly and followed Jonah and Mark out to the barn, and I donned an apron and went to work on the pies beside Fannie, smiling and laughing when Hannah and Emma tried to get information out of me. Fannie smiled with me, seeming to know by either the flush of my cheeks or maybe her own experiences as a newlywed, long ago.

She knew we were happy.

She knew we were fine.

It wasn't until Nathan came inside for a drink that perhaps my willpower wavered.

He was dirty and sweaty, after all.

I offered him a tall glass of water and watched as he drank it down, always mesmerized by his long neck and how he swallowed. When he looked down at me, his eyes said it all.

Was it time to go home yet?

He looked needy.

And that look set off a spark inside me. He had me with just a look.

Leaning down he kissed me by the corner of my mouth, his hand touching my cheek briefly before he headed back outside, leaving me to look after him, dazed.

"I think we need to have an early supper, Mother," Hannah said, waking me from thoughts.

"Why is that?" Emma chimed in, grinning.

"Because I think Nathan wishes to get home before the sun sets."

I blinked and looked over at Hannah, narrowing my eyes at her.

"Like you didn't do the same thing on your first day of wedded bliss," I shot back at her.

Hannah rolled her eyes at me trying to brush off her embarrassment. Finally, she just shook her head and joined in on the laughter, the four of us finally falling into a more relaxed atmosphere as we cooked and readied the kitchen for supper.

And as we all sat around at the supper table, enjoying the food and the company, I was relieved to see how easy it was to slip into the everyday routine with my new husband. Nathan held my hand just as Mark and John did their wives'. He smiled and leaned in to whisper to me every now and then, and when it came time to leave, just as the sun was setting, I didn't feel sad at leaving my family behind.

We waved at them as we walked up our hill, Nathan holding me close so that I could stay warm in the chilly air. He lit the lamp, smiling as he closed the door.

"Home again," he murmured and pulled me in for a long kiss.

We slowly made our way upstairs, returning to the bed we had left hours ago as if no time had passed at all. Nathan was sure to be attentive, aware that I was tender from our first night together. Just as the previous night, he took his time, and we fell away together into bliss. Weak and spent, we both lay there in the bed, exhaustion coming easily. He struggled to roll off of me, pulling the covers up to keep us warm in the night air. His arm pulled me close, his mouth finding my neck for an instant before reaching my lips, kissing me tenderly.

"Promise we will be like this until we are old and gray," he whispered against my cheek.

I smiled into the darkness and hugged him tighter to me.

"Why stop at old and grey?" I giggled, enjoying his lips against my neck.

"I love to hear your happiness," he murmured.

"You make me happy," I replied sleepily.

He hummed and relaxed against me, mumbling against my

cheek, but I could tell he was already drifting off, his arm growing heavy across my waist. I adjusted against him, so that my head lay on his chest, closing my eyes so that I could listen to his heartbeat against my ear.

I was beginning to drift away when he spoke again, in just a whisper.

"You make me the happiest man ever."

I fell asleep smiling, holding him close as he slept underneath me. We had so much to look forward to, and so much to enjoy now that we were together. There was nothing that we could not accomplish now that we were together.

Life was perfect.

19

It was going to be a busy day; I could feel it before the sun had even risen.

My nerves fluttered in my stomach, so much so that keeping my breakfast down was a challenge. It was not every day I would have every member of my new community in our house, seeing what I had done with my in-laws things. It was not every day that I had so many people there to help us make a fresh start.

In two days, I had experienced the grace of my new world, and today I wanted to prove to them that I was a good wife and member of our community.

I finished making up the tea just as Fannie and Emma walked in, arms full of breads and pies for the day. I smiled at them and filled another pot full of water, preparing it to boil. The sun had barely risen and already we were readying ourselves for the day.

"You have been very productive this morning!" Fannie exclaimed as she surveyed the kitchen.

"We were up early," I replied, shaking my head when I noticed Emma's smirk.

So what if Nathan had a biological clock that had him up at four in the morning.

It gave us a little time before we had to really get up and start our day. I rather enjoyed waking up to Nathan Fisher's internal alarm. It put a little pep in his step as he had ventured out to take care of the morning chores before the community converged on us.

"Well, you seem to have things in order so far. Have you eaten?" Fannie said, coming up to hug me before she looked around again to see any remains of breakfast.

"We had some cereal. Nathan wanted to get out before dawn," I said, not wanting her to know it was more my nerves than Nathan's eagerness to start the day that left us with a simple breakfast.

She nodded and motioned us toward the door. I heard the horses and the wagons, the community prompt about starting early on the task of the day. I couldn't wait to see our barn become a reality. The sky was just beginning to lighten when we stepped out onto the porch.

"Pleasant morning, Katherine Fisher!" Benjamin announced as he climbed out of his buggy, the first one to stop in the yard.

I beamed at the sound of my new name and took Benjamin's hand happily. He seemed much more comfortable around me than he had the day before, with his playful eyes and bright smile.

"Pleasant morning to you, Bishop Yoder," I replied. "You've brought quite the gathering."

The buggies and wagons continued to come, many faces I had never seen before, even at the Sermons. Nathan joined me, holding me close as the people introduced themselves before setting to their tasks. When young Bishop Zachariah Ropp from Friendship stepped up, I took his hand in surprise.

"Pleasant day, Nathan. Katherine," he said. "I announced to my congregation that there was a barn to be raised. We know how important this is, and many wanted to come help."

He introduced us to several in his community, the faces I had not recognized as they moved among us. He introduced so many, I knew I would forget so many of their names; I could only hope to guess as the day progressed. Nathan stepped away from me with a quiet word and headed toward the men, a small group of them appearing to be the architects of the group. I could tell the different skill sets as I watched them for a moment, some with hammers and nail bags, others with thick gloves and waist belts as if they would be the ones carrying the heavy loads.

Orders were called out, and the men divided to organize different tasks. I was awed by the organized chaos before me. I couldn't tell what the plan was. Planks of wood were moved from here to there, and horses were hooked up to large beams that I was sure would become the center supports for the large barn.

Nathan stood with Mark and John, bending over with his hammer and nails to begin the task of nailing the tremendous beams together. I was amazed to see so many men moving about before the sun had even crested our hill. Over and over again, Nathan shook hands with a man as he passed, his smile bright and true as he spoke his appreciation to the men working beside him.

Nathan seemed overwhelmed by the outpouring of kindness as the men set to work and the women followed me into the house to set up the feast for later. I could understand; it was extraordinary to witness the generosity of our neighbors and strangers alike. I found myself time and again overwhelmed with gratitude.

Naomi Yoder and Fannie stood beside me as we directed traffic throughout the house.

There were too many people to set everyone up in the basement, so we decided upon two locations for meals — the basement reserved for the women and children, and the outside for the men.

Soon the oven was heating up the house, the smell of roasts and bread strong as we busied ourselves throughout the morning. I met many new women, including Zachariah's mother and sisters. Sarah Jensen took over setting up platters of food outside, while I spoke and directed and smiled to so many people. The time rushed past, the morning closing toward noon, the sun high in the sky.

I had so little time to simply sit back and breathe.

One moment I was in the house, helping Sarah and Fannie with water and lemonade. The next I was talking like a Mayor's wife to the new people who filed through my house and out in our yard. So many people, many we had never seen, and many who brought food or help and a friendly smile.

I didn't expect to freeze in the middle of the yard when I turned around to find myself staring at the vision before me.

In the bright sun, the sky an amazing blue for November, the beginnings of our barn had already taken shape. I stood there, the glasses of lemonade forgotten as I watched the men of our community climbing around the two standing ribs of the barn. The men climbed with ease, hoisting large beams up to the men on top, hammers shining in the sun as the men fastened the lumber into place.

And up there at the very top, in that fresh straw hat, was my Nathan.

I smiled as he worked, watching the fluid swings of his hammer driving the large pegs to hold the spacer beams in place.

Swing. Connect.

Swing. Connect.

So beautiful in his grace.

He caught my eye as he looked down to call out for the next one.

A smile lit up his heated face and warmed me as I waved to him. I laughed when he winked and tipped back his hat. I followed some of the other women, handing my lemonade off to the men on the lower level, eyeing my glasses as they made their way to the top.

To my husband and to Mark, who sat just below where Nathan straddled the beam.

Quenching his thirst, he passed the glass back down, winking again at me before returning to work, the wide smile remaining on his face as I walked away.

My own grin was proof that we knew how to please one another.

I couldn't wait until after sundown when we were alone again.

I planned on showing my husband just how much I loved him.

"You make your husband very happy."

I turned to find Benjamin standing beside me, smiling toward the men working.

He glanced my way, the playful twinkle in his eyes once more.

"We make each other happy, Benjamin," I replied, feeling I might burst with the joy I felt.

"It is good to see my friend in high spirits. I am grateful for your love for him. I know that with this new start, the two of you will prosper," he replied, his eyes growing contemplative as he regarded me.

I touched his arm gently, my eyes never leaving his.

"Well, now it's time to find the Bishop a good girl to settle down with," I whispered, and patted his arm lightly when he flushed and cleared his throat.

"In time, Katherine," he said and looked around as if in search of an escape.

"It will happen, Benjamin. I have faith," I replied and stepped away, watching the young women hustle around our property, thinking surely one of them would be a good match for our Bishop.

He was a good catch after all.

I'd have to employ Fannie to help me with that. Seeing her with Emma, I steered my way toward them as they made their way back into the kitchen. I caught the tail end of their conversation when I caught up with them.

"She will have to stay clear of the kitchen until she feels better, Emma. Have some consideration for your sister," Fannie said as she stepped into the hall.

"I have consideration for my sister. I just think if she is not feeling well, she should not get the rest of us sick by being here," Emma retorted.

"What's wrong with Hannah?" I asked, looking around for her.

I had seen Mark, but not Hannah.

Was she ill?

"She will be fine," Fannie said reassuringly. "She stepped out to the garden to gather up the last of the squash for you."

"Is she okay?" I asked, looking out toward the garden and not seeing her there.

"She will be fine after midday meal," Fannie replied and returned to gathering up the next platter to take outside.

I looked over at Emma who shook her head and leaned in close.

"She was ill yesterday most of the day, and this morning. Refuses to simply stay in bed. It is not like Mother to be so relaxed about her daughter's illness!" she huffed and stalked after Fannie with a basket of bread in her hands.

I looked again toward the garden, still not seeing her among the buggies and the dying vines there. I had thought I had stripped the last of the squash from the garden the day before. I made my way out the garden to see if Hannah needed help.

I didn't like the idea of her being here if she was ill.

I grew more alarmed when I found her huddled beside a buggy, kneeling as if to hide from us.

"Hannah?"

Her head lifted up and I could tell that she had been sick. Her eyes were puffy and her lips were puckered as she wiped them on her apron.

"I am sorry, Katherine," she mumbled hoarsely. "I thought I would be better today."

"You shouldn't be here if you're sick, Hannah," I said softly and rubbed her back when she turned from me to heave once more.

She leaned back and closed her eyes when the nausea passed.

"Mother says it will pass. I do not wish this on anyone, Katherine. The nausea," she muttered and wiped her mouth again.

"Was it something you ate? What did you have for breakfast?" I asked, grimacing when she turned quickly to try and heave the bile from her stomach.

"Please," she groaned. "Do not talk of food."

"Sorry," I whispered and returned my hand to her back as she coughed and heaved once more.

When she sat back again to look at me, she let out a weak laugh.

"I am sorry. I should have stayed out of the kitchen this morning. Every smell sets my stomach turning. And Mother just smiles and says it will pass, like she knows," she groused.

I blinked and sat there in front of her for a moment, the clues clicking into place.

"Oh my goodness, Hannah! You're pregnant!" I exclaimed.

Her eyes softened and a weak grin appeared on her face.

"Two months, I believe," she said quietly.

"Hannah! This is wonderful! It's just morning sickness!" I laughed and hugged her tightly.

"Except it lasts much longer than simply the morning, no matter what Mother may think," she grumbled into my shoulder and hugged me back weakly.

I looked down at her, seeing her a little differently as she sat there. She was pale, but already I could see her face and body had filled out a little more. Something you might think better eating could do, but it was obvious she wasn't holding much down lately. She looked a little tired, but her smile and glimmering eyes told me she was happy for this news.

"Does Emma know?" I asked, sitting down beside her.

She shook her head.

"I was going to say something this morning, but we have been so busy, and she was upset when I disappeared from the kitchen," she replied.

"Emma thinks you are really sick, you should say something," I whispered, pulling her hand into mine and squeezing it hard.

"I told you I would be first," she sighed and her smile warmed at her success.

"I would hope so. I'd like to have older cousins for my kids to look up to, after all," I said, beaming. "I'm so happy for you, Hannah. Mark must be proud."

She grunted and nodded.

"I am surprised he has not announced it to everyone yet."

"And Fannie must be so excited!" I said, thinking how much she wanted to be a grandmother, even if she was too young in my eyes for that.

Hannah rolled her eyes and let out a breath.

"She is already making clothes and pulled down the cradle yesterday," she said, shaking her head carefully.

"So this morning sickness lasts a while, then?" I asked, wondering how Nathan would handle it when it happened to me. It would worry him to death.

"I wake up starving, I try to eat something simple like dry toast, and it comes right back up," she explained. "The nausea is worse when I smell food cooking. By supper I can eat something simple, most days."

"Well, let's give you something to do away from the kitchen then," I said and helped her up slowly.

"I suppose I could carry water," she replied.

"And the kids are playing over by the pasture. Maybe you can watch over them," I suggested, watching her smile widen.

"Thank you, Katherine. I do not know what I would do without my sisters," she whispered and hugged me to her again.

"Thank you for being *my* sister," I murmured. "I am here for anything you need, okay?"

"Just do not let me near food. And tell that husband of mine to be kinder to me or I will hurt him when he sleeps," she grumbled.

"What has Mark done?" I asked, laughing when she scowled at me.

"He could have waited a month or two before he got me with child," she huffed.

"Well, I think he loves you," I replied and pulled her toward the pasture where the children played. "I have a feeling he wants nothing more than to please you."

"Then he needs to stop smiling like a fool every time he looks at me," she said, scowling toward the men working.

"He loves you, Hannah. You both have every reason to be proud of this news. You are going to have a little one!" I said excitedly.

She nodded and wiped at her eyes, trying to disguise the tears from me.

Still a tough Hannah, but now with a tender side to her.

"He will be unbearable, you realize. Acting like he is the first man to get his wife pregnant," she sighed and offered me another weak smile when we drew up close to the children playing.

"You'll keep him in check," I retorted, laughing with her for a moment before leaving her with the kids, her color returning as she occupied herself with a task that didn't trouble her stomach.

It was difficult to see Hannah as a mother until I watched her interact with the kids. She might have been a little gruff, but she kept them in line and even smiled when the smaller children drew her into a game of Duck Duck Goose.

When I returned to the business of laying out food for the midday meal, I caught Fannie watching me, her smile broad and her head nodding slightly. She glanced to Hannah, and I knew she had watched us as we walked. I nodded and laughed quietly to myself, returning to the kitchen to put more water on the stove for dishes later.

When the mealtime bell rang out, a skeletal formation of a barn stood before us.

Nathan took the towel I held for him after he had rinsed off, his eyes taking me in while I watched him. We sat at the same table as Benjamin and Fannie and Jonah, while Emma and John sat with Hannah and Mark one table over. Emma and Hannah must have talked, because Emma was constantly whispering into her sister's ear with a brilliant smile, while Hannah looked to be in much better spirits.

Benjamin held up his hands to quiet down the congregation, his eyes falling on us as he spoke.

"So much love here today, I surely feel blessed! So many of you have come today and put forth so much energy to help our newest couple in need," he started, smiling at us before he continued.

"I have so much to be thankful for this day. A loving community that comes together on this beautiful day. I am thankful for my friends that, again and again, show me what it means to live in the light. Nathan and Katherine are two of the kindest souls I know, so it warms my heart to see their love for one another, and to know that this barn will be a good start for their future.

"Evil may try to pull us down, but we rise up from the ashes better men. Stronger and more resolute in our beliefs. What happened here was a tragedy. But from the remains come hope and life. From hope and life comes solidarity. Thank you to so many for coming today to help Nathan and Katherine begin their life. When one is in need, we come together. That is so true today. From far and wide, we have come, and I know that God sees that. We are all truly blessed today.

"So let us enjoy this feast that so many have worked to provide," Benjamin continued. "And let this new barn be a start that the Fishers can enjoy for many years to come!"

There were many murmurings of "Amen" around the yard and soon we were eating happily beside one another. Nathan's hand brushed against my thigh many times, his smile glowing under his slightly flushed face. Benjamin and Nathan spoke about the coming winter, while Fannie and I spoke quietly about plans for the animals as soon as the barn was finished.

"We can keep half the cattle, so that the burden will be less for the two of you," she was saying. "Once the snow falls, you will not want to be out in it for long."

Truth be told, I didn't want to be out in the cold much at all. I smiled into my cup at the idea of keeping warm inside with Nathan.

"The Snyders were asking about the cows this morning," Nathan said as he listened to our conversation.

"Who are the Snyders?" I asked, noticing Benjamin's sudden

blush at mention of the name.

It was an interesting reaction.

"They live in Friendship," Nathan explained. "They own a successful dairy farm there. Something my father had always wanted to do. But it is not what I want. They offered a good price for most of the cows, and offered to deliver us cheese and the like whenever we wished."

"That sounds like a good deal," Jonah said. "Keep a few for yourself and have them provide you with the product. Much better than having to learn to make your own cheese."

"I can go with you to speak with the Snyders if you like," Benjamin added, his smile wavering when he caught me watching him curiously.

Nathan nodded and continued with his meal, smiling down at me with ease.

As the meals finished up, and as the desserts disappeared, the men returned to the task looming in the afternoon sunlight. I watched as they prepared the last, large truss, running ropes through a point at the top. The men grouped together, the larger men pulling on the rope to raise it while many others braced it with large lengths of wood to keep it from falling back.

Up in the rafters again stood my husband. Nathan braced against a beam and hammered in the span for the last rib, all concentration as his arm worked. I knew he would be tired tonight. Climbing and balancing, and then hammering and sawing things into place the old fashioned way had to take a lot out of a person. He would feel accomplished, but he would be sore and tired also.

I smiled at the thought of preparing a bath for him and busied myself with clearing away the dishes, joining my close friends in the kitchen to begin clean up. Dishes were done much more quickly when there were several hands to do them. I tried to offer the women all the leftovers we had, but Sarah and many of the elder women refused to listen to me, wrapping up much of the food to place in the freezer for deep winter.

Looking at our bursting cupboards and now our full freezer, I had no doubt we would have a better winter than Nathan had ever hoped for.

We made many sandwiches with the meat and bread left over so that the men had something to eat late in the afternoon while they worked. Unlike at the Wittmer Frolic, many of the men chose to stay late so that the outer walls and roof were completed on our barn.

The women helped around the house, clearing away anything that had come in from the day, even to be so helpful as to help me organize our closets upstairs. I found several coats and heavier dresses in the lot the women had brought the day before, so as the afternoon sun slowly dipped into the hill behind us, I sat with Hannah and Fannie on the porch to take in some of the dresses for me. I was standing with my third winter dress on when I looked out over the yard to find Benjamin speaking with a woman I didn't recognize.

He was fiddling with his hat in his hands, looking down often as he spoke. I was pretty sure he didn't catch half the smiles she threw at him because he was so busy toying with his hat. But I didn't know the dark-haired girl. She was about my age and tall, almost as tall as Benjamin, and her smile seemed to only be for him.

"Who is that girl Benjamin is talking to?" I asked.

Fannie looked up from her pins and pulled the few out of her smiling mouth.

"That is one of the Snyder girls. She is the youngest of them, I think. I cannot remember her name though. Look at him, so nervous," she said, the teasing tone of a mother clear in her voice.

I raised my eyebrow at Fannie, remembering the conversation earlier about the Snyders being interesting in our cows, and then Benjamin's blush.

"She has brought him lemonade all day," Abigail chimed in, grinning.

"I am amazed he has not turned into a lemon for all the drink he has endured with her," Emma chuckled.

"Perhaps our new Bishop has found a purpose," Hannah mumbled against my hip, pinning up the expansive waistline.

"Well, he deserves it. I think I need to meet her," I said.

"Leave them be for now, Katherine. He is not doing so badly, even with his nerves. She looks quite content to remain in his company. Much like you did when you courted Nathan," Fannie replied and smiled knowingly before returning to the base hem.

"Well they better finish that barn soon then," I murmured, catching Emma's giggle at my words.

There was no reason why Benjamin couldn't take advantage of a little barn time on his own. And the corn was long gone, so he really had nowhere to walk with the Snyder girl. So they remained standing by the buggies, talking and offering one another a timid smile before they would look away again.

It was cute to watch.

I hoped their community wasn't too far away. With Zachariah Ropp marrying Naomi Yoder at the end of the month, perhaps there would be another reason to see the Snyders. And the selling of our cattle would be yet another chance. Benjamin would be a part of that to be sure. I smiled and tried to watch them discreetly; excited that my friend had perhaps found someone finally.

Benjamin deserved a good woman.

And this Snyder girl looked like she would be good to him.

There was hope that maybe he had indeed found the right girl.

The sun was setting when I shook the hands of the last group of men from Friendship who had remained to finish the exterior planking of most of the barn. Only one side remained exposed, and Nathan was already talking excitedly with Mark and John about finishing it in a day or so.

Mark and Hannah said their goodnights, Mark holding her close as they disappeared over the hill toward their home. John and Emma left soon after, and Abigail with Fannie and Jonah, leaving us to stand alone before our new barn. Nathan sighed and took off his hat in the fading sunlight, wiping away the sweat that lingered on his forehead. Taking his hand, I walked toward the huge expanse that would soon be doors leading into the stables.

The layout would have to be figured out. When we stepped inside, it was dark and wide open. We would have the chance to make the barn into whatever we wished it to be. Nathan's arm wrapped around my shoulder, holding me to him as we looked around.

"The stalls will go over here on this wall," he said quietly, pointing toward the wall closest to us. "And there will be a room for storing feed. My workshop will remain in the back, as well as a new storage area for tack and the like. And the hayloft will be above us here."

At the mention of a hayloft, I felt his arm tighten, pulling me into him as his mouth descended. His lips tasted salty from the long day of work, his body overheated from the sun. But his arms were still strong as he held me tightly, his mouth searching. I felt the new wall behind me, felt his body press up against mine with delightful strength as he pinned me there between the barn wall and himself. My hands roamed across his chest, tugging on the suspenders. His head pulled away, eyes dark and breath heavy as he watched me slide the suspenders down along his sides.

"I am dirty," he whispered hoarsely.

"Filthy, I know," I whispered back, pulling his shirt out from his pants.

"You do not mind?" he asked and groaned when he felt me tug him closer.

My mouth on his was proof enough that I did not mind the smell of him. My hands wound up into his hair, knocking off his hat, feeling him push me up against the wall with a little more enthusiasm as our mouths moved together. The cool air of the closing night washed over my legs, Nathan slowly tugging my skirt up my hip to move against me a little more firmly.

"I missed you today," he whispered against my cheek as his lips trailed along my skin.

His lips found my throat, and any words were lost when I felt his teeth graze my neck. Whimpering, I arched into him, wanting him closer.

I needed him closer.

And judging by his hard body and throaty moan as he moved against me, he needed it as much as I did. I felt his hands work their way up my waist, ghosting over my breasts before cupping my head to deepen the kiss once more. When he drew away, he was breathing heavily.

"I want you," he breathed, licking at his lips as his eyes drank me in.

"So have me."

He let out a heavy breath and leaned in to kiss me again when we heard a buggy pull up just outside and the familiar voice of our new Bishop call out to us. I felt Nathan sag against me and sigh across my temple.

"Remind me when he is newly married to be sure to call on him at the most inopportune moments," he murmured, joining me in laughter as we pulled apart and straighten our clothes before venturing out to a slightly abashed Benjamin.

"Sorry, did I interrupt plans for the barn?" he said, fighting his smile.

"We got a few things worked out," I said, watching Nathan slowly draw up his suspenders with a scowl.

"I just wanted to say that the Snyders will be at the Yoder wedding. And they are definitely interested in the cows. Could be a good trade before winter," he said.

"Excellent," Nathan said, his voice only a little strained as he held me a bit tighter.

We stood there looking after one another, feeling the awkward tension in the air as the silence grew. Finally Benjamin let out a nervous laugh and took a step back toward his buggy.

"Well, I promised my mother to visit this evening. I should go before it is too late," he said and shuffled toward his buggy.

"Thank you, Benjamin, for everything," I called out, smiling after him as he waved to us.

"It is my pleasure, to see you happy and well. I will see you in a day or two, Nathan?"

"Not tomorrow," Nathan called out, grinning.

I heard Benjamin's laughter and knew they were sharing in an earlier conversation.

"I will be sure you are left alone tomorrow!" he called out as he turned his buggy in the drive.

"Do I want to know what that meant?" I asked when I felt Nathan guide me toward the house. He chuckled and leaned in to peck me on the temple.

"Just that I would like to spend some time with my wife tomorrow, that is all," he murmured and walked me into the house, his arm tight about my waist.

"We'll see how long Fannie lets us spend time alone," I joked.

"They will understand. Jonah has said he will not expect us tomorrow," he whispered, pulling me up the dark staircase.

"Are you hungry?" I breathed when his fingers glided over my arm when we reached the bedroom.

"Later."

"Bath?"

"If you join me."

Nathan's lips trailed over my cheek to my lips as I turned on the water to the bath, his hands moving over my body as if to memorize it. I pulled away for a moment to check the temperature only to find his arms wrapping around me from behind, his mouth attacking my neck with renewed energy. Turning in his arms, I worked his clothes free of him, pushing him toward the steaming tub with a laugh.

"You are really dirty," I said with a smile against his lips.

"I told you," he chided while he fingered the hooks to my dress.

"Get in and relax. I will go get towels and come back," I whispered and worked my way out of his arms to go grab fresh towels and to give myself a moment before I gave in to his desire. I wanted it too, but I could also tell he was sore and tired from the long day.

When I stepped back in a few minutes later, he was comfortably propped against the side of the tub, eyes closed, with just his head above the water that now threatened to overflow. I turned the water off, smiling when his eyes slowly opened to watch me in the room. I lit the lanterns by the door, conscious of him tracking me back and forth.

"You let the water get too high for me to get in with you," I whispered, sitting alongside the tub by his head.

"I can easily drain it," he replied and moved his toe toward the drain plug.

"Stay like that for a bit. It will help with your sore muscles," I said and let my hand trail across his submerged shoulder. My eyes wandered, his body clearly visible in the water. My fingers worked their way up his neck and into his hair, cupping his head gently as I watched him relax in the soothing water.

He closed his eyes with a sigh and leaned his head into my wet hand.

"I would not have thought I could feel so at ease with my wife beside me while I bathed. I have no worries when you are with me," he mumbled, a contented smile playing on his lips as he leaned a little harder into me.

"You are nice to look at, Nathan. I'm a lucky wife," I replied, wagging my eyebrows at him.

He opened his eyes wide, laughing low in his throat.

"Do enjoy what you see, Kate?" he asked, the mischief clear in his voice when he sat up straight to wrap his arms around me quicker than I could pull away.

"Nathan! You'll slosh water out!" I exclaimed when he shifted to cause waves in the bath.

"Only if I do this," he said and pulled me in with him, fully clothed. I cried out and laughed in surprise at feeling the water soak into my clothes. Only my feet remained out of the tub, as well as my head that reached up to his in a heated kiss.

"We will need to clean this up," I breathed around his lips.

"Later," he whispered, his mouth moving once more to my neck. "How is it that you taste better every time I kiss you?"

I giggled at the stubble on his chin as he moved along my neck, trying hard not to move so as to keep from splashing more water out of the tub. I didn't want to spend precious time after his bath cleaning up. I wanted a repeat of our time last night in bed. Nathan groaned against my collarbone and tipped his head up to look up into my eyes, the tender expression in them making my heart pound.

"I cannot get enough of you," he whispered. "I want to take you to our bed and stay there all night worshipping you."

I was more than happy to grant him his wish, splashing water everywhere as I scrambled out of the bathtub, Nathan not far behind. I peeled away my wet clothes there on the flooded floor as he dried himself off, and was turning to grab a towel for myself when I felt his arms wrap around me, the towel enveloping me as he did so.

His mouth against me once more, the counter at my back, Nathan's hands slowly dried me, my hands idly playing in his wet hair. He stood before me in only a towel, eyes travelling over my naked body as he worked. When he dropped to his knees, I stood frozen before him. The towel dropped from his hands, allowing them to trace up my sides and over my shoulders before fingertips glided down across my front.

I let out a stuttered breath when he traced my nipples, his lips following immediately after.

Nothing felt better than Nathan's touch.

He hummed against my skin, fingers continuing down to spread out across the expanse of my stomach. He hummed again and pulled away to watch his hands move.

"I love to feel your skin against mine. Promise me we will always sleep skin to skin," he said, his voice deep and rough.

His arms wrapped around me then, his mouth covering mine in a passionate kiss as he drew us toward the bedroom. We collapsed onto the bed and he entered me eagerly. He groaned into my lips and pulled away to watch as he thrust into me again and again in need. I knew he was close, his breath ragged as he grunted and whispered my name over and over again, lifting up onto his elbow to move a little deeper, a little more urgently. My hands glided across his body, feeling the muscles along his hips move with purpose. I loved to feel him move; it was like experiencing a beautifully carved statue come to life.

His mouth found my shoulder, lips running along my neck until he groaned and froze against me, buried deep and tight against my body so that I could feel him tremble and tense. The heaviness of him only lasted a moment before he rolled us over until I was on top of him, his heart hammering against my breast as he caught his breath. He licked his lips and let out a soft moan, wrapping his arms around me in a warm embrace.

"I could do this every day forever," I whispered and snuggled into him, letting him stroke my head lazily as we let our bodies slowly relax.

"I look forward to forever with you, Kate. I want to enjoy everything with you," he whispered.

I listened to his heart slow down, and his arms relaxed against me as he slowly drifted off, the long day finally catching up with him. I pulled the covers up over us as the chilly air made me shiver, and watched my husband in the dim light from the lantern in the bathroom.

I would have to get up eventually and clean up our mess, but for the moment I wanted to simply lay there and watch as Nathan slept with a contented smile on his face, his body relaxed, and his dreams hopefully pleasant as he lay beneath me. So much of our life had been dramatic and in many ways painful. It was nice to have this time of ultimate bliss.

I knew we had a lot to face as a young married couple.

A long winter.

Daily life in our world that was still so very new to me.

Struggling crops in the spring.

Sean's friends out there still.

None of that would trouble me.

As long as Nathan and I had each other, I could face anything that came our way.

We had each other.

We had love.

We had faith.

And that would see us through.

20

In my old life, sleeping in meant not eating breakfast until it was almost lunchtime.

They called it brunch.

If you didn't wake up with the sun, you simply started your day later; the day went on without you. You stayed up a little later perhaps, to finish that load of laundry in the dryer. You threw the dishes in the dishwasher to do later. You waited to go to the grocery store.

It was the most valueless part of my life then.

Just getting by in order to find something better.

Something that had meaning.

Waking up before the sun became that meaning.

What used to be thankless chores were now a measurable part of my life.

And every task had value.

Waking up to Nathan's heavy arm as he snuggled against me had meaning.

Making love to my husband had meaning.

Living this life had profound meaning.

The Amish didn't believe in brunch.

We believed in living every moment and giving thanks for those moments. Even if it was over the laundry that needed to be put on the line before noon in order for it to dry in time before you went inside for supper.

Every day of this life was fulfilling.

Nathan and I found our rhythm in this new life. And with each morning as we woke up together, I felt more in touch with my place as Mrs. Fisher. Nathan and I seemed to know just what the other needed, from a soft kiss as I made breakfast, to the unspoken team work in building our new barn, to the quiet need to be one as the cold settled outside of our blankets at night.

We lived very well together.

And once we had the rudimentary beginnings of the stalls for the horses built, we were able to add to our daily list of chores. Horses taken care of, house tended to, fall crops salvaged. I walked over the hill every morning to help Fannie and Jonah with our cows, and Nathan joined us for breakfast.

Soon, with the onset of winter, it would be more difficult to go visit every day.

I hoped that Nathan would be able to sell his cows to the Snyders. We could handle a few. We could not handle the dozen. And Fannie and Jonah had their own worries. So as we made our way to the Yoders on a blustery Thursday, hands full of pies and treats for after Naomi's wedding, I thought about the fields that Nathan had let rest because they were too much for him.

"Nathan?"

"Yes, my wife?" he asked, smiling down at me.

I smiled and shook my head at his charming mood.

What was I thinking of just then?

Oh yes. Fields.

"This is serious, Nathan," I said, pretending to scold him.

He fought to hide his smile in a serious pout, but failed at it.

Instead he looked like he was sucking on a hard candy, which was just as distracting when I thought of how he looked when he sucked on other things.

"I am sorry, Kate," he murmured, trying to be serious for a moment.

I looked out over the barren field that lay between our house and the Yoder's. It was large, and looked to have been abandoned for some time.

"This is your field, right?" I asked, nodding to where we walked.

"It is our field, yes," he corrected and nodded toward an outcropping of trees far on the other side of the far hill. "It extends to the trees there. It is about fifty acres on this side."

I looked back the way we had come. Our house was obscured from the hill but I could make out the other side of his fields behind us.

"And back there?" I asked. "How many acres do you have total?"

He looked at me curiously and shrugged.

"About eighty total. Why?" he asked simply.

Had it been any other man, I might have bristled at why he asked. But with Nathan it was genuine curiosity that he asked me why.

"How much did you plant this year?" I asked instead, a plan forming in my head.

He frowned and looked ahead.

"Only about five acres. But I plan on doing more in the spring. We will be fine," he said, his voice more determined.

"That's not what I meant, Nathan," I said softly, drawing his eyes back to mine. "I had an idea that could help."

He was quiet for a moment, perhaps afraid of what I could be thinking.

"Go on," he replied finally.

"Well, in the old days, they had sharecroppers," I started, watching him to see if he was following. He nodded for me to continue.

"The land got used, and the owner took a percentage while the people planting and tending took the majority of the profits," I explained, and smiled when I saw his mind working hard behind his eyes.

"So," he said and paused. "You think we should offer up the land we cannot maintain for a small fee in order for someone else to grow crops?"

I nodded, wondering if maybe this went against some code.

He was quiet as we walked, looking out over the land.

"It is an interesting idea," he murmured, and then leaned in to kiss me on the forehead. "You have very good ideas, my wife."

I laughed and rolled my eyes at him.

"You like saying that, don't you?" I asked, smirking.

"I love to call you my wife," he whispered, and even in the cold breeze, I felt myself warm considerably from his heated gaze.

"I am glad, my husband," I said. "Because I love it when you say it."

His smile broadened and we walked happily the rest of the way to the Yoders, every moment together making us more and more comfortable as we learned how to please the other. We had learned much in just a week or so.

I wondered what more we would learn this winter. Alone.

I smiled and winked at my husband as we parted ways at the porch steps, Nathan going out to help the men with benches for the basement while I helped the ever present Sarah Jensen and Mrs. Yoder with laying out the food for the inside buffet.

The house was teaming with people, it being too cold to hold the wedding outdoors.

It would be cramped quarters and we would have to eat in shifts.

"At least this is the last wedding of the season," Sarah said, sighing as she wiped at her brow.

"This is a late one, right?" I asked, curious to learn more of my world.

"Just for this reason," Mrs. Yoder explained. "It is too cold to do much else than Sermons. Naomi reduced her invitation list to accommodate. But Zachariah did not ask for much, he simply wishes to marry."

Both women smiled at that and continued with shuffling food around the tables in the kitchen. I stepped in to carve one of the three roasts resting on the counter. Even with a short list of invited guests, there was enough food in the kitchen for about a hundred people.

Sitting with Nathan in the warm basement, it was obvious there were nearly that many people wedged into the large room. Perhaps because of that, Benjamin kept the Sermon short, allowing Nathan to lead in song before we were presented with the husband and wife.

Naomi and Zachariah made their way through the tiny aisle to the front of the room, her eyes already bright with emotion. Zachariah looked nervous, as most young men seemed to in that moment. But as soon as they were announced, both of them seemed to beam with the excitement.

I understood the feeling well.

Especially when Nathan came up and walked with me out of the basement and up the stairs. I was shocked to find the kitchen cooler than the basement with so many people in attendance. But soon those people were making their way through the house, plates in hand and finding any surface to sit on or lean against. The basement was full, and the happiness of the newly married couple spread through those of us staying for the meal.

It wasn't until I was storing the leftover foods that I noticed the young woman who had taken lemonade to Benjamin during our barn raising. I watched her from the corner of my eye as she helped gather dishes from the house, her smile timid as she interacted with the people around her. There were few people from her town due to the cold weather; she must have felt a little out of place.

And I was curious.

Maybe even a little devious.

As she drew near to me in the kitchen I turned and smiled

toward her, her eyes widening a bit when she noticed me. She slowed down, walking with care as she drew close.

"We have not yet met," I said, smiling and extending my hand. "I am Katherine Fisher."

She looked sheepish as she took my hand and looked down toward her feet.

"I know," she whispered. "You are Benjamin's friend."

I nodded, still smiling at how nervous she seemed.

Was I like this when I first arrived?

"He is more of a brother than a friend, really," I said simply.

She blushed and nodded.

"I am Judith Snyder from Friendship."

"Welcome, Judith. Would you like to sit with me while we let the men talk? Aside from my sisters, I do not have many I can sit and speak with, and my husband looks busy," I said, glancing at Nathan, who was in deep conversation with an older man and Benjamin.

"That is my father," Judith replied and walked with me to the front room. "He is interested in your husband's cows."

I smiled and pretended to be surprised.

"Oh really? That would be nice. It is a lot to handle for the winter with just the two of us," I said casually, settling us near the corner of the room so we could talk.

She looked around the room, at the groups of women as they talked quietly, some with knitting already out, others catching up and laughing amongst themselves.

"So," I said, startling her as she turned to look at me once more. "You are from Friendship. I have never been there. Have you lived there all your life?"

She relaxed some and nodded.

"I was born there. Father and Mother were some of the first to move there, along with the Ropps," she said. "But I hear you are new to the Way."

I smiled and nodded.

"I am."

"You have settled in so well. And found a nice man," she said and let out a quiet sigh.

I was itching to ask her about Benjamin, but I held back, wanting to find out a little more about her first. She seemed nice enough. Maybe a little quiet, just as I was with strangers. So I opened up to her.

"Nathan was very kind and had faith that I would enjoy this life. I cannot see myself anywhere else. I am glad he took that risk with me," I said.

"The men in West Grove seem to be very sensitive," she murmured and blushed when I grinned.

"I am sorry," I said quickly. "I think you might be right. At least from where I am from, there was no one like Nathan."

"It has been nice to come and visit with your friends," she said, looking down bashfully.

"You are welcome anytime, Judith. And perhaps, if it is not too forward of me, I can invite you to supper after Sermon sometime. I have a feeling we will see more of one another, what with Naomi married to Zachariah, and Benjamin being Bishop," I said, trying to provide her a way to discuss Benjamin.

She glanced around and was quiet for a moment before leaning in to whisper.

"Benjamin seems like a nice man. I do not understand why he is not married. What with being the Bishop," she said quietly.

"He was newly made Bishop," I explained.

"But you have had a Bishop Yoder for years," she said and then nodded to herself, blushing. "Of course he would not have been Bishop for years. He is not that old. Still strange, a man his age not yet wed."

I patted her on the hand to ease her embarrassment.

"Perhaps he is waiting to find the right woman to balance his life. Someone that can give him hope and love," I whispered back and offered her a friendly smile.

I liked Judith.

There was something about her that just seemed calm and loving.

Something that Benjamin needed.

He had seen the other world.

But he lived in ours.

He needed someone who would strengthen his hold on our Way.

I watched as Benjamin and Nathan stepped into the room, Judith's eyes tracking Benjamin as they drew close, only to drop her gaze when they stood before us.

"Katherine, you have been entertaining Judith, I see," Benjamin said, a brief look of fear in his eyes before he recovered and offered a tremulous smile when she looked up at him, smiling.

"Katherine was telling me how much she has enjoyed coming to West Grove, Bishop Yoder," she said, and I smiled behind her when I looked up at Benjamin's blush.

She had said his name a little breathily.

Nathan tried to hold back his grin behind Benjamin, but it was clear that he was enjoying this as much as I was. We sat together, speaking quietly about the Sermon, Nathan and I asking questions to the shy couple in order to get them talking. I felt his finger trace across my shoulder once or twice, and that simple touch made me feel all the love he had for me while we sat with our friends.

All too soon, the afternoon drew near. Those from Friendship bade farewell, a long trip ahead of them by buggy. I pulled Judith close while Nathan shook hands with her father, the deal for the cows done and arrangements made.

"You will have to come and see us, Judith. Perhaps when Benjamin and Nathan bring the livestock to your farm, I will come and visit?" I asked, happy to see her smile light up.

"I would like that," she said and turned to her father's buggy, a small smile playing on her lips when Benjamin helped her in. I held back a chuckle when Benjamin shook hands with her father and then drew back, letting out a long breath.

As the buggy slowly made its way down the road, I stood

quietly with Nathan at my side, Benjamin on the other. Nathan and I both glanced at our Bishop, his concentration on the disappearing buggy.

"I go to deliver the cows on Monday next," Nathan said, trying to appear serious. "I will need help."

"I would be happy to help," Benjamin said, looking back at me nervously.

"Perhaps she will have lemonade," I teased and pulled Nathan with me to our home, a wide grin appearing on his face as he waved at his friend.

"He is enamored of her," Nathan said into the cold wind as we walked.

"She fancies him," I replied calmly.

"I think it was meant to be, then," Nathan said, and pulled me close to kiss me against the temple.

"We will have to figure out where they will live," I replied, hoping that it would not be with us.

I liked Benjamin, and Judith was nice, but I wanted my alone time with Nathan.

"The community will help with that. The Yoders own the property across from me, where the gazebo sits," he said simply.

The idea that they would be our neighbors would be perfect.

A new friend for me, and Nathan's best friend.

Right next door.

21

I bundled up against the wind as I stepped outside, looking to see if Nathan was back from picking up supplies from town. I noticed Magnus in the pasture as I made my way toward the barn, where the wagon sat, half unloaded. Peering inside I heard him above me in the hayloft.

It didn't sound like he was pleased.

Nathan never used foul language.

At least that I knew of.

But he was muttering in German, and I knew enough to know they were not glorifying words.

A forceful groan and a sudden clink nearby caused me to leap out of the way before something fell on me. As it was, a large hook with some kind of lashing fell from above, making me let out my own form of exclamation.

Something we Amish didn't say, in English anyway.

"Kate?" I heard above me. Looking up I saw Nathan's face peek over the side, his eyes wide.

"Did I drop that on you?" he asked, the worry clear in his voice.

"No," I called up to him. "I should have told you I was here. I am sorry. But I was amused by the noise up above me."

He scrambled down the ladder and reached for the rope hanging beside me, his face flushed and lips tight as he pulled the knots loose.

"If Benjamin was here, I would be finished and comfortable inside with you, instead of raising these bales one at a time and situating them myself," he grumbled.

If he weren't in such a sour mood, I would have laughed. He was cute when he was frustrated. I thought better of teasing him.

"I can help," I said instead.

He pursed his lips and shook his head.

"It is too heavy for you to lift," he said and moved back to the wagon to strap in another hay bale.

I followed after him.

"I can unhook them up above, Nathan. I don't need much strength to guide them and untie," I replied, hands on hips.

He turned to argue, only to laugh and shake his head when he looked at my stance.

"I should have learned by now not to argue with you. You are far too stubborn to deny," he said.

"We are a team, Nathan Fisher," I retorted. "I am not stubborn. Just persistent."

"And beautiful when you are so," he murmured and leaned in to kiss me.

I pulled away and hiked my skirt up a bit to climb the new ladder leading to the hayloft. When I looked down, Nathan was smirking, his eyes on my backside. I rolled my eyes and hoisted myself up onto the floor of the loft, the action much harder in a long skirt. Sometimes I missed the jeans and sweatpants of my previous life.

But then again, watching Nathan's eyes trail up my legs was enough to make me forgo pants forever.

"So I will raise it, you must grab it with the hook there at your feet and guide it back onto the floor beside you. We can stack them when we get a few up there," he instructed.

I nodded and wielded my long hook device, watching as Nathan pulled on the rope, raising the heavy bale up toward me. I had to remind myself that I was there to work and not ogle my husband's arms. The bale came level with the floor, and I reached out to hook one of the straps. Tugging it in wasn't too difficult, Nathan knowing to keep it floating above the floor until he couldn't see it and then he let the tension go some to let the bale rest hard on the floor.

I struggled for only a moment with the straps, figuring out that they unhooked from one side and then had to be tugged from underneath before I could let them go with the rope. Nathan pulled them back down to him and told me to wait a few moments before he would be ready for the next one.

Looking around, I saw almost a dozen bales lined up behind me, stacked up three high. I looked at the bale and thought about how difficult it would be for Nathan to land the next one unless I moved this one first. Grabbing at the twine straps that bound the bale together, I tugged on it, managing to move it a few feet with a couple of loud grunts. Getting behind it, I was able to shove it closer to the neatly stacked ones.

Another hard shove and I had the one lined up to form the base of the next stack.

Proud of myself, I stepped back to the edge with my hook, just as the second one leveled up with the loft. More quickly, I let it go and shoved it back to the new row.

Another bale came up, and I moved it all by myself.

I was feeling accomplished.

"Do you have room for one more?" he called up to me.

"Keep them coming!" I called down, smiling at him when he eyed me curiously.

"You have room?"

I nodded and waved him to keep going.

Another and another, and soon I had my base row full.

The next one arrived and I pushed it to the row, contemplating for a moment how I could get it up to start the second row. Flipping it on its end with a grunt, I managed to topple it onto the bottom row. It wasn't as neat as Nathan's row, but with a little pushing and shoving with my backside, it was close.

I was almost late to retrieve the next bale; Nathan had to call up to me. I grabbed the bale and pushed and flipped, this time with more gusto.

Again Nathan called up to ask if there was room and again I told him to keep them coming.

There was no way I could make a third row, but as I finished the second and started another base row, I heard a chuckle from the ladder. Looking behind me, Nathan peeked over the edge of the floor and took in my progress. He nodded, laughing again, before he disappeared back down onto the ground.

We resumed our hauling, until the wagon was clear and I was panting as I pushed and shoved another bale up onto the second level of another base row. The hay made the ground a little slippery, and as I had grown tired, my hard shove catapulted me to fall onto the long row of hay in front of me. The last troublesome bale tipped over and landed back on its side.

I let out a tired huff and flopped onto the hay, not caring if I got it in my hair.

I just wanted to be horizontal for a minute.

When Nathan's warm body covered mine there in the hay, I wasn't worried about how straight my rows were or whether I was just a little too weak to make a third row.

His lips covered mine, searching slowly while his hands travelled down my side past my hips, tugging at my skirt to free up my legs. I could feel his grin against my lips before he drew away to look down at me.

"Benjamin is at the mill until late," he whispered, his eyes gleaming.

I raised my eyebrow at him.

"And?" I said, playing ignorant.

My skirt moved up a little higher, his smile wicked.

"And you have made such a nice place to rest," he whispered, his lips moving down my throat until his nose edged across the top of my dress.

"It is quite comfortable up here," I replied, slipping my fingers through his suspenders to slide them down over his shoulders.

"It is better than the old loft," he mumbled, his nose drifting further down until his face lay nestled in between my breasts. "No one will find us up here."

His overheated body felt good against me in the cold air, and I moaned when he adjusted against me.

"Is this all right?" he murmured into my skin. "I must confess I have thought of you in the hayloft with me since before the last time we ventured up."

"What did you think we might do up in the hayloft?" I asked, breathless and eager to see a more adventurous side of him.

He chuckled and looked down at me with mischievous eyes.

"I think my ideas have grown now that you are my wife."

Pulling him up to my mouth again, I held him close as he moved against me, his hands slipping under my skirt to explore me. I sighed when I felt his fingers slide against me, so confident in their swirling touch. I lifted my hips up to him, helping him remove every barrier. His low-throated chuckle into my shoulder had me tugging at his pants, eager to feel him against me. But he was unbearably slow as he traced those fingers.

Was it wrong that I wanted to be a little frantic?

We were outside the bedroom, and Nathan was being wicked.

"Nathan," I whined.

"Mmhmm?"

I managed to get his pants unbuttoned, my fingers slipping inside. He groaned deeply and moved against my hand, keeping a slow and steady rhythm to his own exploration. His lips returned to mine, deep and slow.

He was taking his time.

It was maddening.

Gone was the timid man who had run from me that first day. In his place was a man I loved, who was excited to learn everything about pleasuring me. A man who wasn't looking for merely the end result, but for the pleasure of the entire experience. I knew I was lucky in having Nathan as my partner. He was more willing to be daring than I assumed most men of his upbringing might be.

"Nathan," I whispered, this time a pleasurable sigh when I felt him sliding us both up against the bales of hay.

Slow and deep, hands holding one another close, we connected. Nathan's soft humming groan ventured no further than the bales of hay, and my quickening breaths were muffled against his half open shirt. Tipping my head up, I caught him looking down at me, a tender smile playing on his lips, his eyes heavy as he moved above me. I closed my eyes when I felt his thumb lightly trace along my cheek, at the heat there from my need for him. I could feel my lips curve up, so much affection working through me at his touch.

"You are so blissful in this moment," he whispered. "Do I do that for you?"

"Always," I breathed, and opened my eyes to find his had grown heavy with desire.

His lips captured mine once more, his rhythm growing more urgent, and his hands more possessive as he thrust into me. Clinging to him, I met his desperate movements with my own, my hips finding a matching rhythm, both of us gasping when we felt our pleasure build. He ducked his head against my neck, a whimper vibrating against my throat as he quickened his pace.

I clung to him when I fell away, his body shuddering against mine before slipping off to my side with a satisfied sigh. Opening my eyes, I found his crinkled in his contentment. Tracing the opening of his shirt I tucked in close to him, enjoying the moment.

"I think we should work together more often," he said, laughing when I raised my eyebrow at him.

"I think if that's the result, you need to cook with me more often," I retorted. "It's warmer in the kitchen."

Nathan wrapped his arms around me and pulled me in for a kiss.

"I will happily help you in the kitchen. Or anywhere else you wish," he said, his grin becoming ever wider.

I felt the heat build at that thought.

"I am finding that I enjoy everything with you, Kate," he murmured and sighed into my neck.

I relaxed in his arms, the two of us simply content to rest there for a time. The cold finally got the better of me, even with heat of Nathan beside me. I groaned and sat up, sliding my skirt down over my cold legs. I was aware of Nathan watching me as he propped up on one elbow. I looked back at him, lying on his side, his pants undone but covering him, and his shirt as it sat open to reveal his chest underneath. He was beautiful to look at as he smiled and watched me move. I wanted simply to sit and watch him, just as he was.

But there were things to be done.

"I should head back inside and make sure I haven't overcooked the chicken," I said quietly.

I stood and dusted myself off, trying to work the straw out of my hair before going back inside. Nathan stood and helped me pull the hay out of my clothes, his hands lingering along my neck as he looked back at the job we had accomplished together.

"Thank you for coming out to check on me," he murmured. "I would have been only half done at this hour without your help."

"You know I will do anything you need," I replied, holding him close.

He nodded and looked away, bashful.

"I am afraid to say I thought you could not do it," he whispered and blushed a little deeper.

I pursed my lips at him and tried to look annoyed. But truth be known, I would be feeling my muscles rebel in the morning to be sure. I had a lot to learn about running the farm.

"I'll forgive you if you promise to let me help you from now on," I said.

His timid smile crept up and he let out a playful laugh.

"You are more enjoyable to watch than Benjamin, especially when you are shoving at a bale that weighs as much as yourself!" he exclaimed.

Rolling my eyes, I turned and headed to the ladder. As I took the first rung, I looked back at him, full of mischief.

"I should hope I am more interesting to look at than our Bishop," I said. "And maybe we can continue with these little moments after each chore is done."

I winked and descended the ladder, not waiting for his comment.

It was worth getting hay in my hair this time.

22

"It is snowing."

I looked out my window at Hannah's glum comment and smiled.

I was happy to see the snow.

Snow meant that things would slow down on the farm front. The ground would be too hard to work, the crops taken care of. I had spent the last week canning with Fannie. We had made our last run to the butcher and the market for goods, and with our savings, we had stocked the barn for our horses and few cows. Nathan had even built a secure chicken coop, Jonah giving us a few of his own chickens to get us through the winter.

After the long two weeks we had with getting the barn weatherproofed, and preparing for winter, I was more than ready to spend the winter indoors with my husband. We had a lot to learn about one another, and I wanted the time alone with him in order to do that.

"I love the winter. I have a feeling it will be very memorable this year," Emma said happily beside me as she chopped the potatoes for supper.

I looked at her with an arched eyebrow, and she grinned.

"We are all married, Katherine," she said simply.

"Starting a household," Hannah said, her voice muffled.

I turned to find her taking a large bite out of the leftover biscuits from breakfast.

She hummed and took another bite.

"Did you make this pumpkin butter?" she mumbled and spread more of it on the tiny remains of the biscuit in her hand.

"Sarah Jensen gave me the recipe last week. Fannie and I salvaged some of the pumpkins in the fields," I said, chuckling at Hannah's newly voracious appetite.

Apparently she wasn't suffering from morning sickness anymore.

"It is good," she replied and popped the last of the biscuit in her mouth, peeking under the cloth to see if there were any more. Her frown told me she had eaten them all.

"We can make more biscuits if you want," I said, laughing when she pursed her lips at me.

"Just you wait, Katherine," she growled. "I finally find something I can eat and I want nothing more than to devour them. You will see."

I leaned into her and offered a nudge like sisters do, enjoying her old character once more.

"I have a few jars of the pumpkin butter you can take home," I whispered and watched as she eyed the empty basket.

I knew I would be making biscuits for supper.

"The men will be inside soon. The snow is coming down a little harder," Abigail announced as she looked outside at the darkening sky.

"I suppose that means we will see a little less of one another, but that could be a good thing," Hannah replied, smirking at the two of us.

"You are beginning to sound like Mother," Emma grumbled and tossed the potatoes into the boiling water.

Hannah simply shrugged.

"If you are not already, you will be soon. There is not much to do in the winter months."

I realized then what they were talking about. Glancing at Abigail, she was oblivious while she played in the window, making pictures in the condensation. I busied myself with clearing away the bowls and utensils from preparing supper, my mood shifting back to what it had been this morning before they had arrived.

Surly.

Frustrated.

A little embarrassed.

I hadn't realized the date, and Nathan had overreacted at the blood.

Of course I didn't react well to his reaction.

I had never been good at talking about it, and with his embarrassment, mine doubled when trying to explain it to him. Which then made me frustrated and irritable. I rarely snapped at people when it was that time, but perhaps with marriage comes elevated hormones every month.

Regardless of how many women had once occupied the Fisher home, Nathan had a lot to learn about them.

Their cycles. And their hormones.

Of course, maybe that was something Amish men didn't think about.

Was it a taboo conversation? Like in the old days when women would be shunned for the week.

Did they simply ignore us then?

I doubted Mark understood. Hannah was pregnant within the first month of being married. Emma had not been married much longer than me, but I assumed she would tell us when she became pregnant. Judging by her sudden silence as Hannah discussed the discomfort of her first few months of pregnancy, I concluded that she had not become pregnant yet.

My own issues were put aside as I suddenly wondered if Emma could even have children, given the cancer and her treatment for it.

"Hannah, can you check in the basement and see if there is another jar of bean salad? I only have one here and it won't be enough," I said, cutting off her lecture on bloating and nausea.

She nodded and disappeared, Emma's loud sigh echoing across the room.

"Thank you," she said and closed her eyes as if to regroup.

"I'm not ready to hear about what it might be like, to be honest," I whispered. "It's stressful enough to have everyone assume."

Emma opened her eyes and regarded me thoughtfully.

"It is still early for us. Sometimes it takes time," she replied, and I could hear the worry in her voice.

"What will happen will happen, Emma. I think Hannah just wants to share in her excitement," I explained, although I didn't really want to think about children, especially today when my ovaries felt pummeled.

"I just worry that I may never..." she started and closed her mouth, afraid to finish.

I went to her and hugged her tightly.

"I think Fannie showed us another path if that is the case, Emma," I whispered.

She sighed and nodded against me.

"I know it is difficult for John to understand. He knows it may take some time, but the rest of it, I hope he does not feel like he lost something when he married me," she said softly.

"I think John is a lot more perceptive than that. He loves you, Emma. He'd walk through fire just to be with you. He reminds me a lot of Jonah," I replied.

"I snapped at him last week," she mumbled. "It was not on purpose. It was just that I was sad that my monthly had come, and he could not understand my sadness."

She hugged me a little tighter.

"They do not understand how it affects us, I think," she said and blushed.

"Well, it's up to us to educate them. And I get it, Emma. Believe me, I get it," I said and nodded to emphasize I understood her. She laughed and hugged me a little tighter.

"Maybe John and Nathan can compare notes!" she giggled. "I was not a pleasant person last week."

I grunted and pulled away.

"If they don't understand they'll have to learn the hard way when they are stuck in the house with us," I said and we both laughed as we turned back to the food cooking just as Hannah returned.

Mark, John, and Nathan finally came inside, Fannie and Jonah with them from next door. Mark brushed his giant hand lightly over Hannah's cheek, smiling like the summer sun at his wife. John leaned in and pecked Emma on the cheek before going to the sink to wash up.

Nathan kept a safe distance from me, a timid smile on his face as he watched me work.

I felt a little guilty.

We had not talked much since this morning, and he had been uncomfortable talking. And I had jumped right into work as soon as Hannah and Emma came over.

Sitting down at the table beside him, I felt his hand brush against my leg tentatively, his eyes watching me for a sign. I clasped his hand in my own for a second, squeezing it to tell him we were all right. His smile brightened, and the rest of the night the tension around us seemed to lighten.

At least until I crawled into bed that night.

It was the first time I wore a shift to bed.

Nathan rested against the headboard, his eyes a little downcast while I slipped under the covers. It didn't go unnoticed that he was in his cotton sleep pants. I sighed and snuggled in alongside him, resting my head on his chest while he played with my hair.

"I am sorry for this morning," he whispered.

"No, I'm sorry. I didn't think about how it might be for you," I replied.

"It is not something we talk about. I should not have reacted so strongly," he continued.

I lifted my head to look up at him. He still wore a pained expression on his face.

"Nathan," I said, drawing his eyes to me. "It's a natural thing. It'll last a few days and be over. Can we just forget about this morning and move on?"

His frown tightened for only a moment and then he nodded, slipping us down under the covers. He remained quiet for a while, his hands floating lightly over my shoulder and down my back idly. When he finally spoke, his voice was low and rough.

"I do not like being this far away from you."

I turned to look up at him, confused.

"I'm right next to you, Nathan," I replied.

He swallowed and his lips pursed.

"I miss the touch of your skin on mine."

I sat up beside him and touched my shift, debating how I felt about lying there without it. Somehow it made me feel protected. Perhaps we both had something to learn of my body. I closed my eyes and pulled the shift over my head, leaving me in only my underwear. I felt his fingertips trace over my shoulder and down.

Opening my eyes when he traced the swell of my breast, I watched him regard me with silent reverence. Across the top of my breast, sliding along the side, the backs of his fingers dragging over my stomach until his hand disappeared around my back, reaching and drawing me toward him in a loving embrace.

"I do not fear your body, Kate," he whispered. "I want to learn."

As uncomfortable as I felt all day with my body and its natural reaction to life, Nathan's words wiped those feelings away in a moment and I snuggled in beside him, enjoying the pleasured sigh from him when our skin connected. He pulled the covers up over us and wrapped his arms around me protectively.

"What does it feel like for you?" he whispered.

I turned my head to meet his eyes.

"What do you mean?"

"I mean when this happens to you. Besides your emotions, how does it affect you?" he asked.

I smirked when he mentioned my emotions. Nathan was at least poetic enough not to call it a mood swing. But the rest — how do you describe your monthly cycle to your husband, who has no idea?

"I feel crabby and bloated and tired and gross and sensitive and headachy," I said in a rush.

Honesty always seemed to work best with us.

He looked a little perplexed and I had to giggle. He looked down at me, even more confused.

"It passes, Nathan. I feel a lot better now than I did this morning. Can we just stop discussing it now?" I pleaded, shaking my head with growing embarrassment.

He nodded and pulled me back to him, but I could tell he was still thinking about it. I let him dwell in his quiet thoughts until I couldn't stand it anymore.

"Ask your questions, Nathan," I said, a little exasperated.

His arm tightened around me, a soft chuckle echoing in the room.

"I wondered why you were less enthusiastic this morning when we woke up. I was afraid perhaps you had grown tired of me," he said, and I could hear the mirth in his voice.

"Maybe just this morning," I said, pretending to sound grumpy.

"So we should not make love," he stated.

My head shot up off his chest, his statement catching me off guard. His eyes widened and he looked a little fearful.

"I just mean now," he said hurriedly. "That this is not a good time to share ourselves."

I stared at him.

"What?" he said, worrying his lip.

I continued to stare at him.

"I mean, you are not feeling like yourself, so it would be wise, right?" he continued.

I finally closed my mouth long enough to swallow in order to answer.

"You surprise me every day, Nathan," I whispered.

"I surprise you?" he asked, genuinely confused now.

"Just when I feel like I should be treated like I have the plague, you say something like that," I said.

He shifted in the bed and shrugged.

"I do not understand how it works, Kate. This is not something I would ask Benjamin or Mark. Maybe Jonah, since he is a healer," he said, pursing his lips.

"I just thought you'd be disgusted by me when I'm like this," I said, wrinkling my nose.

He laughed and shook his head, pulling me close to brush his lips to mine.

"You will always be desired, Kate," he murmured.

I slid in next to him once more, my hand resting on his chest while I thought of what he suggested.

"I think I'd like to just be like this on these days," I whispered, still a little uncomfortable with my own body at the moment.

"All right," he said quietly, and hugged me a little closer.

I thought about what Hannah had said earlier in the day. That it wouldn't be long before we were all pregnant. At the rate Nathan and I were going, that seemed likely. And in some ways that frustrated me. I liked our time together, and becoming pregnant would shorten that intimacy. But then again, it would stop this awkwardness between us every month as well.

One thing or the other.

Either way it would affect the two of us.

It seemed silly to worry about my monthly now.

"Just this month," I amended. "We'll see about next month."

"Whatever you wish. I am just happy to have you in my arms,

Kate," he replied with a yawn.

I let him drift off to sleep, thinking about the future.

And how Nathan would react when the monthlies stopped coming.

I wondered if I was ready for that.

My dreams that night were full of vivid images of extended bellies.

And pumpkin butter and biscuits.

Hannah was right. I'd soon see.

23

With winter comes the cold. That bone chilling cold that seeps into you and refuses to let go.

December started with our first snowfall, and with it I learned that snow in California and snow in Iowa were two very different things. In California, it was wet, soaking into your clothes and leaving you forever cold no matter how dry or warm you tried to get. In Iowa, the snow was drier, mostly. But with the Iowa snow also came the wind.

Travelling to the new barn and back, with the snow swirling around me, the wind cutting through my layers made me question which was worse.

Wet or wind?

And to hear that this winter had started late only disheartened me more.

Nathan spoke of snow from November through March.

Five solid months of cold bracing wind.

And all I could think about was that I needed more stockings and sweaters.

I needed to learn how to knit.

It was difficult to stay warm in the large house, except perhaps at night.

At night, Nathan laughed at me with my socks and extra blankets while I snuggled into him, at least until I slid in one night without my socks and snuck my cold feet up on the backs of his thighs. I snickered and threatened to wear my full stockings unless he let me keep my socks on.

Skin on skin was fine, but my toes would be frostbitten if I didn't have my socks.

Nathan suffered through my need for some clothes; as long as he could feel me against him he seemed content. And making love to him before we gave in to our exhaustion from the day was always a pleasant way to warm the bed.

As promised, with the winter snow came more time alone in the house. Chores were limited to taking care of the livestock and keeping the house. We worked as a team in the barn, Nathan mucking out the stalls while I milked the cows or groomed the horses. Magnus preferred his warm cozy stall to the pasture, but they spent many days out in the field burrowing their noses through the snow to find a scrap of grass before making their way back to the barn, fresh hay and feed waiting for them.

Magnus may have become a bit plumper than Nathan liked.

But I held up my promise to my big black horse and spoiled him every chance I could.

He especially liked the warm mush I brought him on Sunday mornings before we hitched him up to the buggy for Sermon. He was more willing to brave the cold for several hours with a warm belly.

By early December, Hannah was showing signs of being with child. Emma and I were still without, and while Emma fretted about not being pregnant, I silently thanked the powers that be that I was not yet with child.

Was that wrong?

I knew Nathan wanted a family.

I knew that our way thrived on having large families. It was how we survived on such a large farm. But on nights when I watched Nathan fall away into bliss as he released into my body, as I felt my own passion explode within me, I wished for just a little longer in getting to know my husband before we took that next leap.

Perhaps it was God's way of allowing us that bit of pleasure.

Unencumbered.

Just husband and wife.

Perhaps it was meant to be.

We would still get by, even if our family was delayed a bit, just like Fannie and Jonah, and Nathan's parents. We would see a way through the spring and the following harvest.

Just Nathan and me.

The beginning of January came with the big storm everyone was dreading. A heavy wet snow that fell for three days, the first day marked with dark clouds and a cutting wind that nearly blew me to the ground when I tried to walk to the barn.

Nathan insisted I stay inside, so I hunkered down and tried to warm the house by cooking, and sealing the windows as best I could. The draft in the front room was especially bad on the first night; I finally tacked up a thick blanket to the window and pulled out a quilt from the closet to keep me warm on the sofa while I tried to finish knitting my long socks.

With the snowstorm came the inability to go to Sermon and to even walk to the Berger's. We didn't mind so much, preferring to stay inside wrapped up in each other. I learned quickly that Nathan didn't mind leftovers if I made enough for a couple of days, and he could take care of the animals in the same amount of time it took me to make us a hearty breakfast. So after that first day with the wind and three feet of snow, Nathan didn't complain about following me back up to our bedroom and snuggling under our quilts.

On the morning of the third day of the snowstorm, Nathan woke early, whispering for me to stay in bed. I was exhausted from the night before, so I murmured in agreement and was soon fast asleep once more. It was only when I felt an icy nose in between my shoulder blades that I woke up fully and yelped. Nathan's cold body snuggled into mine, my own fighting to keep from shivering.

"You're so cold!" I exclaimed and wriggled against him to try and create a little heat.

"It is freezing out there," he grumbled and tucked in tighter to my warmth.

His cold hands enveloped my breasts and I gasped at the shock of it.

And the incredibly intense feeling it offered.

He chuckled and brushed across my hard nipples playfully.

"That was quick," he teased and rolled his thumb over them, causing me to moan at their aching.

"Because you are like an ice cube!" I growled and took his hands and moved them down to my stomach, pushing further down.

One thing you learn in the wilds of California is that the warmest part of one's body is the lower abdomen. And perhaps in between one's legs.

He groaned and wiggled his fingers in between my thighs, the heat of me warming him and the movement making me hotter still. I giggled when he tried wiggling them closer to the heat. It wasn't like I didn't know where we were heading. We had spent most of last night wrapped around one another. So as I turned around to face him, I knew instantly from his playful smile and wandering warmed hands, we'd be a while before venturing downstairs for left over breakfast casserole.

"I am cold in other places as well," he whispered before kissing me.

Oh yes, warming one another in the dead of winter was perhaps my favorite thing about the season.

I never wanted to leave the bed.

Unfortunately, our daily lives still included things like eating and taking care of our livestock, even if the rest of the time could be spent together. But as the nights grew colder, and the days grew shorter, I found myself wishing for the bed more and more, if only to sleep in the warmth Nathan provided.

I yawned over the stew I was making and shook my head to wake myself.

I didn't know why I was so tired. I had slept well the night before, Nathan taking pity on my sore body and simply snuggling with me all night. It was a little strange; I nodded off shortly after dinner for the last few days, and our nights of keeping warm by making love had left me in need of a day or two off to recuperate.

So when Nathan noticed I was dragging from fatigue, he showered me with gentle caresses and let me sleep. He took over the barn duties completely, worried I might catch a cold in the still bitter weather outside. I knew he worried about me getting sick, so I didn't argue.

And truth be told, the less I went out into the cold, the better I felt.

So I stayed inside and baked and cleaned and sorted out plans for the spring.

But the yawning needed to stop.

I heard the back door open and close, listening as Nathan stomped his feet in the mudroom before venturing into the kitchen.

"If it is possible, it is colder out there!" he called as he pulled off his coat and layers of clothes.

I shivered when I felt his arms wrap around me, his nose burying deep into the crook of my neck in what was becoming his favorite way of warming his face when he came inside.

"You are so warm," he hummed and took a deep breath. "And whatever you are making smells amazing."

I smiled and offered him a spoon to taste.

"I used to call this Hodge Podge at home," I said, smiling when he took another spoonful and nodded in approval.

"What is in it?" he asked, licking his lips clean.

"Anything you want to use to get rid of," I said smiling. "We had a few vegetables and ground beef I wanted to use up, as well as tomatoes, corn and noodles. It's a hodge podge of goodness."

He pulled me close and kissed me sweetly, grinning down at me as his hands wandered.

"I will be fat like Magnus if you keep this up," he joked.

I shook the spoon at him and scowled.

"You better still be feeding Magnus my goodies. I promised him," I said warningly.

Nathan pulled in behind me and held me close while I stirred the pot once more.

"He is a horse, Kate. He will be fine with all I give him," he said and I simply shook my head.

Magnus was a lot more than simply a big, dumb plough horse.

I wasn't going to argue that with Nathan, though.

Especially when he was currently cupping my breasts and kissing my neck.

"You feel good against me," he groaned and cupped my breasts a little more firmly, making me jump at their sensitivity.

He pulled away and looked down at me worriedly.

"Did I hurt you?"

I shook my head and pulled him close again.

"No, I'm just a little sensitive today," I said and smiled. "I am probably close to my monthly."

He nodded and chewed on his lip at my mentioning the dreaded monthly event.

He was still a little unnerved by my moods when they came.

I was sure that was why I was so tired as well, as I thought on it.

I turned and plated up our supper, while Nathan cleaned up from his chores.

Supper was a quiet affair, Nathan watching me thoughtfully as I fought back a few yawns and picked at my meal. I wasn't especially hungry, having snacked on the pumpkin loaf I had made earlier. He didn't say anything about my appetite, but I could tell by his watchful gaze he worried about me. Again I assured him I was simply tired and we made our way early up to bed to snuggle and enjoy simply holding one another.

I slept hard and woke up feeling tired again the following day, and then the day after that as well.

Fannie and Jonah came over to have Sunday meal with us, the weather still too troublesome to go much farther than the neighbor's house to visit. We settled into our meal and caught up on how things were developing in the community. Jonah, being the healer, got out much more than anyone else.

"Benjamin has been staying with the Yoders," Jonah began, smiling.

"He is getting along better with his father, then?" Nathan asked as he speared a potato.

"It seems so. They have been busy with plans for the mill, and Benjamin has asked about the land across from yours. It seems he wants to settle down somewhere," Jonah replied simply.

I listened as the men continued to talk, feeling Fannie move in beside me with the rest of the dishes to help clean up. She was quiet, but I could tell in my periphery that she was watching me.

I finally turned to her and tilted my head in question.

She chuckled and shook her head.

"You look tired," she said. "But you glow as if happy. Has Nathan been keeping you up late?"

I blushed and turned back to the dishes.

"I've been a little tired the last week or so. I think it's the combination of being holed up in this house and my monthly coming," I said and frowned as I thought on that a little harder.

Fannie noticed my frown and cleared her throat, drawing my attention back to her.

"Winter does that, true," she murmured and smiled again.

She slipped into conversation about Hannah, and how she was showing signs of having twins. She had grown in size in just the last month, and when the road cleared, Jonah planned to take her to the clinic to have an ultrasound.

"You should come with us," Fannie suggested with a smile.

"To get you out of the house."

I nodded and asked about Emma. I missed my sister.

"She and John are doing well. They should be at the house next week if the weather improves," she said and changed the subject to other events around town.

I knew she didn't want to discuss how worried Emma was about getting pregnant.

But I had faith that it was just a matter of time.

After all, I wasn't pregnant yet, either. And it was already late January.

Fannie and Jonah left after dessert, Fannie hugging me tightly and reminding me about joining them in town with Hannah in a couple of days. We waved them off and quickly hurried back inside to the warmth of our home, Nathan ushering me up the stairs when he noticed me yawning.

We collapsed into bed, Nathan propped up on his elbow as he traced his fingers over my skin. We had spent the last week or so simply enjoying one another's touch rather than being more amorous. His hand lingered over one breast, his eyes enthralled when he cupped it lightly.

"You look beautiful right now," he whispered, leaning in to brush the top of my breast with his lips. "Your breasts look fuller tonight."

I scoffed at him and made to brush his hand away teasingly.

"I'm gaining weight from eating so much and not working," I retorted.

He let his hands move down my waist and lingered on my hips, his eyes growing darker as he took in my body before him.

"It is not a bad thing," he whispered. "There is more color in your skin, and heat."

He leaned down to kiss my hip, skirting his fingertips across my belly before he laid his head against the softness there, watching as his fingers as they glided across my thighs. I felt my body responding to him, the heat building as his fingers traced slowly upwards.

"Are you too tired?" he whispered, and I knew he was asking

if he could make love to me.

"I would never deny you. I need you," I replied huskily and sighed when he moved against me, slow and tender.

He was gentle as he made love to me, whispering softly against my ear as he found me. My name tripped off his lips again and again as we moved against one another. When we finally needed more, he simply held me tighter and rocked against me with a little more enthusiasm, sighing into my ear when he felt me quiver beneath him. He curled up against me, one hand lazily thrown over my stomach as he relaxed afterwards. He was quiet for sometime, his mouth leaving soft kisses against my neck. His quiet voice broke me out of my reverie.

"It has been over a month. Is that typical?" he asked against my neck.

My hand stalled in his hair at his question.

"What do you mean?"

He lifted his head up and looked down at my body once more, a deeper love in his eyes than I had ever seen.

"Jonah said something tonight that made me think," he said, his brow creasing slightly.

"What?" I asked, growing a little anxious at his serious look.

"It has been over a month, Kate. And your body is fatigued. Jonah mentioned your color was more pronounced," he continued, tracing his fingers over my stomach once more.

My brain slowly clicked into place, at where he was going in the conversation.

His eyes travelled back up to meet mine, a tender smile on his face as he laid his had gently over my stomach.

"Perhaps," he whispered and leaned in to kiss me when my eyes grew wider at the thought as it popped into my head.

I was late.

I was tired.

I was glowing.

Nathan's smile seemed to confirm it. Like he could sense it.

I was pregnant.

Following that night of revelations, his demeanor changed in regard to everything I did. Every day he asked how I felt, and over and over again he denied me certain jobs around the house. Normal chores that I would have always done, he now took over for me. First it was too cold. I might get sick and that was bad. Then I couldn't carry the laundry down the stairs, I might fall. I couldn't carry it back up the stairs either, for I might hurt myself straining. Now it was the horse stalls.

"I will do that, you should not exert yourself."

I rolled my eyes and handed him the shovel roughly, too tired to fight him on whether or not I was too fragile to scoop up horse poop.

"Can I feed them while you do that then? Is that too strenuous?" I asked in an exasperated sigh, and I knew he would take it hard.

I didn't mean to be mean, but I was finding that all I could do lately was stand around. Maybe cook if it didn't involve carrying a heavy roast.

And I didn't want to think about the sex.

Nathan would get me all bothered by him touching me, tracing my skin and fondle my apparently bigger breasts, only to say he didn't want to hurt me and then tuck me firmly into his arms so I could rest.

I was ready to burst from need.

I didn't need more sleep. I really needed more of him.

Maybe I was feeling more now that I was pregnant.

Well, we thought I was pregnant.

The roads were clear enough so that we could take Hannah for her ultrasound. I would find out tomorrow for sure. But it had been six weeks now since my last period; I had finally marked it down. There was no denying it anymore.

I was most definitely pregnant and being treated like a piece of crystal.

Nathan hadn't said anything in response to my quip about feeding the horses, but when I went out to grab the feedbag, he was right behind me, hauling it over his shoulder so I didn't have to carry it.

I turned and left him in the barn.

It was obvious nothing in there was safe enough for me to do.

I made myself busy gathering eggs and taking them back to the house.

I'd just cook then.

And maybe mop the floors, for the tenth time in two days.

Men infuriated me.

And I really missed my passionate Nathan who liked having sex outside the bedroom now.

Well, not now.

That could hurt me.

At least the floors would be clean. And there was always baking.

I had enough loaves of bread in the freezer now to feed a small country.

Stupid overprotective men.

Even on the day of our trip, he seemed overprotective.

"Do you want me to go with you? I can go. You might need me."

Nathan had asked me so many times now I almost wanted to simply say yes so he would stop asking me.

"No," I said dismissively for the hundredth time. "I'm going with Fannie and Hannah. I'll be fine. And you have to meet up with Mark and John. I will be fine."

He frowned as he did every time he asked and held me a little closer when we knocked on the Berger's door. I know he wanted to hear the news first. And in many ways I wanted him there with me, but I was also afraid that if the news was negative, he would have to hear it then, and I didn't want to see his disappointment with Hannah there. I would feel like a failure. I had spent the last few days being either immensely excited or terrified about the prospect that I was pregnant.

And now that we were heading to the clinic to get Hannah checked out, I knew that Fannie had intended to confirm what everyone suspected. Nathan stayed near me while we made arrangements to leave. Hannah quirked her eyebrow at me when he helped me into the buggy, but I ignored her silent question. I was nervous enough without having to explain his obsessive care of me.

Jonah was climbing into the buggy when we heard another rolling in beside us. I watched as John and Emma climbed out, John looking after Emma as she scrambled up, wedging herself into place beside Hannah and me.

"I thought we were picking you up at your home?" Jonah asked as he waved to the young men left behind and started us out.

"John wanted to come here. He said he had to speak with Mark and Nathan," she said quietly and looked back where we had come.

I glanced back to see all three of our husbands looking after us as we left, Mark the only one smiling as he pretended to punch Nathan in the shoulder. I shook my head to the thoughts milling around in there and turned to Emma.

She seemed deep in thought as we rode, her arms wrapped around herself as if cold. It was indeed cold as we travelled toward town, but I knew she had to be withdrawn by the circumstances of our town trip. I wrapped my arm around her and drew her to me, feeling her stiff body in my grasp.

Perhaps I was not the only one who was nervous for this visit.

Had Fannie asked Emma to come also? Could she possibly be pregnant?

I hoped Emma was pregnant. It would be exciting to go through this with someone close, and Hannah was so far along already, she'd have her babies before I was even showing. I glanced at Emma again and caught her looking at me.

Her stare caught me off guard. It was a little glazed as if she was daydreaming.

"What is it?" I whispered.

She blinked and looked down, blushing.

"I was thinking about what it would be like if you and I were with child," she replied softly and nodded toward Hannah.

"Look at how happy she is," she continued and I looked over my shoulder at Hannah, who was knitting as we rode. It looked like a small pair of booties in her hands. But her face was radiant and she wore a small smile on her face while she worked.

It was true.

Hannah was happy.

"You seem happy as well," Emma whispered, drawing my attention back to her.

I nodded and smiled.

"I am. Nathan makes me so. I have never been more happy," I replied and knew that was the truth. I had never been happier than I was living here.

Emma sighed and leaned into me, as if she had lost all her energy. It was worrisome how much she seemed defeated and forlorn suddenly. I held her close to me on the trip, knowing that when we got to the clinic, things would change.

We'd find out about Hannah.

And everyone would find out about me.

And instead of being overjoyed about it, I worried.

I worried that Emma would not get the same news.

So as I sat there in the exam room, I couldn't help but listen to the conversation in the room beside me. The walls were extremely thin and I could hear the sound of the ultrasound beating away. I heard Hannah's laughter, followed by Fannie's, and knew that they had confirmed the possibility of twins.

Hannah was asking about whether they were boys or girls.

I was distracted from the answer by a knock on the door. I relaxed when I saw Jonah step in.

"How are you, daughter?" he asked softly and sat close beside me in the empty doctor's chair.

"Nervous," I said truthfully. "How is Emma?"

He looked down at his hands to hide the sad frown.

"She is getting changed and said she would meet us in the front," he replied quietly.

He didn't need to tell me what her little stick had said. I held mine in my shaking hand.

Definitely positive, the doctor had said brightly with a smile and a nod of congratulations. We were just waiting on the real test they did with my blood to confirm it.

"She'll be sad," I said, his head nodding for a moment before he sighed.

"She knows it will take time. She has been through much the last two seasons. It will take some time," he said and looked up at me with a soft smile.

He patted my knee and glanced at the stick in my hand.

"You and Nathan were expecting this answer?"

I nodded and swallowed.

I was still feeling some worry interlaced with happiness.

How did I act around Emma?

"It is good news, I know the family will be overjoyed."

I smiled down at my adoptive father's proud eyes and reached out to put my free hand over his. We heard the doctor finish up with Hannah, and a few moments later he came back in to speak with us. He glanced at Jonah with a broad smile and shook his hand.

"You will be a busy man this season! With the twins and then with your daughter here, I know Fannie is beside herself with preparations already!" the older man said as he settled in to the seat that Jonah had vacated.

"It will be a busy time that we will welcome," Jonah said and looked at me thoughtfully.

"Would you like me to stay?" he asked softly.

I blushed and shook my head.

I still had to get used to the idea that he would help deliver my baby. But I had questions I wanted to ask the doctor that I didn't really want my father hearing. He nodded and smirked before stepping out, leaving me alone with the doctor.

The doctor looked over my charts, his glasses falling down his nose many times before he finally looked up at me with cheerful blue eyes. He was grey and clean-shaven, which was a little odd to look at now that I had lived in the community for so many months, but he had a kind smile and was friendly as he spoke to me.

"The tests are positive," he said simply. "Probably about four weeks, if your last cycle was about six weeks ago."

I nodded and he continued.

"Jonah tells me you came from the outside world, so I assume you had some health classes that your sisters may not have?"

Again I nodded. I remembered the class in high school about childcare. I had hated that silly flour sack child we had taken care of. Now I had wished I had paid more attention in the class. And maybe not dropped the sack so many times. I was doomed to drop my child one or several times.

"Any questions you have that maybe you can't ask your father?" he asked gently.

"Um," I said, hesitating.

It was awkward even to speak with the doctor, knowing he knew Jonah.

"Is your husband excited about this?"

"Oh, yes. Very much so. He's been very careful with me this last week or so, since we suspected," I said quietly and felt the blush rise in my cheeks.

"Careful how?" he asked. "You know that the human body is fairly sturdy, and being pregnant doesn't necessarily precipitate needing to bubble wrap you."

I laughed at the image. It was a little like what Nathan had done all this week. It had been maddening.

"So I can still help out in shoveling out the barn and things like that?" I asked, smiling.

He laughed and nodded.

"I am always surprised by the Amish women, to tell you the truth. I see pregnant women out in the field beside their husbands up until they give birth, sometimes returning to the work with a newborn wrapped tightly against them," he said and leaned back. "But the young couples are usually very careful with their first time. The husband doesn't allow her to do more strenuous chores, or even have sex during the pregnancy. But it is perfectly safe for someone as healthy as you."

I sat up a little straighter.

"So, I can work around the house as usual and still be intimate with my husband?"

I whispered, to which he laughed and nodded.

"With moderation, of course. Typical chores will actually help to keep you in shape and healthy. You should not overwork yourself. Nor should you be overly affectionate in your private activities. Perhaps different positions when it becomes difficult for you as you grow," he said and cleared his throat.

He looked at me intently, trying to clarify without using words as to what he meant.

I had a pretty good idea.

I simply nodded.

He let out a breath and looked back at my chart, moving on with his lecture. I supposed he wasn't used to an Amish wife asking about having sex with her husband. It wasn't something we talked about after all.

"Your iron levels are low, so I am giving you prenatal vitamins to take, you should be sure you are eating enough meat and vegetables too," he continued and went down the list of basic prenatal things a new mom needed to know.

I listened in a sort of daze, excited by this news even more, now that I knew I was not some fragile thing that Nathan feared I was. The last few days had been a challenge for me with him. I knew we'd be having a talk when we were alone.

I fully intended on taking back some of my duties.

Outside and in.

24

Emma was quiet as we rode back, listening to me answer some of the questions and advice Hannah had for me. I felt uncomfortable talking to Hannah about what to expect, thinking again and again that it was something that Emma and Hannah should be sharing, not me. I distanced myself from conversation finally, holding onto Emma's hand in a quiet way to show her that I cared.

She squeezed my hand and offered me a tender smile, but stayed quiet for the rest of the ride.

It was more somber than it should have been.

Hannah was having twins, and I was with child.

The Berger home would be crawling with grandbabies before long.

But we knew talking about it would upset Emma.

So when we finally made it home, I hugged Emma as she made to leave with her husband. John seemed to know what the results would be. He quietly congratulated me and took his wife in his arms, spiriting her off as only John could. I saw the beginnings of a smile on her face, the first of the day, and knew that they would be working hard to catch up. That in itself made me smile.

Emma had a good husband in John. Always supportive and loving unconditionally.

I glanced at Nathan as I said my own goodbyes, his smile beaming while Mark slapped him on the back again. Hannah was neatly tucked into Mark's giant one-armed embrace, his eyes beaming down at his proud wife. We had all been amazingly lucky with our husbands. I felt a moment's guilt in thinking Nathan was being too protective of me. He had been only trying to take care of me.

My internal argument with him fizzled as we walked hand in hand back to the house, his shining smile reminding me again what he had said.

He would be there for me. No matter what, and he was.

We just needed to set some ground rules now that another person was involved.

He was quiet as I made a quick supper from leftovers. As I brought the food to the table he finally pulled me into a hug and held me hard.

"Are you still upset?"

I pulled away a little and looked up at him in question.

"What do you mean upset?" I asked.

He held me around the waist, looking down between us, his eyes bashful.

"For being so protective of you. Mark laughed at me for half the day when I told him what I did," he mumbled.

"Do you tell them everything?" I asked, a little irritated. I didn't tell my sisters everything.

His eyebrows shot up at my tone and he shook his head emphatically.

"No, really I do not," he said in a rush, relaxing some when I patted him on the cheek and pulled him down to sit.

"What did you say then to make Mark laugh at you?" I asked, my tone reassuring that I wasn't upset with him.

He rubbed at the back of his neck and let out an embarrassed laugh.

"I told him you were upset with me for not letting you do the chores," he started and I nodded in agreement.

"I was upset with you, but we're going to fix that right now," I said, watching his eyes widen once more. I shook my head and put up my hand.

"I understand you want to protect me, Nathan. But the doctor says I can do my share of the chores," I argued.

He let out a breath and I couldn't help but scowl when I saw his brow furrow.

"Can we discuss that?" he asked.

"Why don't you want me doing the chores in the barn, Nathan? Or carry clothes, or hitch the buggy? I can do those things," I said, my determination growing stronger.

"I overreacted," he whispered, and then his eyes drew up to capture mine, and I saw it then.

That fear he had. The one I saw when we talked about his family, or when I had been kidnapped.

He was so afraid of being alone.

"I don't want to lose you. Is it wrong that I want to make sure you are safe, always?" he asked, almost pleading.

I touched his cheek, my ire suddenly gone. His family's deaths would always be his burden.

"I'm not going anywhere. I won't get hurt by doing my chores," I replied softly.

"What if the horses spook?"

"They won't."

"What if you fall?"

"I won't."

"What if you get sick? You are more susceptible now."

I took his head in my hands and kissed him hard, shutting up his nonsense.

"Women have been doing this for a very long time, Nathan. I

can do this," I whispered.

He closed his eyes and let out a long breath.

"That is what Mark said," he replied. "Can I at least be the one to muck out the stalls?"

"No."

He opened his eyes at my answer, shocked by my resolute answer. I shook my head at him.

"Partnership, Nathan. We are in this together. And the doctor said I could do these things, within reason. I can do my fair share for a while still," I replied.

He thought about my request for a while, rubbing the back of my hand as he processed my words.

"Just promise me you will not over do it?" he begged, a hint of a smile fighting his lips.

"I won't go join the rodeo with Magnus, okay?" I said, trying to be light.

"I will always worry, Kate. Just promise me you will not try to prove yourself. You have done so much for me already," he asked, still serious.

"I promise."

He tugged me close and kissed me tenderly, our dinner long forgotten until he finally broke off the kiss with a low moan.

"Kate," he groaned and let out another long breath. I could tell he was struggling to behave.

"Oh, right. That's the other thing," I said, his eyes opening up to find mine.

"What other thing?" he croaked.

I let my hands slowly trace beside his suspenders, holding him in place when I reached his trousers. He swallowed and made to pull away, only my hands had a firm grip on his waistband, barring him from distancing himself from me.

"Another thing the doctor told me, Nathan," I whispered, raising an eyebrow at him when he jumped at my hand as it ventured further south.

"Kate."

"Don't 'Kate' me, Nathan Solomon Fisher," I growled. "You and I are getting naked tonight and I am going to show you that it's okay to make love to your wife while she's pregnant. Doc says so."

His mouth opened and closed, as if he were fighting a losing argument.

"He said it was all right?" he asked instead.

"Yep, he even suggested different positions when I get all big and gross," I said, matter of fact.

Nathan's grin broke out across his face, and I didn't have time to react when he scooped me up into his arms and all but ran up the stairs into our bedroom. He laid me down on the bed carefully and slid in over me, careful not to crush me.

"Firstly, Kate," he said against my neck. "You will never be big and gross, you will be beautiful always."

His mouth found mine and he kissed me fully, leaving me breathless.

"Is there a secondly?" I asked breathlessly when his lips moved to my jaw.

He looked down at me with his playful eyes and grinned.

"Secondly," he said, reaching for the clasps to my dress. "Secondly, I have some catching up to do. I have neglected you for too long and I want to discover these new positions with my wife."

I let out a low moan when his hands found me, so sure and earnest in making me want to feel pleasure.

"Supper?" I gasped, my thoughts scattering at his touch.

"Later. This is what I wish to feast on," he growled and his lips moved down to find my breasts.

Supper was long ruined before we even thought to eat, breakfast perhaps being the better choice given the hour that we finally chose to venture out of our bedroom.

It was difficult to tell. It was still dark out, and a heavy snow was falling once again.

Nathan didn't argue when I dressed with him and made our

way to the barn to get the morning chores completed.

Many hands make fast work, after all.

And I had every intention of getting those chores done quickly.

Our warm house was calling.

That warm house was a Godsend when it snowed, non-stop it seemed, for half of February.

Not that I minded so much.

It was cold when we went out to Sermon. It was cold when we had chores to do.

But the rest of the time it was very, very warm.

Nathan made sure of that.

We used our fireplace in the sewing room on many nights.

And the sewing room now had a permanent stack of pillows and blankets to lay on in front of the fire. Nathan always tried to pass off our fireplace lounging as an excuse to read and cuddle. But that usually lasted about as long as getting through one or two pages of verse before I was kissing him and slipping my hands under his shirt and down.

My hormones may have been a little off kilter.

I thought Nathan had been the insatiable one.

But once the initial fatigue wore off, I was full of energy when it came to being with Nathan. There was something about his scent, while he lay there cradling me in his arms with a roaring fire beside us. Or when he laid in bed, exhausted from making love, warm and relaxed beside me. Or when he came in from outside and his cold nose trailed along my neck.

There was a lot about Nathan Fisher that made my heart race.

But it was amplified now.

I could smell more. And his scent when sated only excited me more.

I could taste more. And I really enjoyed the taste of Nathan.

I could feel more. Every touch on my skin aroused me.

And Nathan loved to touch me. Every inch of my skin he

traced, every night. It was as if he wanted to mentally document every little change in my body.

My breasts grew fuller within the first month.

My hips were more pronounced the second month.

And into the beginning of March, his hands cupped the small bump along my belly, his eyes always so full of wonder at my changing body.

He swore I glowed.

He kissed every new part of me he noticed had changed, and every day he whispered against my belly. I couldn't hear what he said, but I know whatever it was made him happier with each passing day.

Every day he said I was more beautiful than the day before.

Every day he traced my stretching and growing skin.

Every day he made me feel the love he held for me.

Every day I felt something new.

One entire day I cried, panicked that I would be a horrible mother. Nathan ultimately had to hold me all night, whispering that I was everything he wanted in a wife and the mother of his children.

Another day I was frustrated and moody. It was a good time for Nathan to go with John to mend the Wittmer barn. By nightfall I was myself again. And the house was extra clean.

Yet another day I slept the day away, comforted only by Nathan's soft touch and whispered words in my ear while he read to me.

My hormones were the hardest part of my pregnancy. I had been blessed to have no signs of morning sickness and the only craving I truly had was for butter. Nathan made a deal with the Snyders for more butter and I was content. And I ate a lot of butter lately.

On bread.

On biscuits.

On everything I could.

I wondered if perhaps that would change when spring finally

came and we could eat fresher foods. I looked forward to spring and its fresh, clean air. I had been cooped up for long enough in the house for winter. I wanted to start planting and preparing our farm again.

It was with the first thaw that we heard the news about Emma.

She practically danced into the Berger home, her energy brightening an already cheerful kitchen. I knew instantly. Call it pregnancy code.

Fannie seemed to already know as she hugged her youngest daughter tight and cried happy tears at the news.

John stood proudly, so like Nathan had, and Mark before him.

Proud fathers-to-be stood around the kitchen table while their precious women hugged one another tight.

Emma held me for a long time, crying softly into my shoulder until she could finally breathe and looked up at me with glistening eyes.

"It will be the best thing," she whispered and looked between Hannah and myself. "We will have each of our children within a few months. Mother will have her hands full with grandchildren and our babies will grow up together, like one large family."

It was a wonderful feeling being in the arms of my sisters, making me a little nostalgic for my own sister in the English world.

Often on days where I felt truly blessed in the ways of my Amish family, I wondered about my sister, Stacy, and what she was doing. And how I hoped she had found a similar happiness as I had. My Amish family had given me so much, and we continued to grow.

A large family offered bountiful love for all.

Something I had never known, but now knew would be how I should have lived all my life. Children running around, full of life and love. And a wonderful husband who looked at me each day the same way he had the first day he knew he loved me.

As winter fell away to spring a sense of excitement coursed

through us as life began again. A new life with a new start. The snow that had covered the sleeping ground soon melted into the earth, nurturing it so that it would be ready for seed.

Nathan spent most of his days in the fields, preparing them for seed while I looked to the garden. Left to myself, I could decide what to plant for the season. The year's crops were more complicated than I imagined, having never worked on a farm before.

Nathan patiently talked through the necessity for fast growing vegetables versus a garden full of slow growers, and soon we had varying degrees of growth in our new garden. It was amazing to me to find that within a month or so, I had the beginnings of a menu from which to pluck fresh vegetables, setting aside the canned greens for fresh ones.

With spring also came less time for idle hands, and I soon discovered that working on a farm, and trying to make some sort of wage to keep that farm successful, came with the price of alone time with my husband. We woke early, sometimes eager, but most times tired, and hurried to start the day to get as much done as we could with only our own hands.

Nathan opened up his acreage to others, delighted that the Bowmans and the Wittmers were the first to accept our sharecropping idea. I saw much of John and Mark as the tilling and planting commenced, which meant my sisters joined me many times a week to help with feeding their husbands. When they were not in our fields, I visited Hannah and Emma in their homes and helped out where I could.

It seemed pregnancy favored me more than my sisters as spring crept forward. I seemed to have more energy most days, eating more but never having any serious cravings like my sisters did. I enjoyed baking more, much to Nathan's enjoyment, and the fact that he filled out well in the winter and spring was noted by many women at Sermons. I gained a new respect from the women of the community for taking care of my husband during the long winter. The only downfall to being pregnant seemed to be my urges, which again, Nathan enjoyed as much as I did.

Emma was put on bedrest in her fourth month when she was told she had an irregular heartbeat due to the pregnancy, and that any hard work, given her medical history, could cause her to lose her child, or her own life.

John was more protective over her than Nathan had ever been with me, but in her case, I did not blame him. She pouted and put up a fuss at first, but with Hannah and Fannie watching over her almost daily, she finally gave in and volunteered to be the seamstress for our families while we handled more rigorous chores for her.

It was what we did, helping each other. My daily walk to visit with my sisters became something I enjoyed immensely. I was able to see the growing green around me start from dark rich earth, sprouting forth in tender vibrant green, to grow and flourish to that rich emerald that covered the landscape around us. Life was thriving everywhere I looked. I had never been so in love with the idea of green before coming to Iowa.

Hannah, with her twins, became more uncomfortable in her own skin as the months passed, and by the time she was at eight months, she waddled slowly here and there and scowled at me when I could still manage to climb into the buggy without assistance to go into town. But for all her fussing, she still smiled more and cradled her giant belly when she thought people were not watching her. I knew from the way Mark doted on her that they would be fantastic parents. Hannah would be stern and protective, while Mark would surely be more carefree, carrying his children on his shoulders whenever he could.

I seemed to expand every day, with proud observations by Nathan whenever we settled into bed at night. He had taken to laying low beside me, one hand tracing over the rise of my belly while his lips worshipped every mark, every change in my skin. I was often left giggling before he would move up to silence my laughter with a searing kiss. Nathan seemed to love me more and more each day, even as I felt myself growing more ungainly. The happiness on his face whenever he glanced my way was worth every cramp and new mark on my body.

His happiness was my happiness, and with each day I grew more excited for every new life lesson I found with him.

We worked together when we could, early mornings in the barn caring for the animals, and often I helped him in the field, having learned to handle the wagon with Magnus. Magnus worked hard for me, much to Nathan's bewilderment. My grandmother had been right when she said a little sugar went a long way to getting a male to do what you wanted.

Be it husbands or stallions, they both enjoyed the sweets I offered them.

As the summer neared, we had the beginnings of a flourishing crop. Nathan helped Jonah every other day with his own lands, leaving me to spend time with Fannie when I wasn't travelling to the Wittmers. Fannie and I developed a blossoming baked goods business that seemed to do well at the Amish co-op. Fannie beamed whenever she had her daughters with her, and when we all spent time at her house, she would nearly burst with excitement in seeing her children come so far.

There was much joy in the Berger household.

Life was good, and getting better with each new day.

It was just a matter of time before the family grew.

25

Screaming.

So much screaming.

Was that normal?

Or was this something more dire?

I swallowed hard and shut my eyes tight, trying to focus.

Screaming again.

I can't.

What was I thinking?

No pain medicine.

Home birth.

All that pushing and screaming.

I can't.

"Kate, it is all right. Breathe."

"That is my job!" Hannah hissed from the edge of her bed before she clamped her eyes shut and started panting again.

I seemed to be panting with her as I stood there helping to hold her knee.

Too close.

Watching, breathing with her. I could almost feel every contraction with her.

And in a few short months I would be in Hannah's place.

"AARGGGHHH!"

Deep breaths.

Something about peaceful images.

"I cannot!"

I opened my eyes to her plaintive cry and her iron grip on my shoulder.

I looked over to find her eyes pleading with me.

"It is all right, Hannah," Mark breathed against her ear, my partner in holding up her knees while she struggled to breathe and push. "He is almost here. Just a little longer."

"I cannot," she whimpered, shaking her head, making her hair stick to her face as it moved.

He wiped it away lovingly and kissed her sweetly against her temple, whispering softly to her as she whimpered at the next contraction.

"Hannah, my sweet wife. It is close, you are doing so well, my Hannah."

My eyes welled up at the interchange between the two.

So much love and affection in this moment; I felt like an intruder.

His soft terms of endearment getting her through the next contraction were enough for her to push again, gripping me harder.

"I cannot!"

Again she looked to me, so scared.

"I am so proud of you, Hannah," Fannie encouraged from in front of us, sitting on a stool with Jonah at the foot of the bed.

I still found the notion of Jonah and Fannie delivering

strange. It was too awkward to see your parents in that position, waiting to catch, as it were.

Soon enough.

I cannot.

"I cannot!"

"Yes you can, Hannah," I said finally, my courage or my absolute terror of what I saw offering me words.

If Hannah couldn't do this, what chance did I have to do it?

"I cannot," she cried and leaned toward me, needing more support.

"You can, Hannah," I continued. "Think about how beautiful they will be when you can finally have them in your arms. Come on, Hannah, you can do it."

I had no idea where the inspirational words came from. Maybe it was what I would want to hear when I was in her place. To hold that life that had been wriggling in your belly, making you eat and eat, and sleep, and wish for an air conditioner under your skirt.

To finally be able to see your feet again.

Hannah choked out a laugh and looked up at me with a strained smile.

"I miss seeing my feet, it is true," she said and then hissed again with the next contraction.

I had no idea I had been talking out loud.

"Push, Hannah! I see a head!" Jonah exclaimed.

"Push, Hannah!" I cried, looking down finally and seeing the dark hair of her first boy showing.

"Almost there!" Mark choked, overcome with emotion seeing the first sight of his son.

Hannah cried out as she pushed, and Mark and I watched in awe as first the head, then one arm made its way out.

"Push!"

And with that third or fourth push it was like a slick football in the rain and mud sliding out.

I understood now why Fannie and Jonah were both there to help.

Slippery and covered in stuff I didn't want to think about, the tiny little being wriggled and arched, Fannie wrapping him quickly and clearing some of the gunk from his mouth with enthusiasm before a tiny little cry lit up the room.

It was the first little cry, followed by two grateful ones from the proud parents.

"Is he?" Hannah asked hoarsely.

"Beautiful," Mark and I chorused.

I turned to look at her as Jonah cut the cord and Fannie pulled away to wipe him down more thoroughly. She brought him over to Hannah and Mark, the moment precious to the both of them as they looked on the first of their twin boys.

"Little Isaac," Hannah whispered.

Mark took their son carefully, a brief bit of fear flitting across his face before the little bundle made a sound. Then Mark was hooked. His eyes lit up and he laughed quietly as he looked between his wife and his new son. That look said everything.

Mark would spoil these children.

Absolutely.

Of course, little Isaac was only the first. There was scarcely any time to spend before Mrs. Bowman took her grandson, and Mark and I were back to coaching Hannah, her face a mixture of joyous determination as she worked to see her second son into the world.

Tiny Simon came a little easier, and a little louder, much to the joy of Mark.

I could see his chest fill with pride as he held Simon in his arms while Hannah looked over at Isaac.

I quietly took the soiled towels out of the room, leaving the new parents and new grandparents to have their private moment. I let out a breath as I closed the door, my emotions scattered. What had started as my daily visit to see Hannah turned into an event where I saw one of the most amazing and terrifying things in my life.

How would I be able to do that?

How had I thought this would be easy, giving up hospitals and epidurals?

"Come, child. I will help you with that," Mrs. Bowman said softly.

I opened my eyes to see Mark's mother waving me toward her.

I offered a weak smile and followed her downstairs to the basement so that we could set the towels to soak. We were silent as we worked, Mrs. Bowman one of those women who seemed intimidating because of her blocky face and tall stature. But she was a strong and loving woman, just more reserved.

"You are blessed this day," Mrs. Bowman said out of the blue.

I turned my head to her in confusion.

"The birth is usually reserved for the husband and Fannie and Jonah," she explained. "Although it was wise to have another hand there. With two babes, you would need another catcher."

"Catcher?" I asked, imagining a baseball catcher in full gear sitting in between my legs.

It was not too far from the truth, judging my Fannie's duties.

Mrs. Bowman laughed and nodded.

"Once you have four or five, it is simply a matter of catching!" she said and made a motion like future babies would just pop right out.

"That is if you even have time to call for one," she continued, seeming to enjoy my wide eyes. "Mark came to me between midday meal and supper. I tell him I sneezed and there he was! And then I was putting the roast in the oven!"

I must have whimpered, because she pulled me close and laughed, sounding like the female version of her son.

She had certainly passed her sense of humor off to her son, Mark.

"It will be fine, Katherine," she chided and helped me up the stairs. "Your husband will be there, and your parents, and you will see. It will be everything you hoped for."

I hoped for painless.

I definitely didn't want to scream like Hannah.

For hours.

Everything I hoped for.

I suppose that meant I would have to endure some pain.

Nothing so incredible could come without hard work.

I was sent to deliver the news to Emma and John, returning just as the afternoon sun disappeared behind the hills. Nathan caught up with me just as I crested the hill to our home. He slipped into step with me, taking my hand tenderly as we walked.

"I take it they have arrived?" he asked, his smile spreading when I nodded.

"Did you see them?" he pressed.

I nodded again.

I saw it all.

"And?"

"It was amazing," I whispered. "And frightening."

"Frightening?" he asked, frowning when he looked down at me.

I was quiet for a moment, trying to put my thoughts together. Everything I had seen was something that women had gone through since the beginning of time. But to see someone as strong as Hannah break down like that, it was frightening.

"I do not know if I am strong enough," I whispered, suddenly ashamed of my fears and reservations.

Nathan wrapped his arm around me and I felt his mouth against my hair for a moment before he pulled away enough to look down at me with such tender eyes.

"You are the strongest woman I know, Kate," he said. "I fear I will be the nervous one when it is our time."

"Why would you be nervous?" I asked.

His face slowly slipped into that worried pucker I saw whenever he thought of his life before I arrived.

"I do not wish to lose you."

I hugged him tight and tossed aside my fears.

"You won't lose me," I replied and held him harder as if to squeeze the thought out of his body.

"We will be together," he murmured. "We can do anything as long as we are together."

And like that, my fears were gone. Brushed aside by Nathan's faith in us.

For now, I was sure we could do this.

Even if it scared me to simply have nothing but faith.

And no pain medication.

Yes. Yes, of course we could do this.

~~~~~

"I think Isaac looks like Mark," Abigail said happily as she folded another pile of diapers in the kitchen. "Simon looks just like what I imagine Hannah looked like as a small baby."

I shook my head and laughed to myself.

The boys were identical twins. And while I knew that Hannah seemed to be able to distinguish between the two, I couldn't. I supposed it came with parenting. Mothers could just tell those things.

What would happen if I had twins?

I touched my belly, already uncomfortably large at seven months and I was only having one baby. I wondered how big Nathan had been when he was born. His mother had had issues giving birth. Perhaps the Fishers had incredibly huge babies. I swallowed and rubbed at my belly once more, hoping for a small and agile baby who could do contortionist acts in order to get out fast.

I had remembered the health classes with the birthing scenes.

And stories of a cracked pelvis, or a fractured tailbone, or ripped...

"Katherine? Are you all right?"

I looked up into Emma's worried eyes and tried to smile.

"Sorry, I was just thinking about having twins," I mumbled. "That must be really hard."

Emma eased herself out of her chair and came over to give me a tender hug.

"I am just happy to have this one. It is up to Him to see if we can handle something like that," she said and then leaned in close. "Hannah can sometimes bark the loudest, so perhaps He thought she could handle a litter."

We both laughed and pulled apart when the men walked in, Mark and John carrying the little bundles and laughing.

Mark had been showing off the boys to Nathan and John, allowing Hannah a few quiet moments to clean up. Judging by their faces, something funny had occurred. Nathan looked a little less amused as he stepped past me to wash up at the sink. His shirt was damp and he began splashing his face with water over the sink.

Mark and John, on the other hand, were dry and grinning.

"Isaac has good distance," Mark said proudly, laughing a little harder when Nathan made a noise over the sink.

"You could have warned me," he groused.

I looked over at Mark with suspicion.

I had an idea of what had happened.

"Did you not warn my husband to cover Isaac before pulling off the diaper?" I scolded.

"He had a younger brother!" Mark explained.

Emma and I both looked at them and shook our heads, pretending to be perturbed.

But it was nothing that hadn't happened to us, either.

Hannah and Mark both seemed to enjoy springing their boys' fountain impersonations on unsuspecting parents-to-be. I had at least ducked and thought to cover little Simon when he tried to pee on me.

I took one baby gently to give John a chance to relax. I

settled into a seat beside Emma so that she could lean in and watch as I rocked Simon to sleep. I only knew it was him from the little cap on his head. His was dark blue, and Isaac's was light blue. It became quiet in the kitchen as the babies settled in our arms. Glancing up, I caught Nathan's eyes on me, the smile creeping onto his freshly washed face as he watched me with the baby in my arms.

It was a special moment, like a brief look into the future when it would be our baby I rocked. Nathan moved closer to me, his hand moving gently to tuck some of the hair that had worked loose back behind my ear. The look in his eyes as he continued to watch me made my heart dance.

This would be us in three months.

And his smile and bright eyes told me that he would cherish every moment.

"May I hold him?" Emma whispered to Mark.

Mark eased Isaac over to Emma's shoulder, her eyes lighting up as she carefully rocked him while she patted his back. I chanced a look at John and saw that same look of adoration in John's eyes. It was strange for me to think that this was not something I had personally experienced in my former life.

Had my dad looked at my mom or me like that?

I turned away and squeezed Nathan's hand in a brief need for comfort. He seemed to sense my distress and leaned in to kiss me tenderly near the ear.

"I cannot wait to have this in our lives," he murmured.

Just a few words and Nathan could make me feel at peace once more.

Thoughts of my biological parents slid away and we enjoyed the afternoon with Hannah and her babies before returning to our own homes. John held Emma more closely as they drove off in his buggy, and Nathan and I slowly made our way back home. The sun had begun to dip, much to my own relief. The early August heat was as I remembered it when I first arrived here over a year ago, and by the time we stepped into our house, I felt like I had walked through a rainstorm.

"You should rest, you look overheated," Nathan commented

as we stepped into the kitchen.

"You have not had supper yet," I replied, rinsing my hands in the cold water. I was tempted to dip my head under the water to cool my neck.

As if he knew, I felt Nathan move behind me, his arms reaching around me with one of the dishcloths to wet it under the cold water. He placed it on my neck, eliciting a long sigh from my lips. I leaned back toward him, rewarded with a brush of his lips along my jaw.

"I think we can finish the bread and the fresh tomatoes you picked for a light supper. Then maybe a cool bath?"

I moaned at the idea of a bath. I felt gross with the constant sweating these days.

The sticky trickle of sweat that would run down my legs as I walked from house to house these days made me think fondly of air conditioning and cool swimming pools.

"All right," I breathed. I couldn't argue with his logic.

He disappeared to draw the bath while I made quick work of sandwiches for supper. It was simple, but perfect on a hot summer night. We retired to the bath, Nathan insisting I enjoy it by myself while he brushed the cloth over my back to cool me off.

How did people in the English world think that we did not have comfort in our simple ways?

Aside from making love to Nathan, having him massage my aching back and cool me down with a wet cloth felt like heaven. He smiled and chuckled with each subtle brush over my sensitive areas, his own needs put to the side in order to please me, even if it was just a touch. I hummed quietly and leaned into him, my hand brushing across his thigh outside the tub. He sighed and bent to kiss my bare shoulder, a smile of contentment on his face.

I stepped out of the bath finally, much cooler and perhaps a little pruny, but Nathan's soft sigh as he slipped into bed with me and snuggled in close made me feel more beautiful than perhaps my ungainly figure made me seem.

"I love to see you like this," he murmured and moved toward his spot by my belly.

His hands caressed over my taut skin, while soft kisses made their way down from my shoulder to the top of my belly. He lingered there, eyes closed and lips heating up my skin, just above my flattened belly button. And then he started with his quiet murmurings.

I chuckled at the tickling of his hair against me and traced my fingers over his forehead, pulling his hair up some so I could see his eyes that were now looking up at me.

"What do you talk about down there?" I whispered, amused.

He looked up a little and the smile on his face made his eyes crinkle.

"That is between me and our little one," he whispered, laughing when I groaned and moved to drag him up.

Nathan crawled up beside me, his hand lingering over my belly as he spooned me close.

His lips were close to my ear.

"I tell him how blessed we are and that I will always be there for him. I tell him I envy him some days, how he gets to be there inside of you and how I wish I could every time I desire it," he whispered breathily against me.

I moved to turn to look at him and he offered me a bashful look.

"I haven't said you couldn't, Nathan," I whispered and moved to turn.

He shook his head and looked a little embarrassed when he held me in place, his body tight against me. I knew he had needs, and I had pleased him many times with my mouth because he asked. But I was beginning to wonder, now that I was so huge, if maybe he didn't want me because of it.

"Do you still want me like that, Nathan?" I asked, my voice a little too soft.

His eyes held mine intently.

"Yes, but," he stammered. "But I do not want you to be uncomfortable. These last couple of weeks you have been aching and tired."

"Never enough to not want you," I argued softly and reached

around to hold his hip to me.

"I do not want to hurt you or him," he mumbled.

"You won't hurt me," I said reassuringly. "We just need to be gentle. And you are always gentle."

His head disappeared behind my neck, kissing between my shoulder blades and working their way back up to my shoulder, his body tucking in a little closer to me.

One hand made its way to my hip and lower, teasing me as he had learned early on would bring me closer to pleading for him. He was quiet against me, just soft breaths and gentle kisses as he moved slowly, my leg cradled in his hand as he adjusted and groaned at the feel of me.

It had only been a few weeks, but the loss was real when we both felt the energy play between us as he found me and pushed inside slowly. I sighed and melted against him, having missed this closeness. Cradling me as we moved, no words were needed, just the touch of our hands on one another's body, and the gentle press of lips against skin when he could manage it between breaths. I trembled against him and let out a soft cry when I felt myself let go, his own stuttered gasp heating up my shoulder.

It was a warm night, and the soft sheen of sweat on our bodies should have been uncomfortable, but I smiled as my fingers slipped over his hip, still tight against mine.

"We shouldn't let this go for so long next time," I said softly.

"I agree," he chuckled and hummed against me.

We were quiet, listening to the breeze flutter through the window in the night.

"Soon we will have less time to ourselves," he whispered.

"Yes," I replied and hugged him closer.

"I will savor this time then, and promise you that we will have it whenever we can," he replied and snuggled in.

Was I afraid we would lose this bit of intimacy after the baby was born?

Absolutely.

So for him to say that made me smile and hope for every

minute I could have alone with Nathan.

I let out a contented breath and relaxed against my husband, my thoughts drifting.

Before I slipped into sleep, a thought occurred to me, something Nathan had said earlier.

"How do you know it's a boy?" I asked, turning toward Nathan's closed eyes.

He smiled and kept his eyes closed.

"Because I know," he said simply.

"You know?" I asked, amused by his smile and brilliant eyes that flashed in the moonlight.

"It just feels like a boy," he said and slid his hand across my stomach again.

"And if it turns out to be a girl?" I asked, a little nervous.

"Then she will be our pride and joy," he replied and leaned in to kiss me again.

I couldn't argue with that. I planned on treating this child as I had wanted to be treated all my life.

Whether boy or girl, it would be so very special.

26

I looked out into the field to find Nathan near the top of the far end, Magnus pulling him along as they tended the soil from the latest harvested crop. We had already harvested the wheat and had thriving winter crops bursting through the ground. We were ahead of the game this year.

I smiled as I filled up the water bucket and looked out over our flourishing farm.

A year ago it had been a wreck. Too much for one man. It was still too much for just the two of us. But with Mark, John, and even Benjamin, we had planted five times what Nathan had accomplished on his own. We had our first earnings from the wheat and it had helped get us through the summer. Soon the corn would be harvested and come late October, we would be able to begin harvesting the pumpkins and squash.

It would be a good winter this year.

I pulled at the water bucket, hoisting my sack over my shoulder a little harder before I stepped into the nearby cornfield toward where Nathan worked. I walked purposefully, ignoring the prickling fear I always felt when I had to walk through the corn. Old feelings, never truly buried, even though the reasons for those fears were long gone.

Sean would always be in my memory, regardless of how much I tried to push thoughts of him aside. And the corn only reminded me of the last time, around this time of year, when I had almost lost everything.

I took a shuddering breath as I tiptoed over the dark, rich earth that Nathan and Magnus had turned. I gained a little strength in seeing Nathan turn his eyes toward me and smile as I approached. Magnus came to a halt, biting at his bit and shaking his mighty head as if to object to stopping.

"What is the water for?" Nathan called as I trudged closer.

"You are not the only one working hard in this heat," I said.

Magnus nickered softly and bobbed his head when I drew close, his lips covering my palm in greeting. He had become more careful around me as my belly grew, as if he understood I was more fragile now. I held the bucket out to him and let him drink before I looked up to Nathan, who was shaking his head and laughing.

"You have spoiled him!" he accused, only to smile a little wider when he noticed the bag on my shoulder.

"I can spoil you, too, if you like," I replied and handed it to him, his tongue licking at his lips as he dug through it.

He pulled out the thermos and drank deeply, wiping at his mouth when he had drained it.

"You spoil me every day," he whispered and looked out over the field he had been working on, a thoughtful smile on his face.

"You have done a lot today," I commented, looking out with him.

"It is still not enough. John was supposed to come and help but with Jonah insisting on taking Emma into town to watch her more closely, it has been difficult for him to help," he replied, a frown appearing on his face.

"You cannot blame him, Nathan," I chided. "She is at risk of delivering early."

He looked at me in surprise.

"Oh, I am not upset with John!" he exclaimed. "I am just worried that I am out here, and you are alone inside and then what if something happens? You need help, too."

I smiled up at him and sighed.

"If it will make you feel better, I will ask Fannie to come and visit every day, but I cannot stop doing my tasks because you are worried," I admonished.

He took a bite of the sandwich I had brought, his eyes back on the field.

"I was thinking that," he conceded. "Or maybe Abigail could spend the days with you. She is out of school in a week."

I laughed and nodded.

"That would be nice. We can prepare her for becoming a babysitter," I teased. I had missed Abigail, only seeing her lately when she came after school.

He leaned down and kissed me on the forehead.

"I will ask Fannie and find out how soon she can be here," he murmured before straightening up and handing me the bag once more.

"Do not be too late in the field today, Nathan," I said as he got Magnus moving once again.

He waved to me and lowered his hat over his eyes, settling in once more on his task. I returned to my work in the house, staying out of the hot kitchen for as long as I could before preparing supper. The laundry took more time to fold, thanks to my stomach getting in the way of folding the sheets.

Yes, it would be nice to have a pair of hands to help here.

That night, Abigail was abuzz with energy at the news of coming to help me during the day. I was used to her enthusiasm, but it was amusing to watch Nathan's wide eyes as she ran around the room listing all the things we would need before the baby came.

He looked as if he was regretting his idea already.

My stomach hurt from all the laughing.

I rubbed at my belly and tried to quiet down. It was a strange feeling, sort of a pinching low under my belly. Nathan was by my side in an instant.

"Are you well?" he asked, eyes looking up at me from where he knelt.

I nodded and cleared my throat.

"Yes, just too much laughing. I am fine," I said as the pinching ended.

I would have to be more careful. I was close to term, and anything could set my body into motion. I squeezed Nathan's hand and smiled down at him. He nodded and the worry slipped from his face, lingering only in his eyes before he turned and addressed Fannie and Abigail.

"Perhaps we should call it an early day, we have much to do in the next few days," he said.

Fannie stood and moved to give me a tender hug, drawing away to look down at my belly.

"You will need to be more careful these next few days," she teased. "With Jonah away with Emma, you will let me know if you feel anything?"

I nodded and laughed dismissively.

"You will know the second I do," I said and glanced at Nathan. "He keeps a constant eye on me these days when he can."

"And so will I!" Abigail exclaimed and turned back to Nathan with her demands on what was needed for her to babysit properly.

Fannie smiled and hugged me once more before herding Abigail out the door.

Nathan came to me and held me close, his hand automatically going to my stomach.

"Abigail will be more protective than I will, if she has her way," he chuckled.

"She is most serious about taking care of all the babies," I replied, finding her enthusiasm sweet.

Nathan's hands stroked the swell of my belly repeatedly.

"Are you sure you are all right?" he asked.

"I think so," I said, looking up at him. "It was just a pinch and then it was gone. I just need to curb the laughter until after the birth."

He nodded and looked out to the setting sun.

"It is close. We will need to be sure Fannie comes to check you each morning," he whispered and drew me quietly inside.

Not long now, it was true.

The idea of that, with memories of Hannah and her birth, just made me more nervous.

How hard would it be for me?

It seemed it was no time before we found out. I woke with a start that night, the pressure low in my stomach making me gasp.

Nathan was up in an instant, his hand on me but his body halfway out of bed, as if he was preparing to sprint for help. I let out a few relieved breaths as the pain passed, closing my eyes and letting my head rest against the pillow once more.

"Was that?" Nathan whispered hoarsely.

"It felt like one," I breathed, threading my fingers in his around my belly.

"I should get Fannie," he said and moved to stand.

"It is early still," I said and watched while he pulled his trousers on.

"But this could be it," he said, the excitement and fear clear in his voice.

"It would be nice to have her here," I conceded, my own trepidation building off of his.

A quick kiss on my forehead and he was out the door, setting off at a run down the stairs and up the hill. I lay there in our bed for several minutes, my hands around my stomach as my little person nudged me once or twice and then settled down once more. I found my shift and put it on, not knowing how Fannie would react should she find me naked in our bed.

It was not long before I heard the door open and their hurried footsteps on the stairs.

I saw Fannie first, her smile broad as she stepped in, wrapped in a coat over her sleep shift. She came up to the bed and sat beside me, looking me over.

"How far apart are the contractions?" she asked. I frowned and thought about it.

"There's only been the one," I said, blushing when I saw her eyes narrow at me.

"I will forgive you this once, Nathan, because you are new and I said to let me know should anything happen," she said, never looking away from me. "But it is normal for mothers-to-be to have occasional contractions days before labor."

Nathan and I both looked at Fannie sheepishly and apologized for waking her only a little after midnight. She tutted and leaned over to kiss me sweetly before standing and drawing her coat around her once more.

"In the future, when the contractions are no more than six minutes apart, then come and get me," she said and smiled up at Nathan as she passed him.

"Yes, Fannie," he murmured and followed her back down the stairs, only to return a few minutes later.

He looked thoroughly abashed.

"Sorry," I whispered and pulled him down into bed, his clothes still on.

"I just did not want to be too late," he replied and let out a long breath. "Fannie is so like my mother it scares me sometimes."

"What does that mean?"

He chuckled and rubbed at his face.

"She would have told me the same thing. That I worry too much," he groaned.

"I am sure we are not the only nervous couple Fannie has had wake her up in the middle of the night," I said, touching his chin with my hand.

"Still does not make me feel good about having her come all this way for nothing," he whispered.

I patted him on the hand around my hip and nestled into him further.

"She understands, Nathan," I whispered. "We are ready for this."

I felt him smile against my throat and he relaxed beside me.

"We will be better prepared."

"Exactly," I replied simply.

Nathan fell asleep quickly, and I lay beside him contemplating the next time. It would not be long, I knew. Every day that we drew closer to our own occasion seemed to garner exciting news from everyone else.

Fannie came to breakfast at our house with news that the hospital had decided it would be best to induce labor with Emma, a month early. Her blood pressure had risen in the last few days and they worried that she would have more issues the closer she came to her due date. In the race to see who would have their child first, it seemed Emma would beat me to it.

It was both exciting and frustrating.

I waddled around, uncomfortable in my skin and always hot now. I never seemed to stop sweating, and the baby was bumping my bladder on a regular basis. All I wished was for that big day to finally come, regardless of the fears of the unknown. I had only suffered a couple of small contractions in the morning, and with each one, a wave of nervous excitement coursed through me in anticipation for the next one. It wouldn't come and I would be forced to continue to waddle and sweat and wish my bladder was higher in my body.

I was working in the garden as the midday sun beat down on me when I felt the dampness run down my legs. Groaning at the never-ending sweat, I moved down the line of green beans and felt the warm flow increase. I paused, looking down at the dry earth as it dampened under my skirt. I looked up, scanning the horizon for Nathan. He had said he would stay close, but I couldn't see him.

That nervous bit of excitement turned into panic at not seeing him.

"Nathan!"

I heard it echo off the barn, a frantic cry that I realized was my own.

I walked carefully toward the barn, hoping to find him there. I was not alone. I knew he would not leave me alone. But for a fleeting instant, I worried that he had.

"Nathan!"

"Kate?" I heard, his voice in the barn before he stepped out, carrying a bucket and looking for me.

When he saw my face the bucket dropped and he was running toward me.

"Now?" he breathed, his hands reaching for me like I was suddenly breakable.

I nodded just as the first real contraction hit.

"Whoa," I gasped and clutched at him as the tightening in my lower stomach increased.

"Inside, I need to get you inside," Nathan said and all but carried me toward the house.

My feet felt like they glided over the hardwood floors as he helped me upstairs and to the bedroom. He looked around and pulled the sheets back as I slipped into the bed, the contraction gone and my body simply damp now.

"I need to change, Nathan. Go get Fannie while I change," I instructed, strangely calm.

He froze in front of me, looking from me to the door.

"I do not want to leave you," he started, but I shook my head.

"She said every six minutes, Nathan. We are still beyond that, but my water broke," I explained, still so calm. "You have time to go get her."

"Are you sure?" he asked, edging toward the door.

I nodded and moved to strip.

I heard the door close downstairs and knew he was probably halfway up the hill already.

I was down to my shift when the next contraction came, forcing me to lean heavily into the bed before it let up once more. I let out a relieved breath and tried to ignore the fact that the contractions were faster than six minutes apart.

I softly counted as I continued to change, stepping into the bathroom to start the water in the bath. We'd need water, and towels. Another contraction, this one at four minutes as I pulled the towels down out of the linen closet. I clutched at the towels and tried to breathe through the clenching.

How long had Nathan been gone now?

Three contractions.

Almost fifteen minutes.

And then another.

This baby wanted out.

"Kate?"

"Nathan!"

I heard the footsteps and then saw Fannie and Nathan, picking me up from the hallway amidst the towels that had fallen.

"Katherine, what are you doing?" Fannie asked as she settled me into the bed. She propped me up with pillows against the headboard but I shook my head.

"Three minutes," I panted, feeling the tightening starting once more. "Three minutes apart."

She looked at me in surprise before turning to Nathan.

"You said she had just had only one," she said.

He nodded and looked at me with worry.

"And her water," he added.

I groaned and clutched at the blanket beside me as the next wave hit.

"Nathan, go and wash well. This will be quick and I need you to be ready," Fannie said, her voice taking on the same authority I recognized from the night Hannah gave birth.

He paused for only a moment before he hurried into the bathroom to clean up. He was back by my side again with a cool towel to put over my now sweating brow. I looked up to find him worrying his lip. I nodded and reached for his hand.

"It's okay, Nathan," I panted, trying to smile, only to grimace with pain as another contraction squeezed at me.

"Nathan, help me to move her to the front of the bed,"

Fannie instructed, Nathan holding me in place as Fannie shifted the pillows.

"Why is it happening so fast?" I hissed, breathing heavily and shutting my eyes tight when I felt the pain shooting down the backs of my legs.

Fannie let out a grunt and shoved the pillows hard against me to hold me semi-upright.

"Would you rather have it last for days? It seems this baby wants into this world sooner than later," she said and grabbed a number of towels to place on the floor before me.

"It took so long for Hannah," I said and whimpered at the weight that seemed to be bearing down on my lower body.

"It is different for every woman, Katherine," Fannie said and looked up at me with proud eyes. "Soon, Katherine. It will be soon."

The idea that this would be over quickly was squashed with the pain that shot through me once more. I cried out and grabbed at Nathan, who held my hand and whispered urgently into my ear. I didn't hear all that he said, only catching the important words like love, and his everything.

Anything else was lost in my heavy breathing and the rushing of blood in my ears.

We seemed to go like that forever, soft words followed by my cry and an unbearable pressure down low. Then a moment to relax, Fannie checking on my progress, and Nathan wiping away the sweat before we did it again.

It was probably only an hour, maybe two, but it felt like all day. My only measure of time was the sun as it progressed over the floor of our room. It was disappearing from our window when Fannie looked up with excited eyes.

"I can see hair, Katherine. You can push on the next contraction," she said, looking over to Nathan as she moved my feet a little further apart, showing Nathan how to hold my leg so that I had something to push against.

The next contraction came, forcing me to cry out with the need to push. Nathan held me tight to him, his eyes jumping from my face to where Fannie looked in earnest. The pain vibrated through me, making me cry louder as I felt the pressure build in me. I clenched my eyes shut and pushed a little harder.

"Good, Katherine," Fannie chanted. "Again, you are so close."

"I cannot," I moaned, the pressure too much.

I had a moment to breathe, my eyes opening up to search for Nathan's, looking at me with that intense look I remembered so many times before.

When we first met.

When we first kissed.

When he came to get me in California.

When I saw him in the burning barn.

When he said he would be mine forever.

When we first made love.

"Nathan," I breathed, the tears welling up at seeing his soul laid bare in those brilliant green eyes.

"Push, Kate," he whispered and kissed my lips like a promise.

The pain shot through me again, breaking off our kiss with my cry and I pushed, holding onto my husband as he called my name again and again. When I thought the pressure could not get any worse, it peaked and I growled to push past that pain, feeling another sudden burst of pressure as Fannie cried out.

"The head is out! Good, Katherine! Just a little more!"

"Come on, Kate. Just a little more," Nathan echoed in an urgent whisper, looking down as Fannie reached for more towels.

"Push Katherine!"

"Push Kate!"

I felt Nathan's support, heard his voice, and pushed, crying out as I did. A sudden release and Nathan's quiet whimper forced my eyes to open to see there, in Fannie's arms, everything we had worked for these last several months. Small and surprisingly long, a shock of dark hair mashed down and wet.

And then as Fannie cleared the airways, a soft cry that went straight to my heart.

Our child.

"It is a boy," Fannie said brokenly, sobbing as she held the small baby in her arms.

The room was filled with noises, laughter mixed with tears. Crying that never sounded mournful.

"Little Jason," I whispered and clutched at Nathan's hand while Fannie cleaned our son up a bit.

I felt her slipping him up to settle on my chest, Nathan looking over both of us with adoration once more, his brilliant green irises and a smile that made his eyes crinkle up with joy. Our son wiggled against me and we both looked down to see our son's eyes flutter and struggle to look up at us.

"Our son," he whispered softly against my ear and kissed me so tenderly I thought perhaps I had dreamt it.

My idea of reality was slipping as I sat there with the tiny little man in my arms, and the man of my dreams at my side. The soft cry of my son called to me and I touched him lightly with my fingers, his skin soft and pink and warm. He wiggled in my arms and I laughed, the feeling of him there in the flesh such a wonder.

"Our son," I repeated, smiling over him.

"And so the Fisher house fills up once more," Fannie whispered, tears in her eyes as she took in her children before her.

And so with little Jason, our family began to grow.

Epilogue

"They should have been back by now," Hannah huffed, ignoring the heavy sigh coming from Fannie.

"Will you step away from the door and help to finish this order of pies, Hannah!" Fannie called.

I snorted and shook my head.

Even after living on her own with Mark for over a year, she still had not perfected pie making. We were safer with her by the door.

Emma let out a long frustrated growl and slapped her dishrag on the counter.

"Hannah, do you see Katherine or me worrying? They will get back before the snow falls any heavier!" she cajoled in a strained whisper, only to shake her head when we heard the cry from the other room.

"I will go," Fannie said and wiped her hands. "Hannah, come. We can look after the babes while Emma and Katherine put in the last of the pies."

Hannah made one last effort to look out the kitchen door and then followed her mother to the adjacent room where one of the babies had woken up from his nap. I knew it was a he because it sounded suspiciously like Simon. But soon we heard little Mary chime in and Emma let out another sigh.

"If she had just stayed asleep for another ten minutes," she grumbled and moved to the refrigerator for the bottles for Hannah. With two boys who seemed to consume more than their father did, it was harder for Hannah to keep up with them.

"They will all be awake in moments; that is the way," I replied and shoved the last of the pies into the oven.

Fannie came out with Mary and Jason in her arms, Hannah with the twins on her hips as they wiggled and squirmed against her. Emma and I both went to Fannie and relieved her of her burden with a smile so that she could help Hannah with her boys.

Mary quieted almost immediately as soon as she was at Emma's breast, and Jason gurgled a smile up at me as I settled into a seat to feed him.

It was quiet in the room as the babies fed, Fannie burping one twin while Hannah fed the other. Smiles played on our faces as we watched our children enjoy even the simplest of things that we could provide. It was a good life. A quiet one. A few gurgling burps, a soft whimper from one twin who was not yet ready to give up on his feeding against Hannah's breast, and perhaps a contented chirp from a full and sleepy baby.

We were settling the babies back into the other room when we heard the men entering through the kitchen. They had learned by now to enter the house quietly, after Mark had once startled the babies from their first good nap of the day with his loud and boisterous laugh. I was the first to step into the kitchen, catching sight of Nathan by the sink as he cleaned up. He glanced my way and smiled brightly, so at ease with showing his affection towards me now. His eyes conveyed the unspoken words of affection he always shared with me when alone.

Jonah started talking as soon as the others were in the room.

"Our Bishop is all settled into his home," he started, laying a kiss on Fannie's forehead. "He sends his apologies for not joining us, but promises to come around in a few days after he returns from seeing Bishop Ropp in Friendship."

I smiled to myself and turned to the pies in the oven, removing them to cool on the counter. I wondered if perhaps young Bishop Yoder was visiting a pretty dark-haired girl in Friendship as well. He had been very secretive regarding his time there, and spent more and more time in conferences with Bishop Ropp than his father had ever done.

And it did not go unnoticed when the Snyders came to deliver cheese and butter to us, that their youngest daughter accompanied them, and our dear Bishop always called on us at the same time.

Nathan brushed past me, his hand lingering along my back in a silent promise of continuing when we returned home. With Jason sleeping through the night finally, we had quality time alone once more, if only late at night. At least until I began to swell with the newest addition growing inside of me. I matched his mischievous smile and glanced around to see if anyone might have caught us.

Emma was smiling up at John as he leaned down to tuck away a long lock of her dark hair that had escaped out of the bun on her head.

Fannie and Jonah seemed to be having their own moment together as he leaned in to kiss her again.

And Mark was brushing one of his giant hands over Hannah's stomach tenderly.

Hannah was smiling with her eyes closed at her husband's touch.

It seemed we would know about another child soon enough, if I had to guess.

I looked around the room at my family, so much larger than I had ever dreamed it would be.

And happy. So much happiness.

Of course we had our down days.

We had our sorrow.

Ezekiel had passed on just before the new year, dying

peacefully in his sleep with his youngest child, Sarah Jensen, by his side. It had been a great loss to our community, and the first funeral I had been to with my people. Sarah for once did not supervise the reception afterwards, the community coming to her side in her time of grief. I had held her for some time with Fannie as she cried beside her father.

Ezekiel had touched so many people.

It was up to us to take care of his own, and to remember him in our hearts.

This life had shown me how to live, and how to love. How to grieve, and how to have faith that we would thrive.

That was our way.

That was the Amish way.

It was simple here, perhaps.

Those outside might not understand it.

But it was where I belonged.

I looked back at Nathan, his eyes full of love and faith in me.

The same look he had given me so many times before.

So much like the beginning.

When I stepped out of that world of violence and sorrow, and into his.

Because this is where I always belonged.

In our world.

~~~~~

The *In Your World* Series Continues:

FINDING LOVE

Coming soon

Judith Snyder never thought she would ever find a man she could love enough to marry.

Of course, that was before she met Bishop Yoder.

Bishop Benjamin Yoder from West Grove was kind, handsome, and from a good Amish family. From the start, she found him easy to adore. A girl could do right by marrying a Bishop.

But Benjamin Yoder held himself apart from others, and while he smiled and seemed to enjoy her company when they bumped into one another every chance she could muster, he avoided making any offer to marry her.

A dark past made her father dubious to the pairing, what with the Bishop's liberal views of agreeing to allow an English into their community. Bishop Yoder avoided conversation about his life before becoming Bishop. He was a messenger of God now, his past to be forgiven and forgotten. His contemplative being and soft spoken words told Judith he was a good man, perhaps just in need of a woman that saw the love inside of his soul. He just had to learn to love again.

Judith Snyder must set out to woo the Bishop.

And offer him a chance at finding love.

Acknowledgements

This story would not be possible without the love and support of my friends and family, and my incredible readers who have stood by me through every word.

To my loving and amazing husband, for believing in me and being patient while I diligently researched, and to my sweet boy, who always knows how to make my heart melt with his sweet romantic suggestions.

To Leah, who nudged me to take that first step.

To Jess, for reminding me of what was important and providing sanctuary.

To my girls on Twitter and Facebook and the forums — thank you for providing so many hours of love and support, laughter, and inappropriate inspiration to keep me going.

To Claudia, Teddi, Traci, Terri, Staci, Sarah, Kris, and Mandy for the moment of conception on this sweet boy: suspenders and big black hat, shy smile and all.

To Amy, Mary, Jen and Jayme for holding my hand through the editing process and lending me your most trusted opinions.

To my amazing models, Brian and Jessica — you two are stunning together!

I love you all, and I have been so blessed to have you all on this journey.

ABOUT THE AUTHOR

Jennyfer Browne has always been a sucker for a good love story — a complex recipe with a dash of dashing, a pinch of heroism, and a hefty dose of outside forces that test young lovers. Seasoned with tears and laughter, followed by a sprinkle of happy sighs fill out the perfect recipe.

Jennyfer also enjoys pie.

Ms. Browne lives in California with her wonderful husband and adoring son, where she enjoys the beach and sailing off on further adventures. A member of the Romance Writers of America and blessed with an overactive imagination, she writes sweet and savory romances with a twist of tart that always come to a happy ending.

You can visit Jennyfer Browne on her Facebook page at
https://www.facebook.com/jennyferbrowneauthor

Books by Jennyfer Browne:

In Your World Series:
Healing Faith (Book One)
Renewing Hope (Book Two)
Finding Love (Book Three)

CPSIA information can be obtained
at www.ICGtesting.com
Printed in the USA
LVOW13s1742300617
539951LV00012B/1234/P